SUPERWORLD

SUPERWORLD

—— BOOK 1 ——

BENJAMIN KEYWORTH

Podium

To Dad
Who was there, always

Copyright © 2022 by Benjamin Keyworth

Cover design by Podium Publishing

ISBN: 978-1-0394-1312-2

Published in 2022 by Podium Publishing, ULC
www.podiumaudio.com

Podium

SUPERWORLD

PROLOGUE

The Earth stood unaware.

Silent and alone, a blue-green marble floating in the black. Across its surface teemed humanity and everything humanity brought: chaos and noise, movement and life. But out here, from far enough away, mankind's machinations faded into irrelevance. Watched from afar, Earth was peaceful.

A silent sphere swimming through an ocean of stars.

To the people who called it home, it was their everything. Most never looked beyond it, convinced without convincing that everything worth watching was already happening here—their neighbors, their nations, their needs, their enemies, their families, their dreams. Every fragment of their lives come and grown and gone on the world beneath their feet. Few looked beyond their homes. Few watched outside their lives.

And, so, few saw when it drew near.

The date by human time was July 6, 1963.

And a wave of golden light was billowing toward the Earth.

Aakesh Singh's back ached. It always ached when he was digging, but this morning the ground seemed particularly cold. Maybe it was coincidence—maybe he was just getting old. Aakesh straightened, feeling the muscles crunch in his back. A callused hand rested on the shovel, the other wiping sweat from his brow.

Strange. The morning had barely begun, but the sun shone unusually bright. He lifted his head, shielding his eyes with a hand—and then stopped, struck still. The sun was no brighter than usual. His field was the same as yesterday.

But above, the sky danced with golden light.

"This goddamn council," Nora swore in Norwegian, striding through the halls toward the sound of crying. First the trees and now—floodlights? At this hour? What possible reason could there be, other than to deprive them all of sleep? Unbelievable. Even with the curtains tightly drawn, wisps of light seeped in around the edges.

"Erik!" she shouted as she drew closer, the cries growing louder. "Erik, where are you! Can't you—can you talk to—just ridiculous," she muttered under her breath, her bare feet flashing from underneath her silk nightgown. She glided into the nursery and swooped down over the crying bundle.

"Yes, my darling, I know, I know, Mommy's here. I'm sorry, I'm sorry, my baby, yes, you were trying to sleep." She rocked the mewling Asta against her shoulder, one hand pressed against her tiny head, hushing. "Sleep now, my baby, sleep. Erik?" she called, not as loud this time.

"Out here," came the reply. And as she glanced around the nursery, Nora saw the window open and her half-dressed husband standing out on the balcony.

"Erik, what on earth is . . . ?" she started, moving to join him—but the moment she saw the world beyond their apartment, the words fell from her mouth.

She stopped. "Oh, my love," she whispered, and without knowing it, she stood next to him and their hands intertwined.

"It's beautiful," he murmured. "Asta, look." Nora turned so the newborn's eyes could face the shining city, so she could watch, as everyone around her was watching—watch, without understanding, as golden rippling waves illuminated the night sky.

"I know it's everywhere. I don't need to hear it's everywhere; just tell me what the hell it is and who's behind it."

General McCulvic's face was bright red, and patches of sweat seeped through his white shirt at the armpits. The cigar that drooped from his mouth had gone out, but neither he nor anyone under his command seemed to have noticed.

"Pentagon, sir," called a junior—Dickson maybe, he could never remember their names—seated at one of the workstations. Each station had a monitor and a headset phone, knobs, dials, and connections to the outside world, and swarmed with government staff. "They're requesting an update; they've got nothing."

"Got to be the Ruskies," someone whispered to McCulvic's right, but the information flying in thick and fast cut them off.

"Word from the Kremlin, they're saying it's not them. Repeat, they're saying this is definitely not them, and they're asking us to confirm the extent of our involvement."

"Our involvement is nothing, and we know nothing," McCulvic barked. "And let those red bastards know it before the nukes start flying. God knows, this doesn't need to get any more out of hand," he muttered under his breath.

"MI5 confirms phenomenon the same over London."

"Wire from the Antarctic station, sir, it appears to be worldwide."

"Looting in Detroit."

"Japan's called a state of emergency."

"Beijing on line five; they want to know what's going on."

"NASA's got no idea; they think it's some sort of space wind or solar flare."

"That's impossible. It's not a goddamn aurora. How's it everywhere at once?"

"Get everyone on highest alert," McCulvic ordered, the words clenched through teeth and cigar. "Ground everything. I don't care where it's flying. Get it out of the sky and on the ground now." He paused, chewing without even thinking. "Move the president and chiefs of staff to the bunker. Close schools; lock down the roads. Emergency broadcast, all channels, tell everyone to stay in their homes." His eyes narrowed, glaring across the darkened room at the images flashing across the screens. "Until we know what the hell is going on here, we're not taking any chances."

"Marry me."

He opened the tiny velvet box and pulled out a ring, held gently between his thumb and forefinger. They were alone on the hill, under the tree where they'd first kissed, their initials still engraved in the bark. Alone at sunset on a woolen tartan blanket, with fruit, chocolate, and a bottle of too expensive wine. A scene straight from a movie—textbook, postcard romance. It would win any girl's heart. Should.

"I . . ."

What was she supposed to say? *I love you, but I can't marry you? That you're sweet, kind, and gentle—but if I say yes, then we'll never grow, never change, never leave? Because I love you, Walter Reid,* she wanted to say, *but I need more than just love. I need to make a difference. I need to be more than just your wife.*

She looked down at the ring in his hand, at his hopeful, besotted smile. With the sun at his back, the world beyond him glowed—and he was overshadowed. This man who loved her more than she could ever love anything. Who would happily do nothing for the rest of their lives, so long as they did it together.

The diamond sparkled, a golden star, the rays of sunlight reflected and refracted through its tiny heart. She loved him. She truly did. But she couldn't accept the life he offered, no matter how much it hurt, how brightly it shone, how much his proposal lit up the world and made it seem like the sky was awash with gold . . .

"Oh my God," she whispered.

THE CLAIRVOYANT

Thirty-Seven Years Later

Juy 6, 1963."

Matt Callaghan snored.

Flat on his back, mouth open, his limbs kneaded through a tangle of sheets and blankets, Matt slept soundly as the first glimpse of daylight snuck in underneath the gap in his blinds. From the other side of the room, a small, square television blared, perched almost forgotten atop a chest of draws. Oblivious to the room's tranquillity, its old-timey announcer's voice and black-and-white images streamed on.

"To the people of Earth, a day like any other. But this is no ordinary day. For today, the destiny of mankind changes . . . forever."

The narrator paused, and the images of 1960s men and women going about their daily business gave way to dramatic footage of a sky engulfed in undulating ripples, the intensity of their golden color diminished somewhat by the graininess of the recordings. Matt mumbled something indistinct and rolled over onto his side, eyes still closed.

"The Aurora Nirvanas. From the deepest reaches of space it comes, a wall of golden light blanketing the Earth, causing amazement, wonder, and panic. Scientists have no explanation. The United Nations convenes an emergency session. Some call it a solar flare. Others, a sign of Armageddon. A stranger phenomenon the world has never known . . . yet stranger still is yet to come."

Suddenly, images of streets, homes, and offices filled with motionless bodies.

"Mass lethargy. An urge to sleep so powerful, it overtakes everyone. Mere hours after the Aurora's arrival, the human race succumbs to unconsciousness."

The small screen flashed with shots of people with their eyes closed in parks and cars—dramatic reenactments intercut with off-center footage from antiquated security cameras. Men in suits curled up on the floor of the New York Stock Exchange. Kennedy and his aides asleep against a desk.

"The Great Slumber. Six days mysteriously lost from human history. Five billion people, miraculously unhurt and unharmed. And when humanity awakes, it finds more miracles await."

Matt's eyes twitched underneath his eyelids.

"Superpowers."

A man, staring in black-and-white wonder as flames flutter around his upturned palm. A housewife outside a white picket fence, hesitating only briefly before rocketing up into the sky, the strings of her apron fluttering behind her. A tiny hunchbacked old woman wobbling unsteadily, one hand trembling on a cane, the other lifting a car above her head.

"Everyone, men and women, young and old, gifted with abilities beyond science and nature. No pattern. No explanation. From African royalty to Soviet peasants, a power for everyone . . . and chaos for the world."

The screen darkened, and images arose of burning vehicles, broken buildings, injured bystanders, and superhuman fighting. Guns tearing themselves from soldiers' hands. A mother, her skin turned to rock, fiercely clutching her child.

"Crime. Uprisings. Madness. Society teeters on the brink of collapse, powers running loose, unchecked. Nations descend into civil war. For a time, it seems the superhuman age might be over before it has even begun."

A bank robber dressed in a stereotypical ski mask and black shirt levitates a helpless teller into the air—but then, in an instant, a blur speeds around them, and the reenactment criminal finds himself hog-tied underneath the foot of a bright-lit, airbrushed policeman as a dozen superpowered men and women storm in behind him.

"But after almost a year of unrest, there is hope. City by city, state by state, the good people of America take their nation back. Law and order return, as mankind learns that its greatest power lies not in these new-found gifts, but in uniting for peace with one's fellow man."

Matt grunted and rolled over to face the TV, clutching a pillow to his chest.

"And so, the world rises anew. Different, but not destroyed. Wary, but hopeful of what could lay ahead. Untapped potential. Advanced technology. A newfound drive for social justice. The uncharted waters of a society of the superhuman, united by the promise of the new world, and a single shared belief . . ."

Matt's eyes opened.

"All powers to the people. And to all people, a power. This . . . is the Impossible Era."

The documentary's title flashed on the screen. Matt groaned, halfway between a yawn and a moan, and fumbled clumsily for the remote sitting on the bedside table. His sleep-heavy hand finally found the Power button, and the old television set atop his dresser faded to black.

For a moment, Matt just lay there with his eyes closed, one hand still lolling out from underneath the covers, reveling in the newfound silence.

It was Tuesday. Even smothered by the tentacles of sleep, he knew it was Tuesday. His eyes opened a fraction and wandered reluctantly to the red LED of his bedside clock: 6:13. Matt rolled back over and closed his eyes again, allowing himself the precious indulgence of the last few minutes of sleep.

That he'd fallen asleep with the TV on didn't surprise him; that he'd fallen asleep at all did. Times like these, troubles like his—he'd expected sleep to elude him. But, he supposed, in the end, he was only human.

That was the problem.

Six fifteen arrived, and the alarm went off, blaring electric tones into Matt's ears like the wailing cries of Satan taking a soccer ball to the groin. More than anything in the world, he wanted to hit Snooze, roll over into his nest of bedsheets, and go back to sleep—to lie here forever, safe, warm, and far away from the real world and its unpleasant truths. Maybe if he stayed in bed, maybe if he hid beneath the blankets, time would go on without him and everything would just go away.

But denial had never been Matt's strong suit.

He reached out and turned off his alarm, then with little more than a grunt, rolled out of bed and stumbled blearily across his room, past the

Bloodhound Gang and *Big Lebowski* posters, out the door and across the hall into the bathroom and the shower. He stood there for four minutes, letting the hot water rush over his shoulders, hair, and face until his brain was starting to approach something resembling consciousness. Matt moved through the motions. Water off. Dry off. Towel on. Step out. Face the mirror. Breathe.

Breathe.

"My name is Matt Callaghan, and I am a clairvoyant."

He said it as little more than a whisper. Matt closed his eyes.

"My name is Matt Callaghan, and I am a clairvoyant."

A little louder this time, a little firmer. He opened his eyes, wiped steam from the mirror, and stared into his reflection. An unremarkable-looking young man stared back, of middling height and slightly stocky build with light skin, short milk-chocolate-colored hair, and only the occasional freckle. Matt was not a distinctive person; he could have sat in any Starbucks in America and used the Wi-Fi without ever being asked to buy something. But right now, he stood alone in the bathroom, watching his reflection and focusing on his words.

"My name is Matt Callaghan, and I am a clairvoyant."

He felt it as he said it. He believed it, felt it hard and fast and firm inside his mind, a coating of iron. Knew what it meant, the facets of it, knew it as unshakable truth.

"My name is Matt Callaghan, and I am a clairvoyant."

He moved on to his other mental exercises. Thinking of everything he could think of. Thinking of nothing at all. Breathing deep and searching for stillness and silence within himself. Focusing on a single point of feeling in his little finger. Reciting songs. Moving and holding his thoughts in order, then rearranging and holding them again.

From 6:20 to 7:00 a.m., Matt Callaghan honed his mind in front of the mirror, just like he had done yesterday and the day before and would do every day for the rest of his life: forty minutes in the morning, forty minutes before bed, and a set or two throughout the day whenever he could find time. Was he tired? Yes. Was his mind sluggish and sleep-deprived? Definitely. But that was almost the point—his thoughts needed to be unassailable, no matter what. Any time, every time, he needed to be ready and able to believe a single fact.

"My name is Matt Callaghan, and I am a clairvoyant."

Because today was the last day he had.

Everyone else was already up by the time Matt made it downstairs.

"Toast's on the table, honey!"

"Thanks, Mom." He sat down next to Sarah, who was eating her piece with both hands.

"We're out of Cheerios, though; your father finished them yester—JONAS! No phones at the table!"

Kathryn Callaghan rounded the kitchen bench and snatched the cell phone from her youngest son's hands. Jonas let out a wail and turned to his mother.

"But, Mom, I—"

"No buts! No phones at the table! Drink your milk!"

Jonas Callaghan looked like he was thinking about replying but gave up at the look on his mother's face. She was wearing a pantsuit today, which meant she had a meeting, which meant she was in a rush, which meant she had exactly zero time for arguing, thank you very much.

"Jonas, listen to your mother, no phones please." Michael Callaghan didn't even look up from his newspaper. A knife no one was touching spread butter over a piece of toast floating three inches above his plate.

Jonas leaned back into his chair and sulked. "He's texting a *girl*," whispered Sarah. Matt looked at his little sister with an expression of mock horror, and she giggled.

Thus were mornings in the Callaghan household. Matt's mother would rush around the kitchen, putting on toast and making Sarah's lunch—Matt and Jonas made their own by now—and generally keeping things moving, while Matt's father sat and read the paper, unless things were particularly late or stressful, in which case he would be up and helping without a word, sending things telekinetically flying into bags, dishwashers, and pantries. Habitually organized and perpetually busy, Kathryn Callaghan was a lean, slightly taller than average woman, with a head of long brown curls that tumbled over her shoulders like a lion's mane, the ability to move just as quickly in heels as she could in flats, and a propensity to swear ferociously at traffic jams. By contrast, Michael Callaghan was a soft, good-natured man, with large hands, a head full of hair like otter fur, reading glasses that slipped to the tip of his nose, and an unconditional love for Matt's mother, though he almost always forgot their anniversaries.

While his father read and his mother rushed about, Jonas Callaghan, fourteen, would sit on his phone, bicker with his siblings, and use the small fire he could summon from his fingertips to turn his toast to charcoal, which he insisted he liked, though no one believed him. A regular teenage nuisance, Jonas was probably going to end up taller than his older brother, but for now was the splitting image of a younger Matt, aside from his crop of black ringlets and disdain for deodorant. Sarah Callaghan on the other hand, being only ten, had not hit her annoying teenage years yet, and so was content to sit at the table and ask her parents lots of questions or tattle on Jonas for things he may or may not have done. Sarah liked fairies and horses, and despite being slightly small for her age, had done well at athletics, which gave her family the inkling that she might turn out to be a speedster once her powers manifested.

"Matt, honey, can you pick up Sarah from the bus this afternoon?"

"What's wrong with Jonas?" Matt asked, teeth sticky through a mouthful of jam.

"What isn't wrong with Jonas?" his dad joked, shooting a smirk over the top of the paper at his youngest son, who scowled.

"Jonas has soccer 'til five; Dad's going to pick him up."

"Yeah, that's cool, no problem." Matt turned to his sister. "I'll wait on the corner, okay?"

"Can I have a piggyback?"

"No. Well, maybe, but only if you piggyback me first."

"You're too heavy!" Sarah whined. She turned to her mother. "Can we get ice cream?"

"No."

"Please?"

"No. Finish your milk."

Sarah looked downcast.

Jonas leaned over. "Piggybacks are for babies."

"You're a baby!"

"Mike, it's almost seven thirty."

"Yes, right!" Matt's dad started folding his paper. "Can't keep Tony waiting." He stood up and drained the last of his coffee. "You kids have a good day, okay?" There was a general murmuring of consent. He turned to Matt.

"Lucky numbers?"

"Four," Matt grunted, not particularly in the mood.

"I'll buy a lottery ticket." His father chuckled, the master of inoffensive sarcasm. "Bye, honey." He got up from the bench and kissed his wife on the cheek. "Bye, everyone!" Matt's father waved as he walked out the front door. A few seconds later, there was the sound of male voices greeting one another, and not long after that the recognizable *pop* of a teleporter departing with their ride-alongs.

"Sarah, honey, finish your milk," Matt's mother commanded, untying her apron. "Bus will be here soon."

"Do I have to go to school?"

"Yes, Jonas, you have to go to school. Brush your teeth, both of you, let's go." The boy grumbled all the way up the stairs, his sister close behind. Kathryn looked at Matt. "You all right? You seem a bit down this morning."

Matt made a face. "Just tired. Up late finishing that history essay." The lie came naturally, without hesitation or remorse.

"Well, whose fault is that? That should've been done a week ago."

"Thanks, Captain Hindsight."

"You need to be more organized."

"And people in hell need ice water." He glanced up at his mother in her gray blazer and business pants. "Meeting or flushing?"

"Meeting then flushing."

"Ouch. Why?"

"We keep losing pressure around Seventh Street; department wants to investigate."

"Ah, the glorious life of an aquamorph."

"It's a living." She bent down and kissed her eldest son on the head. "Make sure to lock up when you leave."

"I'm almost eighteen, Mom. I know to lock the door."

"I'm just saying."

"I'll get into the Legion of Heroes before I leave the house unlocked."

"Not if you keep leaving your assignments to the last minute. Come on, kids!" she shouted up the stairs. Jonas and Sarah came trundling down with their backpacks.

"Mom! Jonas called me a rude word."

"We'll talk about it in the car. Bye, honey!"

"Bye, Mom," Matt echoed back as the three of them piled out. The door slammed, and the house was suddenly silent, leaving Matt Callaghan alone to contemplatively chew on his toast.

Normally, Matt took the bus to Northridge High, but this morning he wasn't interested in public transport. He wanted to be alone, and he wanted to walk, irrationally gripped by the neurotic delusion that if he could delay getting to the next part of the day, he could delay the day's passage itself. Sure, it was idiotic—but you don't grasp at straws when you've got something better to hold on to.

Matt strode out the front door, hands in his pockets and backpack over his shoulders, not even bothering to put in his earphones. It was stupid really, he thought as he turned onto the footpath—passing the house of their neighbor Mrs. Mailer, which was as usual engulfed in inky smoke—though he was loath to admit it. Time wasn't the issue—he was.

Still—and he clung desperately to the thought—there was one day left.

One day. A vain, insane sliver of hope.

The world woke as Matt walked. Garages swung open, cars pulled out of driveways, husbands kissed wives and wives kissed back, curtains opened, neighbors greeted neighbors, children ran shrieking or trudged grumbling toward a school bus. The usual clusters of teleporting ride-alongs, generally about five or six but sometimes more, gathered on street corners for the morning jumps, the sound of "Morning, Sue!" and "Morning, Jack!" as they linked arms punctuated by distinctive *pops* and the smell of sulfur. Passing the turn-off to Brown Street, Matt waved half-heartedly to Rufus, Mr. Ngyuen's chocolate Labrador, who was nudging open the mailbox with his nose. The dog didn't return the wave, obviously, but Matt felt like it recognized him by now. Rufus seemed like a smart dog, and though Mr. Ngyuen was technically a faunapath, Matt thought after thirteen years of bringing in the mail the pooch probably had the routine down pat. A few minutes later, he also waved at Brad McNamara, one of the clerks at the local court, who did wave back before looking up into the clear blue sky and flying off without a moment's hesitation, the stars and stripes over his doorstep fluttering in his wake.

Inadvertently, Matt knew all the fliers on the walk to school. He'd stopped to talk to all of them at some point—not as part of any grand plan or anything, but because he honestly couldn't help it. The words just seemed to come out. Only friendly conversation, you know, nothing weird; just enough to get a glimpse into their fantastic, magical lives, where with a single thought they could lift up and be soaring among the clouds. Matt had always wanted to be a flier, even as a kid, sitting in class, staring out the window at the great blue beyond. What would it be like, he'd wondered—the wind rushing through your hair, the world fading beneath you? That feeling like you could go anywhere, free as a bird. He'd dreamed about it for years.

But Matt hadn't developed the power to fly. Technically, he hadn't, but Matt scattered the next thought to the wind as soon as it started to formulate.

Matt also knew every psychic on his school route, though this was precaution, not passion. It might have been illegal to listen in on other people's thoughts unauthorized, but so was Napster, and that'd filled up half his iPod. He knew where the psychics lived and knew what the tiny little tingle in his frontal lobe felt like as their minds, not focused on anything but merely open like an ear to background noise, washed over his. He didn't recoil, didn't slam down his walls the moment they made contact—that would draw attention, like tripping draws attention to a crack in the pavement. Most people didn't feel telepathy like he could—most people couldn't be bothered practicing, despite the Board of Education mandating annual mental protection training. Most people didn't worry about psychics, and most telepaths didn't randomly snoop, lest they drown in an ocean of endless thought-noise. Everyone's powers were dangerous, and telepaths' no more than others'.

Unless you had something you really, really needed to hide.

"I'm telling you, man, she's hiding from me," said Taylor. He smoothed his hair back with one hand and winked behind him at Jessica James, who (a) he wasn't even talking about, and (b) didn't appear to notice.

"What a gift," grunted Matt, looking sourly in front of him. "Women flee from you."

The line to get into Northridge High was somehow moving both faster and slower than Matt would have liked. Faster, because the longer it took Matt to get to the start of first period, the longer it took to get to the end of the day and the longer Matt could indulge his delusion that there was really nothing wrong with him. Slower, because it was still standing in a line waiting for a dull, underpaid security guard to check his ID and—looming crisis or no—Matt was not immune to boredom.

"Name and power," muttered Dyson Brady, the dullest and least shaven of the Northridge mandatory security force, able to grow claws but apparently not cut his fingernails. He glanced up at Matt from behind a flimsy wooden desk.

"Matt Callaghan, clairvoyant," replied Matt. Dyson's eyes slid sluggishly down his list, and he nodded before penciling a small check mark.

"Next," he mumbled, looking up at the next student in line and waving Matt absentmindedly through the sorry excuse for a security check. Taylor stepped forward.

"Taylor McDermott, copper-midas," he enunciated clearly as Matt took a few steps down the hall and then stopped, turning to wait for his friend. What exactly Congress expected these checks to prevent had eluded him since kindergarten. Yes, the guard on duty was supposed to keep an entry log and report anything suspicious, but Matt personally doubted whether a human porpoise like Dyson Brady would notice if the Black Death himself rocked up wearing a fake mustache and calling himself Stu Dent. He definitely had no problem letting in Aisha Parkes, and she was invisible save for a faintly rainbow outline. But, Matt supposed as he stood waiting, safety bred complacency, and he probably shouldn't be complaining about any lack of scrutiny, given the circumstances.

Taylor passed through the checkpoint without incident and their conversation resumed unbroken.

"Only because she's into me."

"You think everyone's into you."

"Only 'cause it's true, bro. Everybody wants a piece of this." He grinned as they paused by Matt's locker, Matt's fingers already spinning the combination. Taylor watched Matt grab his math textbooks by their beaten spines and slam the locker door closed, then they turned and started to walk together down the crowded hall. All around them, people rushed to and from classes, their conversations and footsteps backdropped by the sound of a hundred others.

"If she was into you, wouldn't she have, I don't know, said something?" Matt asked over an armful of books.

"Nah, man, she's playing hard to get. You know how girls are."

"Uh-huh."

"Man, quit doubting me. You'll see."

"This isn't doubt, it's healthy skepticism."

"Whatever. You get history done?"

"Yeah, at like two in the morning. Ending's a bit crap."

"It's history, man, who cares? It has all already happened, not like writing about it is going to change anything."

"It'll change my grade."

"Oh, I forgot, you've got to maintain your illustrious B average."

"Screw you, Mr. GPA."

"Get in line, baby." Taylor grinned at him. "Any plans for tomorrow?"

"Kill myself?" Matt suggested, only half-joking.

"Well, duh." Taylor chuckled, not noticing the half part. "But after that, you know, any plans? Fiesta? Major moves for my main man's big day?"

"It's a Wednesday," replied Matt, unenthused. "Can't party on a Wednesday."

"Not with that attitude."

Matt shrugged half-heartedly. "I don't know," he lied. "I think there's something planned with the family."

"Friday then," insisted Taylor. "Blitzed with the boys."

"Play it by ear," Matt replied, remaining deliberately uncommitted. They turned a corner. This was his room. They stopped, and he and Taylor bumped fists. "See you."

"Have fun. Lemme know if you see me getting with Chrissie!" Taylor called as he walked away.

Matt couldn't help himself. "Sorry, bro, all I see in your future is big, burly men."

His friend turned and gave him both middle fingers. Matt chuckled and pushed open the door to math.

* * *

Power Development, or PD, unfortunately didn't yield visions of either of them getting with any girls. In reality, it didn't yield visions of anything. But Matt wasn't about to let that stop him from predicting the future.

"I'm seeing white," he told Timmy Lopez, a short Puerto Rican kid from the seventh grade with Nike shoes and a cowlick, who was sitting nervously on the edge of his seat hanging on to Matt's every word. Matt scrunched his face up into a grimace of false concentration. "Does that mean anything to you? A white car maybe, a white house, a white dog?"

"My grandma has a white dog," Timmy said. He looked at the older boy anxiously. "I don't really like it."

"How is your grandma?" asked Matt, pursing his fingers and leaning back.

Timmy hesitated. "She's . . . all right, I guess," he answered. "She lives by herself in Fairfield . . ." His eyes grew wide. "Is something going to happen to her?"

"It's difficult to say for sure," Matt said, leaning forward with a fake sigh. He'd found weary to be a convincing emotion. "The vision isn't clear. But I think you should visit your grandma more."

"I should?"

"Definitely. Sooner or later, she's not going to be around. You should try and make time for her. She'll appreciate it."

This was Matt's PD. For every other kid in school these periods had structure, with lesson plans and syllabi and competent teachers and the like. The fliers practiced flying and got drilled on altitude sickness and cold-weather gear; the speedsters worked on track times; the pyros learned the finer points of shaping fire into useful forms. Even the flora-mancers had a curriculum teaching them about native plants and the best practices for sustainable accelerated crop growth. But there was no pre-approved education plan for clairvoyants because the Department of Education had never encountered a clairvoyant before and so nobody knew how best to hone their abilities. And so every PD period, while the telekinetics were off bending spoons and the kids who could shoot lightning were off electrocuting one another or whatever, Matt Callaghan sat on a wooden chair behind the teacher's desk in an unused classroom and gave his best advice regarding the future to anybody who wanted it. Or if no one came in, he finished his homework and played *Bubble Spinner* on his phone.

Ironically, Matt didn't view these periods as a complete waste of time. Well, okay, they were a complete waste of time for him—but for the people he saw, he could generally do some good. Even if they didn't know it, most people came in with predetermined problems on their minds—a concern or goal, which a little probing and open-ended, suggestive questioning could invariably reveal. From there, it was less about clairvoyance and more about counseling: working through problems, identifying issues, and dispensing good common-sense advice. Matt was amazed at how many people really just needed someone to listen to them, to provide an outsider's perspective or even to just reassure them that they weren't going to be total failures. For the younger kids especially, telling them they were going to turn out okay often paradoxically gave them the confidence to actually go and live better, happier lives. Some teachers even came in for a "reading" occasionally, their reluctance to discuss their personal lives with a student overcome by the allure of knowing the future. They had nothing to worry about, of course. Matt was an excellent secret keeper, and a good clairvoyant never divulged what they saw.

Of course, "saw" was a strong word. Matt the clairvoyant didn't "see" the future—he only caught glimpses, flashes of this and that, colors, feelings, or common household objects. Nothing solid, nothing disprovable. On the contrary, Matt's "visions" were so broad they were applicable to pretty much anything. He'd "see" a "vision" of a girl in someone's future—and then how could that not come true? Was the boy he was making the prediction to going to depart human civilization and never encounter a woman again? Inevitably, he'd have a crush on someone or someone would crush on him, or he'd make friends with a girl or work alongside a girl, or engage with a girl in some way—and then the "prophecy" would come true and the blanks deliberately left in Matt's "prediction" would be filled in by the boy's own mind. It was the same principle as people seeing star signs; really, it was just a bunch of random dots, but the human proclivity for spotting patterns meant people saw crabs, lions, and all kinds of nonsense.

Matt spent a few more minutes espousing the importance of making time for family to Timmy before the "visions" "fell silent," and he sent the kid out with an enraptured look on his face. He then ushered in his next subject, a redheaded girl from the year below named Jenny Deane. Jenny was a regular.

"How're things, Jen?" Matt indicated to the empty chair and sat down opposite the junior.

Jenny looked bummed. "I don't think Gavin likes me."

"Sure he does. He might just not like you like you like him, that's all."

"What if I, like, just go for it? Like, I'll just kiss him, and then there's no way he can't know."

"Well, the future's never certain." Matt closed his eyes and pretended to envisage Gavin, who for the last year and a half had been asking for predictions about the best time to come out. "But I'm getting a distinct sense of disappointment."

"Nothin' but disappointment, I'm telling you." Taylor held up the broccoli on the end of his fork and rotated it in the cafeteria light. "Seriously. Tuesday's supposed to be goddamn tater tots."

It was lunchtime—usually one of Matt's favorite times. Today though, it was only a terrible reminder of how much of the day was gone.

"Loofs life somefing thaf'd grow on yourf balls," added Marcus, terramancer, through a mouthful of food.

"Damn, Mark, you need to see a doctor," said Carlos, his glinting brown eyes giving no indication of their ability to see through walls. Everyone around the table laughed and Marcus went red.

"I difn't"—he swallowed—"I meant it looks like . . ."

"You know you're meant to wash down there," said Brodie, who could secrete superglue and had already finished everything on his tray.

"With soap."

"And water."

"And not fondle sheep."

"Or chickens," added Pat the electromorph, looking up from his assignment.

"Really, man, any farm animals, definite no-no."

"Screw you all." Marcus scowled.

"Mark, we're just looking out for you."

"Yeah, bro, show your poor body some respect. And antifungals."

Marcus drew himself upright and turned to Matt, who up until now hadn't been saying much, more interested in keeping a lid on his looming feelings of despair. "Matt, they're bullying me. They're damaging my mental health."

"Guys, please." Matt sighed, looking up and forcing himself to engage in the banter. "We're hurting his feelings. Mental health matters."

"Mental health matters," the other five boys echoed, though semi-sarcastically. Next to Matt, Taylor still hadn't eaten his broccoli.

"This junk's harmful to my mental health, swear to God, goddamn rank-ass vegetables."

"Gotta have a brain before it can be sick." Brodie chuckled.

"Hey, screw you, man. Matt, you gonna let them talk to me like that? It's damaging."

Matt didn't look up. "Everyone, be nice to Taylor; he's very delicate."

"That's right."

"He's a beautiful sensitive flower who needs constant nourishment and praise."

"Damn straight. Poet's soul, right here."

"We have to hold him when he cries. Love his tender heart."

Taylor grinned. "You know I love you, Matt. You're my number-one girl."

"The one and the only." Brodie smirked.

"Hey, screw you, Brodie, you ain't ever even smelled a woman."

"I've smelled your mom. She smelled like old cheese."

Pat snorted with suppressed laughter and milk shot out his nose.

"Gross!"

"Damn!"

"Godddamnit, Pat, gross!"

"Anybody got a napkin or something?"

"Sorry, guys, my bad."

The bell went off.

Matt walked out of last-period history still not feeling any different, but at least confident he'd achieved a B in his assessment. In retrospect, he probably could have gone into a bit more detail—discussed some of the ramifications of the newly superpowered economy or discussed causes of deaths in the Year of Chaos. Given more examples of technological acceleration or societal restructuring, or maybe something about communism. Mrs. Colbert loved communism. But . . . oh well. That would have meant more work, and Matt was nothing if not efficient.

All around him, the sounds of people rushing to leave school rang out: laughing, slamming doors, starting engines. He threw Taylor a wave as they walked in opposite directions, he heading home and his friend to soccer practice.

The bus home was about three-quarters full. Matt took a seat somewhere toward the back and sat quietly with one arm resting on the windowsill. Two stops after Northridge, a man with a row of ivory spines running down his back, poking out from what looked like every vertebra, moved into the seat in front of him. Matt found himself watching the spikes rising and falling in gentle, rhythmic movements in time with their owner's breathing, lulled away from his thoughts. Around him, children and people his own age laughed and shouted, but Matt didn't join in—content to just sit and stare at the silent stranger's supernatural protrusions. Abilities that manifested as physical abnormalities were often a sign of some kind of congenital disorder, but Matt wondered if these spines were reversible, whether this man with his tangled hair could retract them into his body but simply felt cooler leaving them out. If not, he'd spend half his life leaning forward for fear of impaling the furniture. The jacket he was wearing, Matt noted, was custom, with steel-ringed holes sewn into the leather, each perfectly aligned to let out one of the stranger's spikes.

As the bus rolled ever forward, Matt found his head pressing against the dull vibrations of the window, watching superpowered society pass by—the teleporters appearing on their lawns, the technopaths driving hands-free in their cars, a woman holding three brown paper bags of groceries suspended in a bubble-like force field. He saw Brad McNamara fly down from the sky and land on his doorstep, briefcase in one hand and a carefully wrapped bunch of daffodils in the other. He and Julie would probably have kids soon, children who'd one day develop powers and grow up as part of a superhuman world.

It was almost four o'clock. He had eight hours left.

Eight hours, he told himself, before he gave up on a miracle.

"Ice cream?" were literally the first words out of Sarah's mouth the moment she got off the school bus.

"No, I'm Matt. Your brother? Sarah, please, we've been over this."

His little sister made a face. "Noooo, can we *get* ice cream?"

"I thought Mom said no."

"Pleeeeease?"

Despite himself, Matt smirked. "Well, all right, maybe we should check with Mr. Cohen, see if he's got anything on special," he said, knowing full well the outcome of that particular examination.

"Yay!" They linked hands, Matt's big fingers engulfing Sarah's little ones, and headed down the road toward the corner store, which was on the way home anyway.

Inside, while Sarah threw her torso into the ice-cream trough, Mr. Cohen, the superstrong, wizened old Polish owner, greeted Matt with his usual friendly wave and long, unsolicited conversation, which today centered around his shop's newly upgraded security. The clacker on the door had been fixed apparently, and thus the entryway would be impenetrable to people moving at superspeed—none of whom, Matt resisted the urge to point out, had actually tried to rob Mr. Cohen at any point. Then there was the new D5, freshly affixed to the roof in the middle of the store, which would similarly stop any teleporters or intangibles attempting to phase through the walls.

"Why do you need a D5, though?" asked Matt, squinting up at the black box, about the size of a grapefruit. "They're like five grand, what's wrong with a D2?"

"Pah," the old man spat, dismissing the notion with a wave of his hand. "Disruptance Two use more electricity. More noisy. Disruptance Five quiet as whisper and make teleporter who try to get in end up on front path throwing up his guts."

"Well, what does that achieve?"

"Then teleporter no run away. I come outside and kick him into next suburb."

"Or her," Matt added for political correctness.

"Maaaaatttttt, can I get the chocolate?" Sarah chose that moment to call from waist-deep in the freezer chest. After confirming she hadn't gotten stuck this time, Matt bought the ice cream and the two of them walked back out into the fading afternoon.

By the time Matt's mother got home, dinner was finished and the four remaining Callaghans were already cleaning up. Michael kissed his wife hello and floated out the plate of shepherd's pie he'd set aside for her. She looped an arm around his waist and laid her head on his shoulder.

"Calcium build-up." She sighed. "I've been telling them for years they need to do something about it. They're going to have to replace the piping." She shook her head. "Although Lord knows they don't want to. They're having me go back down the pipes on Thursday just to confirm what we already know and waste everybody's time."

They sat on the couch and watched TV as a family—Mom leaning on Dad, Sarah leaning on Mom, Jonas and Matt on their own chairs half-following, half-looking at their phones. *The Simpsons*, then the news, then Kathryn got up and walked upstairs to put the sleeping Sarah to bed. Michael made Jonas put his phone on silent because the constant *ping*-ing was "annoying everyone." Half an hour into his dad's favorite cop show—he'd seen this episode before: the killer was a replicator who had literally been in two places at once—Matt said good night and made his way upstairs. He stripped down, threw his clothes into the laundry basket, brushed his teeth, flossed half-heartedly, and washed his face. Then he drew a long, deep breath, looked into the mirror, and began: "My name is Matt Callaghan, and I am a clairvoyant."

Matt sat alone in his bedroom. The room was dark, the house quiet—the rest of his family were asleep. They probably thought he was in bed too, but there was no question of sleeping now. Not tonight. Instead, Matt simply sat, waiting, leaning on his desk chair, his chin on his hands, staring quietly at the red glow of his bedside clock: 11:58.

It'd been a fruitless hope, in the end. One, if he was being honest with himself, he'd never really entertained. Matt had known, truthfully, since he was thirteen—since he'd lain in this exact same room almost five years ago the night after sex ed, mentally going through the checklist of puberty. It hadn't made any more sense then than it did now. But the inconvenient thing about the truth was that even if you didn't under-stand it, even if it wasn't fair, it didn't stop being true. Normally, Matt was pretty good at accepting this, but he guessed there was just some-thing about a closing deadline that made you reexamine things you'd long since come to terms with.

For the past five years, he'd focused mainly on the plan, putting the "how" and "why" of it to the back of his mind. In retrospect, the fact that Matt's gut reaction had been to adapt to an impossible problem rather than seek help probably should have clued him in that, deep down inside, he knew who he was and who he was always going to be.

But still, heck, maybe stupidly, he'd held out hope. Maybe, just maybe. Stranger things had happened, hadn't they? People manifesting slowly, developing later in their teens. It wasn't impossible. But as the months turned to years, Matt's beacon of hope had faded—until barely a spark remained.

And tonight, that spark finally extinguished.

11:59.

Is this how a death row inmate feels? Matt wondered. *Alone, counting the hours, knowing logically no last-minute reprieve was coming—but still desperately waiting, unable to give up that final scrap of hope that some miracle might occur.* It was an odd feeling, this mixture of defiance and resolution, acceptance and despair. No one to bargain with, no way to fight—only the waning, terrible wait and the relentless march of time.

In the quiet dark of his nightstand, the alarm clock gave a single beep. Alone and unseen, Matt leaned back, closed his eyes, and let out a long, shuddering sigh. That was it. Time's up. His fate was sealed.

It was midnight.

Matt Callaghan was officially eighteen.

And he did not have a superpower.

Matt sighed.

"Happy birthday," he muttered to no one in particular. Then without further ado, the only true human in the world climbed unceremoniously into bed.

Unaware that from outside his window, he was being watched.

EMPATHY

"The Powers That Be"
New Scientist, September 1999

Almost as soon as humanity gained supernatural abilities, there followed the desire to understand them. How did they work? Where did these abilities—which so often defy our understanding of not only nature, but physics—come from? Why is the power a person manifests seemingly random?

Such questions have troubled scientists for years and have never been satisfactorily answered. Despite decades of research and tens, if not hundreds, of billions of dollars in funding, the ability to understand how our powers function, and to replicate them artificially, continues to elude, with scientists seemingly no closer to finding the answers to fundamental questions now than they were forty years ago.

How do our abilities function? It is universally accepted that all people develop a single power that first manifests at puberty, but a rarely acknowledged addendum to this fact is that one "power" may, in fact, consist of several supernatural attributes. Take, for example, someone able to move at superhuman speeds. To do so, they must also logically possess not only the ability to move incredibly fast, but an unnatural bodily resilience (to avoid being incinerated by air friction and so they can stop without being killed by their own momentum) and accelerated cognitive processing (to navigate their surroundings at superspeeds). Does that mean, therefore, that a speedster, in fact, has three abilities? Likewise, take those able to shoot lightning from their hands—a feat that, if replicated by science, would likely leave the caster deafened and severely burned. Yet electromancers do this without suffering burns and without creating the momentous explosions of sound associated with naturally occurring lightning. Do they therefore possess some limited form of sonic absorption and thermal resistance?

From where do our powers draw their energy? Observationally, they seem to rely on an individual's bodily stores to function and continued power use will, like any activity, eventually tire the user out. On the other hand, many of the extraordinary abilities demonstrated in the world today logically require so much energy as to render the explanation of an intrinsic fuel source impossible, leading some scientists to suggest that the energy is drawn not from ourselves but from molecular bonds, subatomic instability, or the very fabric of the universe itself.

Why do people develop the abilities that they do? Comprehensive surveys spanning decades and continents have found no pattern from race, location, diet, childhood, association, or even family—despite popular belief, children are no more likely to possess the powers of their parents than any other ability. Powers do not appear to follow phenotypical patterns. The child with a father who can turn his body to fire and a mother who can turn her body to ice will not have the ability to turn themselves into steam. Nor are they associated with someone's mental or physical characteristics. A small and sickly man is just as likely to have super-strength as a body builder. Powers appear in essence to manifest completely randomly—a conclusion that is as unpalatable to scientists as it should be to the natural world.

However, while a complete understanding of the fundamentals remains elusive, certain discoveries have been made and certain developments recognized—despite perhaps their unquantifiable causes. The rise of the "antipath," for example—an individual with the specific ability to counter telepaths but without telepathic abilities of their own—is a development limited only to the last twenty years. Prior to 1978, there are no records of anyone demonstrating antipathic abilities, meaning today's antipaths are exclusively born several years after the Aurora Nirvanas. What does this mean? Some claim it shows that antipathy requires lifelong exposure to whatever effects the Aurora left behind, while others, like Professor Jordan Rothwell of Cambridge University, have speculated that antipaths have developed as a reaction to telepathy—a sort of societal immune response but on a randomized, individual level. Such theories, however, create more questions than they answer.

The inevitable conclusion about our powers is simple—we don't know. We don't understand. Despite their omnipresence in our lives, despite their everyday use and despite their impact on the world, we are no closer to understanding the science behind our abilities than we were in 1963. Powers offer us many challenges and many more opportunities; but not, it seems, the chance to understand.

Ironworks Gym sold itself on always being open. Twenty-four hours a day, seven days a week, rain or shine, holiday or disaster.

And every morning, without fail, the girl was there first.

She ran, three miles, sometimes four. Punched the bags, the pads, the speedballs; circled, weaved, kicked. Push-ups. Pull-ups. Endless sit-ups. Barbells, dumbbells, machines, and ropes. No rest. No days off. Didn't matter how hard she pushed one day or hurt the next—she was always back, always training. Never saying a word to anyone, not a syllable. Even if someone was crazy enough to come in early and use something she wanted, she never spoke—just moved on, did something different that day. She was the ghost of 5:00 a.m. A tall, lean, bronze-haired ghost in a gray hoodie and worn sneakers who entered, trained, and left.

Nobody engaged her. The few staff there avoided her, never giving more than a nervous glance in her direction. Theirs was a mutual, unspoken agreement: You don't see me; I don't see you. I pay my bills; you leave me alone. Nothing more needed saying.

Because the tattoo on the girl's cheek said it all.

It was raining this morning—cold, wet, and miserable. When the girl stepped through the door of the gym, she was sopping wet, drenched through and thorough, head to toe. She didn't complain, just removed the old ragged towel from her backpack with the missing zipper and dried herself off as best she could. Pulled off her hoodie in the showers, then put her sneakers and socks next to the radiator where it was warm. Then she started: running, then punching, her bare feet barely whispers as they struck the ground.

An hour and a half later, the rain hadn't let up. Her socks were dry, but her shoes were still damp. She put them on anyway and made for the door as a middle-aged man entered wearing a Gold's singlet, balding but muscular. He started to hold the door for her with a friendly smile—but the second his eyes touched her face, his color drained, and he froze. He stared at the girl, wide-eyed and breath held. The girl didn't stare back. She saw him, but she tried not to see him, because he didn't matter. None of them mattered.

She ran home in the rain with her hood up, keeping the rain from her face and her face from the world.

Her home was not close. Not to the gym, not to anything. It was a bad house in a worse neighborhood, a worn-down cement box with a brown lawn and weeds pushing free between cracks in the cement. Empty driveway. She pulled open the rusty screen door and turned her key in the lock.

The house was dark and quiet, and the girl did nothing to change that. Her leggings were flecked with mud, her sneakers covered in it. She took them both off in the doorway and carried them to the sink—the smell of the kitchen musty in her nostrils and her wet socks slippery on the linoleum. She flicked the switch on the electric kettle, then started rubbing the mud off with her hands. By the time the last shoe was close to clean, she'd realized the kettle wasn't working. She flicked the switches, pulled out the plug, and tried the toaster. No, the kettle was fine—the power wasn't working. Fine. The girl rippled her fingers as if rolling an invisible coin between them. Then she clenched and made a fist. She uncurled in a slow release—and a blue line of electricity flickered between her thumb and forefinger. She fed it gingerly into the prongs of the power plug and the kettle began to boil.

The girl ate her porridge in silence and dust on a small metal table with uneven legs.

There wasn't any hot water—she only realized this after she'd gotten into the shower. Maybe the furnace was busted again, or maybe the power bill hadn't been paid. It didn't matter. She rippled her fingers, the invisible coin rolling to a different gap, then she raised her hand to the spluttering showerhead and opened her palm into a disc of fire. Her arm stayed up, the disc kept burning, and the water that spat through it was as hot as steam. She washed the sweat from her bones.

She dressed, quickly and quietly, in ill-fitting jeans and a shirt that still smelled like a thrift store. Pulled the knots from her hair then tied it up back and tight. A sweater over the top and a dry pair of socks that wouldn't last a second against the wet sneakers she was putting back on. Done. She turned to leave, but her eyes caught the mirror.

The girl couldn't help it. She stopped. Paused. Caught by the eyes of the person looking out at her from the little black-and-white photograph tucked into the mirror's frame. Punched in the stomach again by the stunning, smiling woman.

Look at how grown up you are. Look at you. My beautiful baby girl.

The girl's eyes flickered onto the reflection staring back at her—this gray, brown, wry, soaked creature with the hideous mark on its face. Then she turned and walked away, leaving the photograph behind.

Her father was walking in as she was walking out, reeking of chemicals and smoke. She looked up to meet his eyes, then caught herself. They both said nothing, just shuffled past each other awkwardly in the hallway, him coming in, her going out. By the time she'd laced up her cold sneakers, she could already hear the TV blaring away in the background.

"I loved you like a brother, Viktor. But the Legion of Heroes cannot let this evil stand."

The girl left her home alone. It was still raining.

The bus was six blocks away and took fifty-five minutes to get to school. She didn't sit next to anybody, or more accurately, nobody sat next to her. She was one of the first on the bus, so it was not her choice whether somebody shared her seat. Nobody ever shared her seat, no matter how crowded it was, or how many had to stand. It was a positive, she supposed. Plenty of legroom. She could put her bag on the seat. May as well, wouldn't make a lick of difference.

But she never did. She always left the spot open. Because . . . well, she didn't really know. Just in case.

She stared out the window at the world dripping by. She was an idiot.

Someone had gotten in early and tore the door off her locker. The girl felt her jaw clench as her fingers traced the bent hinges. Trying not to care. It didn't matter. Jokes on them, nothing in there of value. Except they'd stolen her math textbook—she'd have to go to the office and get another one. It was only a few minutes until class. She turned and walked away, leaving the twisted door lying where it was on the ground.

"You need to stop losing these," snapped the office lady, her eyes reduced to slits at the sight of the creature before her. The girl nodded curtly, a familiar clench in her chest. It wasn't her fault. It was never her goddamn fault. It just . . . breathe. Just breathe. The toad-faced woman stared at her, her jowls pursed in a sneer. "This is going on your account." The girl just breathed.

She was late to class. Mrs. Roberts looked up, her lips parted and poised to lecture, but when she saw who it was, she caught herself mid-breath. The girl made her way to her seat at the back quietly and without incident. A minor miracle. Mrs. Roberts's voice wafted out toward her. ". . . so if we see here x's coefficient . . ." She was glad she'd gotten a seat in the back. Nobody behind her to flick paper or spit or throw things at her. Eyes forward, back to the wall, just sit there and learn like you're supposed to. Like a normal person.

The girl liked math. The indifference of it. Numbers didn't care what you were. Numbers were detached, black and white. There were no opinions, no prejudice, only the truth, right or wrong. Maybe that's why she was almost kind of good at math. She'd be better if they'd stop taking her textbooks. But that was her own fault. She should have taken it home, not trusted the locker. Never trust anything. Rely only on yourself. She pulled a nub of a pencil out of her pocket and solved the problem.

She sat alone in the cafeteria eating her lunch in silence. She liked it better this way, she told herself. If anyone tried to sit with her, she'd leave. She chewed with her mouth shut and kept her eyes forward, focused on nothing, floating alone, her own little island in a sea of people. Today's meat loaf was chewy and the rice was mush, but it was food and it was free, so she didn't care. *Just a little longer*, she thought, *just a little longer*. She had the grade, and the Legion would eventually notice. They had to notice. Just a little longer.

She ate everything on her plate and dropped her tray in the bin. Then she went to the restroom, washed her hands, rinsed her mouth, splashed her face. A group of girls walked in just as she was leaving. Her steps quickened, putting distance between them, but not before she heard them muttering:

"Freak."

By the time she got back to her locker, someone had spray-painted PARASITE in red on the inside.

The whistle blew, and the head coach's voice echoed around the gymnasium as children of all ages scrambled toward their designated sections.

"Remember this is Week B! You are doing your Week B activities! Look at your schedule and—"

"Sir, where do you want me?" The girl's voice was level as she stepped forward. Firm, unwavering. She looked straight ahead, not making eye contact but not backing down. The coach, a six-foot-three forty-eight-year-old man with gym shorts and a beer gut looked back at her like he might look at dog crap stuck to the bottom of his shoe.

Every PD session, he "forgot" to designate her, and every PD session she asked him direct where he wanted her to go. It was either that or stand there, unacknowledged, waiting on recognition that would never come, and end up doing nothing. She wasn't going to let that happen.

The man glared down at her. The girl looked straight ahead, unblinking. "Join the cryomancers," he finally spat. "That's one of your tricks, isn't it? East side oval."

"Thank you, sir." Swap "thank" for "screw" and it'd be more accurate. But he'd relented, like he always relented, and she'd won like she always won. Smash your head into a wall long and hard enough and you learn two things: the strength of your head and the strength of the wall. And her head was hard, like the rest of her. The girl rippled her fingers and started jogging toward the oval, ready to make ice from the rain.

She didn't change or shower after PD. Other people did, but other people didn't get their clothes stolen. So, she was cold, wet, and hungry—again— when she got on the bus, and she stayed like that all the way home. She sat in the back, right in the corner where nobody could touch her. Most didn't want to. Most took one look at her face and stayed as far away as they possibly could. But there were always a few who took it upon themselves to mess with her. Fear did funny things to some people: some felt it so deep, hated it so much that they had to act against it to prove they weren't cowards, sometimes to others but mainly to themselves. To them, her presence wasn't just undesirable, it was an affront, and they would never be satisfied until they'd made sure she knew it. Generally, at first, not to her face. But eventually, after a few weeks or months of her not reacting, of not getting the rise they wanted, things would escalate. They'd take her inaction, her submission to their torment, as a sign that she couldn't fight back or wouldn't. No matter how well she took it, no matter how peaceful she stayed, it didn't matter. She'd tried to explain that to her dad a hundred times. Inevitably, it would get worse. Insults within earshot. Books knocked out of her hands. Her stuff stolen or broken, her locker set on fire or her lunch telekinetically thrown across the cafeteria. Then came the threats, the stalking, then finally, the violence.

Was it wrong that she actually looked forward to the violence? Looked forward to the day those stupid, arrogant, preening, privileged, thick-skulled scumbags finally found the guts to do what they'd been telling their idiot friends for weeks they were going to do? It was a perverse kind of anticipation, the kind where you're looking forward to something you shouldn't, something you know is wrong. But it was the catharsis. Those few, blissful seconds, built up to over months at a time—those few, fleeting moments of unrestrained release.

Sometimes, they came with intentions of nothing but violence. Sometimes, especially if it was a group of burly, sexually frustrated knuckle-draggers, they came intending a more intimate violation, as weak men often want to inflict upon strong women. Either way, it made no difference. Once they crossed that line, the leash came off. By law, once they attacked, she could defend herself. Not even the mark on her face could deprive her of the right to fight back.

Well, not "fight back." "Fight" made it sound like they stood a chance. The girl got off the bus and walked home in the rain.

The TV was still on—she could hear that much before she walked through the door. What a surprise. Her beloved, responsible father, snoring like an animal in his recliner, a bottle drooping from his hand, still in his overalls. It was efficient, she supposed. This way he could just wake up tonight and stumble out to work without a moment's bleary thought. She stormed past him into her room and slammed the door.

She changed into something less wet. Sat at her rickety desk and did what little homework she could get done. Then it was almost five o'clock, and she needed to put on her uniform, the black pants and striped shirt signifying someone who was utterly replaceable. She didn't hate her job. It paid a wage, and her manager wasn't unkind—he let her stay out back flipping burgers, out of sight. So what if her coworkers were drug addicts and criminals? The franchise would hire pretty much anyone, and they fit the bill. As did she. Drug addicts, criminals, and her. Society's most hated, even though she'd never asked for it, even though she'd never done anything wrong, even though none of this was her fault. Her fingers dug into her fists. The sound of her father's snoring pierced the bedroom, and for a moment she just wanted to roar, to shout and scream and let loose, to destroy everything and everyone, burn it all to the ground . . .

But then the picture on the mirror caught her eye, and once again she was staring at that face, that smile. Her heart rose up and caught in her throat.

My beautiful girl. My strong, beautiful girl.

The knot in her chest softened and the girl's shoulders slumped. Slowly, she unclenched her fists. The house was cold. She sniffed. Quietly, the girl rose, tugged the blanket off the top of her bed, walked out of her room, and lay it gently over her father. Then, without a word, she left the house, closed the door behind her, and stepped out into the rain. One step at a time.

It took three months of passive endurance, but finally they came for her. There were five of them. One she knew was called Randy, the fat thug with a face like a squashed potato, but she didn't know the others. She'd never really taken much time to get to know her classmates.

"The hell do you think you're going?"

They started following her after PD. She'd walked away, back toward the front of the gymnasium. Not running, but leading, leading them to somewhere isolated, somewhere that had cameras. Actions spoke louder than words, and video evidence exonerated fast.

"I said where the *hell* do you think you're going!"

He threw in a few profanities that would have made other people jump but which slid right off her. She made herself ready.

"Are you deaf? Are you *deaf*, you cut-faced freak?"

"No," the girl replied curtly. She turned to face them. They'd boxed her in, or so they thought. She put her back against the wall, keeping them all in view.

"Oh!" Randy chortled, a sound like a wet rag slapping cement. He was clearly the ringleader. His posse echoed his laughter behind him. "The freak speaks."

The girl said nothing. Randy's face darkened. He took a step forward.

"You're not welcome here." Low and murderous, echoed by the mutts behind him.

"I don't want any trouble." Not true. She wanted trouble. Her chest was a pounding drum of fire, and she had a lifetime of frustration and rage ready to set loose.

"You don't have a choice." It was funny how one of them always seemed to do the talking. "We're sick of you." Murmurs of agreement. "Sick of you sneaking around. This is our school. Our neighborhood. You're just a parasite."

"I don't want to hurt anyone." Again, a bald-faced lie.

The five of them howled with laughter, the smell of alcohol wafting on underage breath. The girl readied herself.

"I am legally entitled to take whatever measures I feel are reasonably necessary for the protection of my person," she articulated, clear and concise. She sounded like a robot, but sometimes that sentence alone, the strangeness and artificiality of it, was enough to make people take pause.

Not this time. "Screw you. Screw the law." Randy's snarl turned silver as steel spread down his arms. Behind him, powers arced across his companions.

The girl rippled her fingers and snarled. "Bring it on."

"This type of behavior is not acceptable at our school." Principal Garren's tone was severe, his mustache trembling. He didn't show it much, but he was afraid. Good. "We don't condone it and we cannot allow it."

His assistant principal nodded her agreement, slapping a stack of letters down on the principal's desk.

"We've received numerous complaints. Parents simply don't feel safe with your daughter here. Randy Misch's mother, in particular—"

"Randy Misch?"

Any competent parent would have interjected, *The boy who attacked my daughter unprovoked with a gang of four others? Has he been expelled yet?*

But the girl's father said nothing.

"She feels that, given her son's . . . condition . . . allowing your daughter to remain a student here would be . . ." The assistant principal's sentence trailed off. The principal picked it up.

"The boy has suffered severe cardiovascular trauma. He was only this morning moved from intensive care. He's going to have to be fitted with a pacemaker. His football career is essentially over."

He tried to kill a lightning thrower with a body made entirely of metal. What the hell did you expect?

The words unsaid, the silence pointed. The cowardly mustached man behind his cherrywood desk began thumbing through a stack of papers.

"Billy Thompson has third-degree burns to seventy percent of his body. Juan Alvarez needed three pints of blood before they could close all his lacerations. John Chu's femur is fractured in two places. And Mark O'Donnell is possibly going to lose his genitals to frostbite—the doctors are still uncertain."

She always liked it when they laid out all her accomplishments. It was like reading the sports highlights.

"Now in light of the, ah, nature of the incident, the school will not press charges . . ."

Because you know it was self-defense. Because you know you did nothing to stop it. Because you'd lose.

"Nevertheless, we feel it would be better for everyone if your daughter"—the principal looked at the girl for the first time since they'd walked in there—"finds alternative education arrangements."

She looked at her father slumped in the chair beside her, unshaven, bleary-eyed. Smelling of soot, oil, and grease. He wasn't looking at her. He wasn't looking at them. He wasn't looking at anything.

"We'll go," he said simply, finally. Relenting. Like he always did. Backing down from a fight.

He pushed himself out of the chair, and they left.

"They attacked *me*."

"I know."

"They were trying to kill me."

"I know."

"Or worse!"

"I know. I know, I know, I know."

They drove in silence. The rain poured down the truck's windows. This was the first time he'd picked her up from this school since she started.

"It's not my fault."

"It's never your fault."

"It never is!"

"I wasn't being facetious." Her father's old, tired eyes never left the road—just stared straight through the rain and the *swish-swish* of the wipers. "I know you didn't ask for this. For any of it."

But even though they both knew it was true, it didn't sound like he believed it.

More road and more silence.

"We'll find a new school. There was a flyer in the mailbox about this place in Northridge." A pause. "Give that a go."

"Great."

"And just"—her father's voice suddenly rose—"look, I know it's not your fault, and I know you're not doing this on purpose, but please, just . . ."

"Just what? Keep my head down?!"

"Keep your head down, stay out of people's way, just try and . . ."

"I am trying!"

"WELL, TRY HARDER!" The shout echoed around the truck's cab, ringing and reverberating into nothingness. And then there was only silence. The girl leaned back in her seat, a harshness in her throat and a stinging in her eyes. She stared away, watching the raindrops trickle slowly down the window.

Her father sighed. Ran a hand through his fading hair.

"I'm sorry, I didn't mean to . . . I just . . . I'm hanging by a thread at work. I don't need this, I can't . . . we can't . . ."

He paused, and for the first time in a long time, turned to look at his daughter.

"I just need you to do this. Just this once. For me. Please, Jane. I'm begging you."

They drove on in silence through the rain. The rusted, broken man and the fierce, beautiful girl with the E tattooed on her cheek.

FEAR AND LOATHING

Empathic Individuals Regulation Act 1990 (Federal)
Selected Extracts

Section 2: Purpose
The purpose of this Act is to control and regulate both empaths and empath behavior for the protection of the American people, by ensuring that empathic individuals are visible and known to the communities in which they reside and prohibiting the unauthorized copying of powers . . .

Section 7: Definitions
Subsection 1. In this Act . . .
"empath" means a person who has the ability to copy, mimic, acquire, or absorb one or more abilities from other individuals, irrespective of the manner in which the abilities are copied, mimicked, acquired, or absorbed. . . .
"mark" refers to the indelible imprint required to be displayed by empaths at all times . . .

Section 8: Act Applicable Irrespective of Age or Capacity
Subsection 1. Any section of this Act that could be applied to an empath under the age of eighteen applies to that empath as if that empath had attained the age of eighteen.
Subsection 2. Any section of this Act that could be applied to an empath save for that empath temporarily or permanently lacking capacity applies to that empath as if that empath had full capacity at that time . . .

Section 16: Empaths to Be Marked

Any person designated as an empath or possessing empathic abilities must be affixed with an indelible mark upon their right cheek.

Subsection 1. This marking must be imprinted immediately after empathic abilities are discovered.

Subsection 2. The penalty for an empath remaining unmarked is up to twenty years imprisonment . . .

Section 17: Mark to Be of Certain Quality

The mark indelibly affixed to an empath must be that of an upper case alpha-numeric "E" not less than three inches in length and one and a half inches in width.

Subsection 1. The penalty for an empath failing to immediately rectify an insufficient mark is up to fifteen years' imprisonment . . .

Section 18: Mark to Be Visible

An empath's mark is to be readily visible to the unassisted eye at all times.

Subsection 1. An empath's mark is to remain uncovered and unobstructed and must not be obscured, hidden, disguised, or healed under any circumstances.

Subsection 2. The penalty for an empath failing to ensure their mark is clearly visible is up to twenty years' imprisonment.

Subsection 3. The penalty for assisting an empath in obscuring, hiding, disguising, or healing their mark under any circumstances is up to ten years' imprisonment.

Part a. This section applies irrespective of whether the assistance is provided by a licensed healer . . .

Section 37: Empaths to Require Express Consent

Subsection 1. An empath may not under any circumstances copy, mimic, acquire, or absorb the ability of another without:

Part a. That individual's express and informed consent, and

Part b. That individual having capacity to provide consent and being free from undue influence or duress.

Subsection 2. This section applies regardless of whether an empath copies, mimics, acquires, or absorbs the powers of others through touch, proximity, or intake of genetic material.

Subsection 3. The penalty for a breach of this section is imprisonment to a term of life.

Part a. The penalty for a second breach of this section is a sentence up to or including death . . .

"All right, Mr. Callaghan. When you're ready."

Matt smiled with a warmth that was serene, confident, and utterly insincere. He drew a deep, semi-dramatic breath, took the old lady's cold, wrinkled hands and closed his eyes.

In the silence of the deserted classroom, Matt Callaghan and Carol Blithe sat unmoving on opposite sides of the desk, her peering inquisitively—if not a little hopefully—over the top of her full-moon spectacles at the young man's face, and him mentally counting *one Mississippi, two Mississippi* . . . until an appropriately mystical amount of time had passed.

Matt opened his eyes and calmly took his hands back.

"I'm seeing green," he told her. "Green growing to red and fading to brown." His brow furrowed and he put a hand to his temple. "I think it's leaves. Plants. Red flowers."

Across the desk, Carol's eyes widened—and despite what Matt could only presume were her best efforts a look of comprehension dawned across her face. "And the brown?" she asked despite herself, in little more than a whisper. Matt faked a frown.

"Potential. Tomorrow or the next day. There'll be a package and . . ." He scrunched his face up so that he appeared slightly confused. "You shouldn't use it. It's born of jealousy. Withering. There's brown inside and out." He looked up at Carol, still intentionally frowning. "Sorry if that doesn't make a lot of sense."

The examiner nodded mutely and made a little note on her notepad.

It was five days after Matt's birthday, the rain had finally let up, and his powers of clairvoyance were being tested. Unlike most people in most schools across the country, Matt's PD grade wasn't assessed through standard grading, because clairvoyants it turned out were so rare—rare, in fact, almost to the point of nonexistence—that nobody had ever developed any standardized tests to evaluate them. This put Matt's teachers and the Board of Education generally in a somewhat difficult position—because it was one thing to have a student not subject to a strict lesson plan or actually learning anything about their powers, but it was a different matter entirely for the school not to be able to grade them. A PD mark was essential for getting into college and a key performance indicator tied directly into Northridge's funding, not to mention a potential discrimination lawsuit if they denied Matt the opportunity to earn one. As a result, the school district was placed in the unenviable position of having to test Matt's clairvoyance without any clue how to do so, and Matt was placed in the unenviable position of having to have his clairvoyance tested without actually having any.

In the end, the Board of Education and Matt's parents had settled on half-yearly assessments, conducted by a specialist assessor brought in from outside the school district. In theory, this was supposed to provide Matt with a blank and unknown subject on which to focus his second sight in order to accurately gauge its progression and extent. In reality, the assessments were a game where the assessors were unknowingly played from the word *go*, and where Matt, his life and lie on the line, had no intention of playing fair.

Without warning, Matt reached over and placed his hand on Carol's cheek, causing the examiner to flinch. "There's someone in your life whose name begins with M," he informed her, his eyes once again closed. "And they're going to need your support. Soon. Or sometime in the future. I . . . time is vague; I can't see exactly. But they'll need your help, and you can't be reluctant to give it." He withdrew his hand and opened his eyes just in time to see a look of comprehension—unmistakable this time—flash across his assessor's face. Matt forced himself not to smile.

It had all started with a phone call. Matt, his voice deliberately slowed and mumbling, had called up the Board of Education offices under the pretense of being one of Northridge High's security workers and requested the name of the visiting examiner so it could be "added to the authorized personnel list." It was a trick he'd used a dozen times before, and the bored receptionist on the other end of the line had yet to question it, especially when Matt provided the identification number he'd memorized off Dyson Bradley's badge.

And once he had a name, Matt Callaghan, child of the Internet age, got to work.

The Board of Education website gave him Carol Blithe's work email and biography. An online phone book gave him her phone number and home address. From Google Maps, he pulled up a view of her house and the surrounding neighborhood, and from her social media profile (on which, like so many older citizens, she had neglected to update the privacy settings), he compiled a rough outline of her interests, hobbies, family and friends, and indeed, her entire life.

Carol Blithe was a lifetime teacher of decent yet modest means (judging by her home, which was nice but not too nice, as well as her recent five-day trip to Florida) with two adult children and a parakeet—a kind woman and successful educator (judging by the size of the bouquet her graduating class had got her last year), who lived alone and could resonate various materials by humming at different frequencies. (Thank you, Department of Powers Registration open search function.) The school where she normally worked was a four-hour drive from Northridge, and Matt had been sure to have a double-shot soy cappuccino (her regular order, from a marker scrawl on a cup in a picture of her lunching with a friend) waiting when she arrived.

"Knew you'd be tired from the journey," he'd said the second she walked in, smiling kindly and passing her the Styrofoam cup.

And from there, she was putty in his hands.

Successful assessments legitimized Matt's deception; so when it came to assessments, Matt brought his A game. The "M" person he'd alluded to was Mrs. Blithe's youngest daughter, Melanie, who social media informed him had just started interstate at Brown and who, by simple deduction, would at some point require her mother's assistance. The green with red flowers, of course, had been a reference to the rosebush blooming very visibly in Carol's front garden, a magnificent and robust specimen that could never have grown that large without continual attention and care. The brown package, on the other hand, was a "free sample" of "lawn vitamins" Matt had put into the mail only yesterday, which was, in reality, potent plant poison—poison that would arrive at Carol's 49th Street home in a day or two and from which Matt's "prediction" would now "save" her prize flowers.

But he wasn't done yet. Not by a long shot.

"There's a man in a black coat," he proclaimed. "A long black coat. He's older, determined. I see him clearly." Matt paused and looked across at the examiner. "Do you know anyone like that?"

"I-I-I," Carol stammered—Matt knew she wasn't supposed to give away any details about her life. But he didn't need her to.

"If you don't know him yet, you will," he continued confidently, not in the least bit concerned about the probability of an older, single woman from a colder town at some point running into an older man wearing a black coat. "He's facing a choice—though there isn't really one. He won't change, he can't, not now. There's a person around him, someone he's linked to. He's connected, but not connecting." Mystic-sounding contradictory nonsense and good old-fashioned vaguery. Carol ate it up.

As the assessor continued to scrawl hurriedly on her notepad, Matt leaned back in his chair and folded his arms, allowing a concerned shadow to pass over his face. When Mrs. Blithe eventually looked up, she found the young "clairvoyant" staring warily at her.

"What is it?" she asked, an edge of fear creeping into her voice. Matt paused thoughtfully for a few seconds, apparently lost in contemplation, before slowly shaking his head and answering.

"I'm seeing growth," he predicted, his eyes half-narrowed and his voice measured. "Somewhere around you. Someone, inside someone, growing internally. Except it's not good." Carol's shoulders stiffened. "It's insidious." Matt let the corner of his lips droop slightly. "I'm sorry."

"What do you mean?" the examiner asked, her mouth half open, her pencil no longer scribbling notes. "Insidious, what do you mean by that?"

"Inherently wrong," replied Matt, his gaze sympathetic yet unwavering. "Dangerous. Corrupted or corrupting. It's not immediately obvious, but, given time . . ." His voice trailed off, and he watched with discreet satisfaction as the older woman's mind churned through the implication of his words.

This, Matt felt, was one of the cleverer "predictions" he'd come up with. "Growth" and "internal" in reference to a person would generally lead someone to think of one of two things: babies or cancer. Cancer, one of the few diseases still capable of killing in an age of superhuman health care, was still common enough to be worrying, and at fifty-eight, Mrs. Blithe and her peers were its prime target—without knowing a thing about her, Matt could have practically guaranteed that she would or did know someone who'd be diagnosed. If Carol's mind had gone to cancer, the first person she heard of being afflicted would be confirmation of Matt's power—and if she took it to mean a baby, well, inevitably she'd know someone who was pregnant, and then it would be twenty-something years before Mrs. Blithe could properly rule out the child she'd applied Matt's prediction to being some kind of kitten-drowning psychopath. Alternatively, she might run into someone who'd miscarried, which would practically confirm Matt as a modern-day Nostradamus.

What kind of messed-up life am I living, he thought ruefully as Carol's pencil scratched shakily across the paper, when I'm wishing death upon a stranger's unborn baby. He gave a small sigh and glanced discreetly as the clock on the wall hit 11:17, then watched with an expression absolutely lacking in any kind of surprise as the sound of Mrs. Blithe's phone ringing pealed out from her handbag.

"Don't worry," he assured her matter-of-factly, making a face as the examiner jumped half a foot in the air. "Nothing bad. It's a telemarketer. Home insurance. One of those recorded calls."

Which, thought Matt, smiling to himself as he watched the wide-eyed woman fish the phone out of her handbag and hold it up to her ear with trembling hands, it unquestioningly was—since he'd programmed the robocall to go through from his computer last night.

It took Matt barely twenty minutes to earn a very respectable grade for his preparation and performance and to successfully discharge his PD examination obligations for another six months. Freed from his assessor's scrutiny and having wished Mrs. Blithe safe driving in the wet (the Bureau of Meteorology was claiming a 98 percent chance of precipitation about two hours north, where she'd be passing through on her way home), Matt spent the remainder of the period polishing off some overdue math equations, before packing up and exiting the deserted classroom at the sound of the lunch bell, the evaluation form clutched firmly in his hand.

If Matt had been the type of person to talk about his "powers" to his friends, he would have been keen to talk to them today. He wasn't, for obvious reasons. Matt had never told anyone what he really was. Still, he thought ruefully as he pushed his way through the crowded hallway towards the school office, it would've been nice, if for no other reason than to get some appreciation for all his hard work. Five years of pulling off a successful con didn't feel nearly as impressive without someone to boast to about it.

Matt pushed open the door to the front office and was greeted by a rush of air-conditioning. "All done." He smiled at Miss Cambridge as he strode over to the reception desk, sliding the assessment form across the countertop. The fit thirtysomething-year old woman said nothing and made no move to acknowledge his presence other than to look up at him with a nauseated, slightly panicked stare.

Matt's smile faded. Miss Cambridge was normally very cheerful.

"Everything okay?" he asked, glancing around the otherwise deserted room—but before the receptionist could answer a man's voice barked "Mr. Callaghan!" so loudly the pair of them jumped.

"Mr. Callaghan," repeated Principal Rance, half-shouting through his office's open door where he stood stock-still behind his desk, hands clenched on the back of his chair. His piggy eyes burned into Matt as if he was afraid the boy might at any moment turn tail and flee. "Matt. Just the man I wanted to see."

Matt didn't like the sound of that, and he liked Principal Rance's wide eyes and unusually sweaty jowls even less.

"Sir . . . ?" he extended reluctantly, but the pasty, gray-suited man shook his head and beckoned furiously at him to come over. Against his better judgment but not wanting to disobey, Matt moved reluctantly toward the principal's office, shooting a look back at Miss Cambridge, who was watching him go with the terrified expression of someone seeing the family cow walk to slaughter. Matt stepped into the office to find Northridge's principal flanked by his assistant principal, who seemed, if possible, even more nervous than his boss—and who shared Rance's wild-eyed avoidance of looking at the third person in the room, a bronze-haired girl in a light gray hoodie who was sitting silently in the plastic chair in front of Rance's desk, staring straight ahead.

"Sir?" he said again, confused by the obvious tension but even more confused by the way the girl did not in any way acknowledge his existence. "What's the . . . ?"

"Matt!" Principal Rance yelped in a voice that was several decibels too loud for enclosed spaces. "This is Jane. She's new!"

"Hi . . ." Matt started to say, but before he could even glance at the girl Rance's irrationally high voice made him start back around.

"Jane, Matt will show you around!" he continued, racing through the words as though they were hot coals in desperate need of spitting out. "Won't he?"

"Sure." Matt shrugged, turning properly around to face the girl, not getting why they were all stressing out over some new . . .

It was then that he saw the E.

A pool of black ice crashed down into Matt's stomach and he involuntarily stepped back, seized by a rush of panic. An empath. An actual empath. It took every ounce of Matt's self-control not to run.

It was like seeing a tiger or bear up close. He'd read about them, seen them on TV, but it didn't prepare you for the sight, the actual knowledge that the thing was right there, alive and dangerous and ready to kill you. That E, that symbol, the warning and reminder of not just power and imbalance, but genocide—of half a billion souls snuffed out in an instant. The darkest day in human history. He'd only been a kid, but Matt could still see it, still remember, the sky black, the sea burning. People running, fear, everywhere, palpable. Talk of the end of the world.

If she had noticed Matt's visible recoil or his compunction to flee, the empath didn't show it. Instead, she merely sat where she was, her face blank, staring straight ahead at nothing.

"Can I go?" she asked dully. She made no attempt to meet Matt's fixated, horrified gaze or in any way acknowledge his existence. Rance's hands fumbled across the neck of his chair.

"Of-of course," he stammered rapidly, wiping sweat into the leather. "The, ah, the cafeteria is . . ." But at the first hint of dismissal, the girl was up and out the door into the main office, gone before the pudgy principal's sentence had time to wither and die. A billowing silence expanded in her wake. Matt's head swung ashen-faced between the door and the two men, his mouth agape.

"I . . ."

"Thank you, Mr. Callaghan, for agreeing to this," gushed Murphy.

"I-I-I," Matt stammered, struggling to find the words. "Um . . ."

"You're a model student," Rance assured him, covering his discomfort with a stiff cough. "And she, ah, needs a companion. Someone to . . . to keep a close eye on her." Matt turned back around to find the principal and his assistant principal staring at him with desperate, uncomfortable intensity. "A close, *comprehensive* eye."

"What do you . . . ?"

But suddenly, the penny dropped—and in a rush of multilayered terror Matt realized why he of all people had been picked to stay close to this dangerous newcomer.

Crap, the so-called clairvoyant internally swore.

Matt wandered out of the school office so caught up in a feeling somewhere between dazed and terrified that half a minute later he almost ran into the back of a Mexican sophomore with retractable dragonfly wings who had abruptly stopped moving forward—blocked, Matt saw as he looked up properly for the first time, by a crush of bodies backed across the hall.

"Excuse me," Matt mumbled, fumbling past, not really thinking. Was there a spill or something? He shot a glance at the floor as he made his way between the muttering students, but he didn't see anything out of the ordinary and his shoes weren't sticking. Matt kept pushing through absentmindedly. He couldn't smell smoke—it didn't seem like one of the pyromancers had set their locker on fire again. But people were just stopped, standing there, blocking the way to the cafeteria like stupid statue sheep, whispering among themselves. It didn't make sense.

Then Matt reached the front of the crowd, saw the girl and realized he knew exactly what was going on.

She was sitting at their table. Weirdly, this was the first thing Matt noticed, and it sent a little flicker of completely irrational annoyance running through his mind. They always sat there, and here she was, a foreign invader. Of course, he conceded a split second later, she wouldn't have known it was their table.

The second thing Matt noticed was the space. The area around where the empath sat was completely and utterly empty—the students of Northridge High bunched up in a perimeter around her like fish skittering around a shark. An increasing feeling of panic fluttered through Matt's stomach as he watched the empath sitting alone, surrounded by empty tables, eyes blank and picking half-heartedly at her food. What was he supposed to do? Rance had explicitly told him to keep a "close eye" on this girl, but that wouldn't just put him in danger, it'd single him out in front of the entire school. So far everyone was just standing there, silent and horror-struck, and Matt understood why. They'd come back from a seemingly normal day to find a monster in their midst, a creature that wasn't just empowered like they were but who could copy their identities, their very essence, and use it against them. And he was supposed to monitor this thing?! How?! God, she could do anything, be anything, steal from anyone!

Except me.

The thought popped out of nowhere, unbidden—so clear and sudden that it almost shocked Matt to think it. Anyone except him. That big spikey E was an imbedded, lingering warning—but to him, the girl may as well have been wearing a T-shirt that read "I steal ovaries." Cool, good for you, but Matt had none to steal. She was a thief, but he was bankrupt.

Suddenly, Matt found himself suppressing the bizarre, hysterical urge to laugh. It was like in an instant the whole world had flipped upside down. Everyone was standing here watching this new kid, terrified— and for the first time in his life, he had less reason to be afraid than any of them. What was she going to do, copy his nothingness? Oh sure, she had powers—but didn't everyone? Was someone walking around with four guns who much more dangerous than someone walking around with one? What was she going to do, kill him twice?

Honestly, what could this new girl do that anyone else couldn't?

Because she was just a girl, he realized now, and it was like his eyes suddenly adjusted and for the first time he was actually seeing the totality of the person in front of him, unobscured by the mark. She was just a girl. A tall, lean, auburn-haired girl wearing a ratty gray sweater and sitting all alone at a table meant for eight, gazing straight ahead while an entire school stood ten feet away staring at her like she was Satan.

She hadn't asked for this, he realized. Nobody got to choose what powers they got. He knew that better than anyone. And yet there she was, alone and despised just because she'd happened to be born a freak like him. The whole school was afraid of her. Heck, Rance was so scared, he'd implicitly ordered Matt to watch her future. The canary in the coal mine, whose job it was to die.

Or, he suddenly realized, to keep singing.

And in an instant, Matt made up his mind.

He strode forward—out behind the girl, past their table, and off toward the serving area. A sea of eyes and low murmuring followed him as he walked, the first one to break ranks. Matt could feel their gazes burning on the back of his head, but in a way it didn't matter. He suddenly knew what he was doing. He moved with confidence, chin up, chest out. The lunch lady filled up his tray, going through the motions with a look of stunned surrealism. Matt smiled, said thank you, then turned around, walked back . . . and sat down opposite the empath.

The girl glanced up at him for a few seconds with an expression that was halfway between weary and confused. He looked back at her and smiled, then bent down and started to eat. There was a low mumbling behind him. Out of the corner of his eye, Matt could see Taylor mouthing swear words and furiously shaking his head. Matt ignored him.

They ate slowly, in relative silence. The girl stopped looking at him and Matt kept his face forward, acting—no, being—like this was just another normal lunch. Around them the shock, or perhaps the novelty, was starting to wear off, decaying under the pressure of time and inaction. People were beginning to realize that they were actually hungry, and hey, the world hadn't actually stopped spinning. The bell would be ringing soon, and they'd all be trapped back in class. So, after a few minutes, people slowly began to move, hesitantly, in dribs and drabs, though giving Matt's table a wide berth and many nervous looks.

Sound, the buzz of conversation, slowly began to echo through the hall. Matt pinched open his carton of milk and took a sip. The girl forked blankly at a piece of broccoli. The tables around the room were filling up, no one voice distinct now, the sound louder, more normal. Movement, color, and life returned, albeit somewhat confused and subdued, with every second eye fixed very intently on the two of them.

Finally, quietly—once the background noise was enough to cover it—the girl glanced up at him and spoke.

"What're you doing?"

Matt's composure never wavered, and his posture remained relaxed. "Eating."

"You know what I mean. What is this?"

"Lunch." He put down the carton of milk and pulled the corner off one of his cookies, popped it in his mouth, and looked up at her, smiling genially.

The girl looked back at him, her thin brows arched in evident hostility. Not too much hostility, though, not enough to be visible to anyone else. She might have been angry, but the girl wasn't stupid. She was quite pretty actually, thought Matt, maybe even beautiful. It was hard to look at anything other than the big, ugly E tattooed on her face, but if you get past that, she actually had quite striking features—gray-blue eyes, a small nose, and elegant cheekbones. No makeup to speak of, or at least none Matt could see, which was kind of impressive in its own way, though it meant there was no disguising the dark rings under her eyes.

"I'm not going to sleep with you."

If he hadn't been being so deliberately composed, Matt might have choked on his food. As it was, he just coughed a little, caught himself, and swallowed.

"What?"

"I'm not going to sleep with you." The girl's voice reminded him of a flagpole he'd licked one winter.

"Well, never say never," he said with a smile. Her eyes narrowed. Matt's smile faded and he leaned back a little. "I'm joking."

"I'm not. Go away. I don't care what stupid bet you've made with your stupid friends." She glared at him. "Leave me alone."

Matt was taken aback. "What are you talking about, what bet?"

"Your bet. Your bet, or dare, or stupid bro-initiation 'first one to get the empath girl' hazing trash to prove you're a real man. You think you're the first? You're. Not." She punctuated her words with her fork, jabbing it at his chest with discreet viciousness. "So, go back to the other idiots and tell them whatever you like. Tell them you failed. Tell them we made out. Kill yourself. I don't care. Just go away."

Matt blinked, stunned. "Anyone ever tell you you're kind of rude?"

The girl didn't reply but instead looked down and stabbed violently at another vegetable.

A silence stretched out between them while Matt tried to form a coherent sentence.

"Okay," he said finally. "Well, first, I'm not trying to sleep with you. Second, how do you know you don't want to sleep with me? We've only just met. I could be adorable."

The girl glared daggers at him.

"Again, joke," Matt continued, moving hurriedly on. "I'm not trying to sleep with you. And nobody bet me anything." Although that wouldn't actually have been a bad idea, he avoided adding regretfully, he could have made like fifty bucks.

"Oh yeah?" Heavy sarcasm slathered in contempt.

"Yeah, actually."

"Then why the hell are you sitting here?"

"The principal told me to."

"He told you to show me around," she replied, then rolled her eyes around the room. "Oh, look, the cafeteria. You showed it to me. Well done. Now go away."

"And," Matt continued matter-of-factly, "this is my table. This is where I usually eat lunch." He kept his eyes steady and his movements calm and deliberate, matching his voice.

Silence . . . punctuated only by the sea of background chatter, then, "Is this some kind of joke?"

"No."

"Well, are you stupid? Or blind?" She pointed, savage but discreet, at her cheek. Matt stayed focused on his meal.

"Neither."

"You know what this is."

"Was that a question?"

"It's not a fashion statement."

"I don't know much about fashion anyway."

"You can goddamn see it."

"I can," he replied, calm and neutral. "And so can everyone else. They can all see exactly what you are." He looked up and into her eyes. "What else can they see?"

For the first time since he'd sat down, the girl hesitated. "What do you mean?"

"When they look at us, at you, right now." He waved his fork around idly, subtly indicating the entire room, his gaze very deliberately not following his implement. "What do they see?"

"I don't know, what kind of stupid—"

"They see you," Matt interrupted without raising his voice in the slightest, "and me, sitting here eating lunch like it's nothing. Like it's the normal-est thing in the world. Heads up, I'm going to take one of your tater tots." He reached over and pierced the piece of fried potato with his fork, then drew back and put it in his mouth. The girl didn't move, though she stared at him like the fork had gone into her leg. Matt forced himself to chew, swallow, and keep going.

"Now what do you think they think, seeing us here, sitting, talking, acting normal? What do they assume? What do they know? They know you're an empath. You can copy people's powers; they know that from the tattoo on your face."

The girl's mouth hardened, but Matt pressed on toward his point. "And they know who I am," he continued. "They know I'm a clairvoyant." The girl's eyes got maybe just a little bit wider. "Because I've been going here for years." He paused and shook his head at her. "I'm going to take another tot because it really doesn't seem like you want them."

The girl said nothing, so Matt reached over and took it. It needed salt. "So, they see you, and maybe you're all rigid and tense and dangerous— but me? Look at me." He sat up a bit, squared his shoulders. "I'm casual, man, cool as a cucumber. Ain't got a care in the world. And I'm a clairvoyant. I can see the future." He relaxed slightly and went back to his food, slow and deliberate. "And if me, who can see the future, is totally relaxed and unphased around you, then you obviously aren't going to hurt me, or I wouldn't be here. They don't know what you're going to do, but I know, and they know I know. And I know you're not going to hurt me. And I know you're not going to take my powers. And that's that."

For about half a minute, the girl didn't speak. She'd stopped picking at her food. Matt ate in silence, looking up occasionally to watch her process.

"Why?" she said finally.

Matt swallowed a mouthful of weakly gravied meat. "Well, for one . . ." He shrugged, keeping up his cover. "The future's the future. Are you going to hurt me?"

"No," replied the girl, chewing reluctantly on the word.

"Right," confirmed Matt. "And I wasn't planning on hurting you, so there we go. Two, well, I got told to. Three, table. Four," he said, holding up three fingers and a fork, "I don't know, because I'm nice? Because it's the right thing to do?"

"I don't need your help."

Matt pointed with his fork. "See those guys over there? That big table of African dudes who're staring at you like you killed their dog? No, don't turn around, look subtly." He waited for the girl to get a glance in at the four young men, tall, dark, and furious. "See them? Yeah. They're Ugandan. And I'd imagine—but, you know, this is just speculation—that they don't feel the greatest amount of affection toward empaths."

The girl's eyes fell to her tray. "What's your point?"

"My point is that right now, they're sitting over there thinking about trying to kill you. And they're probably not the only ones. Everyone's afraid of you and fear can make people stupid."

"You're worried I'll get hurt?" the girl scoffed.

"Aren't you?"

"No. Anyone comes at me, I'll destroy them."

"Yeah, maybe you will." Matt leaned in. "But see, these are my friends. They might be stupid, they might be scared, and they might be bigots, but they're still my friends. And I don't want them to get hurt any more than I want you to."

"You don't know me."

"I don't know a lot of people. Doesn't mean I want them to get hurt if I can help it."

"And this, sitting here, eating goddamn pudding cups, this is doing something?"

"Yes. It's normalizing. It's showing everyone they don't need to be afraid."

A silence stretched out between them, the boy eating as calmly as he could, the girl glaring coldly at him.

"I don't need your help."

"Who's helping? I'm just eating lunch."

The girl's hands clenched the ends of the tray, and for a second Matt thought she was about to launch across the table at him—but then she just stood up, turned around, and walked off.

"Are. You. Insane?"

Taylor was on his arm like a leash on a dog. This was probably the most agitated Matt had ever seen him; his shoulders were arched, and his eyes darted around the hallway as they strode toward fifth period. Suddenly, they were the center of attention—people stopping, pointing, whispering to one another . . . at him directly, Taylor vicariously through being beside him. Matt kind of loved him for that, being loyal enough to walk into the middle of a maelstrom. If he'd been less practiced controlling his thoughts, Taylor's agitation might have been contagious, but Matt just concentrated on walking and breathing as calmly as possible.

"She. Is. A. Goddamn . . . !"

"Empath. She's an empath. So what?" He tried to avoid looking back at a scale-skinned girl who was gawking open-mouthed at him as they passed.

"So what?!" hissed Taylor. "So"—he loosed a string of profanity—"What?! You know what those people can do!"

"And I know she's not going to do it. I *know*." He said it firmly, like he believed it.

"You don't." Taylor stopped suddenly. He stared at Matt. "You know?"

"I know. Hundred percent. Heart of hearts."

A steady stream of staring faces continued past them.

"You're sure? Like not even a little?"

"No doubt. Not an inch. Nobody here needs to be afraid of her."

"Man . . ." Taylor glanced around at either side, then gritted his teeth and breathed out a torrent of swear words.

"Okay. All right. Okay. I trust . . ." Taylor looked at Matt, face hard. "I don't trust her. But, man, I mean, this is your thing, right?"

"It is."

"Seeing stuff, being right, this is . . . this is what you do!"

"You know it is."

"All right. Okay. All right. I trust you. I trust you, and if you say it, it's on point, that's your thing, you . . ." Taylor shook his head and looked at Matt almost pleadingly. "But do you have to go sitting with her, man, I mean come on . . ."

Matt shrugged. "I'm sorry, man. I just see it how I see it. I've got to hang around; she's got a part to play in my future."

"It's not tempting . . . ?"

"Fate? I'm a clairvoyant, numbnuts, I own fate."

"Yeah . . ." Taylor let out a big, pent-up breath. He was wavering. "Yeah, I suppose, right, if you know, yeah, it wouldn't be . . ." He shook his head. "Just, damn, man, you know I have to worry 'bout my boy. You know I love you."

"Gay."

"Screw you, I hope she murders your ass."

"Bet you twenty bucks she won't."

The staring didn't let up in fifth period, but the silence did. Even muted, Matt's phone was buzzing so much he could have used it to seduce bees.

He spent the entire fifty-five-minute class with his eyes buried in his lap, tapping out replies to the torrent of messages as fast as he could while remaining inconspicuous.

No shes not a murderer shes just new felt sry 4 her. Shes cool all g

Luckily, he'd manage to snag a desk second row from the back, which put him out of Mrs. Colbert's immediate attention without looking like he was trying to hide. The only downside of this was that it meant Abby Sanders sitting behind him was able to keep tapping him on the shoulder and trying to hand him scraps of paper. Matt kept waving her away as discreetly as he could.

No notes dude just msg srsly whats wrong w u fug

Whatever historical event they were supposed to be learning about today, Matt didn't gleam a bar of it, although he was quietly grateful that Mrs. Colbert had the good sense not to decide right now was the perfect time to revisit the Black Death and Africa.

Im not tryna bang her u idiot just eat lunch say hi. She at our tbl. Not dangerous no prob

Thank God, his phone had unlimited messaging. He snapped out a reply to Rebecca Grayson, who was asking if his nose had been bleeding, implying he'd been psychically possessed. Him, honestly. And this coming from Rebecca Grayson, the same girl whose mental defenses their Thought Protection teacher had described as "paper-esque." The nerve.

A+ in ment def rmbr? Im not stupid, shes not even psy

Technically, Matt didn't know if the new girl had telepathy or not. Actually, he didn't know what she could do. Jeez, he didn't even know her last name. That was a bit of an oversight.

Dude relax dont worry know wat im doing

Buzz. Buzz. Buzz. Dear Lord. What had he gotten himself into?

The girl's full name, it turned out, was Jane Walker. He'd learned that when his science teacher, Mr. Swaim, had, his eyes very much averted and with much adjustment of his bow tie, called the roll in sixth period. Still buried in his phone, Matt had been very nearly late, and upon entering had found the entire lab fixated on one bench up the back, its sole occupant, and her glaring spikey E. Suppressing a sigh, Matt had dutifully hitched his bookbag up on his shoulder, pulled himself a little straighter, walked right over, and sat next to her.

Jane had just glared.

If it had been any other new student starting the teacher might have introduced them, asked them where they were from, all that boring kindergarten stuff. As it stood, Matt was actually impressed Mr. Swaim even said the empath's name—the coward's way out would have been to just ignore her or skip roll call entirely, but despite his quivering and unseasonable buildup of sweat, the young teacher hadn't.

Jane, of course, didn't seem to care about making it any easier either. The girl didn't say a word to him at all in class, which was quite a feat considering they were setting up an experiment together. She also, as an aside, resoundingly sucked at science—she clamped the wrong cable onto the electrode and her answers to the written questions were so poor Matt had eventually just taken the sheet off her and done them all himself. "Do you want a hand with those?" he'd asked politely, but Jane had just scowled and kept on writing copper as CO. So, she was definitely stubborn, and possibly stupid. Great.

The girl disappeared after class, and Matt made no attempt to follow her. Still enduring the many stares, he'd packed up his belongings and trudged out past the suspicious gazes of the security staff and onto a bus where he was just as irritatingly ogled as he had been all afternoon. After twenty uncomfortable minutes, Matt Callaghan managed to escape the whispers of his onlookers and finally found himself, for the first time in hours, in the company of someone completely oblivious to his newfound celebrity-pariah status.

"Ice cream?" Sarah asked, immediately and predictably, her Powerpuff Girls backpack bouncing on her shoulders.

"No," her brother replied, annoyed and stressed. His phone was still vibrating like it was trying to burrow its way through his right butt cheek. "I'm broke."

"You're okay." Sarah hugged his leg.

"No, Sare, that means . . ." Matt sighed, then gave up and smiled down at her in spite of himself.

Jane Walker arrived at Northridge High School midway through Monday morning. By lunchtime on Tuesday, despite having sat with her for three classes and two meals, Matt had given up trying to make her speak. They continued to sit in complete, uncompromising silence, each ignoring the other's existence and playing the "I'm ignoring you ignoring me" game. Matt was a late entrant to this particular event but felt like he had a leg-up on Jane, who would still occasionally shoot him venomous glances when he texted, moved, or existed too loudly, while he, for his part, maintained a perpetually calm smile, like the empath was just an unremarkable yet pleasant summer breeze.

He sometimes wondered what he was doing—why he was going so far out of his way to keep hanging around this cold, obstinate person. It wasn't like he needed the attention—quite the opposite, in fact. Matt was keenly aware that his legitimacy as a clairvoyant relied substantially on avoiding any form of heavy scrutiny, and a part of him was beginning to think he might've actually messed up by sitting with the empath in the first place. But now he was committed—half because the moral snowball of normalizing her existence was loose and rolling down the hill, and half because Jane's sheer bloody-minded stubbornness and resistance to his presence—when he was just trying to help—was so teeth-clenchingly annoying that it left him no choice but to persevere. He'd come offering aid, and she'd thrown up a wall, and that irritated Matt so much that now, so help him God, he was going to break down that stupid wall if he had to headbutt his way through.

On Wednesday, Taylor sat with them for lunch. It was, after all, their usual table.

"Hey, uh Matt, uh hey, how's it, you know, g-g-going!" he stammered, half-tripping over the table leg. He sat one butt cheek down gingerly on the very edge of the bench that was diagonally opposite where Jane was sitting, as though scared the contact would burn him.

"Hi, hi there!" He threw a hasty, stunted wave at Jane, who glared once (Matt's running theory was one glare for "yes," two glares for "no") before returning to her geography textbook. Taylor looked across at Matt, who just shook his head and rolled his eyes.

"So, uh, what's, uh, you know, what's new w-w-with you, m-m-man?"

"Not much, dude." He extended a fist and Taylor bumped it. "Fish again." He refrained from telling him to sit properly because he looked like he was trying to work the bench up his butt—he was too proud of his friend for summoning up the courage to be there.

"Yeah, man, damn two, uh, two days last, um, last week as well, it's some, uh, yeah, some nonsense."

"Who likes fish?"

"Nobody, man, damn, you know, like, p-p-penguins, a-a-and stuff. Nobody."

By the end of lunch Taylor was sitting pretty much normally and, despite still shooting the occasional worried glance at Jane's spikey E, was no longer speaking like a stammering moron. When the bell rang and the girl picked up her things and left, Matt clapped Taylor on the back. His friend just half-shrugged and gave a weak smile.

Carlos joined them on Thursday. His tactic was to stare unblinkingly ahead like he was trying to activate X-ray vision on the wall of the girls' locker room. He sat so close to Taylor on the opposite end of the table to Jane that he was practically sitting on his lap.

Brodie was a bit more reluctant to return to the fold.

"Nah, man, screw that, man. She's an empath. She's gonna steal my powers the minute I look at her."

"Brodie, your powers are lame; nobody wants to steal your powers."

"Go to hell, no, not in a million years."

"Come on, dude, don't be a baby. You're scared of a girl."

"I'm not scared! Screw you, you're scared."

"Bet you ten bucks you can't even sit down without wetting yourself."

Brodie hesitated mid-head shake, and Matt saw the conflict tearing away at his brain. See, Brodie liked weed. Weed cost money. This was easy money. Brodie liked money.

Brodie sat with them on Friday. Matt handed him a ten-dollar bill without a word.

"Hell, yeah, showed you!" He pocketed the ten, grinning from ear to ear. "Aren't you supposed to see the future or something?"

"Oh, god-freaking-damn it," groaned Carlos, walking up and seeing Brodie sitting on his corner. He sat on the other side, pulled a twenty out of his wallet and handed it to Matt. "Why do I even make bets with you?"

On the far side of the table, Matt could have sworn he saw Jane suppress a laugh.

Despite these small victories, by the time Friday rolled around, Matt was well and truly done. Thankfully, this week he had last period free, so after fifth ended, Matt went immediately to his locker, grabbed his stuff, and prepared without hesitation to head home. With the weekend on his mind, he stepped through the double doors, semi-racing to catch the early bus—when out of nowhere he felt something collide with his legs.

"Oof!" Matt winced, the heavy sound of a staggered crash cascading on the pavement around him. He looked down to see a little blond boy laying sprawled on the concrete, surrounded by a scattered pile of fallen books.

"Ah, I'm sorry, little man," Matt apologized. He dropped into a squat and started picking the kid's books back up into a pile. "My bad, I wasn't watching."

"*It's okay,*" the little boy murmured, sounding slightly teary. His tiny pale hands helped Matt reassemble the multicolored literary tower. Once all the books were stacked, Matt helped lift them back into the kid's arms.

"*Thank you,*" mumbled the boy. Matt smiled down kindly at him.

"Happy reading," he said. He watched the skinny kid wander off inside, then glanced up. Down the end of the street, the early bus was pulling away.

"Son of a—" Matt started, before remembering there were children present. Well, there went that plan. Technically, he could walk but . . . ugh. Honestly, this week . . .

Matt pursed his lips, trying to think of what he could do until the next bus came in an hour. He didn't want to walk. He supposed technically he could go waste time in the library—but the prospect of either more studying or more staring revolted him.

Oh, wait, he realized, PD. Friday afternoons were generally Sparring for PD, which Matt didn't mind watching—the grandstands were usually empty, and it made a good backdrop for doing assignments, or procrastinating when he was supposed to be doing assignments. What the heck—at least in the chaos of the gymnasium, he'd go relatively unnoticed. Matt turned back inside and started down the hall.

There was a restless, last-period impatience in the air when Matt entered. He climbed up through the rows of metal bleachers lining the gym's far side and took a seat about two-thirds of the way up, his eyes wandering out over the mess of people below.

"SINGLE STRAIGHT LINES!"

Coach Barton's distinctive twang echoed up through the bleachers. The man himself stood in the center of a horde of students with a silver whistle around his neck, well built and muscular, if not slightly gone to seed. Matt had never seen him in anything besides track pants and a sweatshirt, and today was no exception.

"COME ON, PLEASE, SINGLE FILE, AND THE FIRST CELL PHONE I SEE OUT WILL BE USED FOR TARGET PRACTICE! THANK YOU, MISS EVERGREEN!"

"Sir?"

Matt's head snapped up at the sound of a voice he hadn't heard since Monday.

"Sir, where do you want me?" Even from the grandstands, Jane's words were clear and audible. From where he was sitting, Matt could see her, standing at the gym's edge, looking straight at Coach Barton— ignoring the throngs of people parting nervously around her. She'd ditched her usual wornout hoodie for a somehow even more worn-out singlet and bike shorts. And seeing her exposed skin for the first time took Matt somewhat aback. Jane was fit—unusually so. Standing at her full height, her arms bare, Matt was struck by how muscular the girl was, almost Amazonian—she had better biceps than he did, he thought, feeling simultaneously envious and confused.

But seeing her standing there caused new, previously unexplored thoughts to enter Matt's mind. What *did* an empath do in PD? Practicing stealing powers sounded very much illegal. And if they had more than one power, how did they pick? Flip a coin? Draw straws? Was there a syllabus for empaths?

"Miss Walker." Coach Barton's tone was wary, but not confrontational. Matt saw his eyes flick, probably unintentionally, to the E. "Your powers, again, are . . . ?"

"Fire, lightning, ice."

"The classics. Okay, well, let's see . . ." The coach bent down and flipped through pages on his clipboard. Suddenly, he let out a huge, erupting laugh.

"No." He looked back up at Jane. "Is this a joke?"

The girl said nothing. Matt craned his head to see what was written on there that was so funny, but the contents of the page were obscured by the angle and distance. Whatever it was, Matt watched as Coach Barton rechecked it, then started chortling.

"All right, look." He laughed, shaking his head. "I don't know where you've been, but here we do real assessments. Accurate grades. Not"—he looked down again and snorted—"not whatever this is."

Jane didn't respond. Barton's smile faded slightly.

"JACKSON!" He snapped his fingers at a nearby boy. "You're a pyro."

"Yes, Coach!"

"Show the new girl how Northridge does fire. CLEAR THE CIRCLE!" He pointed at Jane. "Flame on flame only." The girl just nodded, expressionless.

There was a mad scramble as dozens of feet stampeded to get clear of the practice ring painted onto the floorboards. Henry Jackson, a six-foot beefy-faced freshman, bounced on the balls of his feet, grinning from ear to ear. Jane remained impassive, immobile, directly opposite. From his place in the grandstands, something tightened in Matt's chest.

"COMBATANTS! READY?!"

"YES, SIR, COACH!" Jackson roared. Jane said nothing.

"Show me how it's done. GO!"

The whistle blew and Jackson punched, a wall of flames shooting from his hand—but Jane was already gone. She leaped, fire exploding from her feet, launching over Jackson's attack, closing the gap between them before the boy could blink, drawing back her fist and striking forward with a . . . BOOM!

An explosion burst down into the gym floor like a meteor, and Jackson's body flew backward, tumbling, splintering the wood before skidding to a halt, brown and smoldering. Jackson groaned. A pair of student healers rushed to his side.

Silence. Stunned silence. Jane rose wordlessly from where she'd landed, one knee on the ground.

Coach Barton found his voice.

"DALIA! SHINON! GO!"

There was no pause, no whistle this time—the two pyromancers launched in, twin plumes ripping from their palms. Jane leaned backward, and the fire streaked past her. Then she turned, springing toward Shinon, rolling underneath a whip of flames and launching the Jewish boy upward with a burning uppercut that carried her over Dalia's next attack. She landed horizontal, flat to the floor, then twisted, one hand on the ground, kicking a pillar of flame into the other girl's chest, blasting her off her feet.

"CRAWDON! BROWN! LAN-YI!"

There were three of them now, running at her, shouting, streaming fire from all sides. Jane exploded upward, ten feet in the air, arcing over their heads while their flames converged where she'd been, landing, skidding, feet whispering on the floor, opponents in front of her, back to the wall. The three didn't hesitate; they attacked in unison, three streams crossed and consuming Jane in a wave of fire. She was surrounded, engulfed, and for a moment it looked like she'd been overwhelmed. But then the inferno began changing, shaping, funneling into a sphere around where Jane had been and from where she emerged, legs locked, arms turning, circling, bending her opponents' fire around her, untouched, untouchable . . .

"Holy . . ." whispered Matt.

But not just around her, toward her, between her hands, tighter and tighter into a ball, brighter and brighter, the three attackers panting and sweating, their streams of flame wavering, until suddenly they stopped, stumbled, stared—and in that instant, Jane twisted, blasted the ball up twenty feet in the air over the middle of the circle, over them, where it . . . BARRROOOOOOM!

An eruption, no, an avalanche of fire, a tidal wave of flames pummeled downward, smothering Crawdon and Lan-Yi's helpless forms.

Brown was faster, dived to the side, rolled back onto his feet—just in time to be punched in the chest by a column of fire from the other side of the room.

"LIGHTNING THROWERS, GO!"

Coach Barton didn't even give names, didn't give any warning or any time for Jane to switch abilities—just pushed them in, four of them, sparks flying from their hands.

Jane danced. She ducked under a blast from Ramirez, caught a bolt from Graves and redirected it into Weiss, turned a bolt from Jones into a crackling blue shield, vaulted over another bolt, skidded to her knees, grabbed Weiss by the throat and punched him in the chest with blue lightning, sending him flying over the arena and slamming into Graves, then crossed her arms across her chest, fingers drawing horns, and in the split second while Jones and Ramirez hesitated, watching their companion fly across the room, two crackling, snaking bolts arced out and hit them in their guts.

"GET HER! *GET HER*! SOMEBODY, EVERYBODY, AUTOMATIC A PLUS TO WHOEVER CAN HIT THIS *GODDAMN EMPATH*!"

Chaos. Raw unrestrained chaos as dozens of students clambered against one another, half-running to take a shot, half-running for their lives. A storm, a hurricane of fire, ice, lightning, water, metal, and flying objects, blurs of speed, sound, and light, and in the middle of it, Jane, ducking, weaving, boxing bursts of fire, weaving lightning, cracking ice through the air, freezing, sliding, and slicing as she dodged, jumping, kicking off one girl and slamming a flaming heel down into another, launching above the melee on arcs of lightning, sparks crackling through her hair, ducking, spinning, striking . . .

SCREEEEEEEEEEEEEEEEEEEEEEEEEEEEEEEEEEEEEEEEEEEEE ECH!

The shrill screech of Coach Barton's whistle cut over the noise. Everything—everyone—skidded to a stop, except Julie Finch, who decided that the whistle meant now was a good time to attack Jane from behind.

Jane kicked her into a wall.

"ENOUGH!" Barton roared. He was panting slightly, his face the color of fresh-fallen bird droppings. His eyes traced around the room, between the numerous blackened, shaking, moaning bodies of his students, the healers racing between them, the splintered wood, roasted paint, and twisted seats—and Jane, unmarked, standing in the middle of it all, feet apart, fists locked at her side, steady and centered. He gaped at the empath.

For a few seconds, the surreal silence simply lingered. Then the coach shook his head like a dog trying to clear water from his ears and started giving orders.

"Kinetics, clean this up. Podawlski, go to the office and tell Ms. Brownlow that whoever's got detention this afternoon is doing maintenance. Healers, good job, good responses, keep . . . keep it up. Miss Walker . . ." He turned back to Jane but couldn't seem to focus. "I . . . you . . . that's enough. You're . . . you're dismissed. For uh . . . for the day."

The empath simply nodded, turned on her heel and left.

Matt didn't remember going back to his locker. He didn't remember pulling his phone out of his pocket and starting to message "Holy mother of" to Taylor. He sort of just woke up halfway through typing before backspacing the entire thing.

Words couldn't do it justice. Dazed and confused, his eyes stinging, a ringing in his ears from all the lightning, Matt stood in front of his locker, the corridor deserted, trying to put his thoughts back in order. He blinked his eyes open and shut a few times, trying to snap himself out of it, but his mind kept staggering. That . . . that was amazing. Off the charts, hands down, coolest thing he'd ever seen—

And also, maybe, absolutely, the most terrifying.

Jane Walker was not just an empath. Jane Walker was insane. Insane, talented, insanely talented. How many people had she just beaten? Twenty? Three dozen? And not just beat—destroyed. Wrecked, trounced, mopped the floor with, he'd . . . God, he'd thought she was going to die. Right there, with the all-engulfing ball of fire, he had really thought Coach Barton was going to let them kill her. No. Nope. Nah. Not a chance.

Matt squeezed his eyes shut, trying to calm the adrenaline surging through his chest.

He needed air.

He shouldered his backpack and half-jogged off down the hallway. What was he going to tell people? Jane hadn't done anything wrong but shoot, he thought, and a slight unease curdled inside him, this would not go down well. Powerful normal people got scholarships; powerful empaths got lynched. Or hunted down by Captain Dawn.

Don't think like that, Matt reprimanded himself, *it doesn't help. It's not accurate.*

Probably.

Matt pushed through the front doors and out into the afternoon breeze, his thoughts swimming. Was this bad? It definitely wasn't good. He had maneuvered himself, his friends, close to a very powerful, very dangerous empath. Forget not wanting to prove Jane right—this was about their lives. His life! This girl could kill him, really, truly kill him, with practically no one able to stop her, if she woke up one day and decided to. And would she? What was her mental health like? In his rush to help her it'd never crossed Mat's mind, but now it was all he could think about. Jane clearly had issues. She was clearly isolated, a loner, very, very angry, and to the best of his knowledge without any supervision, at least that he'd seen . . .

But . . .

Matt turned a corner, bag straps digging into his shoulders. But, fear aside, he tried to think logically, did this really change anything? His reasons for trying to normalize Jane's presence were still valid—admittedly tipped less toward "protecting her" and more toward "protecting everybody else." Woe befall the fools who got stupid enough to try and jump her after class. If anything, this made what he'd been doing even more important.

Still, it was hard to shake the smell of burning classmate from his nose.

A sudden stumble jerked Matt back into the real world. Cursing, he bent down to retie his shoelace. Where was he going? Was he walking home? What was the plan? The bus didn't come for another half an hour. That's why he'd been inside in the first place.

Matt looked up from his retied shoe and almost yelped with fright.

Jane. There, just down the road, back in her hoodie, a worn backpack over her shoulders. She must have come out from the locker room behind the gym. Matt stiffened, frozen for a second, then, when she didn't turn around or even glance in his direction, realized he was too far away for her to see him. Or maybe she was ignoring him like she always did. Matt let out a small sigh of relief and straightened back up, watching her walk away.

Then his eyes widened and his heart sunk.

Because at that moment, around the same corner, stalked four tall Ugandans.

They came for her sooner than she'd expected. It'd barely been a week, but it didn't matter. They still came, four of them, tall and black like polished stone, the hate they were carrying warping and distorting their faces into monstrous masks.

They didn't say a word. They just followed her. Teeth clenched. Breathing. Low, fast, and murderous.

They'd started following her after PD. Alone, she'd heard them move behind her, through the back paths and onto the street. Jane didn't run. She'd meant to lead them somewhere with cameras, but now that wasn't an option. She didn't know where she was going, and they were gaining fast.

Hard footsteps behind her. An alleyway to her left.

She turned, found a lane, a fence, a redbrick wall. This was it. Her feet mounted the curb, twisted, and put her back to the wall. She turned to face them, and there they were. Huge and looming, the whites of their eyes pearls in the abyss. They'd boxed her in, or so they thought—really, she'd put her back to the wall and had them all within view.

There was a pause—a silence in which the world seemed to hold its breath. She wasn't afraid, not of them, but maybe of what would come after. Investigations, expulsions, maybe even a trial. The disappointment on her father's face at another failure, again, so soon. But it was inescapable. These men meant to kill her. Not hurt, not humiliate. Murder. Cold and bloody. She saw it in their eyes—the rage, the grief, the madness. They hated her, and she understood. Their loss, at least, was real.

For once, she spoke first. "Stop," she said. No preamble. "I don't want to do this." It was true. Not here, not now, not them. Not like this.

The foremost man snarled, a sound like a blade dragging through timber. "You . . ."

He took a step forward.

"You . . . you here . . . no. Not while I live." Low and murderous. "Not while I remember."

"It wasn't me. I was a child." The truth, but it didn't matter. They hated her mark, not her. Who she symbolized. What he'd done. Her chest was a slithering ball of cold, and she had neither rage nor frustration, only grim determination, and the will—the need—to survive.

"You are a monster. You take our homes. Our families."

"I didn't do it. I don't want to fight."

The four of them said nothing; they merely clenched their fists and stepped forward. The girl closed her eyes and drew one final, shallow breath, then leaned back and readied herself. She opened her eyes.

"I am legally entitled to take whatever measures I feel are reasonably necessary for the protection of my person," she articulated, clear and concise. She hoped it would stop them.

But their minds were consumed by Death.

"I don't care." The air began to vibrate.

The girl rippled her fingers. "I'm sorry."

"All right," came a voice from their left. "Let's everyone just hold up a second before we all do something stupid."

Five heads spun, and five sets of eyes swept over Matt Callaghan as he stood at the mouth of the alleyway, wearing an expression of mild concern. For a moment, all five just stood in stunned silence. Jane's eyes narrowed slightly, and one of the shorter Ugandans at the back of the group opened his mouth to say something but stopped halfway and instead glanced at his companions for direction. The rest stared stonily at the new arrival. Matt leaned back on his heels and took his hands out of his pockets.

"I'm serious." He spread his hands wide. His breathing was slow, his shoulders loose, his face casual, though his heart was hammering. "Take it from me. This is a very, very bad idea."

For a moment, Matt thought they were going to ignore him. The Africans and the empath stood at a stand-off, stuck in place a split-second away from powering up and murdering one another. You could cut the tension with a knife, but Matt didn't have a knife. All he had were words. Silver words and an outsider's eyes, ready to bear witness to the ugliness threatening to unfold.

Sometimes that was enough.

After what felt like an eternity, the tallest Ugandan turned slightly toward him. "You."

"Me.

"I know you."

"I know you do."

"You sit with her." He jabbed a finger at Jane, and his face clenched into an expression of pure hatred.

Matt tried to appear unfazed. He'd known that hurdle was coming. "Well, I like to think she sits with me," he replied. "It's my table." Then before they could think, he diverted. "But you know what else I do?"

A pause. A glance between them. "You are the fortune teller," the taller one said in low words.

"A-plus. Got it in one. Matt Callaghan, Clairvoyant. You know me. And I know you too." Matt stepped forward. "You're Kato. From over in Dovington Heights? My friend Taylor—you know, buzz cut, never shuts up—says you shoot three-pointers better than anyone in the district."

The man's face remained blank, so Matt kept going.

"I know all of you, actually. You're Solomon," he said, pointing at the guy behind him. "You took Katie Motro to homecoming last year, but then you never called afterward. Don't know why, man, she was crushing on you hard. Still is, probably." Solomon blinked.

"And you, big, tall guy in the black hoodie, your name's Otim. Your little sister, Maryam, comes to see me now and again. Talks about you all the time. How's her anorexia going?" He looked pointedly at Otim for a reply, who shuffled, uncomfortable at being put on the spot, at having to suddenly think for himself. That was the whole point. Psychology 101—a mob is comprised of people. Remind the people they're individuals, snap them away from whatever they're swept up in, and they start thinking about their actions. The momentum fades, and the mob dissolves.

Theoretically.

"She . . . she is healthier now. Like you told her she would be."

"Healthier and happier I'd think, now that she's ditched that horrible group of girls."

"Yes." An awkward silence drifted out between them. To his right, Matt saw Jane's eyes darting from one to the other. They were no longer looking at her but gazing at the ground. He pressed on.

"And that leaves you, doesn't it? Lucky last, good old Hassan. Hassan the man! You're in my geo class! Remember when Brodie showed up so high to that oral presentation thing that he tried to tell Ms. Peterson there was no such place as Finland?"

Hassan's lips opened into a reluctant smile. "I . . . that was . . . yes. It was funny."

"Exactly! We go way back, don't we? We're old friends. So, you know I'm not messing around when I say, man, you *really* don't want to do this."

The tension, the murderous intent, crept back into the alleyway. Kato's face darkened, and four sets of eyes swung from Matt to Jane. But Matt had anticipated this. He shrugged and spread his hands wide.

"Hey, look, don't get me wrong," he said, drawing their attention back to him. "It's your lives, do what you want. Doesn't affect me. But as a clairvoyant, you know, what I have to do—what is my destiny, my duty, right now—is to warn you, promise you, that attacking Jane here"—he used her name, trying to humanize her—"leads to a very negative future for everyone." He paused, glancing discreetly across their assembled faces, scanning desperately for any sign of his warning taking root. "Simple as that. That is super clear to me right now." He paused again. "Attacking her would be a huge mistake."

For a second, they all just stared—mainly at him, a little at her. There were looks of trepidation, reluctance, a fist uncurling ever so slightly. The words burrowing in, giving pause. Matt tried to appear unconcerned.

"That's it." He shrugged. "That's all I've got to say."

For a while, nobody moved except Matt, who bounced on the balls of his feet with his hands in his pockets—half to appear relaxed, half to hide his shaking.

Finally, Kato spoke.

"You sit with her." It was an accusation, not a question.

"Of course, I do," Matt replied. He added in a small edge of impatience to make it sound like this was obvious. "Principal Rance told me to. I'm a clairvoyant; he wanted me to keep an eye on her. If I stay nearby, then I can see her future and know if she's up to something."

Still rooted to the same spot, Jane's head snapped around to look at him. Matt didn't meet her eyes but could almost hear the gears turning in her head. *Keep your stupid mouth shut*, he mentally urged her, *I am so close to getting you out of this, don't you dare say a goddamn word*. But, of course, she couldn't hear him.

Convoluted as it was, his explanation nevertheless made Kato hesitate. "She is an empath . . ." he said slowly, but the conviction was draining from his voice. "She . . . needs to . . ."

Matt tried to sound sympathetic. "Hey, man, look," he said. "I'm with
you. I hate empaths. If it was up to me, I'd say burn the witch. But I have
to call it like I see it, and this girl is bad news. Anybody who tries to hurt
her is in for a world of pain, I promise. I'm just looking out for you."

There was a moment's silence while the four Ugandans exchanged
uneasy looks. They glanced at Jane, whose combat-ready stance and
general twitchiness was giving off the impression of a rabid fox stuck in
a trap, then back at one another.

"*Hasa diga eebowai,*" muttered Kato. Matt had no idea what that
meant. but it sounded concessional. The tall man turned and gestured to
his companions. "Come. It is not meant to be." There was a general murmuring of consent, and the four of them started drifting back up toward
the main street. "Sorry," Matt said apologetically as they passed. Hassan
just shook his head as if to say "it's not your fault," and Solomon clasped
him on the shoulder. "Watch her," he said. Matt nodded.

His eyes glued to their backs, Matt watched the four figures trudge
slowly around the corner. Then finally, after what felt like hours had passed
and he was sure they were truly gone, he let out a heavy sigh. Matt pulled his
trembling hands out of his pockets and ran them shakily through his hair.
He turned to Jane, who was still standing there, stony-faced and silent.

"You okay?"

"Yes," she said simply.

There was a brief pause, and then, "Thank you."

"You don't have to say it so pained."

"I'm not, I . . . I mean it." She breathed out and her shoulder slumped.
"I didn't want to fight them."

Matt took a deep breath, still shaking a bit. "Because they're African?"

"Yeah." Jane leaned back on the redbrick wall, then slid slowly down
until she was sitting on the cold concrete sidewalk, knees to her chest.
"Is that wrong?"

"No." There was a moment of awkwardness. Matt's hands found their
way back into his pockets.

Eventually, the girl sighed, rubbing her eyes with the heels of her hands.
Any trace of the anger she'd been harboring all week had disappeared.

"I didn't expect it so soon," she mumbled, not looking at him. "Normally, it takes a few months for people to get the courage to . . ." Her
voice trailed off.

Matt grimaced. "This isn't the first . . . well, no, I guess not," he finished, seeing the look on the girl's face. He shifted forward. "That must suck."

Jane shrugged, head on her knees, looking off into nothing. "You get used to it."

A small gust whistled down the alleyway. Jane let out a heavy sigh. "I don't want to transfer again."

"Why would you have to transfer?"

"As soon as the school finds out I was in a fight, I'll have to move."

"Well, there wasn't technically a fight," said Matt. He leaned into the wall, looking down. "And I don't think the school will find out."

Jane glanced up at him. "Why?"

Matt shook his head. "Those guys won't tell. They don't really seem to trust authority, generally. Make of it what you will. But I can't see this coming back to bite you."

They both stared off into space.

"What's it like?" Jane asked after a while. "Seeing the future?"

Matt scuffed his feet absentmindedly on the concrete. "I'm surprised you haven't taken my powers already and found out."

"It doesn't work like that," the girl replied coldly. "That's not my type."

"Your type of what?"

"Empathy."

"There're different types?"

"Obviously." She looked at him with disdain. "I'm touch-based. Empathic mimics are the ones who can copy you just by being in the same room."

Matt glanced around uneasily, unsure of how to broach his next question. "What was . . . ah . . . you know . . ."

"Blood-based," Jane answered curtly. The irritation on her face told him she'd known exactly what he'd been about to ask. "How does everyone not know that?"

"I think they do," Matt admitted. Now that she mentioned it, it sounded familiar. "Guess most people get too worked up to care about the details."

"It's not a detail," she snapped. "It's key. If he hadn't been blood-based, he would never have been able to collect that many powers."

Matt blinked. "I don't understand."

"What type you are decides how many powers you can have," replied Jane, impatient. "Empathic mimics can only hold one. Touch-based can hold two to five."

"How many can you hold?" interjected Matt.

"Four," Jane answered, not slowing down or looking up. "Blood-based are unlimited. And once they absorb enough DNA, the power's locked in for life." She seemed annoyed at having to explain all this, but not enough to be able to stop herself.

"Cool. All right. There you go. Learn something every day." Matt paused. "So you absorb by touch?"

"I just said that."

"So, if you, like, brush my pinkie, you could—"

"I have to get a good grip," she snapped, increasingly annoyed. "Firm, sustained contact."

"All right," Matt said with only a hint of defensiveness. "You ever think of, you know, telling people that? Might make them a bit less reluctant to come near you?"

"Oh yeah," Jane replied sarcastically. "Then they can go from treating me like a plague zombie to treating me like a leper."

"Baby steps?"

"Shut up." The sudden spark of irritation seemed to reignite the anger in her voice. "Why do you care anyway?" Her head snapped round to look at him, eyes narrow and accusing as if she was only now truly registering his presence, standing idly two feet away as she sat on the curb. "Why are you even here?"

"They were going to jump you. I didn't want that to happen."

Jane snorted. "That's right. I forgot. You can see the future. Well, you were right. I would've killed them." There was a pause, and an edge of bitter misery crept into her words. "They were going to try and kill me, and I would've had to kill them."

"I know."

"Must be good, knowing."

"Well . . ." Matt shifted, a little uneasy. "Truth be told, I didn't know-know. Like clairvoyant know. Just between you and me."

Jane eyed him suspiciously. "What do you mean?"

"I had sixth free. I saw you in PD."

"Oh. That." Despite her glumness and irritation, Matt thought he saw a flash of pride streak across Jane's face.

"Yeah. So, a little less clairvoyance and more firsthand knowledge." He paused. "How'd you get so good?"

Jane shrugged, indifferent. "Practice."

"No, but seriously."

"But nothing. I practice. Every day. Most people don't. Most people think, oh, I've got these powers, I'm set. Think they're a natural god-damn artist because they inherited a paintbrush. So, they never learn how to use them properly. Never put in the time." She sniffed and spat. "Sweat more in training, bleed less in battle."

"I guess. And I guess you need to be able to defend yourself."

"It's not for self-defense."

Matt looked at her, confused. "It's not?"

Jane's eyes wandered up toward the darkening sky. "You wouldn't understand."

"Try me."

The girl contemplated for a moment, then said, "I want to be the best."

"The best . . . at fighting?"

"Yes," Jane replied simply.

Matt made a face. "Um . . . why?"

She turned away. "Because I'm good at it."

"My brother's good at making my little sister cry, but I wouldn't suggest he do it professionally."

"I told you, you wouldn't understand. The world doesn't hate you for being born."

"True. They never made me get a big C tattooed on my cheek. What?" he added when she glared at him.

"No," she snarled. "Exactly. They didn't."

Her aggression was coming back, but Matt was finding it less intimidating. "Did it hurt?"

"What?"

"Your face. Did it hurt?"

"No, you"—she threw in a few choice swear words—"idiot, it was one of those completely painless face tattoos that feels like a warm towel when it's carved into your flesh when you're eleven."

"Eleven?"

"Eleven."

"Jeez, how did your parents take it?"

Jane looked off into the distance, still and angry. "I don't know. My dad didn't say anything. He didn't even come when they took me."

"What about your mom?"

"My mom's dead," she snapped. Matt grimaced and ran his hand over the back of his head.

"Sorry."

"Why? You didn't kill her," she retorted, her voice cold.

Matt didn't know how to respond to that.

They lapsed into strained silence; Jane kneading dirt between her fingers, glowering at nothing, Matt just standing, feeling his feet getting sore.

"Come on," he said eventually, shooting a glance up the alleyway then back at the girl. "We should probably get going. I've got to . . . you know . . . home . . ." He looked down at Jane, still sitting on the ground with her arms around her knees. Without thinking, out of reflex, instinctual politeness, he held out a hand to help her up—and without thinking, Jane grasped it.

And for a fraction of second, their bare hands touched.

It was as if time had suddenly stopped. Slowly, in the space of a second, Matt saw a shadow pass over Jane's face, saw her brow furrow, puzzled, and felt his own do the same in reply. Why was she looking like that? Was there a problem? Matt didn't understand—but as he watched, Jane's eyes fell, tracing down to his arm, to his hand, her hand, their hands, clasped together, skin touching. Watched as she looked back up at him, her eyes widening, mangled horror spreading across her face. He felt her arm clench, her grip tighten.

And in an instant, Matt realized his mistake. An instant too late, the penny dropped and his brain woke up, warning, screaming at him not to touch her, to pull away—

But it was too late.

Jane, the touch-based empath, gripped Matt Callaghan's human hand and looked at him for the first time with real, genuine fear, and whispered, "Nothing."

TALENT SCOUT

"A great evil has befallen the world; greater, I believe, than any evil that has come before. The scale of loss defies words; defies comprehension; defies endurance. Never in human history have we faced a tragedy of this magnitude; never before have we, humanity, been so wounded . . .

In this, our darkest hour, we must give thanks to those who struggle, even now, to bring us back into the light. To the citizens of the world who have opened their arms to those in need. To the millions of men and women working day and night to contain the effects of this disaster who have chosen to use their God-given powers for good in the face of such evil. To the valiant members of the Legion of Heroes who lay down their lives to protect us all. And to Captain Dawn, who, were it not for this calamity, this breaking of the world, would have been but the beginning of the end of days."

—President Martin Luther King Jr., Address to the Nation,
October 10, 1990

AFRICA ANNIHILATED
CONTINENT DEVASTATED, 400 MILLION FEARED DEAD
IN BLAST FROM SUICIDAL EMPATH
The New York Times, October 10, 1990

An explosion unprecedented in human history tore through central Africa last night, wiping out entire countries as far north as Libya and as far south as Zimbabwe. There is yet no official count, but UN Secretary-General Sang said an estimated 300 million may have perished, and in the immediate aftermath, the calamity is believed to be the most devastating event in human history.

The explosion came after three days of intense fighting across the African continent between the Legion of Heroes and a single as yet unidentified individual, rumored to be capable of absorbing powers from other people. Around 8:30 p.m. last night, the conflict appeared at an end as Captain Dawn, the sole surviving member of the Legion, gained the upper hand. However, at 8:48 p.m., a blast equal to more than five thousand atomic bombs emanated from a point in northern Zaire, annihilating everything within an almost two-thousand-mile radius and sending shock waves around the globe. Unconfirmed reports from the few surviving witnesses, including Captain Dawn, have described the explosion as the final, suicidal act of the criminal to avoid capture and defeat.

Across the world, death tolls from seismic activity climb into the thousands, and a cloud of ash spreads throughout the atmosphere. Millions of people in what remains of Africa flee earthquakes and radiation. Were it not for the tireless efforts of powered individuals working worldwide to counteract the effects of the catastrophe, Earth would undoubtedly be looking at an extinction-level event. . . .

EMPATH NAMED
DETAILS OF CONFLICT EMERGE AS DESTROYER
OF AFRICA IDENTIFIED
The Washington Post, October 11, 1990

The man responsible for the deaths of up to 400 million people in Tuesday's incomprehensible explosion is believed to be Klaus Heydrich, an empath previously identified by the Legion of Heroes as being responsible for more than a thousand murders believed committed in acquiring a vast array of superhuman powers.

Heydrich, the son of Nazi intelligence officer Reinhard Heydrich—known as the Butcher of Prague and an architect of the Jewish Holocaust—had been slated for apprehension by the Legion to answer for an increasingly uninhibited campaign of terror throughout Africa, in which he is believed to have slaughtered entire villages to gain a single power. At 9:01 a.m. on October 7, members of the Legion tracked down and attempted to apprehend Heydrich, who it soon became clear had access to a vast array of abilities and was far more powerful than originally anticipated. At 9:14 a.m., following the deaths of two Legion members additional reinforcements were called, seemingly to no avail. By 4:42 a.m. the next morning, all initiated members of the Legion of Heroes save two were believed dead, the only remaining combatant being Legion second-in-command, Elsa Arrendel, the White Queen, who continued to fight Heydrich for almost twenty-four hours before eventually succumbing around 6:15 a.m. on October 9.

Following Arrendel's death, Legion head and founder, Captain Dawn, broke his vow of pacifism and left the Academy to engage Heydrich over the Straight of Madagascar. The fight between the two lasted more than fourteen hours before eventually swinging in Dawn's favor, at which point Heydrich, unwilling to be taken alive, is believed to have combined his ability to absorb energy with his ability to imbue matter with explosive force, infusing his cells with unstable atomic power and unleashing an approximately 5-million-megaton explosion. Prior to the blast, the Legion's fight against Heydrich had wreaked havoc throughout the countryside, damage now insignificant compared to the devastation which Heydrich's final act has unleashed upon the world . . .

"Nothing. There's nothing there."

Matt couldn't move. Couldn't breathe. He was paralyzed, overcome with mortal panic. Undo. Undo, undo, undo. Undo the last ten seconds, take it back, don't—

But they were touching. Their hands still together, Jane still staring at him, wide-eyed.

"I can't feel your power . . ." she murmured.

There was a second's stunned silence. Then, finally, Matt's brain snapped into gear and he tried to pull away—but the instant he did, Jane's look of shock twisted into anger, and her hand tightened like a vise.

"Ow!" Matt exclaimed, but the empath's grip was merciless. She raised her free hand beside her head and arcs of blue-white lightning crackled across her palm.

"What are you?" she demanded. Matt winced at the smell of cooking ozone, recoiling, trying to pull away.

"What do you mean?" he cried. "Let me go!" But his feigned ignorance was fooling no one. Jane's face darkened.

"Liar," she snarled, and her hand twisted his wrist, hard, sending pain shooting up his arm and making Matt yelp.

"Ow-ow-ow," he stammered, trying to turn away, but it was useless. The empath was stronger than him by far, and simply held on so that she was practically twisting his arm behind his back.

"What are you?" she repeated, and this time her voice held threats of violence.

Matt still didn't give in. "I don't know what you're talking about!" he cried, struggling the other way—but it was useless, she had him in a lock. "You're insane!"

"Tell me what you are," Jane demanded, bringing her crackling palm so close to his head he could smell the tips of his hair burning. "Or I'll kill you, right here, right now."

That was an escalation. "Okay, okay!" Matt conceded. He held up his other hand. "You win, you win, just let me go!" The girl scowled at him, distrustful, and Matt did his best to put on a supplicating face. Reluctantly, her grip loosened, and Matt's arm slipped free.

"Son-of-a-freaking . . . ow," Matt muttered, pulling back. He rubbed his wrist ruefully, turning away to nurse his wounded pride, but at the same time glancing discreetly at Jane, wondering if he could make a run for it. Apparently, though, this plan was obvious on his face. Jane's eyes narrowed, there was a blast of hissing cold, and suddenly Matt's feet were iced to the road.

"Oh, come on," he complained.

"Talk," growled Jane, folding her arms and curling lightning threateningly between her fingers.

"I d-d-don't . . ." Matt stammered, looking up at her with a vain, pleading shrug. "About what? What do you want from me?" With escape no longer an option, Matt switched roles to terrified civilian. If he could just feign fear and ignorance convincingly enough, maybe . . .

"Talk!" Jane repeated, louder and more dangerously.

"I don't know, I honestly don't, please," he stalled, trying to buy time—desperate, precious seconds—for someone else to come along, to somehow come up with a plausible lie. "I'm sorry I don't understand. I've never been that bright, ever since I was a little kid, you know when teachers would tell me stuff, I'd never get the full meaning. I think I'm on the spectrum somewhere. I mean I've never been tested but . . ."

"Stop," snarled Jane, "stalling. Why can't I feel your power?"

"I don't know," begged Matt, grasping at straws. "I'm not using it right now, maybe you—"

Jane eyes narrowed, and before Matt could react, she'd crossed the space between them. There was a hand on his wrist and another on his throat, and suddenly, he was being lifted, choking and squirming, two inches into the air. Matt struggled, slapping lamely at Jane's shoulders with his free hand, trying to break free. The empath was unmoved.

"You're a good liar," she stated coldly, looking up at him, her fingers crushing into his neck. "But I know what I feel." She paused as Matt's struggles grew ever feebler and more frantic. "I can kill you in a heartbeat."

"You kill me . . ." gurgled Matt, choking the words out between gasping breaths. "You'll . . . go to jail . . . get the chair . . ."

"I'll tell them what I felt."

"Doesn't matter . . ." Matt wheezed, spots dancing before his eyes. "Murder a . . . model student . . . no proof . . . history . . . think they'll believe . . . you . . ."

Jane's face hardened. She stared Matt in his watering eyes, her expression inscrutable. Then all at once, she let go and stepped back. Matt fell to all fours, gasping.

"Ow . . ." he croaked, a weak, hoarse whisper. The world spun. His fingers massaged his aching throat.

"Fine," said Jane. Her voice echoed down over him, imperious and indifferent to his suffering. "Then I'll just turn you in. I'm sure the Department of Powers Regulation would be interested to hear about this."

"No," pleaded Matt, his voice still dry and cracked. "Please. Don't do that." He put one foot forward, then stopped, his head woozy. He looked up at Jane, panting. "Please."

"Why not?"

"Because . . . just don't," he begged her, still too light-headed to come up with some convincing way out. He leaned back, blinking wide, trying to clear his mind. Jane towered over him, her arms crossed, fingers tapping—an immovable, impatient object.

"Are you an empath?" she asked bluntly.

"What?" Matt recoiled as if stung.

"It'd make sense. Maybe it's not nothing I'm feeling, just more of me."

"I'm not an empath."

"Then I'm sure you'd be happy to get tested."

"God, no, I . . . Look, here." Matt held out his hand. Of course, now he realized the full extent of what that would entail, now that it was monumentally too late. Jane hesitated—maybe a little put off by the gesture—but after a second or two, grasped his hand and pulled Matt to his feet.

"Ugh." She shuddered, though she maintained the contact. "So weird."

"There's no empathy," he insisted.

Jane's brow furrowed. Without waiting for permission, she moved her hand along, squeezing the bare flesh of his arms then neck then cheeks.

"Yes, that's my face, thank you," Matt said with only a touch of impatience.

"You're like a child," said Jane, ignoring his discomfort. "All I can feel is skin."

"Do you touch many children?" remarked Matt. She glared at him, but gradually, the glare faded. She dropped her hand.

"I can't feel anything," she murmured. For a moment, they both just stood there as the girl stared off into nothingness, her eyes unfocused. Then slowly she looked up, a curious expression dawning across her face—as if she was truly seeing him for the first time.

"If you have a power . . ." she began, and Matt felt a thrill of horror unfurl inside him as she set the words carefully down, laying out a chain of thought he could already see the end of. "I'd feel it. But I can't . . . I feel nothing. Because maybe there is nothing . . . because maybe . . . maybe you don't . . ."

Matt ran.

Turned and ran as fast as he could, with only a fleeting backward glance. There was no hiss of ice, no crack of lightning, no footsteps in pursuit. Jane just stood there, silent, alone in the alley, watching him go. But Matt didn't stop. He kept running, running until his legs burned and his lungs screamed, until he was home, alone, with the door locked behind him.

What had he done?!

Matt Callaghan stared at himself in the bathroom mirror and gripped the sides of the sink so hard he thought it was going to snap. Idiot. Idiot,

idiot, idiot, stupid freaking idiot! She knew. She knew, she knew, she knew. Oh God. What had he done?

He dipped his shaking hands in the cold, freezing water and splashed it across his face. All his training. All his 6:00 a.m. rises, all that effort, and he throws it out the window with two seconds of chivalry on a psychotic girl. What was wrong with him? Was he insane? Did he *want* to be carted off, harvested, and dissected, locked up in some government facility while scientists poked and prodded at his abnormal DNA?

And of all the people. Oh God, of all the billions of people, he'd picked a vindictive, aggressive, emotionally unstable empath who he knew only slightly better than Timmy's grandma's dog. A week! He'd known this girl for a week!

Oh God. He needed to run, needed to pack a bag right now, get on the first bus out of town, and go start a life somewhere nobody knew his name. Alaska. Alaska or Denmark or the United Abrahamic States, somewhere nobody in their right mind would look for him. He glanced at the back of the bathroom doors, the blue fluffy towels hanging from their pegs. Any minute, any second now, a heavy steel-capped boot would kick down that door, and they'd drag him into the back of an unmarked van. They'd take him, his computer, his family . . .

His family. He'd put them in danger too, everyone, all his powered relatives. An easy case study, compare and contrast. Mom, Dad. Jonas. Sarah. No. No, no, no, no.

He ran his sopping, trembling hands through his hair. He had to tell them, had to warn them, then they could flee together, as a family . . .

Except . . .

Except, maybe not. Except maybe—Matt's hands gripped the sink again and he stared back into his reflection, breathing slower, forcing himself to think. Maybe . . . maybe he'd actually messed up less than he thought.

Not having a power . . . not having a power was unbelievable. Impossible, like saying someone didn't have organs, or bodyweight. Most people couldn't sense abilities. Most people would think it was a joke, an insult, that Jane was lying, and she was an empath. People hated empaths; nobody trusted them. Who was going to believe her when she started spouting such obvious lies?

Matt blinked rapidly, trying to steady his breathing. Yeah. Yeah. It was Jane's word against his. Jane, empath, notorious troublemaker (presumably, given how many schools it sounded like she'd been kicked out of), reclusive, and with a documented irrational dislike of his company, versus him, normal, model student, stable family member, and established clairvoyant. Yeah. Yeah. There was no way anyone would believe such an outlandish claim coming from the likes of her—unless . . . unless he did something stupid . . . like running away to Alaska.

He let go of the basin. He had to stay calm, think this through, not do anything dumb. At worst, he'd get a few questions, which he could play off as Jane trying to cause trouble. Yeah, he could spin that. That was easier to believe than the ridiculous notion of him, a fully functional eighteen-year-old, not having any sort of superpower. This was America, he reassured himself, he was American. They didn't just take people into custody, destroy their lives, on the grounds of a single wild accusation. There were questions and warrants and lawyers, bureaucracy, accountability, rules, not some North Korean nonsense where you misspoke and ended up in a gulag. Right? Right?! If worst came to worst, *absolute* worst, a psychic from the Department of Powers Regulation would probe around his mind, and he could handle that. He could control his thoughts, show them only what he wanted them to see.

Yes. This was survivable. Nobody would believe Jane. Nobody would come looking, and if they did, they'd find him open-mouthed and innocent-eyed. The unsuspecting victim of some sociopath's pranks.

Okay. He straightened up. He could do this. Just pretend like nothing ever happened. He couldn't panic. He mustn't panic. Matt took a deep shuddering breath and buried his face in his hands.

Matt Callaghan did not sleep well that night. Though he knew his decision not to run was the right one—Matt reassured himself of that over and over again—it didn't seem to stop the walls of his bedroom from closing in around him, the whispering sensation of impending doom lingering through the darkness. Every shadow against his window was a government van, every creak of the walls a SWAT team. Matt tried practicing his mental techniques until the feeling of being inside his own head became too much and he had to stop. He tried distracting himself with video games, playing *Rome: Total War* for hours in the dark—but by 3:00 a.m. his eyes hurt and all his non-Italian Peninsula settlements were plagued by corruption, so that, too, had to stop.

He awoke Saturday morning to find the house deserted. Jonas had a soccer match and Sarah had athletics, he remembered as he blearily pulled open the fridge door to get milk. He sat alone at the kitchen table eating Frosted Flakes, secretly thankful for the lack of company.

Alone, it didn't take long before Matt was pacing between the TV, the kitchen, and his bedroom, too on edge to rest and too distracted to do anything useful. He watched ten minutes of the animated Legion of Heroes fighting Ana Bloodbane, with Captain Dawn and his power of limitless energy flying around lifting heavy things and blasting golden light. He went upstairs and tried in vain to study, came downstairs and toasted a Pop-Tart, flopped back onto the couch, and ended up spending two hours half-watching a Discovery Channel documentary about the plight of the few remaining rhinos. Rhinos. A rare and endangered species hunted just because some people wanted something they were born with. Matt drummed his fingers along the arm of the couch as David Attenborough explain the devastating impacts of poaching. They didn't deserve this, he was saying. Why couldn't they just be left alone?

Matt could sympathize.

Matt's family came home around midday, and before too long the eldest Callaghan found himself saddled with a variety of chores, which he normally might have resented but in the circumstances didn't mind, the numbing, routine housework almost calming in its mindlessness. Eventually, as the weekend wore on, the panic of the situation softened somewhat and Matt's years of training reasserted itself, corralling his frazzled mental state. The central root of stress, he'd once read, was uncertainty— the inability to choose between fight or flight. Matt was uncertain of what was going to happen, what Jane was going to do, but that was out of his hands. This stress wasn't useful, he told himself, and worrying about things beyond your control achieved nothing except fraying your mental edges. This was life—you held the cards you were dealt and all you could do was play.

So, Matt forced himself to let go. He took a couple of long showers and longer walks. He messaged his friends and talked with his family. He cordoned off all thoughts of empaths and vivisection, suppressing the urge to run, panic, or Google something incriminating. He was the master of his own mind. So many people had trouble with that concept, but for Matt Callaghan, who stood in front of a mirror practicing mental control for an hour and twenty minutes every day, it was reality. He controlled his thoughts, not the other way around. And he was making a conscious choice to let this go.

And funnily enough, by the time Matt fell asleep on Sunday night, he almost felt like it was gone.

A steady calm pervaded Matt when he awoke on Monday morning, and carried on throughout his walk to school and morning classes. A cynical man might have called it the calm before the storm, but Matt had always thought that saying was pessimistic and trivialized the calm's value.

Come lunchtime, Jane was not sitting at their usual table. Matt wasn't sure what to make of this—it could mean that the empath was avoiding him. Or she was being questioned by the police. *Or,* he reprimanded himself, *it could mean absolutely nothing.* People did stuff for a bunch of reasons. Still, he wondered at the very least where Jane was eating. Matt couldn't see her anywhere in the cafeteria. Maybe she had detention. Maybe she was sick.

Maybe stop speculating, he snapped at himself.

Fifth period came and went, with no sign of the empath anywhere. By the time he had set up and sat down in his empty little classroom for PD, Matt was almost beginning to think he wasn't going to see the girl at all—an absence which in itself was slightly ominous.

He was wrong.

Two minutes before sixth period, the classroom door creaked open, and Jane's auburn hair, gray sweater, and track pants entered through the gap. She glanced back at the small scattering of future seekers she'd cut in front of, then closed the door and spun the lock.

A braver man than Matt would have gulped.

"Figured we should talk," Jane announced. She strode across the room, grabbed one of the plastic chairs with one hand, spun it around, and sat down with the back of the chair facing him, her arms resting on the cusp. Matt took note of her expression, which was . . . not aggressive. Hard, maybe, her blue eyes piercing into him and her brow resolute— but not necessarily unfriendly. Maybe. With her, it was hard to tell.

"And you thought this would be more private than the cafeteria?" Matt nodded. "Smart."

"Actually, I had detention for not handing in a history assignment," Jane replied.

"Oh." He paused. "Sorry?"

"Don't be. I hate history." She paused. "I've been thinking." Matt said nothing, but simply watched as she watched him, her expression drawn and cautious. "I have questions."

"Oh great," Matt replied. Jane ignored his sarcasm.

"Like how."

"How what?"

"How everything. How long have you been like this? How'd you lose your power?"

"Jesus, I . . . Shhh!" Matt shushed. He rummaged hurriedly around in his pockets for his iPod, and he set it on the table, earbuds facing up. His fingers maxed out the volume, and the *da-ba-dee* sound of "Blue" began rasping jankily out.

"I didn't lose anything," Matt hissed, trying to keep his voice low beneath the noise. He hesitated a moment, then sighed. It was no use. The cat wasn't going back in the bag. "I don't have a power. I've never had a power. I am not a clairvoyant."

It was funny; in a way, that actually felt good to say.

Jane blinked and Matt groaned.

"Look, can we not talk about this? Someone might overhear."

"No."

"Then can we at least talk quietly?"

"Fine." The empath scowled and dropped her voice to a murmur beneath the music. "What do you mean you're not a clairvoyant?"

Matt squinted at her.

"What do you mean what do I mean? I am not a clairvoyant. I cannot see the future. At all." Now that he actually uttered it, it seemed pretty self-evident, like saying "I am not green" or "I am not eating a cheeseburger." But Jane was unconvinced.

"Okay . . . then why does everyone think you are?"

"Because I tell them I am."

"But you're not?"

"No."

"Then what are you? Or were you, or whatever."

"Nothing! I'm nothing! I never had a power! *No tengo* power-ino! What do you need me to write it down?"

Jane slowly shook her head.

"Is it like, embarrassing, or . . ."

"It can't be embarrassing," Matt replied, exasperated. "It doesn't exist."

"Is this about me threatening to rat you out to the DPR?" Jane asked, folding her arms. "Because I wasn't actually going to." She pointed to her cheek. "We're not friends."

You don't have to keep pointing, Matt thought irritably.

"I'm telling the truth."

Janes rolled her eyes.

"All right, so what does it say on your identity card?"

Matt took his wallet from his pocket and pulled out the small plastic rectangle. He handed it to her to read.

"Matthew Callaghan. Clairvoyant." Jane gestured at him with an upturned, expectant palm.

"I know what it says," Matt said, sighing. "But I still don't have a power."

"But. Your. Card. Says. You. Do." She articulated each word like he was a six-year-old. Or a moron.

"But. I. Don't."

Jane clenched her jaw. "This"—she held the card up to the light, tilting it so the holographic flashed—"is your authentic, government-issued, mandatory identification card. It says you're a clairvoyant."

"It's wrong."

"Well, why is it wrong then?" she demanded stubbornly, pointing to the picture. "That's obviously you. You obviously got registered. Didn't they ask you what your power was?"

"I lied."

"But don't they, I don't know, check?" Jane replied, frustration evident in her voice. "They did for me. I mean a regenerator can't just walk in and say, 'Hi, my name's Joe and I heal real fast. Can I get a card?' They'd make him cut himself first."

"I faked it."

"You faked predicting the future?"

"Yes. I told them I kept on having visions, but they were confusing and intermittent, and I couldn't work out what they meant."

Pause.

"And they just bought that? Were they six? Or a moron?"

"I haven't finished. I told them I was getting visions of a stern white man standing in front of a podium, addressing the world about impending change as threads of blue and red intertwine."

"Okay. So?"

"So, I held off going to register till half a week before the presidential election. Four days later and they're still processing my application when BOOM, Gore gets elected and everything I said comes true."

"Okay," Jane said again, leaning back and folding her arms. "But doesn't that prove you are clairvoyant? You predicted who the next president was going to be."

"No," explained Matt. "See, that's what's beautiful. I didn't say who was going to win. I never even mentioned the presidency at all. All I said was some general nonsense, which maybe tangentially by association could mean election stuff. I could have been referring to the other guy. Hell, I could have been referring to anything! But that's all it takes. Say something vague and mystical sounding, and let other people join the dots to make whatever picture they want to see."

"What do you mean?"

"Like here, now," he said, gesturing to the empty classroom. "In PD. I sit here, in this supposedly soundproof classroom and when people want their future told, I say something like, um . . ." He waved a hand around aimlessly, gathering thoughts. " 'I'm seeing . . . there's a man . . . somewhere in your life . . . and he's . . . he's struggling with a problem,' and then they go, 'Oh, of course, my dad just got sacked,' or 'Oh, my little brother keeps getting into trouble,' or 'Oh, there's this cute boy in my class . . .' "

"That's stupid," said Jane.

"Yes," agreed Matt. "But so are people."

"But what if they ask for specifics?"

Matt shrugged. "I just say my visions aren't clear and hard to decipher."

"So, you lie."

"Well, what choice do I have?"

There was silence.

"Do you believe me?"

"I don't know. I mean okay, say you're telling the truth . . ."

"I am."

"Well, okay, whatever, you managed to pull one over the DPR. Fine. You still haven't answered my question."

"What question?" replied Matt, his arms just as folded as hers.

"The obvious question! What are you?!"

"I'm nothing."

Pause.

"Jane, you felt it yourself. I've said it like eight times. I don't have a power."

Another longer pause.

"That's impossible."

"Why?"

Jane's expression became strained. "Because . . . because it just is!" she blurted, struggling to find the words. "Everyone has a power! It's like . . . you've got a brain, and you're human, and so, you have a power!"

"*It just is?* Really? After you spent so long feeling me up on Friday?" Jane had no reply. Matt shook his head.

"Fine then," he said, holding out his arm. "Go ahead. Copy my power. Go on. I give you express and irrevocable permission. Touch me. Take it."

Jane's hand jerked involuntarily to her cheek. "Don't joke."

"I'm not joking!" replied Matt. "Take it! Go nuts! I legally permit you! What? You need me to sign something? Swear on a Bible?"

"Matt, I . . ."

"Do it! Grab me! Do what you gotta do!" When she still didn't move, he waggled his arm around. "Come on, seriously. What kind of useless empath are you? Don't be a chicken."

Jane glared at him, but still hesitated. She looked up at his face, then down, as if wrestling with herself—then without warning, took his proffered hand in hers and clamped her eyes shut.

One second.

Three.

Five.

Nothing.

Her eyes fluttered open. Now, more than ever, she looked truly shaken.

"Nothing." A disbelieving whisper.

"I told you," said Matt, not quite sure why he was sounding so self-satisfied.

"It's . . ." She slumped back, almost tipping off the chair.

There was a long pause as Jane considered her response. Then she waved a hand as if shooing away invisible flies.

"Normally . . . normally, when I touch someone . . . underneath their skin, I can . . ." she trailed off.

"Yeah, I gathered."

They sat in silence for a few seconds, Matt watching warily as Jane's face struggled to process the shock.

"But . . ." she eventually managed to force out, as if having difficulty forming complete sentences, "when you registered, couldn't they . . . I don't know, didn't they compare you to others?"

"Others?"

"You know," she said, waving her hand, "others. Out there. Other clairvoyants."

Matt rolled his eyes. "What others?" he asked. "Tell me, honestly, apart from me, have you ever actually met a clairvoyant? A real one?" He took the empath's lack of response as a no. "I mean, you hear stories all the time, a friend of a friend of my aunt's cousin's mother who got advice about her divorce or whatever—but have you ever actually met one?"

"Well, no—" Jane started reluctantly, but Matt cut her off.

"Exactly! No one has! Because it's nonsense! Because they don't exist!"

The empath's brow furrowed. Matt could see the gears turning inside her head.

"This is insane," she muttered finally.

"No, it's annoying. Everybody else gets to have some kind of kickass power, and I get diddlysquat."

Jane ignored him. "Are there others?" she asked. "Other people, you know, without . . ."

Matt shrugged. "I don't think so. I mean, maybe? But nobody I've ever heard of. There's not exactly chat rooms." Jane grunted her understanding. Matt continued. "As far as I know, I'm the first . . . well . . . normal . . . human to be born in forty years."

A prolonged pause stretched out through the room as the two of them sat there, Matt gazing warily at Jane, Jane staring out the sunlit window. "Blue" ended and Matt's iPod earphones began scratching out "Bye Bye Bye" by N'Sync.

"Human," she repeated finally, shaking her head in slow disbelief.

"Can you please not say it out loud?" Matt snapped, perhaps more irritably than was necessary.

"Why not?" Jane shrugged, breaking her gaze off from the outside world and looking back at him. "Why can't I say it?"

"Because," Matt replied through gritted teeth, "it's not exactly something I like to go around just . . . blurting out."

Jane tilted her head and looked at him. "Why? Just out of curiosity. I mean, it's not like it's bad. It's nothing to be ashamed of." She paused. "Nobody chooses their power, so it's the same principle, I guess. You didn't choose to be like this." She glanced up at him. "I assume."

"No."

"Then why?"

"Because I don't want to get carted off to some lab somewhere and dissected by scientists trying to figure out what's wrong with me."

"You really think that'll happen?" asked Jane, raising an eyebrow.

"I don't know," Matt replied, feeling slightly defensive. "Maybe. But even if I don't get kidnapped for gene mapping, maybe I just don't want my entire life defined by this. Maybe I don't want to be 'Matt the Human,' the stunted sideshow who somehow missed out on a superpower. Maybe I don't want to be a freak. Surely, you of all people understand that."

A shadow fell across Jane's face, and Matt immediately rejected his choice of words. "Sorry, I didn't mean—"

"Forget it," Jane said, cutting him off. She lifted her head and looked him square in the eyes. "You're right. I do understand."

There was a second or two of uncomfortable silence before Matt continued.

"So, I mean, I guess I just want . . ."

"A normal life," the empath finished. It might have been his imagination, but for a moment Matt thought he caught a glimpse of a deep, unfathomable sadness passing across the girl's face. But an instant later, it was gone.

"Who else knows?" she continued after a second's pause.

"No one."

"No one?"

"No one. Not my mom, my dad, Taylor, anyone. There're only two people in the whole world who know, and they're both sitting here in this classroom."

Jane looked stunned. "Damn," she said eventually.

Matt rubbed his temples. "Yup."

There was a pause.

"You probably shouldn't have touched me."

"Thanks. I've only been telling myself that all weekend."

Another pause. Jane crossed her arms, though more in a thinking way than an angry one.

"It raises issues though," she stated. "I mean, if you don't want people to know. It's not even a trust thing. I'm not going to go spouting off . . ." She looked seriously at him, and Matt blinked, unable to say anything before the girl continued. "But there're other things to consider. What if I get read? What if . . ."

"Wait, hold up," said Matt, his heart racing, hardly daring to believe his ears. "You're not going to tell anyone?"

"Why the hell would I tell anyone?"

"I don't know," Matt replied, a bit taken aback. "Why wouldn't you?"

"I don't know." The girl shrugged and shifted in her seat, seemingly uncomfortable for some reason. "I guess . . . it seems kind of wrong? You really don't want people to know, so . . ."

Matt blinked. "Um . . . thanks? I guess?"

Jane waved a hand dismissively, like it was an afterthought. "But seriously. What if I get read? I can keep my mouth shut, but my thoughts are going to be a bit harder."

"Just don't think about it."

Jane rolled her eyes. "Have you ever tried not thinking about something? It's impossible. Don't think about purple elephants."

Matt resolutely did not think about purple elephants. "It's not impossible. It just takes practice."

There was an uncomfortable silence while the empath considered his reply with an expression that made it clear she found his answer very unsatisfactory. Matt still couldn't believe his luck.

"You seriously won't tell anyone?" he asked after a few seconds.

Jane shrugged. "Who the hell am I going to tell? The DPR? My deadbeat dad? All of my many, many friends?"

"Right." They lapsed into silence, gazes awkwardly averted. After a few seconds, they both looked up, made accidental eye contact, and quickly looked away. Matt rubbed the back of his head.

"Well . . . thanks, I guess," he said, "for not telling anyone. In advance."

The girl shifted on her chair. "You're welcome . . . I guess. In advance."

A long silence stretched out between them.

"So you can't actually see my future?"

"Ha-ha. Screw you."

"No, I'm serious, I'm disappointed. I was kind of interested to find out."

"You will achieve all your dreams. You will ascend the halls of greatness. You'll fall in love, have three beautiful children, and be a highly anticipated guest on *The Tonight Show*."

"Ha."

They fell silent again.

"What did you want to know, specifically?" Matt asked, half out of curiosity and half just to make conversation. He expected Jane to shrug and give some nonanswer, but instead, the empath looked quietly at him for a few seconds, her head tilted slightly, appraising. Eventually, she spoke, her voice soft but resolute.

"If I get into the Legion of Heroes."

A bubble of laughter burst out of Matt's chest so hard he almost fell backward off his chair. The sound of his laughter filled the empty classroom; he expected Jane to join in, but after a few seconds, when she didn't, he caught himself, his cackling trailing off into weak chuckles as he saw the unwaveringly blank expression on her face.

"Wait. Sorry. Uh, you're, I mean, you're serious?"

"Absolutely," Jane replied coolly.

Matt ran a hand through his hair. "Wow. Okay, sorry, I shouldn't laugh. It's just—"

"It's fine."

He stared at her. "You realize you're insane, right?"

The girl remained mute. Matt didn't think she was getting the point.

"Seriously, they'll accept *me* before they accept you."

"Well, I don't know what your PD rank is," she said stiffly.

"Jane . . ." Matt said, feeling a little flustered, "look, I don't mean to dump all over your dreams, but come on. You're an empath. You figure the Legion might be harboring . . . geez, I don't know, a little resentment?"

"Times change," Jane replied coolly.

"Not that much," countered Matt, thoroughly unconvinced. He paused, considering the impossibility. "I mean, even if you weren't . . . you know . . . the Legion's not exactly community college. You can't just waltz in, you need a rank of—"

"Eleven," answered Jane, looking straight ahead, "eleven point zero before they even consider granting admission."

"Exactly," said Matt. "And, I mean, I don't know anyone above ten . . ." He trailed off, suddenly looking at the girl in a whole new light. "Do you?" he asked, suddenly excited. "Are you in the elevens?"

The girl shook her head. Matt pursed his lips, confused. "But then how do you think they'll even—"

"My rank's not in the elevens," interrupted Jane.

"Yeah exactly, then why—"

"It's twelve."

Matt felt like he'd been slapped. "Well, there you go," he eventually managed.

"Exactly."

The two of them sat there in half-stunned silence.

"It's still a crazy dream," Matt said finally.

"Only kind worth having," replied Jane.

Matt didn't know if it was that they'd shared each other's secrets or the simple fact that the figurative ice between them was broken, but from that point on, Jane the empath became considerably easier to be around. She talked, made eye contact, and occasionally even joked—at first, only with him, but as the weeks progressed, eventually with Taylor and Marcus and anyone else around them. She even volunteered an answer to a question in history one morning—albeit, an answer that was horribly wrong, but it was a step in the right direction.

"I guess ranks don't mean much if you're stupid, huh?" Matt jabbed after class.

"Screw you, you're short," Jane replied, somewhat less eloquent but undeniably an inch or two taller.

"Mean," Matt muttered when she was out of earshot.

Though Jane did have some serious gaps in her education, this soon faded into irrelevance as word of her combat prowess soon spread throughout the school. Initially, the news that the empath was some sort of power-wielding prodigy only further inflamed people's mistrust, but eventually, and especially after Matt suggested she hang back after PD and offer pointers to people who were themselves struggling, Jane's fearsome ability and consistent, uneventful presence earned her a begrudging kind of respect. Matt's friends especially were particularly keen—once they'd overcome their initial phobia—to indulge their curiosities.

"So, like, if you take my power," Brodie asked one lunchtime, his open mouth still filled with chicken, "what happens to me?"

"Nothing," replied Jane.

"But, like, you've taken my power. What do I do? I don't have a power anymore."

"Copy. I *copy* powers." She rubbed her eyes with the back of her hand. "You've still got your power; nobody can take it from you."

"Except a neutralizer," interjected Taylor, who was wearing a baseball cap indoors.

"Temporarily. If you're nearby."

"True, true," Taylor replied. Then he frowned. "If an empath copies a neutralizer, do the rest of their powers not work?"

Jane looked back at him apathetically. "If you're holding an eraser, does that stop you using a pencil?" She left Taylor to ponder that one.

As Jane grew steadily more tolerated, to the point where a few girls apparently even started saying the occasional hello to her when passing in the corridor (not encouraged, admittedly, by Jane's narrow-eyed suspicion of anything vaguely resembling normal human interaction), Matt's PD sessions grew steadily fuller. At first, he had experienced a drop-off in clientele—perhaps afraid he'd caught empath cooties—but after the shock of Jane's arrival wore off, people started visiting his little clairvoyant classroom in droves. Matt's actions had, annoyingly, drawn attention to himself and his "gift"—though it wasn't all bad. Maryam, Otim's sister, dropped off a box of chocolates with an expression of wordless thanks the week after her brother's averted confrontation with Jane, which Matt shared with an ecstatic Sarah and thoroughly ungrateful Jonas. And to his surprise, Matt soon discovered that the increase in people coming to him as a clairvoyant was actually enhancing his clairvoyant reputation.

"It's so stupid," he muttered to Jane one morning when they'd both arrived early, alone at their table and well out of anybody's earshot. "The more people do a thing, the more people assume the thing must be good. Otherwise, why would so many people do it? So, then they do it and people see them doing it and . . ."

"Around and around and around," agreed Jane, not looking up from her English assignment.

"This is why Furbies got popular, I tell you," Matt said, shaking his head. "Lemmings off a goddamn cliff."

"Uh-huh," Jane replied, still not looking up or caring.

The days were getting shorter and colder. It rarely snowed around these parts, but the air acquired a definite bite to it that let you know in no uncertain terms that something was freezing somewhere. Ugg boots emerged from hibernation, the trees started losing their leaves, and the floramancers began walking around with that mopey expression they got whenever the plants were sad. Mutterings began to circulate about homecoming, graduation, and college applications—finals were still a long way off, but the distance was narrowing rapidly. Some were handling the pressure better than others: Taylor was constantly in the middle of various scholarship applications, Marcus was occasionally studying, and Brodie had cut down being high to solely on weekends. Some were handling it worse: Kendra Hatherall had a panic attack during a morning quiz and accidentally turned her desk to liquid, while Mitch Green, whose parents were obviously giving him too much allowance, was caught paying a forty-two-year-old shapeshifter to sit his English mid-semester.

"Like everyone wasn't going to notice," Carlos muttered as school security escorted the red-faced cheater off school grounds.

"You can always tell," Matt agreed, shaking his head as the speckled tubby man was led past. "I mean who calls his classmates 'fellow kids'?"

Personally, Matt wasn't too worried about the future. For one thing, he didn't have to decide whether to pursue a power-requisite or standard career path; he'd considered accounting, or law, if his grades were good enough, maybe even history, where the focus on looking back would hopefully make people less interested in his "ability" to look forward. A job with the tax office, perhaps, something boring and bureaucratic— anything really where he could keep his head down and beaver away undetected.

Jane took issue with this idea.

"So, essentially, you're going to waste your life?" she asked contemptuously when the topic arose.

"I would call it more work to live," he replied, not taking any offense at her tone—he'd long since learned that Jane's seeming lack of courtesy didn't actually mean any disrespect. "But yes, if by 'waste my life,' you mean be a productive member of society who spends his abundant free time doing what he enjoys with his friends and family over and over for decades and decades until he dies happy loved and content, then yeah, I guess I just want to waste my life."

Jane scrunched up her face. "You don't want to . . . I don't know, make a mark? Do something meaningful, change the world?"

"The world seems to get along fine without me," he said with a shrug.

Jane opened her mouth to argue, but at that moment Pat dropped down into the seat opposite her.

"How do you change between powers?" he asked without any preamble at all.

"Why?" she grumbled. Pat grinned.

"Eva Weiss wants to know."

"That junior Swiss girl?" asked Matt, two pieces of melon on the end of his fork. "The one with the huge, uh, ahem, hands?" He quickly caught himself in consideration of present company.

"It's just a mental thing," answered Jane, oblivious to his almost-slip. "Like I'm rolling a coin between my fingers."

"Cool, cool," replied Pat, rocking forward and nodding and undeterred by the semi-awkward silence that followed. "And you have three powers, right?"

"Yes."

"But you can have four."

"Yes."

"Fire, ice, and thunder."

"Yes. I used to have telepathy. I got rid of it."

"I didn't know that," said Matt, looking at her mildly surprised. The girl nodded stiffly.

"Why'd you get rid of it?" Pat pressed.

"I didn't want it anymore," she replied, irritation creeping into her voice.

"How'd you get rid of it?"

"What is this, twenty goddamn questions?" Jane snapped. Pat flinched and leaned back across the table. Jane pinched the bridge of her nose and sighed.

"Sorry, sorry." She looked at him and attempted something that might have been meant to be a smile, but which came across more as a pained grimace. "Any power I don't want, I can just let go. You don't have to do anything special, you just kind of"—she hesitated—"you know when you've been wearing shoes for a while and you sort of don't think about it, but then you get home and you take them off and suddenly you realize there was something on your feet?" She glanced at Pat to see if he understood.

"Kind of? So, it's like taking off a shoe?"

"Kind of. Not really. It feels like shedding a skin you didn't know you had. Except I don't know what shedding your skin feels like so I have no idea."

Pat nodded, satisfied though perhaps not comprehending. "That'll do. Thanks!" He left the table and ran off as quickly as he came.

"Bless his little heart," Matt said as he watched him go. "Going after girls. Trying to be cool." He glanced at Jane. "Being friends with the big scary empath."

"I don't have any friends," Jane muttered into her textbook.

"Uh-huh. How'd you go with the chem equations?"

There was no warning. One moment, they were sitting in fourth-period English, like normal; the next, an announcement, blared out over the loudspeakers—special assembly, would all students please leave their regularly scheduled classes and gather in the cafeteria. Normally, it would have been in the school hall, but the hall was closed for the day, the roof having been caved in by a stray boulder.

"Any idea what this's about?" Matt asked as he slid into the gap at their table between Jane and Taylor. The former said nothing, and the latter just shrugged.

"Maybe it's about the stuff with the hall."

"I swear, man, that was all Freddie P," Marcus swore, although he still looked around nervously at the gathering of teachers.

"Shut up, Marcus."

"Stupid goddamn dirt-wranglers, I swear to God."

"Oh, look at me, I can throw a rock the highest! Oh no, look at me, I can throw a rock the highest!"

"Shut up, it wasn't my fault," Marcus said, slumping into a sulk.

"Ladies and gentlemen!" Principal Rance's amplified voice echoed throughout the room and the buzz of chattering stopped. "Thank you all for coming." The gray-suited man was standing at the middle of the long teachers' table that ran exclusively down one edge of the cafeteria, flanked on either side by what looked like half the staff—and behind him a man Matt didn't recognize. "I apologize for pulling you out of class, however I have just received some very exciting news from a very important guest." He stole an excited glance over his shoulder at the figure behind him, fluorescent light shining off the bald patch on his head. Matt and half the students in the room craned their necks for a better view.

"Is it Steve Austin?" whispered Brodie. Carlos shook his head and Taylor shot him a look. The man being introduced wasn't anyone they recognized. It was weird—Rance wasn't usually this excitable.

"It is my honor," continued the principal, cutting across Matt's chain of thought, "to introduce you all to Mr. Daniel Winters."

This meant nothing to anybody. But the uncharacteristically enthusiastic head apparently knew that would be the case, because he immediately repeated: "Mr. Daniel Winters, managing director of the Legion of Heroes."

There was a stunned silence. Matt looked across at Jane, who had frozen in place, eyes wide, unable to move. Matt didn't think she was breathing.

"What's the Legion of Heroes doing?"

"Who are they?"

The silence broke and a frenetic whispering swept throughout the room, as every student in Northridge turned to the person beside them to ask the question Principal Rance was already answering.

"Mr. Winters is here because one of our students, one of Northridge's"—he emphasized the school name—"students, has been approved for admission into the Legion's Academy."

Beside him Jane's shoulders started to shake.

Rance smiled a huge, walrus-y smile, and turning to the man behind him, extended an open, inviting hand toward the waiting, watching masses. "Mr. Winters. Over to you."

The man stepped forward. He was handsome, early to mid-forties, tall and broad-shouldered without being imposing, with neat salt-and-pepper hair and an immaculate black suit. His smooth, clean-shaven jawline put Principal Rance's mustache and jowls to shame. He gazed around the room, not quickly but steadily, taking in every upturned face, every watching eye. Calm, doubtless, used to being watched.

"Ladies and gentlemen," he said, and his voice was clear and confident, like the striking of a wooden drum, "thank you for having me. The Legion is always excited to find a new recruit." And then his head turned and he looked over the heads of hundreds of students who all followed his gaze, across the room, until it stopped all the way over the other side. Directly on their table. The man from the Legion of Heroes looked right at them—and smiled.

"Oh my God."

Matt couldn't move. It was like his body was rooted in disbelief. He turned to look at Jane, who was sitting there, unblinking, clearly trying to stop herself shaking, shouting, punching the air, or doing anything that could ruin this, anything that would risk taking this away from her. It'd happened. Holy hell, it'd actually happened, just like she said it would. He wouldn't have believed it, not in a million years.

He really was a terrible clairvoyant.

All eyes turned to Winters as he stepped around the teachers' table and started striding across the room—all except Matt's, who only had eyes for Jane. *You know what*, he thought, watching the girl's trembling lips, the loose strands of auburn hair, *good on her. Good on her for sticking with it, for believing in herself in spite of everything. Good on her, and good on whoever at the Legion was open-minded enough—no, who had the common sense—to look past her tattoo and see the talent behind it.*

Winters walked toward them, nearing the edge of their table, his warm, inviting smile aimed directly forward, drawing them in. To his right, Taylor was whispering a steady stream of continuous swear words, while Brodie slowly and discreetly sniffed his sleeve. Matt didn't say anything, determined not to ruin the moment but still unable to keep his face from splitting into a gigantic grin. He looked at Jane, but the girl was still staring straight ahead, eyes unmoving, arms locked awkwardly by her side. Matt didn't think she'd remembered to breathe since the words *Legion of Heroes* had been uttered. His grin grew wider and he fought the urge to slap the empath on the shoulder, to high-five and hug her—because, practically, she'd probably kill him on instinct and then, you know, kill him again for ruining the moment. Heck, he thought, he was actually going to miss her, in a funny kind of way; like how you might miss a spider that'd been nesting harmlessly for a few months eating flies above your curtains.

Daniel Winters had stopped right behind her. Jane's shoulders were so rigid you could've broken a plate over her back without her flinching. The suited man ran one last glance around the room, breathing in the suspense, almost seeming to grow larger upon the undivided attention. He extended his hand and opened his palm.

"It is my honor," he said in that golden, confident voice, "to extend to you the opportunity to take your place among legends." This was all scripted, a ritual—the words known to every child who'd ever watched TV or picked up a comic book. "To take your talents and hone them for a higher purpose; for the highest purpose; for the protection, the betterment of humankind."

He looked out among the sea of shining faces. "Admission cannot be procured. Endurance will not be enforced. And ascension is not assured. But your place in the Legion is waiting, if you are strong enough to take it."

He paused for a single, final moment—then looked down at the boy.

"Matt Callaghan. Welcome to the Legion of Heroes."

THE CHOSEN ONE

"A Short History of the Legion of Heroes"
Taylor McDermott (History Assignment, A+)

"We will do what we must, we few, we great. We, who have the power to save the world, and who will not, cannot, stand idly by while its peoples suffer. We are servants of no nation, but the protectors of humanity. From this day forth, let those who would prey on the weak, the good, the innocent, take heed and beware, for the Legion of Heroes stands against you, and we will not falter." So said the man dubbed Captain Dawn in his now-famous speech announcing the official formation of the Legion of Heroes, an organization that has come to embody not only the pinnacle of post-Aurora superhumanism, but also humanity as a whole.

There are few institutions that can be said to command the same level of respect and admiration as the Legion; nor many which have endured the same devastation. Officially formed on February 24, 1969, the Legion began life years earlier as an informal, essentially vigilante conglomerate of highly talented, socially minded individuals who believed that their powers placed upon them a responsibility to better the world. Led by Captain Dawn and his wife, Caitlin, the group was initially little more than a collection of like-minded acquaintances, but as word of these "Heroes" spread, their ranks quickly swelled to include some of the most powerful and legendary fighters from around the world. Initially viewed with suspicion, hostility, and outright persecution by many governments, eventually the beneficial and popular effects of the Legion's actions, coupled with the collapse of many oppressive regimes and the Legion's sheer unassailability, meant that the group came to be recognized and respected as an independent transnational peacekeeping force.

To examine the history of the Legion of Heroes is to examine many of the pivotal events in modern history, a testament to their involvement and impact. Building on minor cases of small-town justice, the first major act with which the Legion—and in particular its leader, the man known as Captain Dawn, wielder of "the power of a hundred suns"—is credited was the almost single-handed resolution of the 1967 Detroit Conflicts, which had seen the city paralyzed by urban violence. Undeterred by the governmental resentment, this resolution (which the State Department had been striving fruitlessly toward for several years) attracted, the group moved to help stabilize the Mexican–American border before turning its attention overseas and coming to the aid of populist movements the world over. Undeniably, the Legion's presence allowed uprisings such as the Iranian Independence Spring, the Tiananmen Square Revolution, and the fall of the Berlin Wall (which, captured in iconic photographs, Captain Dawn himself had a hand in physically tearing down) to incur significantly less resistance and bloodshed.

In the late 1970s, as the world governments stabilized and adapted to the new needs and irrepressibility of their superpowered citizenry, the Legion's focus shifted away from protecting and assisting peoples revolting against oppressive regimes and toward more disparate threats. As surely as the "superhero" had emerged, likewise it seemed inevitable that some would don the mantle of "supervillain" and seek to use their abilities for personal gain. It was these villains, on which the Legion now focused, and their exploits here provided the brunt of Legion stories enshrined in television, comic books, and other popular culture. There would be few children in America who did not grow up watching and reading about the Legion's triumphs over Ana "Fleshtide" Bloodbane or Viktor "the Mindtaker" Mentok; of their liberation of Broken Hill from the domination of Simon West; the six-day battle against the Children of Silence; or Captain Dawn's defeat of his self-proclaimed nemesis, the Brothers Darkness. In 1981, Morningstar Academy, a college for selecting and training new members, was established in Eastchester County to serve as the Legion's base of operations, becoming not just a home, but a place where the best and brightest from around the globe could be mentored by the greatest champions of the day. In 1983, the Legion gained recognition by the United Nations as an official peacekeeping force—although a cloud was cast over this success several years later by the untimely death of Captain Dawn's wife, Caitlin, in a car accident—embedding their reputation as humanitarian protectors, and ultimately providing the backdrop against which they were almost completely destroyed.

It is beyond the scope of this essay to recount the events of the African Devastation; nevertheless, the impact of Klaus "the Black Death" Heydrich's massacre of the Legion before his defeat at the hands of Captain Dawn cannot be overstated. With the loss of nearly all its full members the Legion, like the world, teetered on the brink of collapse, held together only by Captain Dawn and those recruits not inducted into the Legion's active ranks. As Captain Dawn retreated from the public eye following Heydrich's defeat, doubts raged over the organization's future. However, in 1995, the sealed doors of Morningstar Academy were finally reopened and a new generation of Acolytes allowed inside. Although not (as of writing) officially reformed nor reengaged in interventionist activities, the Legion of Heroes endures, one day to remerge, empowered by a legendary legacy and, as always, the hope for a better world.

"Wait, what?"

Matt looked up at Winters, the smile wiped abruptly from his face. He must have misheard—but the suited man was staring right at him.

"Matt Callaghan, welcome to the Legion of Heroes."

Matt couldn't move—the words didn't seem to be penetrating his brain. Out of the corner of his eye, he caught a glimpse of Jane, her face frozen, wearing an expression like she'd been struck.

"What?"

Winters smiled reassuringly, evidently not unused to this sort of reaction. "You've been selected, Mr. Callaghan. By the Legion of Heroes. Congratulations." And the room erupted in thunderous applause.

For a moment, time seemed to stand still for Matt. The world around him was a photograph—a frozen image from which he was detached, observing, a portrait comprised of a thousand pieces. The sea of people, his friends and teachers, all staring, cheering, every eye focused on him, burrowing into his skin. The polished face of Mr. Winters looming large, his hand outstretched. The elated gaze of Principal Rance, his meaty hands slapping together louder than anyone's, audible across the room. Taylor turning to look at him, wide-eyed and shocked, his arms half-raised as if he was unsure whether to hug or celebrate. Jane, devastated, deflating, her eyes and everything about her falling down. His own face the blank, confused epicenter of this insane storm. For an instant, he was outside it all, watching from afar as it happened to someone else.

Then suddenly, his gut lurched forward, and reality came crashing down.

"What . . ." he repeated, except it wasn't a question this time. Winters mistook his coldness for confusion.

"I know it's a lot to take in," he said, placing a strong, affirming hand on Matt's shoulder. "But you deserve this, Matt. You should be proud."

"No but I . . . I mean . . ." Matt started to raise his hand as if to remove Winters's, but then just sort of waved it around feebly instead, at a loss for words. He felt his face heat up. "I didn't even apply."

"Ah." Winters chuckled, loudly enough for the whole room to hear, now that the applause had subsided into hushed, observant whispers. "I can assure you, Matt, you most definitely did. I read it myself." He glanced around the room. "I think this is what they call shock," he said with a laugh, which the whole school echoed.

"But I didn't," protested Matt, whatever shock he was feeling being rapidly replaced by panic. "I really didn't."

The laughter in the room slowly faded. Winters turned his head slightly, eyes on Matt, but eyebrows furrowing slightly toward the crowd. He reached into his breast pocket and removed a thin ream of folded papers.

"Matthew Callaghan," he read, the papers unfurled, "eighteen. Clairvoyant. Northridge High School." The man in the dark suit paused. "That's you, isn't it?" And to Matt's stunned horror, he held up a completed form, with Matt's school photo stapled to the front.

"Where did you get that?" he whispered, staring into his own eyes with disbelief. But Daniel Winters didn't seem to hear him.

"Look familiar?" He smiled kindly.

"Well, yes," Matt conceded, finally tearing his gaze free from the photograph. All around, he could feel the eyes of the school burning into him. "But I swear, I didn't . . ." His voice trailed off, and the room fell quiet.

Winters broke the awkward silence with a laugh.

"Well," he admitted, "I have to say, this might be a first. Maybe a parent or teacher . . ." He paused, touching a contemplative finger to his lips, then shook his head. "Well, whoever they are, you'll want to thank them. Our invitation still stands."

Matt felt a hotness swelling up in his stomach that was either panic or rage. "I'm not . . . how am I . . . my PD scores suck!"

There was a roll of laughter from the assembled students, and Winters chuckled.

"Performance rankings aren't everything," the recruiter responded. "The Legion looks at an applicant's history, their personality, but most of all, we consider what they could do for the world."

The pin finally dropped. Matt's eyes widened, and he was suddenly gripped by a rampaging, inescapable fear.

Winters leaned down slightly, seeming not to notice, wearing a gentle smile. "Matt, your ability is amazing—quite possibly unique. I feel . . . the Legion feels . . . Captain Dawn"—he said the name louder, with added emphasis and an excited murmur ran around the room—"feels, that with the proper study and training, its potential is incredible."

Oh no.

Clairvoyant.

They thought he was a clairvoyant.

Everyone thought he was a clairvoyant. The National Register said he was a clairvoyant. The Legion of Heroes believed he was a clairvoyant, and given everything they'd gone up against, everything they'd failed to . . .

Oh God. No wonder they wanted him. Despite all their powers, their strength and dedication, the Legion had still been blindsided by the biggest threat in human history and watched half a billion people pay the price. Even though they could do almost anything, beat almost anyone, they still couldn't predict the future . . .

But he could. At least according to his ID.

Oh no.

Understanding and panic flooded Matt. They wanted to train him, hone him, develop his skills. Worse, study him, figure out how his "power" worked, measure the accuracy of . . . CRAP.

He had to get out of this.

Matt looked up.

"No."

"I'm sorry?"

"No, um, thank you?" His throat felt reluctant to annunciate any-thing approaching words, but he swallowed hard and pushed through. "I'd, uh, like to decline."

"Decline?" For the first time, a flicker of uncertainty flashed across the recruiter's handsome face. He recovered almost instantly. "Matt, I understand this might be a bit overwhelming but . . ."

"I'd like to decline," Matt repeated stubbornly. He crossed his arms across his chest, mostly to stop them from shaking. "Thank you, but I don't think the Legion of Heroes is for me."

A ripple of discontented muttering passed through the onlooking crowd. Everywhere, people exchanged glances, turned to whisper. Prin-cipal Rance, still standing at the head of the teachers' table, looked like the boy had just single-handedly murdered his dog. Beside him Taylor tried to subtly tug on his sleeve, but Matt ignored him.

Winters paused, following the murmurs, then his eyes snapped back to Matt. He forced a smile. "Perhaps it'd be better if we continued this conversation in private, just so I can fully understand the concerns you—"

"Here's fine," interjected Matt. If he'd been given the choice, this whole mess would have occurred in private, but the suited recruiter had opted for the grand spectacle, and now Matt had no choice but to follow through. "I don't want to join. Plain and simple." Winters's brow fur-rowed. He paused for a moment and glanced around—then gave a slight shrug, as if to say "as you wish" and spoke.

"If it's danger you're worried about," he proclaimed, maybe slightly louder than he would have had he and Matt been alone, "I can assure you, the Legion will work tirelessly to ensure you and your gift are safe."

"It's not that," replied Matt—although damn, that would've been a good reason, he should have thought of that. He scrambled for a reply. "I'm not afraid."

"Then what is it?" asked Winters, looking genuinely concerned—if not by Matt's rejection, then at least with the idea that anyone could have a problem with his beloved institution. "Mr. Callaghan, I can assure you that Morningstar Academy provides an exceptional education. This isn't a life sentence; this is the best college offer you're ever going to get. You'll emerge trained and empowered, with qualifications and contacts that will allow you to pursue any career you wish. We are fully furnished and ready to accommodate any needs you might have, and if you're concerned about money, don't be—the Legion only offers full scholarships. But even all that aside"—Winters's voice strengthened—"don't you feel like you have a duty? A responsibility to use this gift you've been given to help people? For the good of mankind?" He paused. "I understand this may be daunting but please, Matt"—his voice was almost imploring—"don't let this chance slip by. Don't throw away your future." The crowd fell to a hush and all eyes turned to Matt.

"I-I-I," Matt stammered. He looked around the room, desperately trying to think of a way out, of literally any reason to decline. Some students he didn't know were starting to shake their heads at him. Most were looking confused; a few seemed almost angry. Across the room from him, Pat was silently mouthing *WHAT ARE YOU DOING?* interspaced with a few more profane phrases. On the other side of the table, Carlos was half-frozen in an incredulous shrug. There was a sudden dryness in Matt's mouth that seemed to be sapping his ability to think.

"Um," he stalled, not very convincingly. Something. Anything other than the truth. Instinctively, he turned to Jane, maybe the only person who might be able to help him. But the empath wasn't looking at him— she didn't seem to be looking at anything. She was simply slumped, silent, wearing an expression of profound, broken defeat beyond anything Matt would've thought she was capable of feeling. For him, this was a nightmare, but for her, it was worse. For her, it had been a fleeting glimpse of hope.

And suddenly, Matt had an idea so monumentally stupid it couldn't possibly fail.

"It's not fair," he said. He raised his head and looked up at the confused expression on the recruiter's face. "It's not fair. I'm no better than any of them. Why am I being selected?"

"Mr. Callaghan, I can assure you that doesn't—" began Winters, but Matt cut him off.

"I'm not Legion material," he said. Then he paused for dramatic effect—before pointing directly at Jane. "But she is."

A sharp intake of breath, almost a hiss, ran across the room. Winters glanced down at the girl, who had jerked upright and frozen in place with a bewildered, deer-in-the-headlights look as if unsure whether to run, speak, or just start firing lightning bolts indiscriminately into the crowd. His eyes fell on the spikey E and a shadow flashed across his face.

"Mr. Callaghan," Winters stated as diplomatically as possible, some of the warmth draining from his voice, "I don't know if this is an ill-conceived joke, but unfortunately, the only person I am able to offer a place to today . . ."

"It's not a joke," affirmed Matt. "She's the one you want. She should be in the Legion. She is stronger, faster, and tougher than anyone I know. She can beat a room full of people without breaking a sweat. She is the perfect candidate for the Academy, she actually applied and she"—he made sure to emphasize this part—"has a PD rating of twelve."

There was an outburst of murmuring and a swarm of faces peered over at the girl with renewed admiration. Even the recruiter looked mildly impressed before he managed to get a hold of himself.

"Be that as it may," Winters said, frowning, "her application is not currently under consideration."

"Well, that's some bull crap," replied Matt, causing another wave of muttering (one of the teachers tutted "language"). "Because it should be." Winters's frown deepened, and the managing director opened his mouth to speak, but Matt was already ahead of him.

"If any other person in this school had a rank of twelve, you'd be here for them too. You'd scoop them up without a moment's hesitation. But because she"—he pointed at Jane again, and this time she stared back at him with an unfathomable expression—"is an empath, you don't even spare her a second thought. Well, that's just prejudice. And I won't join a prejudiced institution." He paused, and gazed around the room, daring the crowd to meet his eyes. "Just because she's an empath, doesn't mean she's the Black Death."

The room fell silent. For a second, Matt worried that maybe he'd crossed a line. But he couldn't go back now—the only way through was forward.

"She should be in the Legion," he repeated, and he gave the words a moment to sink in. "She deserves to be in the Legion. And if she can't go, I don't go. Plain and simple."

Half a continent away, a man sat alone, watching in darkness lit only by a white-blue screen. In the cafeteria of Northridge High School, Daniel

Winters blinked, and for a second the room was plunged into blackness, the iris-camera momentarily obscured.

"If she doesn't go, I don't go. Plain and simple." The words hissed through the set, electric and distorted but still sincere.

You had to admire his loyalty—if it was that. An unusual turn of events. The man shifted ever so slightly in his seat. Through Winters's eyes, he stared at this boy, this clairvoyant. What do you know, child? What do you see? Time would tell. But only, it seemed, if . . .

Winters's gaze shifted, so now he, too, looked at the girl. An empath . . . a surly, unkempt, wiry specimen. But . . . fierce. Strong. Driven. He could see that etched into the lines of her face, the set of her jaw. Defiant perhaps, or proud. She did not speak—did not plead her case, though he remembered the intensity of her application. He had dismissed it then, of course, but now . . . now he saw the steel in her eyes . . .

He pushed a button and spoke, in a voice reverberating with power.

"Let her come."

Winters's finger rose to his ear.

"Sir?" he said, not to Matt nor anyone else there. An earpiece, Matt realized. Pale and translucent, almost invisible.

For a few seconds, the recruiter was silent, his eyes unfocused. A slight frown lingered on his mouth.

"Yes, sir," he said finally. Winters's hand dropped to his side. He drew a deep breath, then looked directly at Matt.

"Okay," the man said with a nod. "Both of you."

It was like Matt had been hit in the head with a brick.

"What?" he gaped.

"You and her. Both of you are invited to join the Legion. Congratulations, Miss." Unlike Matt, Winters didn't extend Jane a hand. She didn't seem to care. Jane's arms were trembling, her mouth opening and closing long before she actually managed to articulate any words.

"Th-th-thank you," she finally got out, her voice rasping from disuse. She reached up toward him. "I . . . I don't . . ."

But Winters had already broken off and turned back to Matt. Jane's hand hung limply in empty space.

"If you'll come with me, Mr. Callaghan," he said, calm and professional, "there are papers I need you to sign." He turned on his heel, unflappable, and Matt, in a state of shock, had no choice but to follow.

The room filled with murmurs but to Matt the words seemed a million miles away. As if in a daydream, he followed the fine coat of Daniel Winters across the room of a thousand eyes and through the waiting door.

The door swung open, and a gigantic frosted ice-cream cake practically ablaze with sparklers emerged from its depths.

"Woo-hoo!"

"Mat-ty!"

"Woo-hoo!"

A chorus of congratulatory cries filled the steakhouse, and a swarm of hands mushed over Matt, slapping his back, tousling his hair. Someone smacked his butt. It was like being assaulted by a hand monster. The waitress set the brightly burning cake in the center of the table, right on top of Matt's placemat. The cheering escalated.

"Matty boy!"

"Legion, Legion!"

"You know it, you f—!"

Matt's mom raised her hand threateningly and Marcus sunk sheepishly in his seat.

"Sorry, Mrs. Callaghan."

Even though their reservation had been late notice, the Longhouse Grill (best steaks in the city) had still managed to get them a table. Matt didn't know whether his dad had dropped the name Legion of Heroes, but either way, they'd gotten in. All five Callaghans, Taylor, at least a dozen of his friends, all here and loud and celebrating Matt's induction into an institution that unbeknownst to them would probably end up exposing his secret and getting him killed or turned into a human guinea pig.

"Should we have invited the empath girl?" Matt's mom whisper-asked his dad behind Matt's back, as Jonas helped Matt extinguish the sparklers. Michael Callaghan just sort of shrugged. His wife frowned for a moment, then shook her head and leaned back over to her baby boy.

They probably should have invited Jane, Matt thought. After the call had gone through to Matt's parents, the Callaghan household had descended into a frenzy. There were forms to sign, calls to make, a celebration to organize—and somewhere among all that, between shaking hands and booking restaurants, ordering cakes, and getting Dad an early jump home, all thoughts of the empath seemed to have fallen by the wayside. In his (and he supposed everyone's) defense, none of them really knew where Jane had gone—Winters had said he'd see to her after he was done with him, but Matt didn't know what that entailed. Plus, he didn't have her number. Matt couldn't remember whether he'd actually ever seen her using a phone. Did she even have a phone?

"To Matt!" shouted Taylor. He raised a champagne flute full of Sprite high into the air. "Matt, the superhero!"

"Advocate for empaths!" added Carlos, and there was a ripple of laughter.

"Hey, man, it doesn't stop him." Taylor grinned. "Legion baby, for the good of us all!"

The party cheered and Matt was once again overcome by pats and hair ruffling. He forced himself a reluctant smile. In spite of it all, this wasn't bad. Whatever else may happen, this bit here was pretty nice.

"Cut the cake, you dumb shivering person!" called Pat, glared down mid-sentence by Mrs. Callaghan.

So Matt did. He sunk the knife deep into the sugary sponge cake, then talked, laughed, and ate alongside his family and friends. There were toasts, stories, and recaps from a dozen different perspectives, then the best ribs in town. There was Taylor, in finest form, explaining away Matt's initial refusal as modesty and friendship, a bottle of champagne on the house for Mr. and Mrs. Callaghan when the owner heard why they were celebrating, and several requests for Matt's autograph after he half-jokingly said that it was going to be valuable one day. Pat messaged half the school to organize a rampaging after-party; Sarah fell asleep on her father's lap. And throughout everything, Matt Callaghan sat in the middle, laughing and smiling, allowing himself to be happy, tucking his worries aside, if only for tonight. Because the future was uncertain, but the present was full of light, life, and people who loved him.

Jane sat alone in the quiet and the dark. Alone in her room, on the edge of her bed, breathing deeply, too excited to sleep. No one was home—her father was at work. He'd been asleep when the school called—asleep or passed out. It didn't matter. She didn't care. She was going to the Legion.

She was going to the Legion.

She'd taken the night off work, called in sick. She didn't like to lie, but she was never sick, so they believed her. They hadn't cared. There'd always be someone else to stand out the back and flip burgers.

She was going to the Legion.

It didn't feel real. Wasn't possible. Even waiting, wanting, longing this long, a part of her had never embraced the hope and now couldn't embrace the reality. She clutched the precious papers in her hand, knowing what they said, not needing to look. She'd read them a hundred times over, searching for some fault or flaw they could use to crush her dreams. No. It was real. The forms were signed. She gripped them as tightly as she dared, never wanting to let go but not wanting them to crease. Her totem, her tether to the truth.

She was going to the Legion.

There was a lump rising in her chest, a hot, wet tightness she couldn't describe. She looked up across the room at her silent lonely dresser, at the reflection in the mirror and the moonlight. At herself and at the face in the photo above, looking back at her, the black-and-white woman smiling down.

I did it, Mom.

I made it. Just like you always said.

I'm going to the Legion.

What would it be like? How would they train, how quickly would she progress? She saw herself there, in the mansion on the hill, fighting, proving herself, impressing everyone. She saw the reverence on their faces, the whispered apologies. Saw herself triumph, again and again—saw Captain Dawn himself pin the badge on her chest. His hand clasped hers; he smiled, leaned in, whispered, "Well done." And then he stood by her side as the world around them knelt.

Jane dreamed, and in her dark, cold room her dreams were fitful fantasies of light and hills and gold.

The first rays of sunlight peaked over the hills. Jane Walker sat with her arm resting on the windowsill, listening to the gentle *clack-clack* of the train flowing smoothly around them. She reclined slightly, nesting her head against the crimson carriage seating, watching the countryside go past in a rush of green and gray. It was so quiet, so peaceful—the world barely awake as they stole traceless through it.

The serenity seemed lost on Matt.

"I'm doomed," he moaned. Jane's eyes flicked irritably at the seat opposite her where the boy sat, chest slumped over his knees, head still buried in his hands.

"Stop being such a baby," she muttered, shifting slightly.

Matt resolutely ignored her.

Almost a week had passed—a whirlwind of anticipation Jane could hardly remember. She'd barely slept, barely ate, overtrained to exhaustion—and then before she knew it her alarm was going off at 4:00 a.m. on Monday morning and the time had come.

Matt's week had also been a whirlwind—although less "exciting change" and more "irreparably damage the barn and kill all the chickens." In the space of an instant, Matt's biggest concern had gone from an unfinished chemistry assignment to being trapped in an elite university where the most powerful people on the planet would inevitably ferret out his humanity and ruin his life. He'd had no time to prepare—the Legion of Heroes wanted him, and the Legion of Heroes didn't wait. Matt found the speed at which Morningstar Academy was ready to absorb him almost unnervingly efficient, like having a pizza show up only five minutes after you'd ordered. He suspected, though he had no way to prove, that his consent had been little more than a formality— which did nothing to put his mind at ease.

Frustratingly, the information Matt had on what he was walking into was painfully sparse. Most of what was contained in the information package he had received Matt already knew simply from watching cartoons. Morningstar had been gifted to the Legion by Samuel Barnes, a retired merchant banker whose family had been killed in the Year of Chaos and who, the story went, wished to leave behind a legacy of good. It had been both a home and a college for the Legion, but had been sealed off by Captain Dawn, a notorious recluse, after the African Devastation, only to be reopened five years ago to take in new students. Currently, the brochure told him, there were no "full" Legion members (excluding the captain)—although it failed to specify if, when, or how this was going to change. It was also infuriatingly brief on the exact nature of the "training" entrants were expected to undergo—like the organizers simply expected to be able to drop the name Legion of Heroes and let the rest sort itself out.

All through the week, people had kept on congratulating Matt on his so-called "achievement." And all through the week, Matt had kept scrambling for a way to escape. He'd tried to prolong the seconds, held out until the last minute for a brain wave or Hail Mary reprieve, but instead time flew by like it was out to spite him. And before Matt knew it, it was Monday morning, and he was waking up in the dark with a pounding headache to get ready to leave. After a short and not overly soppy goodbye to his family (webcams, teleporters, and telepathic group calls made keeping in touch much easier these days), Matt's father had driven him to the railway station downtown, where he'd found Jane already waiting, alone, in front of a large freight train with one old-fashioned passenger car. And thus had Matt discovered that the first step to being a superhero was a long, ceremonial, and completely unnecessary train ride.

"Why are we even here?" Matt continued complaining. Even though they were the only ones in the carriage, his voice didn't carry far beyond their seats.

"We're going to Morningstar," Jane snapped back, sick of his whining. "We're joining the Legion of Heroes. Stop asking stupid questions."

"No," contradicted Matt, "I mean why are we on this stupid train?" He glanced up with narrowed, bloodshot eyes at the luxurious compartment as though the wood paneling and maroon upholstery had personally wronged him. "What is this, the Dark Ages? Why can't a teleporter just jump us the entire way?"

Jane knew exactly why they were being made to travel like this, of course, but the reason involved tradition, philosophy, and a very obscure book she'd once read about the Legion's early days and European princesses. She doubted Matt actually cared.

" 'The journey home, savored, is sweetest,' " she quoted, glancing back out the window at the hills rolling by.

"Great," said Matt, rolling his eyes. "So the reason is fortune-cookie bull crap."

"The reason is shut up," Jane retorted irritably. "The reason is we're supposed to use this time to reflect on ourselves and think about what's ahead."

"Right," Matt snorted, laying his head back down. "Because that's never once crossed my mind."

Jane treated his sarcasm with indifference.

"You look bad," she stated bluntly, changing the subject. This was the first she'd seen him in more than passing since Tuesday, and Matt's bedraggled appearance marked him as significantly worse for wear. His hair was tangled, his clothes were a mess, and he definitely hadn't shaved.

"I feel bad," Matt murmured, not looking up. Jane could smell the alcohol and smoke wafting off his breath from here.

"Hangover?" she accused.

The boy raised a wavering finger. "Technically, I think I'm still drunk." To the best of her knowledge, drunk was how Matt had spent the better part of the last few days. Winters's visit had come midweek—from there, there'd been the congratulations party, and then the weekend party, and then the going-away party, the latter of which had only been last night. Jane hadn't been invited to any of them, but she was thankful for that, she reminded herself—parties and people were a waste of time.

Jane pursed her lips. "It's a Monday."

"Of that," came the muffled reply, "I am acutely aware."

The girl paused, considering for a moment whether to launch into a verbal assault about the evils of alcohol, but thought better of it. He wouldn't have berated her, if the tables were turned. "Need anything?"

Matt lifted his head slightly and glazed up at her out of a single bleary eye.

"What?"

Jane felt a flare of impatience. "Are you *okay*? Do you need water or something?" Matt just stared at her.

"Are you trying to be nice?"

"No," spat Jane; then "Yes," she admitted; and finally, "I don't know. I'm not trying not to be nice."

Matt lay his head back down onto his arms. "I'm definitely still drunk."

"I wouldn't know."

They lapsed into silence. Finally, Matt spoke.

"Water. Water would be swell."

Jane swiveled and silently rummaged through her backpack in the adjacent seat for her water bottle. By the time she found it, the boy was sitting somewhat more upright.

"Thanks," he muttered as she handed him the bottle.

"That's mine, so give it back."

Matt rolled his eyes. "I'm not going to steal your water bottle." He gulped down a full half of the bottle, then set it gingerly down on the seat beside him and leaned back with a contented sigh.

For a few seconds, neither spoke, the only sound between them the soft rhythm of the train's wheels. It really was peaceful here, thought Jane, alone in this quiet carriage, with the morning sun streaming through the windows.

"So," Matt said eventually, "why the niceness?"

"What?" she replied irritably. "I can't be nice?"

"Can't," Matt corrected, holding up a finger, "is a strong word." His hand dropped. "I'm not hating. It's just a bit of a change."

Her mouth twitched. "I'm grateful."

"Yeah?"

"Yes. I'm grateful and . . ." She shifted uncomfortably at the next part. "Indebted."

To her surprise, Matt snorted and laid his head back into his hands. "No, you're not."

"I am!" Jane exclaimed, annoyed. "Screw you, don't tell me what I feel, I am grateful!"

The boy waved a hand dismissively above his slumped head, not looking up. "I meant you don't owe me anything."

Jane was perplexed. "How?" she asked. "You got me into the Legion."

"You got you into the Legion."

"Yeah, but if it wasn't for you saying that you wouldn't go unless—"

"I didn't do it for you," Matt interjected, sighing. He looked up, massaging his temples between his thumb and forefinger.

For a second, Jane just blinked. "I don't understand."

"I thought they would say no," explained Matt, looking tired and resigned. He glanced out the train window at the hills rolling past. "I *hoped* they would say no. I needed an excuse, a good way out." He yawned and slumped back down, the exact opposite of her own rigid posture. "I thought there was no way the Legion wanted me in more than they wanted you kept out."

His words sent a tight wad of pain through Jane's chest. She kept her face blank, and the boy didn't notice. "Well, looks like you were wrong," she said stiffly, taking pains to keep her voice level.

Matt snorted. "Thanks, Sherlock, I hadn't noticed," he replied, head in his arms.

Jane stared at him. "Why don't you want to join the Legion?"

"Seriously?" Matt looked up at her, incredulity written all over his face. "Seriously. The Legion of Heroes. The Legion of . . ."—he swore—"Heroes. The pinnacle of superhumans, of refining and studying powers, who have selected me *specifically* for my clairvoyance. Oh no, why would that be a problem?"

He lowered his voice to a teeth-gritted whisper. "This whole . . . facade falls apart the second anyone with half a brain looks too closely at it. As soon as someone starts doing actual, objective analysis . . ." He let the sentence hang. "Which is exactly what the Legion is going to do," he lamented. "They'll want me to predict stuff. *Actually* predict stuff. Not just throw out some 'results hazy, try again' magic-eight-ball voodoo."

Jane remained silent. He wasn't wrong. "So, what are you going to do?" she asked eventually. Matt sniffed, rubbed his temples again and shrugged.

"I don't know. Run away. Kill myself, before they do it via septicemia in some lab a decade from now."

"Don't joke."

"Who's joking?" Matt replied darkly. He paused, then let out a frustrated sigh. "Except I couldn't do that to my folks. You should've seen them, they were so—ah God, just so . . . proud. Their kid in the Legion . . . well, you know what it's like."

"Yeah," Jane murmured, the lie soft and sad. Then she added, "So what *are* you going to do?"

"Ugh," answered Matt, blowing out his cheeks. "Well, so far, I've managed to come up with wing it and lie a lot."

"Genius."

"Do you have a better plan?" he demanded. Jane had to admit she didn't. Matt started counting on his fingers. "Can't run, not going to kill myself, don't have any plausible reason not to go—"

"Bit late for that now anyway," Jane added with a smirk.

"Yes, thank you," Matt said bitterly, once again glaring at the moving train. He sucked in breath between his teeth. "Guess I just hope they think I'm a bad clairvoyant."

They lapsed into silence.

"What I want to know," Jane said after a few minutes had passed and staring at the countryside was starting to get boring, "is who the hell put in your application."

"You and me both." Matt scowled, his eyes cold despite their redness. They flicked to her. "You're sure it wasn't you."

"For the hundredth time, no. Get out your phone if you want, you can record me saying it."

"It just doesn't make sense," Matt muttered, looking out the window, only half-listening. This, too, he'd said about a hundred times. "Mom or Dad would be gloating. Jonas and Sarah couldn't pull it off, none of the teachers . . ."

"Taylor?" Jane suggested with a shrug. Matt shook his head.

"I just can't see it," he said. "He's never expressed interest in any college outside the Ivy League, and it's not like we're joined at the hip. The only person who ever even mentioned applying for the Legion was you, and you say you didn't do it."

"Because I didn't," Jane repeated for the 101st time.

"I believe you," Matt assured her, brushing the statement away with a distracted wave. "The picture they had disappeared from my backpack long before you arrived. I remember, the whole school got their photos, and Mom was annoyed at me for losing mine. I thought it must've just fallen out somewhere."

"Seems you were wrong."

"Seems so," Matt murmured. His fingers pursed on his lips. "I tell you though, if I ever find the person responsible for this, we are going to have some very unpleasant words about them sending me to this hellhole."

"You know," interjected Jane, a little irritated by Matt's continual desire to reject and insult her dream, "if you're that worried, you could have just said you didn't want to go."

But Matt just shook his head. "If I said no, then the question becomes why I said no. People would get suspicious, start thinking I've got something to hide."

"You do have something to hide."

"Yes, but the entire point is to look like I don't."

"You think too much."

"Yeah, well," he grumbled, resting his head back down, "we can't all be psychotically powerful."

Jane wasn't sure if that was a compliment or an insult.

"I'm going to the bathroom," she said, standing up and stretching her arms over her head. "Don't drink all my water."

"I'll guard it with my life." Matt snorted, slumping back down into the seat. He closed his eyes and curled up against himself as Jane left, the sound of the compartment door sliding closed giving way to the rhythmic clacking of the train steaming steadily along. Soon, Matt felt his consciousness wavering, his addled brain lured down toward sleep by the cool semi-silence. He yawned, then, fighting tiredness, forced his eyes back open.

To find another face staring back.

"What in the—" Matt started, scrambling to pull himself upright—because in the seat opposite, exactly where Jane had been sitting mere moments ago, was a child. A small, pale, blond-haired little boy, wearing a white shirt and gray shorts, staring at him with unblinking blue eyes.

Once, a few years ago, Matt had seen an ad at a bus stop about homeless children—lost, forlorn little creatures with downcast faces and clothes that didn't fit. This kid could have stepped out of one of those—sitting there, small hands on his pale, exposed knees, staring up into Matt, imploring.

"How did you—"

The boy said nothing, but instead looked down into his lap, where his small hand clutched a notepad. Slowly, the child lifted it, until the lone word on the paper was level with Matt's eyes: *Death.*

Matt's pulse quickened. He stammered, struggling to speak, but the boy turned, glancing at the compartment door. Then he hunched over the notepad and scribbled on it with a pencil—before again lifting it to show Matt.

Death stalks Morningstar.

"I . . . I don't . . ."

Matt clenched his eyes shut and shook his head, trying to gather himself. "Look, kid, I—" he began, and opened his eyes.

The child was gone.

Matt froze. Stared, stock still at the empty seat where the child had been. He blinked rapidly, trying to clear his vision. Nothing. The kid had just vanished. Heart hammering Matt snapped his head up, sweeping his eyes over the entire carriage. It was empty.

"What the motherf—"

"You all right?" asked Jane, stepping back through the sliding door. She frowned. "You look like you've seen a—"

"Did you see a kid in here?" Matt interrupted, sounding slightly panicked and a little unhinged. He snapped around to look at her and Jane's brow creased in confusion. She squinted behind her and then back out over the carriage.

"A kid? Like a kid-kid? A child?"

"Yes, a child. A small, lost-looking white"—Matt dropped to his knees and glanced underneath the seats, which were boarded—"child." He stopped moving all of a sudden and looked up at her from the carriage floor, his expression incredulous. "He was right here."

"I didn't see him."

There was a long, long pause.

"I'm going insane," Matt finally said, shaking his head. He pulled himself back up onto the seat and Jane sat down opposite. "I'm going . . . Jesus, I must've fallen asleep."

"I wasn't gone for that long."

"It seemed so real."

Jane looked at him with an expression of slight concern.

"How much did you drink last night?"

"Obviously too much," Matt murmured, but still he found himself glancing around the carriage, expecting at any second to see those blue eyes staring back.

The child did not appear again, and by the end of the trip, Matt was convinced it must have been some sort of vivid, mildly disturbing hallucination brought on by excess stress and intoxication. A closer examination of the carriage revealed nothing and there was nowhere, Matt assured himself, anyone could have come from, let alone gone—and besides, what would a kid be doing on here anyway? And why would he write some vague spooky nonsense and then vanish? It made no sense, so Matt tried to forget about it and resist the urge to look over his shoulder every two seconds for the rest of the train ride—which, unfortunately, there turned out to be a lot more of.

It took ten hours—ten excruciating, brain-witheringly boring hours—before they arrived at the end of the line with (on Jane's part) a renewed excitement and (on Matt's part) a newfound hatred of trains. From there, they were greeted, to Matt's incredulous chagrin, by the dark figure of a teleporter popping into existence on the station's edge.

"Hi there!" he called. He was a young, well-built Black guy, maybe a year or two older than Matt, medium build, with very white teeth. "Will Herd. Pleasure." He held out a hand and Matt, suppressing his annoyance, took it. As they shook, the teleporter's eyes found Jane, and his face hardened.

"Empath," said Will, with none of the warmth or charm he'd laid out for Matt. Jane merely nodded. At her acknowledgment, the teleporter stiffly raised an arm.

"This is lead-lined," he told her bluntly. "You won't be able to absorb through it."

"Thanks." Jane scowled, her voice not so much dripping as bleeding sarcasm. Will ignored her, instead turning back to Matt, his charisma returning like it had never left. "These your bags?" he asked, indicating Matt's suitcases. "Here, let me . . ." He grabbed the largest one as Matt wrapped his hand wordlessly around one arm of the teleporter's sweater, which felt oddly lumpy. Jane hitched up her lone, tattered backpack and moved to do the same as Will closed his eyes, envisaging their arrival location.

There was a sudden lurch. The world went black, and a heavy force pulled Matt in toward his hand. There was a rush, his ears popped, and a feeling of all the blood rushing to his head, like being upside down in a wind tunnel. Then suddenly, the pressure on his body subsided, the noise stopped, and Matt's nose filled with the smell of rotten eggs. He opened his eyes, his pupils readjusting slowly to the light—to find them standing on the edge of a forest surrounded by nothing but wind, pine needles, and the sounds of the wild, staring up at the distant shadow of a great building looming high atop a verdant hill.

"Welcome to Morningstar," said Will, smiling.

Jane threw up.

It was bigger than the pictures—that was the first thing Jane thought when she finally looked up, fighting the nausea. Bigger than the pictures she'd seen, the ones she'd once had on her wall. Photos didn't do it justice, couldn't convey the majesty of the building, the grandeur, the glow of illuminated windows in the afternoon light.

It was an old place, modeled after the great manor homes of England, great sandstone stories interlaced with windows and latticework. Built, she'd read, by a rich man longing for the old world, and gifted by an old man dreaming of the new.

It was almost a castle, Matt guessed. Except squarer and yellow-brown, more mansion, less drawbridge. The words *unnecessarily large* came to mind, the type of place where the rooms were named for colors instead of functions because there were too many to practically use.

He glanced behind him at Jane as they trudged up the hill, the only sound the gentle hum of insects moving out into the afternoon air. She was leaning against a pine tree, looking up at the manor with an affection he might not have otherwise believed the empath was capable of—though at least not too enamored to miss Matt's discreet cleaning motion with his hand to get her to wipe her mouth on her sleeve.

They crossed the well-kept grounds toward Morningstar's entrance without pomp or ceremony and entered through a heavy oaken door, twice as tall as Matt, which was already open when they arrived—and through which waited none other than Daniel Winters, resplendent in a charcoal-gray suit, who welcomed them inside with an easy smile.

"Rooms are on the third floor," Winters explained as they moved through the corridors and up two flights of stairs, the suited director in front, Will having left. The walls alternated between sandstone and white plaster, the floors carpeted a dull green. Pictures of Legion members past and present, photos and awards, adorned the walls. "Meals are served in the Grand Hall. Food is available twenty-four hours a day. Our cooks are quite good." He turned a corner, and they followed him down another hall as Matt tried to keep mental track of where they were going. Winters gestured with his free hand at one of the closed doors as they passed. "The central building is mainly living quarters, although you'll also find classrooms, computer labs, and the library. The general rule of thumb is people in here, powers out there." He smirked as if this was funny, but Matt didn't really get the joke.

"There've been extensive additions to the grounds over the years," Winters continued without waiting for or needing acknowledgment.

"Pools, arenas, courses. You name it, we've probably got it. You'll know your way around soon enough. There's a map in your room in case you get lost."

They summited another set of stairs to find themselves looking horizontally along a long row of plain and practically identical wooden doors. "These are not luxury accommodations," Winters said clearly. "But they're soundproof and they're private. Beds are made up and cleaners change them regularly. Each room has a small *en suite* to prevent the need for nighttime wandering." Matt flashed Jane a skeptical eyebrow but lowered it as Winters stopped and turned to face him.

"Mr. Callaghan, you are three doors down there"—he pointed to his left— "the one with the envelope taped to the front. That's your welcome package—read it, unpack, and make yourself at home. Then be at the Grand Hall for your welcome at six." Winters reached into his front pocket and drew out a small silver key, which he placed in Matt's hand with a reassuring smile. "Feel free to greet your neighbors. No one's going to bite. We're all in the same boat—fighters in the arena, friends in the halls."

Matt nodded.

"Welcome to the Legion." The director smiled, and they shook hands. Then Matt picked up his bags and began trudging toward his room.

Winters spent a few seconds watching him go, then glanced at Jane, his smile fading slightly. "You're around the corner," he said. "Follow me."

They walked through the halls without exchanging a word, Winters leading, Jane following. Like Matt, her door had a white business-size envelope affixed to it with masking tape. The director reached into his other pocket and handed her the key.

"Thank you," she muttered.

"You're welcome," Winters replied, inevitably professional. He looked at her, and they made eye contact for the first time since entering the building—the lines of the well-groomed man's face smoothed into an inscrutable expression, neither welcoming nor hostile. For the briefest second, his eyes flicked to her cheek, before he caught himself. He could have been a movie star, Jane thought. He had the look, the smoothness. He carried himself well.

There was a brief pause.

"Six o'clock, Miss Walker," Winters said finally. "The Grand Hall. Don't forget. The welcome." He paused, and his gray eyes glinted with a hint of meaning.

"Yes, sir," Jane replied. The director nodded curtly, then without another word turned and walked away, leaving Jane alone with her backpack, standing silent in front of the door.

For a while, she just stood there, breathing. This was it. She was here. It was real, it was happening. Jane took in a few shaky breaths, letting the reality sink in.

The Legion.

The Academy.

She was inside.

Suddenly, there was a sound to her left. Jane turned her head. Five doors down a tall, thin Eurasian girl with long dark hair, almond eyes and flawless olive skin stepped out from one of the rooms. A blue satin blouse hung loosely around her chest, a white cotton skirt flowing long down her legs. She was beautiful, thought Jane. As if having heard her, the girl turned toward Jane and smiled.

It was a small smile. A smile, followed by a wave, and then in a blur of speed, the girl was gone. Jane stood for a moment, alone in the corridor, watching where she'd been, wondering who she was, where she'd gone— and why, if she could see her mark, the girl had bothered to smile at all.

The Grand Hall rumbled. Even from where they stood, in a small passage off to the side of the main stage, Matt could hear the murmuring of the gathered crowd, glimpse individual faces in the sea of people. Legionnaires, Acolytes, whatever they were called—there were hundreds of them, crowded onto benches either side of six long wooden tables that ran the entire length of the room. Matt forced himself to breathe, running through a few calming routines in his head. He'd never liked crowds, though he seemed to be at least doing better than Jane who, standing next to him in the darkened corridor likewise waiting to be called, may as well have turned to sweaty stone.

"Ladies and gentlemen." Winters's voice rang out, the man himself standing tall behind a lectern in the center of the stage, facing the gathered crowd. "Ladies and gentlemen, if you please."

The murmuring withered and ceased.

Even with his back to them, Matt could tell that Winters smiled.

"Ladies and gentlemen, Acolytes of the Legion, it is my great honor to welcome two new members into your ranks. A brother and a sister in arms—fellow soldiers to our cause."

Jane's heart was pounding so loudly in her chest she could barely hear Winters's words.

"First, Mr. Matthew Callaghan."

In the darkened hallway, out of sight of the crowd, Matt shot a nervous glance back at her, then he swallowed, straightened his shoulders and stepped forward. A smattering of polite applause filled the hall as he strode out onto the brightly lit stage toward Winters, who gestured warmly toward a spot to his left—Jane watched as Matt took his place beside the podium, glancing out over the crowd, his face a nervous, sheepish grin. He gave a small, tentative wave.

"Mr. Callaghan," announced Winters, his voice effortless, confident, and assured, "is one of the most exciting new recruits to grace the Academy. Mr. Callaghan is a person who I think—with the right guidance— could do remarkable things. Mr. Callaghan . . ." he repeated a third time, and his voice rose louder, filling the room with his conviction, "is a clairvoyant."

An audible murmur raced around the room. From where she stood, Jane could see people turning to one another, see their glances, their exchange of whispers.

"I won't labor his introduction any further," said Winters, his voice dropping back down from loud to inviting. "I suspect he will have much to show us himself over the coming months, so I won't say any more." He turned to gaze at Matt with fatherly affection. "Except welcome, Matt. Welcome to Morningstar."

There was another round of applause, louder this time, more forceful. Jane saw Matt give a short, jerking nod, then take half a step back.

Her turn.

Winters paused, turning back to the crowd, and the applause died down.

"Our second newcomer," the director announced, and to his credit no edge of distaste crept into his voice, "is also a promising talent. She has a PDR of twelve and will no doubt make a fine addition to our ranks. Ladies and gentlemen, please welcome, Miss Jane Walker—"

Like in a dream, Jane's feet began to move, carrying her out onto the hardwood stage without thinking, her mind a burning blank. There was sound somewhere, distantly, initial disinterested clapping—and then the shining, blinding lights hit her eyes and her face, and suddenly, all sound stopped.

The hall fell deathly silent. There was no clapping, no whispering. Nobody said a word. Jane kept moving, kept her head forward, her gaze straight, trying not to meet any one of the thousand eyes, the sea of faces staring up at her. She moved to Winters's right, the sound of her muffled footsteps echoing out, alone, into the awful, gaping void, to stand beside the director, who turned back tall and firm to the assembled and spoke the single, unnecessary word.

"Empath."

For what seemed like an eternity, nobody moved. Nobody breathed. Jane's hands clenched at her side, feeling the collective eyes of Morningstar Academy burn into the side of her face.

"May they uphold our legacy," proclaimed Winters. His voice strained against the silence. "May they ever serve the Dawn."

And then, without warning, somebody hissed.

A grating, shuddering intake of breath, raking over tongue and teeth, coming from nowhere but spreading throughout those gathered without exception and pause, until the sound of it seethed through the entire hall. A low, vicious whisper, a tide of anger swelling between hundreds of statues who glared up at her with blazing hate.

"Oh yeah," she heard Matt mutter under his breath. "This is going to be great."

THE LEGION OF HEROES

"Welcome to Morningstar Academy" Introductory Booklet

Page 14: Glossary of Terms

Acolyte: The designation of all students admitted to the Academy.

Arena (Map H3): The primary arena for direct combat, sparring.

Ascension: The selection of an Acolyte to become an active and permanent member of the Legion. (Please note ascensions are temporarily suspended pending further notice.)

Ashes: Acolytes present at the Academy during the African Devastation who continue to support the Legion. The Ashes are here to help you; please show them the utmost courtesy and respect.

Challenges: Academy-wide sparring competitions held at the arena. Please see the notice board for upcoming challenge dates.

Memorial (Map C8): The Memorial to the Legion's fallen members. Non-denominative services are held here every Sunday at 8:30 a.m. If you wish to make an offering outside these services, please refer to the guidelines on page 12.

Morningstar: The Academy's central building. All rooms designated "MS" are within this complex.

Shutdown: A four-day period commencing Thursday, November 23 (Thanksgiving), during which no classes will be held. If you require continuing accommodation during this time, please contact administration.

* * *

Bzzzzzzzzz.

The sound of his phone vibrating slapped at Matt's unconsciousness. He groaned and opened his eyes, the dull morning light momentarily irritating his retinas. His hand slopped blearily across the floor to where the stupid thing and its little blinking light was laying on charge.

Taylor (1)—Hey man how is Legion r u superh . . .

Matt blinked at his screen. The clock read 5:49 a.m. He slid the unlock pattern and typed back an honest answer.

F u not even up

The reply came almost immediately and completely indifferent to his previous sentiment.

Taylor (1)—Send pics

Of what, Matt grumbled to himself. Nevertheless, he obliged, snapping a few photos of his new dorm. It was pretty uninteresting, in his opinion—a plain, narrow, rectangular room with a plywood desk and plastic chair pressed against the left side and a single bed pressed against the right. A small bookshelf on which he'd already managed to smack his skull was nailed into the wall above the headboard, but other than that the only real features was the vaguely vomit-green carpet, the small bathroom, which was the first thing on your right when you came in the door, and the window looking out onto the grounds below.

Matt sent the pictures to Taylor then closed his eyes, feeling the weary residue of a bad night's sleep aching behind his temples. He'd almost convinced himself that he could make it better by falling asleep again when his friend's reply bounced back.

Taylor (1)—Nice

Which means *That's boring, I expected more*, Matt mused. He didn't care though; there were more important things in life than being a constant source of entertainment. His phone buzzed again.

Taylor (1)—Jane dead yet?

No, but I'm sure she's working on it, Matt thought ruefully.

After yesterday's welcome—or Snake Ceremony, as Matt was now mentally calling it—Winters had hurried them both offstage in as dignified a manner as possible and invited them to consider retiring to their rooms for the remainder of the evening. Both Matt and Jane had seen the merit in this suggestion, and thus Matt's first night at the Academy had been one of confined, fitful sleep and gnawing feelings of dinnerless hunger.

Matt rolled over the length of his bed, propping his head up against the wall to stare out the window into the pale green expanse beyond. Morningstar's grounds, the wide-open grassy fields that slopped out and down into an abrupt forest, were doused with a low-hanging, early morning fog that made him thoroughly glad to be inside. Nevertheless, someone was already up and about. As Matt watched, a blur shot across the field, whipping a line through the mist. Ten seconds later, it flew by again, throwing up a cloud of dew drops right to left in the exact same path. Speedster, Matt concluded. He yawned, wondering how many laps they could do before it started to impact the lawn. Though he supposed that's what floramancers were for.

After a few minutes of watching the blur do laps, Matt got up and had a quick shower and shave before running through his mental exercises. His night had been plagued by an endless parade of anxious, anticipatory dreams, full of doors, traps, and hissing lizardmen—though no vanishing pale children—but his morning drills quickly brought those feelings under control, and by the time Matt dressed and exited his room to scout for breakfast, the map in his back pocket, he'd forced himself to relax.

Matt trundled down several flights of stairs to the ground floor, then meandered through the entrance gallery toward the Grand Hall's open doors, which he'd seen but abstained from going through last night. A few people passed by him as he walked, headed in the other direction. Most looked his age, if not a bit older, and most glanced at him with mild curiosity. *Is it because I'm new and clairvoyant,* Matt wondered, with only a hint of trepidation, *or is it because I'm associated with the hiss-magnet?*

The rumble of sound humming out of the hall swelled as he got nearer, as did the scent of fried breakfast food, which was substantially more appealing. Matt passed through the open double doors and immediately there was an audible drop in conversation as a hundred or so faces turned to glance at the new arrival. His pace slowed. For a moment, Matt thought the room might go silent, and he would find himself walking a very awkward gauntlet—but then the moment passed, most of the heads turned back, and the hall resumed its previous volume. Matt breathed a small sigh of relief.

Matt felt like he hadn't got a very good look at the Grand Hall last night, what with coming in from the wrong end and his nerves at being announced. But now that he wasn't being paraded out onstage alongside a tattooed pariah, he could see that the hall was indeed very grand, with high walls and ceilings and large full-length windows running down both sides through which autumn sunlight now reluctantly streamed. The floors were hardwood, with lines of rectangular tables running the length of the room from the entrance to the buffet, which lined the nearest-most edge of a raised platform—the stage they'd been on last night—jutting out of the far wall. The platform had stairs leading up on either side, but as far as Matt could see, nobody was going up there— the dark, wooden lectern standing alone and untouched in its center. Behind the podium rose a vast and unbroken sandstone wall, which Matt could see now was dominated by a ten-foot metal insignia, an eagle with an olive wreath in its talons that stared (Matt thought somewhat menacingly) out over the room. The Legion's famous circular crest of course; but below it, either side of the lectern so that they would have flanked any speaker, stood two outfits, which took him slightly more by surprise. He squinted at the pair of them as he slowly meandered across the room—matching pearlescent-white bodies and golden capes adorning headless mannequins, preserved inside twin glass cylinders. Matt filled up a plate with bacon and beans and, after only a few second's hesitation, headed over to a free space at one of the tables.

"Hi," he said, sitting down as the stranger to his right, a freckly, curly-haired guy wearing a Hawaiian shirt, glanced up at him.

"Hey," said the stranger. He finished chewing a piece of hash brown and looked appraisingly at Matt. "You're the clairvoyant."

"You must be psychic."

"Actually, yes."

"I was joking."

"Nope. Wally Cykes," said Wally, holding out his hand. "Psychic."

"Matt Callaghan," said Matt, shaking it and mentally battening down his defenses. "Clairvoyant."

"Pleasure to meet you," replied the friendly-seeming redhead.

"You too." Matt glanced up at the overlooking podium and pointed. "Whose are those costumes?" he asked.

Wally followed Matt's finger, then turned back to him with an eyebrow semi-raised. "Seriously? You never watch cartoons?"

"No, I mean the one on the left's Captain Dawn's," Matt replied, a little impatient. "Obviously. But who's the girl's?" He glanced back at the woman's outfit on the right. "It's the same colors and everything, same symbol. Does he have a sister?"

"Nope," said the psychic. He raised his fork and bit into another hash brown. "His wife."

"Oh yeah, I forgot he's married."

"Well, he *was*." Wally chewed and swallowed, looking at him matter-of-factly. "She's dead."

"Oh. Shoot. Sorry."

"Relax, it happened ages ago. Car crash." The conversation lapsed for a few seconds while Matt picked at his bacon.

"Bit morbid, don't you think though," he said after he'd given it some thought. "Keeping his dead wife's clothes on display." As soon as the words left his mouth, Matt felt a momentary panic that he might've made a mistake by daring to criticize Captain Dawn, but Wally just shrugged.

"I think it's meant to be symbolic. One uniform for those serving, one for those we've lost."

"Ah." The idea made Matt take pause. "That's actually kind of nice."

"Yeah, I guess?" Wally shrugged. He chewed for a second or two and then pointed at Matt's neck. "You cut yourself shaving."

"Did I? Ah dang, where is . . ." He tried to look down at where Wally was pointing before realizing he couldn't physically see his own neck. "You got a napkin?"

"I gotcha, buddy." He passed Matt a napkin dispenser from the middle of the table. Matt muttered thanks, then spat on a napkin and began dabbing at this neck.

"No wonder everyone was looking at me when I walked in."

Wally chuckled. "I think that's more the clairvoyancy thing. It's got people talking."

"Yeah?" Matt said warily. "That all they're talking about?"

The psychic gave a small, dry laugh. "Not quite. But nobody's going to lynch you 'cause Winters made you stand onstage with an empath, if that's what you're worried about."

"It'd crossed my mind," Matt admitted.

"It's bad timing," Wally assured him. "But nobody's stupid enough to group you together. You'll be all right."

"Thanks," Matt muttered, not feeling entirely reassured. The psychic's eyes grew slightly appraising and he watched as Matt gingerly removed the napkin.

"People are keen to see what you can do," he said after a few seconds.

"Yeah, well," muttered Matt, peering down at the blood-spotted tissue paper, "what I do isn't very exciting."

"Can you predict the lottery, that kind of thing?"

"Everybody asks that," Matt replied. "And no."

"Bummer. What about cards? How's your poker game?"

"Bad. It's a lot more . . . incorporeal," said Matt, preparing a well-rehearsed barrage of nonsense. "I am merely a conduit for visions, perceiving disconnected fragments of truth through the oceans of destiny. To predict with specificity would require anchoring an immutable point within the clouds of time, which by its very definition is flux."

Wally nodded sagely, as if any of that actually made sense. Matt hurriedly changed the subject. "So, how's it all work around here? Which classes do we have to go to?"

"It's college," the psychic answered, turning back to his plate and starting on a fried tomato. "You make or break under your own steam."

"Oh. But there're like . . . teachers, right? Classes?"

Wally sipped from a red coffee mug almost the same color of his hair. "Obviously. Best professors in the world. Plus the Ashes run a lot of stuff. Should all be on the schedule."

"Right . . ." said Matt, a little confused. He pulled the folded piece of paper containing the map of Morningstar's grounds out of his pocket and opened it up to reveal the class schedule on the back. "But, I mean," he pressed on, perhaps against his better judgment, skimming through the list of potential activities, "all these are combat-related. Armed ene-mies, warfare psychology, advanced power groups." He looked up at the psychic. "I'm a clairvoyant. I'm not going to be fighting. What am I going to do, predict someone to death?"

Wally shrugged. "I'm sure they've got something worked out. Don't sweat."

Matt was just about to ask who "they" were when the sound of a steel bell chimed throughout the hall. All around the room, people started moving faster and with a greater sense of purpose, wolfing down the last of their breakfast, closing books, and rising to leave. Wally kept on eat-ing like nothing had happened.

"What's that?" asked Matt, watching the pace pick up around him.

"Ten-to-seven bell. Ten minutes to first class," the psychic replied with marked indifference.

"Jeez, I forgot it was so early."

"That's the way it goes here," Wally said as he shrugged. "Early bird gets the worm." He didn't espouse the ideal with much enthusiasm.

Matt opened his mouth to reply—but suddenly, there was a rush of wind as something streaked between the tables, and a girl wearing yoga pants and a pink gym top appeared from nowhere a heartbeat later. By the time it took Matt to jump, she was already sitting next to him.

"Morning!" The girl smiled brightly, showing a row of perfect teeth. Two plates overloaded with bacon, eggs, hash browns, waffles, mush-rooms, and toast had seemingly materialized in front of her. While Matt was doing a double take, the girl leaned across him with a sly wave. "Hi, Waaally."

Wally smiled, completely unperturbed. "Matt, this is Giselle, speedster."

Giselle was stunning. Tall, slender, and Eurasian, with full lips, dark eyes, and flawless skin, her sudden appearance five inches from Matt's face had him desperately trying to suppress the rush of blood rampag-ing toward his cheeks. It took every ounce of self-control Matt possessed to keep his eyes away from the speedster's chest and fixed firmly on her adorably rounded nose. Giselle smiled a welcoming, radiant smile.

"Matt, I've heard so much!" She rested a hand lightly on his arm, and Matt's heart skipped a beat. A floral scent washed over him. "I'm Giselle, it's so lovely to meet you!"

"You too," Matt replied weakly. He struggled to regain mental control. "I think . . . I think I saw you running around the grounds this morning."

"That's me!" She laughed, a delicate ringing sound that Matt struggled not to find captivating.

"You're very, uh, fast."

"Thank you!" Giselle smiled widely; then suddenly, she leaned across Matt and her voice dropped: "Oh my God, Wal, Greg Dyson won't shut up about the weights."

Wally shook his head, looking down at his food. "He's a joke."

"I know right! He keeps going on about how it's not the right way to break land speed and it's like 'Hello! Who asked you? You're not even fast.' " She scoffed, then turned back to Matt. "Sorry. Have to bitch. Greg's this second year, thinks he's God's gift, keeps telling me how to run."

"Can't even vibrate handcuffs," Wally muttered into his beans. Matt just nodded, having no idea what they were talking about.

"I know, right? Thank you." Giselle leaned back and turned to Matt, her sunny smile instantly remerging. "So, you went to school with the empath girl!"

"Yes," Matt admitted somewhat reluctantly. He wasn't aware that fact had already gotten out.

"I saw her last night; she seems nice!"

"You obviously haven't talked to her," Matt muttered. Giselle slapped him playfully on the arm.

"Stop it. I'm sure she's lovely. Don't you think, Wal?" Wally grunted in what could technically have been agreement. "See? Wal agrees."

Matt was taken aback. "You guys don't hate empaths?" he started to say, but before he could get the words out Giselle's entire body disintegrated into a blur of supersonic movement. A moment later, she'd stabilized and the plates in front of her were empty.

"I might get seconds," she mused, eyeing off the steaming buffet.

"Still like three minutes 'til first," noted Wally with a glance at his watch. Giselle nodded and vanished in a rush of air.

"So how do you like the Academy?" her voice echoed over his shoulder, and Matt spun around to see the speedster strolling leisurely back toward the table, her long tan hair flicking out behind her, both hands carrying plates that were once again laden with food. Matt struggled to find words.

"It's . . . ah . . ."

"He's only been here one night." Wally chuckled. "And he got hissed at."

"I . . ."

Giselle set the plates down and settled back in beside him. "Oh, don't worry about that. People are dumb. You'll do fine; it'll pass; you'll settle in." She blurred again and once more the food was gone. "If you need anything, you just let me know, okay?" She smiled sweetly down at him, because seemingly Matt had blinked and she was now standing up. "And maybe you can tell my future." She laughed and reeled back slightly. "Oh my God, that's actually so exciting." She put her hand on his arm again. "Can you see if I break land speed? Do you see if I get famous?"

"I . . ."

She waved him away. "Tell me later. Got class. I'll show you around! We'll go for a run." She beamed at the two of them and waved. "Bye!" And then there was another blast of wind between the tables and the girl was gone.

For a moment, Matt just sat there stunned as Wally picked at his bacon.

"What was that?" he muttered, more to himself than anything.

"Giselle Pixus." The psychic chuckled, not looking up. "One of a kind."

Jane hadn't slept much. Or well. She could feel it taking its toll. But she didn't care. She hadn't come this far to sleep.

The learning here was self-guided, the pace dictated by the endurance of the applicant. For her, she knew that meant all of it, everything, all the time. She'd already memorized the schedule, figured out the best way to maximize the amount of face-to face hours. Any gaps she'd spend self-training. She wouldn't falter there.

She'd brought a box of Pop-Tarts from home, which she cooked over her open palm and ate silently in her room before the sun came up. Not nutritious, but it was the calories that counted. There was food down in the Grand Hall, but . . .

Jane glanced at her door.

All night, she'd been glancing at that door. At her window. Ready, waiting, turning on every squeak, every creak, and meaningless groan in the timber. All nothing—just normal noises that any building makes, because here she was, alive, eating Pop-Tarts. Still, she kept glancing, as if expecting at any moment for the door or window or wall to explode and for something, someone, to come through to kill her. She hoped that wouldn't happen. But she didn't know.

So, she hadn't slept much.

Jane ate breakfast in her room alone, with the lights off. But then the sun came up, and suddenly she was faced with the reality that eventually she had to leave, that she wasn't here to sit and hide.

And so, heart pounding in her chest, Jane left.

She walked through the corridors quietly, her feet sinking slow and deliberate into the carpet, her breathing barely a shudder, as if by lessening the noise she made she could somehow mitigate her presence. It was idiotic, of course—she was here, she had a right to be here—but still, Jane moved as silently as she could, her footsteps the padding of cat's feet through snow.

She encountered her first person halfway down the second flight of stairs.

It was a large woman, dark and Amazonian, taller and broader than her by a half, with black pupils and white eyes that shone porcelain out from a body of carved obsidian. They passed each other on the staircase, the woman's imposing frame filling the space in a way that rendered its previously adequate width narrow and confined. For a moment, there was a pause, a brief heartbeat of frozen time, as the woman's cold black eyes took in the girl's face, the all-meaning mark on her cheek. Jane saw her breath catch and her chest rise, her face rend in anger—but whatever rage the sight of Jane invoked, it was insufficient to push this unknown woman to attack a complete stranger unprovoked. They passed like enemy ships in the night on opposite sides of a border, no one firing the first shot.

Jane only truly started breathing again once she reached the bottom of the stairs.

She hurried as quickly as she could through the entrance gallery and out into the cold autumn air, almost sprinting to avoid making eye contact. Her hands trembled slightly as she pulled the folded map from within the pockets of her hoodie. Firedome. Far away, on the other side of the grounds. She breathed, faster than she would have liked, eyes darting from wall to tree to twitching blade of grass. She rounded a corner, and suddenly yelped as a gust of wind crashed into her right side, almost slamming her into the jagged sandstone wall, sending her scrambling, firing up her powers—

But it was nothing. Or more accurately, she realized as she steadied, pushing herself off the grass, her hands and trackpants wet with dew, it was gone. Whatever had rushed past—no, come on, obviously a speedster—whoever the speedster was, they were long gone, vanished in the blink of an eye. She was fine; she wasn't hurt. They'd just been running, running a bit too close. *It wasn't an attack*, she told herself. She just wasn't used to this. Powers used with reckless abandon. *But it was normal here*, she reminded herself, *normal and okay and nothing to be worried about.*

She kept walking, breathing hard.

Though the sun had barely been up half an hour, Morningstar's grounds were already abuzz with activity. As she got further away from the front entrance, Jane was struck by the amount of seemingly ad-hoc additions the Legion had built around their institute—from the front, Morningstar Academy was simply a Victorian manor home, but once you turned the corner, the green lawns descended into a sprawling mess of trenches, ranges, arenas, and a host of other structures whose purposes she couldn't properly place. She passed a long metal shed that, as she watched, shattered into splinters and re-formed into a tower around the woman inside; a circular pit in the ground where a small southeast Asian terrapath was directing a swarm of flying rocks at a tall Latino man, who was blasting rings of energy out of his hands; and a square field of what looked like corn, which before her eyes reared and mutated into giant twisting stalks of bulging pods and gnashing teeth at the command of a boy in a trench coat who, a second later, shook his head and disintegrated the fifteen-foot green monstrosities with a disinterested wave. "Pods not glands!" he shouted at another boy sitting nearby taking notes, who called back something about it not being his fault, he just supplied the poison. It was fascinating and chaotic, with little connection between what was where or what was happening, but Jane supposed that was the point. Morningstar Academy was where the best could do what they needed to do without rules or limitations. *Get an idea, find space, do what you want—and when you're done,* she thought as she watched a man refracting the light from his palms through an increasingly complex maze of mirrored shards, *leave it behind for someone else to reuse or re-form.*

Despite being in the middle of work or training, Jane still felt a large number of eyes following her as she passed. Heads turned—a few even stopped to glare as she walked by. Hisses interwove through angry words. Her pace quickened.

The further she progressed around the back of Morningstar, the larger and more permanent the structures throughout the grounds became. She spied a large firing range off to the left, a 3-D fabricator generating a running stream of targets at various points down the line; a small, inconspicuous square of solid concrete on her right, little more than a steel door leading down, bearing the word *Armory* in white paint; and an enormous carbon fiber dome crisscrossed with tessellating struts, which she knew from her reading was actually a sphere, half-embedded in the ground and almost completely filed with water. She glanced down at her map and changed direction.

She passed the front doors to the arena just as a group of three Acolytes, talking and laughing among themselves, were coming out. When they saw Jane, their conversation skidding to an abrupt halt. The man on the right nudged and muttered to his larger friend, who sneered at her, while the girl on the left did nothing but glower as she passed. Jane kept walking, not making eye contact. The leftmost man took a step forward but stopped at his friend's hand on his shoulder and instead just scowled and spat on the ground, where his saliva sizzled and hissed. Despite the cold, Jane felt a bead of sweat trickle across her temple. But she kept moving forward.

From a distance, the Firedome looked like half the other domes that seemed to be the design of choice for the Academy facilities—a large unadorned hemisphere with a small square antechamber entrance jutting out. The difference between it and the surrounding structures, though, was plain to see, or more accurately to feel, because as Jane drew near, she felt her skin growing warm from the heat radiating from the Firedome's walls. By the time she reached the front door, the air around her was so hot she'd been forced to remove her hoodie and tie it around her waist, but even that didn't stop her feeling like her skin was crisping more and more with each step. Jane hesitated for a moment upon reaching the entrance, reluctant to touch the handles, but before her unwillingness could get the better of her, the doors *ping*-ed and slid open on automatic runners.

She stepped inside and the doors slid shut behind her.

The antechamber was cold, bracingly, artificially cold, far colder than it was outside. It also wasn't big—and it wasn't empty.

A dozen pairs of eyes turned to face her as she entered. There was a collective intake of breath—then silence. Utter silence, undercut only by the hum of the industrial air-conditioner, while an entire class of Acolytes in charcoal jumpsuits stared at her.

Finally, one of them, a tawny-haired boy in the middle of the pack, spoke.

"Get out."

There was a murmur of agreement. "Get out," repeated by a discordant cascade of voices, while others muttered "Freak" and "Parasite." Jane kept her eyes deliberately unfocused, trying to breathe steady and let the voices roll off her—but the room was small, she was outnumbered, and they were all very, very close. The tawny-haired boy's scowl darkened.

"I said leave." Jane took a deep breath, her hands almost cramping as she restrained them from balling into fists.

"I'm here to train," she stated simply, looking straight ahead, not meeting any of their eyes.

"No, you're not," replied the boy. He cracked his neck. "Not here."

"I'm not leaving."

"Yes," he corrected, "you are. You're going to turn around and you're going to get out of here, and we"—he gestured at the small army at his back—"are going to forget we ever saw you. Because if you don't, we're going to make you. And we're going to hurt you." He shrugged. "Maybe even kill you."

"You'll do no such thing," came a new voice. The doors on the other side of the room hissed open and a burning figure, wreathed head-to-toe in fire, strolled inside. Without ceremony, the flames extinguished, and the middle-aged man underneath stopped a foot short of the attending crowd and placed his hands behind his back.

The crowd of Acolytes turned and the tawny-haired boy, seemingly their spokesman, pushed through to the front. "Sir," he began, "she—"

"Charles," the man corrected. He was a slight, wiry figure, softly spoken and dressed plainly in black, yet he commanded the attention of the entire room. "Or Mr. Farrington, as you've been told, Julio. Sir is an honorific title."

"I . . . yes, sir, I mean, Mr. Farrington, but she—"

"She is here to train," Mr. Farrington interrupted again, neither making any movement nor raising his voice, yet cutting easily across the boy's words. He paused and peered at him unblinkingly. "As she is entitled to."

"Charles, you can't—"

"She has been admitted to the Academy," the man said simply. "And therefore has the same right to participate as any of you." His turned his eyes across the room, moving from one Acolyte to another until they looked down or looked away. Finally, his eyes stopped on her. The small man's face broke into a welcoming smile. "And she has a name. Which we know. Hello, Jane."

Jane almost forgot to speak. "Hello," she managed. Mr. Farrington inclined his head toward her.

"Hello. Charles Farrington, pyromorph. Is this your first session?"

"Y-y-yeah, y-y-yes, s-s-sir, Mr. Farrington," she stammered.

"Then we shall endeavor to make it interesting." The man smiled kindly. He turned slightly to address the rest of the Acolytes, but Julio remained defiant.

"But, Charles," he protested, "she shouldn't be—"

"Here?" snapped Mr. Farrington, and for the first time an edge crept into his voice. Despite his unimposing stature, everyone in the room recoiled slightly. "She shouldn't be here, is that what you were going to say?"

The tawny-haired boy swallowed, an expression of regret seeping across his face, yet nevertheless he answered, "Yes, sir."

"I have told you, do not call me sir," scowled the man, and the boy flinched. "Tell me, Julio, why is she here?"

"I . . . I don't . . ." he spluttered. He glanced nervously around him for support but the Acolytes beside him had fallen back.

"Yes, you do. How does Jane come to stand in our halls? Is it by accident? By mistake? You think she crept in, and that we simply endure her trespass?"

"I . . . no, Mr. Farrington, I don't."

"Then why," the man demanded, "is she here?"

"I-I-I," stammered Julio. His eyes fell to the floor. "She was chosen."

"Yes," Mr. Farrington said simply. "And who chose her? Who chose any of you? All of you?"

For a few seconds, the boy could only stare at the ground. Then he murmured, "Captain Dawn."

"Correct," replied the man in black, "Captain Dawn." He paused and his eyes grew hard behind his glasses. "Do you question Captain Dawn, Mr. Duante?"

"No, Mr. Farrington."

"Do you question his judgment, Mr. Duante?"

"No, Mr. Farrington."

"No," Mr. Farrington said quietly, "you do not." He began to pace slowly, seeming to grow taller as he did. "I am only going to say this once. Jane is here because Dawn wills it. You will not hurt her, you will not malign her, and you will not lay a hand on her unless training demands it. To do otherwise is to disrespect Dawn and to disrespect the Legion and I WILL NOT . . ." he shouted, and everyone in the room jumped, "abide disrespect of that nature."

He paused and surveyed the cowering students before him. "We are here because of Captain Dawn. We live because of his loss, because of the Legion's sacrifices. If any of you doubt Dawn's choices, then you should leave, now. And if any of you"—his voice lowered—"insults this institution by attacking those chosen by its leader, I will hurl you from these venerated grounds myself."

He stared them down, daring another challenge, and for a moment no one seemed to breathe. Then Mr. Farrington gave a small sigh and closed his eyes, and it was if a spell was broken—the dangerous, fervent being they had beheld reverted to the clean-shaven, understated man standing before them.

"Now then," he continued in a voice both soft and pleasant, "Vanessa, please show Jane the suits. This morning is about physical and mental perseverance." A see-through girl with her hair held back in a headband turned wordlessly toward a gray steel cupboard, where a selection of charcoal jumpsuits was hanging. "The fires within this dome must be endured and your abilities manifested and maintained in such a way as to protect yourself for the duration of the exercise."

"Can we extinguish the fire?" Jane said, almost hesitant to speak.

The man's eyes flicked onto her, and his lips twitched into a smile.

"Are you the White Queen?"

Jane was taken aback. "No."

"Then I sincerely doubt it, but you are welcome to try." He turned to the doors as Jane struggled to pull on the skin-tight jumpsuit. "As you are new, Jane, I request that you communicate clearly if you're having difficulty. Do not overexert yourself."

The man in black blinked and was once more consumed by flames.

"It would be a shame to disappoint Captain Dawn by burning to death on your first day."

Matt Callaghan closed his eyes and imagined he was somewhere warm, laying back on a reclining chair and sipping a nice, cold beer. It wasn't his beer; he hadn't bought it—someone else had left it there sitting in a little fridge. But far from being a bad thing, Matt imagined that this was actually enhancing the overall experience. Nothing in the world like free beer.

"Open your mind," came a soft, melodic voice, low and gentle—not a command but an invitation. "Detach from your physical tethers, that which binds you to the here and now. Disconnect from the eye which sees the world, empty, and find that sight which sees through the waves of time."

Underneath his eyelids, Matt rolled his eyes and tried to imagine himself taking a nap. Maybe if he concentrated hard enough on letting go of his earthly tethers to being awake, he could pass out and sleep through this unbelievably boring waste of time.

After he'd finished breakfast, Matt had hung around chatting with Wally (who seemed nice) for a while, then scraped his plate off and dumped it in the soapy water bucket near the kitchen. At this point, nobody had come forward with instructions or anything, so he'd played *Tetris* on his phone in the hall for an hour before meandering back to his room to check if maybe someone had left something for him there. They hadn't. Matt found this a bit puzzling, but he figured, hey, maybe whoever ran this place was being nice and giving him some time to sleep in, on the assumption that he'd probably not yet be attuned to the Legion's crack-of-dawn schedule.

As ten fifteen rolled around, that notion begun to look less likely. Matt found himself wishing he'd packed his computer instead of all these clothes—his eyes were starting to hurt from looking at the tiny phone screen, and there was only so much *Tetris* a man could play before he went legitimately insane. So, he left his room and wandered, not so much looking for someone to tell him what to do as expecting them to emerge at any minute.

Being by this point quite bored, Matt had almost been tempted to ask one of the budding superheroes he passed if there was, like, an office or something, a Legion secretary or administrative official who could tell him where he was supposed to be. He didn't, obviously, because he didn't actually want to go and do whatever the Legion wanted him to be doing—but still, it was kind of weird. Matt wondered if whoever had designed this "self-paced learning" system had ever considered someone self-pacing at zero.

Just before eleven, Matt wandered down and outside into the pale autumn sunlight and lay in the field for a bit and watched the clouds go by. Then about five minutes later, he stopped doing that, because grass is itchy and clouds are boring and he wasn't even vaguely intoxicated. Instead, he went back inside to the hall and made himself a grilled cheese sandwich.

I feel like I'm being watched, thought Matt, wincing as the hot cheese burned his overly impatient tongue. The hall looked mostly deserted and apart from the odd "oh, there's the new kid" looks, he couldn't see anybody sparing him more than a passing glance.

That's when the man in black had appeared.

"Mr. Callaghan," came a voice, and Matt had spun around to see a fifty-ish-year-old bald man with a broad chest and tanned, leather-like skin standing behind him wearing what could only have been a black bedsheet folded into a toga and a necklace of large round wooden prayer beads.

"I am Selwyn," he said, his voice a low, calm hum that washed over Matt's ears like a warm wave. "I have been assigned to assist you." He glanced down at the half-eaten sandwich steaming cheese onto Matt's plate. "Good. I am glad to see you have already had breakfast."

Well, technically this was lunch, thought Matt, but he refrained from saying anything so as not to appear rude. He got up from his seat and extended his hand.

"Matt, please. Mr. Callaghan is my father."

Selwyn did not shake it but instead placed his palms together and bowed toward Matt, the beads draping from his neck. "And it, too, will be you, in time. We all walk the paths our parents pave." He slowly straightened his back, a serene smile on his hairless face. "Although names are fleeting forms in which we trap and fracture the unity of the world."

Matt had no idea what the heck that meant or how to respond, so he just nodded and tried to arrange his features in a way that looked interested and mildly impressed. If Selwyn was expecting a response, he didn't show it.

"Come with me please," the big man spoke, turning and seeming to glide toward the main entrance with a grace unusual to a man his size. Matt hurried after him, feeling clumsy and confused.

"Who are . . . where are we going?" he asked as they flowed through the corridors and up a flight of stairs. The middle levels seemed less crowded now than when Matt had been wandering them before.

"Who am I? Or where are we going?" Selwyn mused, his smile unchanged. "One might say that to know the first answer is to know the second."

"Um," said Matt.

The robed man laughed. "Excuse my philosophizing. My thoughts have a tendency to wander in tandem with my mind. It seeks abstraction, I fear, to holiday from the omnipresence of reality."

"Um," Matt reiterated.

"Forgive me." He laughed again—a sincere, jolly sound that Matt couldn't help but find endearing, despite having literally no idea what the man was on about. "We traverse the physical world to reach a room on the third floor of this structure, which has been prepared for our purposes."

"Our purposes?" repeated Matt, not sure if that was ominous or not. "What are 'our purposes'?" But the large, weathered man in black robes appeared not to hear him.

They turned several corners and passed through several halls with east-facing windows enjoying the brunt of the morning sunlight, Matt trailing along behind Selwyn, who flowed serenely forward, his bare feet treading noiseless footsteps. Finally, Selwyn turned left into an already open door, and Matt followed him inside.

They'd arrived in a large, square room with a high paisley ceiling, pale wooden floors, and full-length ornate bookshelves painted the same deep blue-green as the walls lining the two sides not taken up by high windows. The room itself was bare and open, illuminated entirely by natural light and offering a fantastic view overlooking the grounds. A variety of large, colorful cushions and an assortment of candles and incense burners, all melted through various stages of their respective life spans, were strewn across the floor. Candles were also aligned haphazardly in front of the worn books along several rows of bookshelves. "Should I . . ." started Matt, glancing at the door then back to the bald monk for cues. None came. The man simply glided into the middle of the room and turned to face him, smiling vaguely, his head tilted slightly to the side. "I'm just going to . . . okay then, yeah, close this . . ." Matt declared after a few seconds, and he gingerly shut the door.

Selwyn opened his palms face up. "Do you see better in light or in darkness?" he asked sincerely.

"What?" Matt replied. He struggled to figure out if that question made sense, but before he could be completely sure Selwyn saved him the trouble.

"I have always found I see better when I can feel the sun's rays upon my skin," he said calmly. "For it aids in preventing disconnection with the world that my soul seeks to explore." He turned and gestured to the long velvet curtains that stood drawn at either side of the windows. "But your sight may function better when freed from such distractions."

"Ah . . ." Matt stumbled, out of his depth, "open curtains are fine."

"Very well." Selwyn smiled. He didn't ever really seem to stop smiling to be honest. "Please be seated."

"Um . . . where?"

"Wherever pleases you," he replied. Selwyn sunk down onto a large maroon cushion in the center of the room, his legs folding together. Matt hesitated for a moment, then flopped down into a big blue beanbaggy one.

For a few seconds, the man in the black robes simply sat with his eyes closed, the sound of his gentle breathing intermingling with the distant noises of the Academy. Then slowly he opened his eyes and stared calmly at Matt.

"The name I have been given is Selwyn Kersey. You may use it if you wish, or you may refer to me in another way which you prefer. I do not mind." He paused and drew in a deep, rolling breath, seeming to savor the very taste of the air. "You are the first of your kind, Matt Callaghan, to walk within these walls. You possess a rare and unusual gift—but I suppose the same can be said of many who come here." He gave a small chuckle as if that was supposed to be funny.

"Nevertheless," he continued, "the intangibility of your power"—Matt's heart sped up—"poses some conceptual difficulty as to how best assist you in its cultivation." Matt let out a tiny sigh of relief. Selwyn appeared not to notice, gazing as he was contentedly out the window at the fields and forest below. "Of all the Ashes, I was thought best able to help you navigate the visions that come to you. They believed, perhaps, that my clarity of sight can be passed on to you." His smile did not waver. "I offer no guarantees. An infinite void exists between all people, a chasm of thought that true understanding can never cross, for to truly know another mind is to know the infinite, which our limited lifetimes deny us comprehending."

Matt didn't really know how to respond to that.

"But I will impart what I can," Selwyn continued after a moment's pause, "and you may take what you please. Wisdom cannot be given but may be seeded for an open mind to nourish. Close your eyes." He leaned back. "And clear your thoughts. Do not try to think of nothing, for the trying in itself is thinking. Simply let go of thought and feeling, and embrace the ether winds of the universe as they flow through you."

And so, it went. For an hour and a half, Matt sat on a big fluffy cushion feeling his butt cheeks go numb while a barrel-chested, leather-skinned monk—who honestly may have been the happiest, most contented person on Earth—talked to him about utter nonsense. For the first ten or so minutes, Matt was afraid that Selwyn might, at any moment, stop and start asking him for specific predictions, but the man never did, and in fact seemed quite unconcerned when, at the end of their meditation or whatever it was, Matt truthfully informed him that he had witnessed no clairvoyant visions whatsoever.

"I thought as much may be likely," he said, his words still projecting the impression of someone who was a little rusty on the finer points of human speech. "Your sight is far more ethereal than my own and changed by viewing. Of course, for most, it defies substantiation." He paused. "My mind wanders through space, while yours treads through time; the former fixed, the latter fluid—presumably, we do not truly know. Regardless, the difference may prove insurmountable. Or it may not. Ours is organic growth, not a path down which to chase progress."

They rose, Matt stiffly. "Make sure to stretch," said Selwyn, in what was possibly the first bit of practical advice he'd given. "The body can cramp after sitting for so long." He then ran Matt through a series of leg and upper body stretches during which the monk demonstrated a level of flexibility Matt would not have believed possible for a man his size.

"Can I ask a question?" asked Matt as he pulled his arm over his head.

"I would even encourage it," answered Selwyn, again in a tone that made Matt think he was making a joke, though he was unable to be 100 percent sure. Regardless, Matt took his reply as affirmative.

"Why do you wear all black?" he said, moving into a quad stretch. A small part of him was concerned about unintentionally disrespecting the large man's fashion sense but on balance he felt it was a pretty fair question—and of all the people he'd met, Mr. Kersey seemed the least likely to get offended about anything. True to his suspicions, Selwyn simply smiled.

"All the Ashes wear black. It is our way."

"Right," said Matt, because that didn't really answer anything. "And what are the 'Ashes'?" Wikipedia had been somewhat vague on this.

"Ashes," Selwyn replied simply, "are what remain when something great is destroyed. By themselves, they appear as dust in the wind. But this is an illusion; for their presence can nurture new life."

He turned and glided toward the door, leaving Matt feeling more confused than before.

Before she had time to think, the world beneath Jane's feet exploded. Shards of rock and dust pelted her nose, her ears, her eyes, sparing her body but showing no such mercy to her head. Pain then blood flowed freely from a gash in her eyebrow, blinding her in one eye.

Get up. She rolled over and pushed to her knees, arms screaming with the effort, her muscles turned to lead. No, not turned—smothered in lead, iron, or some other heavy metal, whatever this damn suit she was wearing was made of. A hundred pounds of superdense material that weighed down every step, every breath.

"Battle," Instructor Sainsbury had said, "does not end because you tire. They who falter first fall first, and those who are tired falter often. So, you will train to fight through tiredness." They would fight in these suits until a hundred pounds of extra weight was nothing, and then they would raise it to two hundred. Fatigue would be a friend they would carry.

REEEEEEEEEEEEEEEEEEEEEEEEEEEEEEEEEEEEEEEEEEEEeeeeeeeeee eeeeeeeeee!

Another wail, another high-pitched scream of an explosive ball rocketing down toward her. Too slow, she planted her feet and pushed, trying to channel fire through her soles, trying to force herself up, out, away—too late, for the orb was already there and detonating before she could get clear, the shock wave slamming into her, winding her, pummeling. She curled her head in tight and felt her back slam into a wall of rock, then gravity caught up and threw her mercilessly to the ground. Her vision spotted and blurred, spots dancing in front of her one good eye. Nothing broken, she felt. Dazed, but not dead. Whatever weighted these suits could take a beating.

"WALKER!" Sainsbury's voice yelled. "GET UP!" Jane could hear her palms hissing, the next orb forming within them.

Get up. Good plan. She wiped the blood from her eyes and pushed forward.

"Push forward a little. There you go. Hold still."

It was 1:38 p.m., and Matt Callaghan was getting his eyes checked.

Well, scanned. Morningstar Academy had an array of discreet retinal scanners that continually scanned the retinas of everyone going through the building. Apparently, Matt had already been scanned thirteen times since arriving, flagging several system alerts.

"I was ready for that, though," explained Edward Rakowski, as bright red light washed over Matt's left eyeball. "Same with every new arrival. Annoying, but shows the system's working."

Edward, or Ed as he'd introduced himself, was the skinny, five-foot-nine resident genius of the Academy, whose glasses and untidy black hair obscured most of his face and gave the impression of a nervous schoolboy peeking out from behind some curtains. He was also single-handedly responsible for Morningstar's Internet, cyber safety, security systems, and gaming nights, which just not enough people were coming to, Matt had been informed without any prompting.

Their mediation session complete, Selwyn had led Matt throughout a series of third-floor corridors until they'd stopped in front of a door marked "317—Computer Lab," which for a moment, Selwyn had just stared at, as if expecting something to happen. He'd glanced down at the handle, stared at it too, for a few seconds, seeming happily puzzled, before finally he extended his large, leathery hand down and turned it open. Matt watched the black-clad man the whole time, unsure whether he was supposed to find this behavior concerning or if his escort was just really, really high.

A gleaming fleet of state-of-the-art computer monitors greeted them as they entered, the screens humming with the uniform blue glow of a log-in page, beside which Ed Rakowski had been setting up a retinal scanning machine.

"Matt, this is Edward," Selwyn hummed. "He will guide you on the next step of your journey. For now, I take my leave." Then he sat down on the ground, crossed his legs, closed his eyes, and went nowhere.

"Don't mind him." Ed had laughed, once he'd introduced himself and explained what was going on. "He's a projectionist. Spent more time out of his body than in it I think."

"He does lighting for shows?" Matt asked, confused. They were making no attempt to keep their voices down, even though Selwyn was right there—but if the strange black-clad man could hear them, his expression of peaceful contentment didn't show it.

"No, a projectionist," said Edward. He peered through a gap between two of the three monitors pulled together in a U-shape that separated him and Matt and saw the blank look on Matt's face. "It's a rare ability. They can project their mind outside of their body, travel the world on the"—he waved a hand to indicate abstractness—"astral plane or whatever."

"Wow," said Matt, actually impressed. He glanced over at the sitting figure. "Cool."

"Yup," Ed agreed, not looking up from his monitors as he typed in a rapid stream of something. "Normally, they get recruited by intelligence agencies, corporate espionage, that kind of thing. Spend their lives ghosting into restricted areas, make a killing, provided a psychic doesn't crush them . . . not Selwyn though. He never cared about money, only ever wanted to see the world." Ed paused. "Man's barely left Morningstar in two decades, and he may be history's greatest explorer."

"Huh," Matt pondered out loud, "I wonder where he is now?"

Edward's fingers clacked across the keyboard. "Last time we talked, he was seeing how far he could get out into space. One day, he could be the first man to spirit walk on the moon." He paused and glanced at the monk. "Or he might have already and not told anyone."

The two of them continued to chat while Ed assembled, calibrated, utilized, and dismantled the retinal scanner. "All done," the genius told him once they were finished, "no more alarms."

"Neat," said Matt.

"It's not rocket science."

"Well, it's more high-tech than my high school." He glanced around the room, trying to see if he could spot any hidden cameras. "Although I'm not sure how I feel about being eye-scanned all day long."

"You'll get used to it," Ed assured him. "There's not much to get used to, the cameras are practically invisible."

"Feels like I'm living in the future," Matt muttered, not exactly thrilled about the sensation. He looked back at Selwyn, still sitting cross-legged and close-eyed on the floor. "So . . . what happens now? Do I need to do anything else?"

"I'll take care of the rest," replied Ed. He followed Matt's gaze. "You go with Selwyn."

There was a pause. Matt glanced down at the black-robed spirit walker, who didn't seem to be going anywhere he could follow, then back at Edward. "Okay," he said, keeping his expression intentionally blank. Behind his wall of computer screens, the genius's face flushed slightly.

They lapsed into uncomfortable silence. Matt rocked back and forward slowly on his chair, massaging his teeth with his tongue and looking around at the computer lab's empty walls. Ed shifted awkwardly where he was sitting, but otherwise did nothing to acknowledge Matt's presence, letting the rhythmic clicks and clatters of his keyboard and mouse stretch out into the silence. Matt rubbed the back of his head and frowned slightly.

"So . . . should I, like, shake him or something?" he asked finally. Ed shrugged, not looking up.

"If you want?" he answered unhelpfully.

Matt glanced over at Selwyn again. He seemed so peaceful, and Matt spied an opportunity to procrastinate. "I don't really feel comfortable . . . you know . . ."

"Yeah, no problem, I just . . ."

"Just met him, not sure if it's like . . . cool, you know . . ."

"Yeah, I get it, totally, I'm just . . ."

"Might just wait a while . . . you know . . . if that's cool . . . check my email . . ."

"Yeah, no, that's fine."

"Long as I'm not, you know, taking up space or . . . ?"

"No, yeah, no problem, I'm just, you know, got to, doing, computer . . . work . . . stuff . . ." Ed's voice trailed off, his face now quite red. He bent down low over his keyboard so Matt could only see the top of his head. They lapsed once more into silence. Matt opened his Hotmail and spent five minutes deleting various spam offers and twice-daily newsletters from websites he'd signed up to years ago. Then, with that done and Selwyn still not showing any signs of life, he started faffing about on the Internet, looking at funny pictures and animal gifs.

"Is he dead?" he asked Ed eventually, when the soppy tentacles of boredom began weighing heavily upon his brain. The genius hadn't said a word the entire time.

"No, he's breathing," Ed replied, not looking up.

"All right," said Matt. He nodded back and forward, twiddling his thumbs.

More silence.

"What are you working on?"

"It's . . . complicated," Ed answered. "Just . . . projects and . . . things . . ." Matt let it be and the room went quiet again.

"Do you want a sandwich? I could go get a sandwich, if you want one."

"No thanks."

"Cool. Might wait then."

And silence again.

"Hey, these computers got any games on them?"

For the first time in thirty minutes, Edward looked over the top of his monitors at him—cautiously, like a meerkat poking out its head to survey the savannah.

"What sort of games were you after?" he asked warily.

Matt shrugged. "I don't know, man, what've you got?"

"I've got *Counter-Strike.*"

"Yeah, dude, I'm keen for *Counter-Strike.* You want to play? Or do you have to work?"

Ed paused, his eyes visible through his lank, dark hair.

"I mean, I suppose I could take a break," he conceded slowly. "It's just ..."

"Just what?"

"I'm pretty good."

"Well, hey, I'm not bad myself."

"No, I mean I will destroy you."

"I'm hearing a lot of talk there, genius."

"I'm not hearing much talk there, Blue!" snapped Higgins. Jane glared with gritted teeth up at where the wiry-haired woman was floating effortlessly, thirty feet above them and the surface of the water. She could barely concentrate on keeping a steady stream of fire going continually down, let alone actually talking with her moronic teammates.

"This is not about hovering!" roared their instructor. "This is not about endurance! This is about communication! This is about all of you, working under pressure, as a team!"

This was goddamn water polo, essentially. Two teams on either side of an arena filled entirely with water, a single ball, and a goal at either end. Rules were simple: Touch the water, you're out. Move with the ball, you're out. Your whole side gets out, you lose the round. Ball goes in your goal, you lose the round. Use your powers to stay up and whatever concentration you've got left to intercept passes.

Jane hated ball games. She hated teams. She hated being new and she hated being picked last and most of all she hated stupid mouth-breathing Josephine Higgins, who just flew there yelling at her while she failed.

"Mark her!" called one of her teammates, a muscular Japanese man with a name not worth remembering. He wasn't talking to her. They were never talking to her. But even if he wasn't talking to her, the red Acolyte he was talking about was close. Jane snarled and pushed downward and forward, fire streaming from her fists and feet.

Too slow. She wasn't used to this, this sustained burn, not a burst but a constant unwavering effort. Every person in the arena was running rings around her, better trained, better prepared, better practiced. And every one of them aching to see her fall. In reality, the teams were an illusion—she was the real enemy and she could see it on every face. Only Higgins's eagle-eyed presence and maybe the natural competitiveness of the other blue-team Acolytes kept the exercise being any semblance of a competition.

Her eyes twitched across the room to where the blonde red-team girl was floating, eying off her mark, the gray medicine ball bouncing in her hands. Jane's mouth formed into a wordless roar, and she slammed down everything she had, pushing forward toward her quarry, this smug smiling red scumbag holding herself aloft with her goddamn telekinesis—

"EMPATH! BALL!"

She turned in the direction of the voice in time to see a dark shape hurtling toward her but too late to stop the sickening crunch as it slammed into her face an instant later. Jane fell, arms flailing wildly, blood pouring from her nose—she hit the water with a crash, suddenly engulfed in freezing, murky silence. The pitch depths of the abyss opening up beneath her, a gaping maw of black-blue darkness—Jane's heart stammered, and she thrashed her arms, trying to move upright, away from the endless deep, a ringing in her ears and a burning in her nose as she writhed, panicking, sucking in water, unable to breathe, unable to swim and—

"Urgh!"

Her head broke the surface and Jane gulped in fresh air, coughing, spluttering, and retching the water from her lungs. She shook and shivered, feeling the darkness of the deep clutching at her legs, flailing her arms to stay afloat. A figure floated over her, blotting out the sunlight coming in through the dome.

"OUT!" Higgins roared as the telekinetic girl sniggered.

"I'm out," swore Matt, running his hands through his hair and surveying yet another abysmal scoreboard. "To hell with this, I'm out."

"I warned you," said Ed, his grin visible from between the monitors. They'd been playing for more than an hour, and in that time Matt had managed exactly zero kills to Edward's . . . one hundred? Two? He'd lost track. All he knew was that he'd never failed so hard at anything in his life. He'd been digitally tea-bagged so many times his mouth tasted like electronic England.

"Hacks. It has to be hacks."

"You just suck."

"I don't suck. You're incredible."

"Hey"—Ed grinned—"I have to do something with my stratospheric IQ."

"How much do you play? Seriously."

"Oh, a bit here and there."

"Bull. Absolute bull. You must practice this like twelve hours a day. Let's play something else. Come on, mix it up. What else you got?"

Ed laughed. "Ah the audacity of noobs. Give up while you're only a little bit behind."

"No. Screw you. You're going down, Rakowski."

They were pretty much completely ignoring Selwyn by now, who was still sitting in exactly the same spot, his black robes draped over his knees, eyes shut in serene meditation, seemingly unaffected by an hour's worth of raised voices and Matt's continuous stream of frustrated swearing.

"You ever played any *Total War*?"

"Yes." Matt cracked his knuckles and shook out his shoulders. "Yes, yes, a thousand years yes. Here we go. This is me. This is my jam."

"Look into your future, Clairvoyant. See your crushing, inevitable defeat."

"I see your mom . . . Screw it, no, let's go, come on."

"Come on," demanded Professor Lun. He looked around the room at the crowd of faces staring at him from all sides of the lecture theater. "Come on. Anybody. Individual presents with fever, shortness of breath, and atypical cardiac arrhythmia. Correct steps to diagnosis are—"

There was a burning underneath Jane's skull, and it had nothing to do with the healer having reset her nose and unfractured her eye socket an hour ago. Everything this man said made no sense. It was like he was speaking a language she'd never heard before, except the words were still English, which just made her inability to understand them even more infuriating. This was supposed to be a lecture on responding to emergencies, but the man was going on about patients and symptoms and a thousand made-up Latin phrases, which he explained briefly once and then flew straight past before she could comprehend what he was saying. She didn't feel like she was learning; she felt like she was becoming actively stupider as everything that was said flashed briefly between her ears and incinerated her brain cells.

Professor Lun, a wiry, forty-something Mediterranean man with a hooked nose and no trace of an accent, who looked like he'd never cracked a joke in his life, stood in the center of the amphitheater with a fifteen-foot projection of a dying man behind him, his suede-jacketed arms crossed over his chest. His eyes swept across the room, taking in the contingent of unenthusiastic Acolytes, and then, to her horror, came to rest upon Jane.

"You there, left of center, Empath. Let's see if you're not entirely useless. Do you defibrillate for tachycardia?"

"I . . ."

"This man's life is in your hands. He's going to die if you don't do something. So, tell me right now, yes or no, do you defibrillate him?"

"I'm s-s-sorry," she stammered, "I-I-I don't know. I'm not a healer . . ."

The professor shook his head at her, disgusted. "I don't care what you are. I care about the fact that the person you came to save"—he pointed at the projected screen—"is now dead because of your incompetence." The whole room laughed, unkindly. "Read a textbook. Learn to do more than hit things."

He turned to the other side of the room. "Now somebody, please. Who's done the readings? Anybody. Come on."

"Come on!" Matt cried in despair as a previously unseen unit of Cavalry Auxilia charged out of the woods and mowed down his Baleric Slingers like a combine harvester through schoolchildren. He clicked furiously, breaking off a unit of spearmen that had been heading to reinforce his front line, only to see their backs treated to a volley of incendiary acupuncture by a solitary unit of Cretian Archers. Okay, enough of this, go for them—at least they seemed somewhat out of formation, or so Matt thought until he tried to charge the ragtag group of archers down with his General's Bodyguard and ran the leader of his forces straight into a wall of hidden Pikemen.

"No! What?! Come on, I . . . do something! WarDogs!" he shouted as his battlelines collapsed and the bulwark of his pixelated army turned tail and fled. Not surprisingly, his words had very little impact and Matt was treated to another battle summary emblazoned with the words *crushing defeat.*

"Goddamn it," he muttered. "That's it, enough. I'm out. No more games with you."

"You sure?"

"Yes, I'm sure. Screw you and your genius-level intellect."

"You sure you're sure?" Edward smirked the smirk of a pool hustler over the top of his monitors. "Because, you know, I've got a GameCube with *Smash Brothers* laying around here somewhere."

"No," Matt declared automatically, then immediately reconsidered. "Wait, seriously?"

"Yeah, man. I'm sure you'd do better at that."

"Yeah . . . that could be a good . . . wait, no!" said Matt, waving a finger at him. "No, no, no, I know that look. You're just going to wreck me again, no matter what we play." He stood up, shaking his head. "No wonder nobody comes to your game nights."

Ed's grin faltered and he looked taken aback. "Wait really? Do you think that's it?"

"Well, duh, Sherlock, obviously," replied Matt, although not unkindly. He pulled out a different chair on the other side of Ed's desk and swiveled around to face him. "Thought you were meant to be a genius. Word to the wise, most people don't enjoy an evening of getting thoroughly demolished. Well, not digitally, anyway," he added under his breath.

"Sorry," murmured Ed, his face downcast.

"Hey, don't apologize, I said 'most people,' not me. I thought it was hilarious. You're insane."

"Ah," replied the genius, looking embarrassed and waving away Matt's compliment, "it's just my power. I didn't earn being smart."

"Don't sell yourself short," said Matt. "Talents are talents, man." Nevertheless, Ed still looked uncomfortable, so Matt changed the subject.

"Do you think he's ever coming back?" he asked, pointing at the still-sitting still-stationary Selwyn.

"I presume he has to eat." Ed shrugged. He craned his neck to get a better view of the black-clad man. "So . . . eventually?"

"Well, that's reassuring," Matt muttered. He flicked his phone out of his pocket then flicked it back in again.

"You posed an interesting case, training-wise," said Edward, sinking back down into his seat. He began clicking and typing as he spoke, doing God-knows-what on his triple-screened computer, which Matt took less as rudeness and more just a superhuman ability to multitask. "The Ashes were at quite a loss how best to cultivate a clairvoyant."

"You don't say," said Matt, very uncomfortable broaching the subject of his "abilities" with someone with an inhumanly high IQ.

"Yeah. They don't come to Selwyn for much, but I guess they felt this something he was suited for."

"Well, we'll see how that turns out," said Matt. He rose to leave before all this clairvoyancy talk turned inquisitive. "Sorry, man, I should get out of here. I've been in your hair long enough."

"Oh," said Ed, stopping typing. He peered up over the central monitor and to Matt's surprise looked fractionally disappointed. "Yeah, sure, no problem. I mean if you want, you don't have to . . ."

"Don't you have to work to do?" asked Matt, raising an eyebrow. "Important genius stuff, inventions that'll save the world, that sort of thing?"

"Well . . . I mean, yes," admitted Ed, though he sounded unenthused, as though he found the prospect of irrevocably improving mankind somewhat dull. "I just . . ." He trailed off then just sort of sat there staring at his computer. Matt blinked.

"If you *want* me to stay here and play games, I will stay here and play games."

"No, don't worry about it," Ed stammered, hiding his face as it turned red. "Get going, it's good, I'm sure you've got—"

"Dude, I'm going to stay here and play games with you."

"No really, that's not—"

"Shut up," Matt commanded. "Go get the GameCube."

The cube was perfectly formed, exactly one inch on every side, or so Jane had been told. At this distance all she could see was a dot. A smudge, a fraction of a blur, a single, grayed-out pixel in her exhausted field of vision. She drew her fingers inward and released, a bolt of lightning crackling across the range.

The light above her station flashed red and a jarring foghorn siren blared, but there was no time for Jane to curse her failure because another horn had already sounded and another cube had already launched. She drew back and fired again, sending another bolt down the line.

Red light, horn. Another.

Red light, horn. Another.

Red light, horn. That one she didn't even see properly, just threw out a fork of lightning in the vain hope that it might connect. Another.

Red light, horn. There was sweat in her eyes and on her fingers but there was no time to wipe it away. Another.

Green light, *bing*. That one had gone long and low, traveling through the air in a flat-hanging arc. Her bolt had been on point, straight down the line—but it'd been an easy shot. Another.

Red light, horn. She was panting now, her breath coming in ragged draws. Another.

Red light, horn. Her vision was blurring, the single gray pixel no longer standing out among the wavering haze. Another.

Red light, horn.

"Ee-nuff," came the voice, and Jane fell to one knee. Her left hand grasped clumsily for support against the wooden railing, the fingers on her right hand still billowing smoke.

"You're not here to praciss missin'," Mac said quietly. He smacked his black-stained lips together, the scent of chewing tobacco and dust rolling off him in waves.

"I'm sorry," muttered Jane. The ground blurred beneath her eyes. "I'm not used to . . . this far . . . normally . . . stationary . . ."

Mac spat into the dirt and pocketed his hands inside his long brown traveling coat. "Useless empaf. I look fo'wad to tha day tha Legion gows up aginst summun thet do not move," he drawled. "But until thet time, you well not demonstrait such incompehtence on muh raynge. Unda'stand?"

"Understood," growled the girl. She pulled herself up, the coarse wood of the railing digging splinters into her hand, then began to hobble slowly back toward Morningstar in the fading light, her firing arm held limply to her chest.

Everything hurt—every muscle, every bone, her joints, her eyes, her brain. The things that didn't hurt she couldn't feel. She needed sleep, she needed water, she needed food. But right now, mainly sleep. She limped toward a side entrance, the cramp in her right calf refusing to shift, too exhausted to go the long way around, too exhausted to avoid the corridors—no energy to care if she lived or died. She just needed to sleep.

Everything else would have to wait.

Oh, God I can't wait, thought Matt, salivating at the plate of food he'd piled high in front of him. Wait no sorry, two plates—there'd been so much that'd looked good at that sweet, sweet buffet, he'd done a Giselle and double-parked. Pizza, lasagna, roast beef, mashed potatoes, chicken carbonara, even these little vegetarian spinach quiches that looked simply to die for. And he hadn't even got dessert yet.

He glanced around for a place to sit—the classic new-kid dilemma. He spotted Wally surrounded by a group of tall, good-looking folk, but they seemed like an exclusive sort of crew and the seats down there were all taken so Matt decided to give that a miss. He would have sat with Ed if Ed had bothered to come down to dinner with him, but the thought of crowds seemed to make the genius uncomfortable and he said he'd prefer to eat later.

He spied a lanky girl with a ponytail sitting relatively by herself at the leftmost table. *That'll do*, Matt thought, and moseyed on down to join her.

"Hi!" he exclaimed, dropping down into the place beside her and setting his plates of food carefully upon the table. She looked at him like he was weird. "I'm Matt. Clairvoyant."

"Celeste," replied lanky-ponytail. Matt offered his hand, and she shook it, albeit with a semblance of reluctance. "Faunamorph."

"Nice to meet you, Celeste. What are you up to?"

Celeste turned her head slightly, as if not sure whether he was being serious. "Reading."

Matt glanced down at what looked like a veterinary textbook on the table in front of her opened up to a diagram deconstructing the circulatory system of an octopus. "So you are," he said. He started cutting up his potato. "What are reading about?"

"Um . . ." replied Celeste, "anatomy . . . of animals?"

"Nice," approved Matt, showing more interest than he actually felt. "Why, ah, what's got you reading that?" He slopped his potato chunks all through the roast beef and gravy.

"I'm a faunamorph," she repeated in a monotone, looking at him like he was an idiot. "I change into animals?"

"Right," Matt said through a mouthful of potato, giving her a friendly thumbs-up. He took in her long face, overbite, ponytail, and small unicorn stud earrings, and had a sudden burst of intuition. "Hey, mad guess, but do you like horses?"

"Oh my God, yes, how did you know?" Celeste replied, almost instantly perking up.

"Clairvoyant," he said smugly, in reality having dated a horse girl in year seven and being able to recognize one a mile away. Matt didn't really see the appeal of horses, but his ex-girlfriend had talked about them nonstop, and he'd unintentionally learned more than he cared to.

"Oh my God, that's so amazing!"

"Oh, well, thank you," Matt crooned, playing at being flattered. "And I bet you've got a particular horse you just love to turn into, right?"

"Oh my God, yes, you're incredible. Palomino!"

For the next half an hour, the "clairvoyant" and the horse girl discussed the minutiae of horses and horse care, the majority of which was spent with Celeste gushing about large farm animals while Matt nodded appreciatively and ate like one. Horses weren't just a passion for Celeste, it turned out—they were the very reason she'd managed to get into the Academy.

"I did a Pegasus," she announced proudly. "Most other faunamorphs, they get stuck on the idea of being real quick or doing a whole bunch of different animals—but I started thinking, right, and I was like 'I can do a horse. I can do a swan. Why can't I do a horse with swan wings'?"

"Wow," wowed Matt. He swallowed a mouthful of pizza and gave an indulgent, little golf clap. The girl blushed. "That's amazing! And that's what got the Legion interested?"

"Yeah. Most people only ever learn to do one or two normal animals, let alone something that doesn't exist."

"I'll bet," said Matt, refilling the lanky girl's glass from a jug of apple juice he'd pilfered from the buffet halfway through the horse lecture. "So, are you like, the best faunamorph here?"

"Oh no," Celeste replied, blushing redder this time. "Well, there's no real 'best.' We're all just Acolytes."

"Oh," said Matt, "well, I guess me too. Acolytes represent." He held up a fist and after some hesitation the girl giggled and bumped it. Matt glanced down at the open book, sitting there practically forgotten. "So, if you can already do a Pegasus, what're you working on?"

Celeste hesitated for a moment, then a conspiratorial grin slid over her face and she beckoned Matt to lean in. "I'm going to be a dragon," she whispered, and then leaned back, beaming. Matt was genuinely impressed.

"Wow, really?"

"Well, that's the plan." Celeste grinned, though her smile faded slightly a second later, and she looked back down at the octopus diagram. "But it's like, dragons are made up of *so* many animals, and I've got to keep all the right parts in my head without getting mixed up. And I've got no idea how I'm going to do the fire. Messing with secretables can be dangerous."

"Yeah, right," said Matt. A niggling thought occurred to him, and against his better judgment he found himself letting it slip through.

"Is there a lot of . . . I don't know . . . danger here?" he asked hesitantly. "Do people, you know . . . get hurt?"

"Well, yeah." Celeste shrugged, seeming unfazed. "But I mean we've got healers."

"Right," said Matt. "So no one . . . dies?"

"Um . . ." Celeste's face scrunched up as she thought. "I don't think so. Not that I've heard of."

"Right," Matt said again, feeling a bit relieved. "So you wouldn't say, like, death stalks Morningstar?"

"What?" the faunamorph snorted. "No. Where'd you hear that?"

"Nowhere. TV. I don't know, I must've misheard. Forget it. Hey, is that ice cream?"

Matt hummed to himself as he strolled alone through the corridors, the upbeat tune somewhat muffled by another spoon of Neapolitan ice cream from the bowl he was carrying. He'd actually come up with two bowls, the bigger of which he'd left outside Jane's door—he hadn't seen her come down to dinner, and a part of him suspected that in all

the excitement she might've forgotten to eat. Now, his good deed done
for the day, Matt meandered back to his own room, ice cream in hand.
Upon reaching the door, he paused to fish the key out of his pocket, then
turned it in the lock and strode through . . . to find the blue-eyed boy
sitting on his bed.

"Je-sus!" Matt yelped, and there was a soft thud as the spoon fell from
his mouth onto the carpet. He squeezed his eyes shut, trying to make the
image go away, willing it to be his imagination—but when he opened
them the child was still there, holding up the notepad.

Listen.

Matt shot a single, terrified glance over his shoulder and slammed
the door behind him, spinning immediately back round to face the boy,
who hadn't moved.

"Jesus Christ, you're real?!"

The child nodded, and in a rush Matt realized the kid could actually
hear him.

"What!" he spluttered, ice cream forgotten. "How? Who are you?
How'd you get in here?"

The boy just shook his head. He glanced around at the walls, like he
could see through them. He bent down over the page.

No time.

"What?" Matt replied, unable to believe he was engaging with whatever the hell this was. "Time for what?" He followed the child's gaze.
"What's wrong? What are you looking at?" More scribbling.

Death.

The boy looked pleadingly up at him and a chill ran down Matt's
spine—though met, a second later, by a flare of irritation.

"Death," he repeated flatly. "Just general, inevitable death. Can you
be more specific?"

The child shook his head, his blue eyes desperate. The pencil flew
across the page.

Why you're here. Why I gave them your application . . .

Matt's jaw dropped and without realizing he stepped forward and
grabbed the boy by his skinny arm.

"That was you?" he cried, fighting the irrepressible urge to punch
a child in the face. The boy nodded, wriggling. Matt's grip slackened
and the boy pulled free, desperate to continue writing. The sound of his

pencil scratched through the silence and then finally he looked up, holding one last message in front of Matt's face.

Stay hidden, Matt Callaghan, or the world ends.

And in an instant, he vanished.

MATTER AND MIND

"Nature or Nurture? How the Powered Become the Powerful"
The Opinion Pages: Room for Debate,
The New York Times, October 12, 1983

Introduction

The official recognition by the UN General Assembly of the Legion of Heroes has shone fresh light onto the extraordinary talents of the Legion's members. Like Olympians and entrepreneurs, the question of how much of their success comes from hard work and how much comes from luck is now being asked of those whose superhuman abilities seem to have so far eclipsed everyone else's. Have they simply trained harder? Or is there something intrinsic which these remarkable individuals are just born with?

You Get Out What You Put In:
An Old Adage Holds True in the New World

When Harsheel Singh was eight, she contracted polio, a disease that, at the time, was still rampant in her native India. The virus bowed and buckled her legs and left her unable to walk without the aid of crutches. Yet, two decades later, she would not only break the unassisted human land-speed record but would become one of the most iconic figures within the Legion of Heroes: "Zephyr, the World's Fastest Woman." Harsheel did not achieve these feats through luck or through being born a certain way, but rather through sheer will and determination, and an irresistible drive to be the best at what she could do. She trained religiously, refusing at every step to accept the prophecies of failure from her doctors and family who proclaimed she would never walk, then never run, then never achieve her dream of being the fastest person alive. Through hard work and perseverance, she proved every one of them wrong.

Singh's journey should be an inspiration to us all, and a lesson that greatness is not given but earned. We often forget that our superhuman powers are not only "super" but "human" as well—and like all aspects of ourselves become mighty through commitment, training, and discipline. It is easy to dismiss extraordinary people such as those in the Legion as simply having been "born that way," but an examination of their ranks shows that this notion is simply untrue. More than untrue, a belief in "the hand you're dealt" is a crutch that the lazy rest on to relieve themselves of taking responsibility for their own inaction. Because after all, if Harsheel Singh can do it—why can't you?

The Uncomfortable Truth of Gifted People

There is a trope in children's television shows that all characters—big, small, smart, strong—must all be, overall, equal. What a person lacks in one aspect, they inevitably make up for with hidden talent in another; and conversely when a person (normally a villain) appears naturally gifted or successful, they inevitably have a counterbalancing weakness to "make up" for it. So, the geek turns out to be a great dancer, the plain Jane a science whiz, and the muscular bully riddled with anxiety—almost as if each person was given a set number of "points" at birth but had them distributed to different attributes.

This, sadly, is wrong. The obsession with latent equality is a childish, fantastical notion that we, as adults, must discard in order to face reality: that some people are simply born better. It is an uncomfortable truth to face, one that runs counter to our natural desire for fairness, but the simple fact of the matter is that be it from genetics, fate, or just plain luck, there have always been those born with gifts no amount of hard work or proper parenting can match. This is perhaps disheartening, but that does not make it false.

The Legion of Heroes stands as a shining example of this. Can anyone honestly say that Captain Dawn, with "the power of a hundred suns," earned his phenomenal strength through the sweat of his brow? Or that the White Queen, Elsa Arrendel, demonstrated anything less than prodigal talent from the moment she manifested her powers of cold? Certainly, there is no denying the benefits of dedication and proper instruction—but at the end of the day, no matter how they're played, a pair of twos is a pair of twos, and a royal flush is a winner.

"Mr. Callaghan. Thank you for joining us."

Matt nodded stiffly. Across the table from him the hard-faced, middle-aged woman in a jet-black pantsuit pursed her lips into a position she probably thought resembled a smile.

"My name is Hillary Cross, audio-light conversion. I believe you're already acquainted with Mr. Winters, flight, and Mr. Kersey, projection." She indicated the two men sitting either side of her. Winters gave a nod of friendly acknowledgment, which Matt returned, while Selwyn simply smiled his dreamy smile.

"We've met. Matt Callaghan, clairvoyant."

"Excellent," Cross said airily. "And I trust you've settled in."

It was his second day. Matt forced himself to swallow a scathing comeback and simply nod.

"Then I won't waste any more time," she continued. "Mr. Callaghan, we are here to discuss your powers."

The Ashes woman had come for him around eight. Matt had barely stepped out of the shower when an impatient rap on his door had sent him scrambling for clothes. He'd opened the door to find this squat, dour woman with short blond hair waiting outside his room, looking like the human personification of an HR department and (a) ordering him to follow her immediately, and (b) noting that he'd cut himself shaving. Matt had scrambled out in a half-jog, struggling to keep up with the power-woman's blistering pace, cursing his stupid blunt first-impression-ruining razor as she led him through a maze of stairs and corridors to what turned out to be Daniel Winters's office. He now sat on one side of a large mahogany table with Cross, Selwyn, and the director himself sitting on the other, staring over at him with varying degrees of imperiousness.

He could have been interviewing for a job, Matt thought wryly. He glanced around at Winters's various diplomas and awards framed on the wall, the high-backed leather chair, silver touch lamp, sleek white computer, and impeccably ordered bookshelf.

"The Legion of Heroes is very interested in you, Mr. Callaghan," Cross began formally. "We wish to do everything possible to ensure you reach your full potential. And as such we have devised a specialized training schedule."

As she spoke the last sentence, Matt was surprised to see Cross's mouth twitch, and she blinked, though continued to stare resolutely forward. Repressed annoyance, he recognized.

Matt's brain worked fast.

He faked a small, dry laugh. "I foresaw this," he stated calmly. "The three of you . . ." Matt paused, nodding as if something finally made sense. "I thought it was weird at the time, because I didn't know you, and you were talking about me. But this decision wasn't unanimous, was it?"

From the looks that passed over their faces—widening surprise around Winters's eyes and the tightening of Cross's lips—Matt could tell he was on the money. Cross's thin fingers curled around her pen, and she took a moment before replying.

"There have been . . . multiple viewpoints on how best to engage your ability," she said diplomatically, avoiding eye contact with the men either side of her. "Captain Dawn has not provided any specific instructions on how you are to be managed and there are some"—the corner of her mouth twitched toward Winters—"who feel this implies you aren't to be given any special treatment." Her posture stiffened. "There are also others who feel any sort of testing . . . any sort of regimentation at all . . . is unnecessary." Matt didn't have to read her face to know which of the three she was talking about there.

Cross's hawkish eyes burrowed into him. "These . . . opinions have been accounted for, but the undeniable fact remains. We need metrics. We need to know the use and limits of your ability, and we need to be able to track your improvement." She paused. "If properly utilized, the benefits of your power could be phenomenal. You could—"

"I could be a warning bell, yes," Matt interrupted, sounding bored. Cross blinked, and Matt was pleased to see she looked mildly taken aback.

"Precisely," said Cross, recovering. "And to that end, Mr. Callaghan, your schedule will be thus. You will attend daily sessions with Mr. Kersey to cultivate your visions. You will attend every non-ability-specific course and seminar available to ensure a level of basic competency. And every two weeks, I will assess, measure, and record your predictive ability. Your first assessment will be today. Are we clear?"

"Can I have breakfast first?" Matt asked, irritable and secretly terrified. Between this and the disturbing disappearing kid, he had a lot to process. Cross opened her mouth to respond but Winters got there first.

"Of course," the director replied amicably. He rose to his feet and reluctantly the pant-suited Ashes woman did too, leaving only Selwyn remaining seated, unconcerned with social cues. "Take your time. I'm sure if you return at say, eleven, the assessment will be ready to proceed. Does that suit you, Hillary?"

Cross rankled at the use of her first name, which Matt thought Winters probably did on purpose.

"Of course," she forced, working her jaw.

"Excellent. Mr. Callaghan, you're excused."

Matt fled before they could change their minds.

Lost in thought, Matt made his way to the Grand Hall on autopilot, where he absentmindedly picked up breakfast before navigating to a free bench. To his surprise, he'd barely sat down to eat his runny egg before Jane climbed into the space beside him.

"Hey," he muttered, "you're not dead. Nice."

Jane didn't respond immediately but just sat there resting her head and arms on the table, looking like Matt felt. The black bags under her eyes seemed to have doubled since Matt had seen her two days ago.

"The Ashes ordered no one to attack me," she mumbled finally, her head still sideways. The effect of her words was undercut somewhat by the fact that half the people in the hall had been staring venomously at her since she'd entered.

"Always a positive," Matt replied slightly warily, struggling to keep his eyes off an Acolyte two tables over who was glaring in their direction and telekinetically weaving a knife through his fingers with unnerving speed. He hesitated, unsure whether to tell her about the strange child and his prophecies of doom, but the sight of Jane's drawn face and heavy eyes made him take pause. It seemed like she had enough problems.

"Yeah," said Jane, oblivious to his internal dilemma. Then she seemed to hesitate, as if unsure how to phrase what she wanted to say next.

"Thank you," she eventually managed to get out, "for the ice cream."

Matt stared at her. "What ice cream? I didn't bring you ice cream. Someone brought you ice cream? Damn. Maybe you've got a secret admirer."

"Shut up," Jane snapped, punching him in the shoulder. "I know it was you."

"Ow, all right fine, you're welcome."

"Idiot." She scowled, punching him harder.

"Stop hitting me," Matt complained, rubbing his bicep. She stopped hitting him and instead sunk her head deeper into her hands.

"You're an ass."

"I was just playing," he said kindly, trying to make peace.

Eventually, she looked at him again.

"Stupid jokes aside, thank you." She paused.

Matt shrugged. "I figured you could use it."

"I did. I hadn't eaten all day." She lifted her head from the table and glanced behind her.

"You know the food here is *free*, right?" Matt said, indicating toward the buffet with his fork. Jane didn't reply but just sat there looking sullen and hungry. From the way she was shifting uncomfortably in her seat, Matt could tell she was in the middle of some sort of mental dilemma— either contemplating whether to risk getting food or deciding whether she was still mad at him.

After a few seconds, Matt interrupted her stewing.

"So, how're you finding it?" he asked. Jane hesitated—still seeming like she was on the brink of leaving—but eventually she shrugged.

"Good. Tough. Lot of stuff I'm not used to, but I'll get better." She glanced around the room, as if trying to catch people watching her. A lot of them were. Matt waited a few seconds for her to ask him how his day had been, before giving up and telling her anyway.

"Well, I've been sitting in a room on some cushions," he told her as if she was interested, "and trying to concentrate on tapping into my innate clairvoyant abilities."

"How's that going?" replied Jane, smirking sideward at him perhaps in spite of herself.

"No progress so far, but it's early days."

"Sure."

"Also, I've been playing a lot of video games and losing."

"It's a tough life," she growled, the sarcasm lathered on thick. "I got my nose broken, my head cut, and two ribs fractured. Plus everyone hates me."

"Yeah, but I don't think you quite understand," replied Matt. "I lost really, really badly." He paused and dropped his voice to a whisper. "Also, they want to test me."

"Clairvoyantly?"

"Yeah."

"Damn." Jane made a face that could have been an attempt at sympathy. "What are you going to do?"

"Lies. Lots of lies. The real superpower."

"Well," she said with measured indifference, "if you get arrested, send me a postcard."

"Hilarious." He gave Wally a short wave as he walked by a row over. Jane followed Matt's gaze over to the retreating psychic, then turned back.

"It's weird," she said, sighing after a few moments. "Being here. I thought . . ." She hesitated. "I don't know what I thought. I guess I was so focused on getting here I never thought much about what it'd be like." She swept a tired glance around the room, at the eyes staring venomously into her. "I guess I never really considered there'd be the same hate here as anywhere else."

Matt didn't know how to respond to that, but luckily Jane didn't seem to need a response. She turned back to him, a crooked smile forcing its way across her lips. "Forget it. You know, it's funny. This is the first time I've ever left a school without being expelled."

Matt chuckled. "You're right, that is funny. How many did—"

And then suddenly, he froze. His eyes wide, his mouth open, all at once awestruck—as like a divine bolt of lightning, the answer came to him.

"That's it," he whispered.

Jane frowned, looking mildly annoyed. "What's what?"

"It . . ." breathed Matt, hardly daring to hope, unable to believe it had taken him this long to figure it out. "Jane, you're a genius."

"Thanks?" she replied, sounding dubious. Then, "Um . . . why?"

"Expelled," Matt murmured, and he turned to face her, his face lighting up. "I'm going to get expelled!"

"What?" Jane growled flatly, her initial shock quickly hardening into contempt. "No."

"Yes!" cried Matt, his voice rising with so much excitement that half of the adjacent table glanced over. Matt forced his giddiness back down. "Yes! Jane don't you see, it's perfect! All this time, I was so set on trying to figure out how to get out of coming here, I never once considered it the other way around." His face flushed. "I don't need a reason not to be here, I need to make the Legion not want me anymore!"

"No," said Jane, holding her face in her hands.

"Yes!" crowed Matt, arms trembling in anticipation. "Oh my God, this is brilliant. I'm going to . . . I'm going to skip class. I'm going to drink. I'm going to do drugs. I'm going to set things on fire. I'm going to be the laziest, worst, most disruptive rule-breaker the Academy's ever seen, and they'll have no choice but to kick me out."

"No . . ." moaned Jane. "You absolute idiot, no." Matt ignored her.

"This is an A-grade institution," he rambled, the ideas now gushing out like he'd struck oil. "Not just an A-grade curriculum, A-grade attitudes. All I've got to do is bring some D-class style, and these paragons of virtue will evict me faster than they can down a protein shake."

"This is a terrible plan," declared Jane. "You're throwing away the opportunity of a lifetime."

"For you it's opportunity; for me it's entrapment," countered Matt, thinking of the weird kid and his enigmatic warnings of death.

Jane sighed. "You can't break the rules," she muttered, rubbing her temples.

"Really?" Matt demanded, sick of her constant negativity. "Is that so? Well, I'd like to see you stop me."

"I could"—she scowled—"but I won't, because you don't get what I mean. I'm saying the Academy has no rules you could break."

"So, you're saying," Matt responded incredulously, "that if I walked up on that stage, dropped my pants, and took a leak on those glass costume cases, nobody here would have a problem."

"I'm saying you wouldn't be expelled," Jane replied, her face hardening. "Because you'd be dead. Because I'd kill you. As would everyone else in this room, you disrespectful piece of crap."

"All right, easy, calm down," Matt muttered, recoiling slightly.

"And anyway," Jane continued with a haughty sniff, "it'd be obvious you were trying to cause trouble. If you did anything that crazy, people would figure out you wanted to get expelled."

Matt paused. "So, what you're saying," he said after a moment's consideration, "is that I can't seem to *want* it."

"I'm not saying that at all," Jane replied, shaking her head in despair.

"I've got to be smart."

"You're an idiot."

"Make it look like I'm naturally incompatible, not out to cause trouble."

"By doing what?" Jane said angrily. "Sex, destruction, violence?" She held up her fingers in a checklist—Matt saw many of them were run down with small cuts. "Everyone here's an adult. They have the best clean-up crews in the world. And half the lessons are people beating each other up!"

"I could attack you," Matt suggested, raising a helpful eyebrow. "Not allowed to attack you outside of class, direct Ashes instruction, you said so yourself. Could punch you square in the tits."

"You could," admitted Jane with a resigned, deadpan expression, "I suppose. If you wanted to."

For a few seconds, Matt seriously considered it—he stared at Jane's sharp, tired face, her auburn hair, tattooed cheek, and piercing gray-blue eyes, sitting right there next to him. It'd be so easy to just reach out, swing at her, fake some sort of ballistic fit, yell abuse . . .

But—

"I can't." He sighed, dropping the idea and his semi-raised fists. "I'm a 'clairvoyant.' They'd think I'd seen you were dangerous or something and then they'd kick you out too. I can't do that." He sighed again, glancing around the hall. "There's got to be another way."

For a few moments, Jane was silent, just staring at him with a funny, conflicted look with not quite enough animosity in it to be a glare.

"Why do you care if I get kicked out?" she asked eventually.

"Oh, I don't know," Matt replied, throwing up his arms. "Maybe because it's your dream? And maybe because that'd make me the jerk who ruined your dream? And maybe because I'd like to think I'm better than that?" He pinched the bridge of his nose. "Stupid conscience is going to be the death of me. Help me think of another way."

"I'm not going to think up ways to get you expelled," Jane replied coldly. She stood up. "Besides, I've sat here long enough. You probably don't want to be seen associating with me." She absentmindedly reached down to take a drink from his orange juice—but the moment she lifted the cup to her lips, the glass shattered. The empath stared numbly at her hand and breathed a defeated sigh. Matt glanced over her shoulder to where the telekinetic's eyes were still burning a few tables over.

"I don't care," he said, but Jane was already walking away, shaking drops of juice and glass from her fingers. For a moment, Matt considered calling out after her. Yet, after a few seconds, he just shook his head, his mind abuzz with disruptive ideas.

Matt met Cross at the door to Winters's office, and she led him with barely a word to a nearby disused classroom. They sat on either side of a small plastic table, and the Ashes woman set down a clipboard.

"We will proceed like so," she said curtly. "You will make predictions. I will record these predictions for analysis. I will ask any questions I deem necessary. Am I clear?"

"You are," Matt said gently. *Be unflappable*, he told himself—confident and unconcerned. "But let me be as well." He gave Cross a kind smile and was pleased to see the short woman appeared slightly perturbed. "I will see what I see. Nothing you or I can do can force the sight. We cannot choose which points are held static in time." He glanced around at the small room. "Can you dim the lights please?"

The sudden reversal from giving orders to taking them seemed to throw Cross. Nevertheless, she rose without a word and walked over to adjust the dimmer. While she was doing so, Matt removed his phone from his pocket and set it face up on the desk, the music player opened to a playlist of deep forest sounds.

"Take my hands," he commanded calmly, holding his palms out face up, as the sound of soothing jungle noise suffused the mood-lit room. If Cross had seemed perturbed before, it was nothing compared to how she looked now.

"I don't—"

"Take my hands please." Matt smiled, the embodiment of mystic calm.

Reluctantly, Cross did as he asked. Matt gently gripped her cold, stumpy fingers and, still smiling, closed his eyes, leaving the Ashes woman sitting stiffly and looking very uncomfortable.

Cross, Matt thought, was a powerful, professional woman. And he'd wagered, both unused to people unaffected by her authority and put off by unsolicited intimacy. Matt slowly caressed Cross's fingers in time with the soundtrack, feeling the tension confirm his theory. And that wasn't all.

They remained in that position, with the sound of an optimist's version of the Amazon washing over them, until Matt felt that a sufficiently dramatic amount of time had passed.

"You're not married, are you?" he asked, slowly opening his eyes and phrasing the question so that literally any answer Cross gave would be correct. But as he suspected, the middle-aged Ashes woman shook her head, her eyes wide and her lips set tight. Matt nodded.

"I see a ring," he continued. "Maybe not soon, but some time. A part of you will want to reject it, a part of you won't. Neither will be entirely right. You'll have to make peace with that."

Of course, Matt had simply felt the lack of a wedding ring on her finger. The rest was pure demographic pandering—any intelligent single woman past a certain age harbored some level of misgivings about not being married, and any intelligent person full stop would have doubts about a proposal. As for the proposal itself? Well, Cross would need to be dead before she could definitively disprove that prediction—heck, he had a great aunt who'd married at eighty.

Matt closed his eyes again and took a deep, slow breath.

"You have so much unused potential," he said quietly, lifting his head but not opening his eyes. Well, obviously the woman was an Ash (Ashe? Ashling); she'd been slated to join the Legion at some point. And even if she hadn't, the fear of not making the most of your life was almost universal. "You will have an opportunity to do great things, to seek your limits. When that time comes, you should follow the color gray."

That was straight guessing. Cross started to say something, but Matt shushed her ever so slightly and kept on with his pretending.

They sat that way for a few more minutes before Matt eventually lowered his head slightly, opened his eyes, and looked directly at Cross. "I also see lies," he said, a little more firmly. "Soon, in your future. You're going to tell a white lie to save another person's feelings."

Literally, everyone did this.

"And," Matt continued, gently releasing his grip on her fingers and folding his arms, "I'm sorry to say, but you're going to be a victim of theft."

This, too, was almost statistically guaranteed.

Matt let out a long dramatic sigh. Then without warning, he turned away and stood up, leaving Cross sitting momentarily stunned, the spell suddenly broken. Matt silenced and pocketed his phone, then crossed the room and undimmed the lights.

"That's all I can see for now," he stated plainly, turning back to Cross, his hands now in his pockets. "I'll let you know if anything more comes up. But for now, that's all I'm getting." Without waiting for her invitation or approval, he turned to leave.

"Oh," he added, suddenly stopping, his hand on the doorknob, as if he'd suddenly just remembered, "except for the dancers."

"Dancers?" asked Cross, still partially shaken but trying to hide it. "What, um, what dancers?"

"A man . . . dancing with a woman," Matt replied casually, holding up an indifferent hand and examining his cuticles. "Not sure if it's you, could be, maybe not. He loves her too much. It's going to get him in trouble."

Let's see her disprove that, Matt thought as he smirked to himself, walking out before the stunned woman could say another word.

Arena was the wrong word for it. It sounded small and personal, and this was closer to a football stadium with a raised square stone platform in the middle, thought Jane. She half-expected some man carrying a heated bin strapped around his neck to be wandering around hawking hot dogs, like in the movies. At least it'd been easy to find—hard to miss actually, being a big random stadium that looked like it'd been picked out of a city somewhere and dropped next to the manor. The Legion's main sparring stadium—her first class of the day.

Around her, combatants milled on the width of grass running uniformly around the outside of the raised central square. Jane ignored their glares, like she ignored the derogatory shouts occasionally hurled down from the smattering of people in the grandstands—her eyes resolutely focused on the gigantic figure looming in front of them.

"Listen up, you scum-sucking pieces of subhuman trash," snarled the man, one foot on the marble stairs leading up into the center ring, one foot on the ring itself. "My name is James Conrad, I am a strongman, and I am a senior. Do you know what that means?"

Nobody answered. His face split into a broad-toothed smile.

"All so shy. You will answer when I speak to you. Sir, yes, sir. Now I'll say again, I am a senior—do you know what that means?"

"SIR, NO, SIR!"

"Good." James Conrad smiled, like a shark before a corpse. He was huge, a monster of a man. Six foot eight, maybe twenty-four, with skin as dark as dusk and every inch of him bulging, rippling muscle. Veins on his arms the width of her fingers, cables in his neck, legs like pistons and a chest that threatened to tear his gray shirt apart. Her whole head could have fit in his hand, and she doubted it would have lasted there long. "Admit your ignorance. I admire that in peasants."

He dropped to the ground, both feet thumping into the grass in a clod of dust and dirt. Even on their level, he towered above them.

"It means I have been here the longest. It means that I have endured and advanced while wave after wave of you pathetic wannabes have washed out." He curled his fingers to fists, cracks popping through the open air. "It means I am the best of the best, and don't you ever forget it."

He looked around at them, over the top of them. Why he needed to make this stupid speech was beyond Jane. She was the only one who was new. Probably. Jane glanced around the crowd of Acolytes, trying to catch a face. Were they intimidated by this act? Did he say this every time they went to fight? But the backs of heads and blank expressions gave her nothing.

James was still talking, though Jane was getting impatient listening. "You will fight who I tell you to fight, how I tell you to fight. You will stay inside the square. You will show no mercy"—he grinned wide and savage—"until your opponent taps out or lies bleeding. I like to see strong. I like to see ruthless." He liked the sound of his own voice, more like. "I like to see contenders."

He started to pace slowly, then stopped. "Who here thinks they have what it takes to be in the Legion?" he asked almost softly. There was a menacing twinkle in his black eyes that Jane didn't like. Nevertheless she, along with everyone there, raised their hands. James's grin widened.

"Well, isn't that appalling. A flock of fools. You think you've got what it takes because you were the best rock-thrower in some hick town?" He laughed. "You need to wake up. And I'm here to awaken you."

He took a step back onto the stairs, his arms raised wide. "I am first among the seniors. I *will* be first into the Legion. And I'm going to make you an offer, fair and square—beat me, right here, right now, and you can take my place at the front of the queue."

A stunned silence fell over those gathered. James smiled a giant's smile, looking down at them with bared teeth. For a second, nobody did anything—except Jane.

Her hand shot in the air. The hulking man's eyes caught it and traced down to her. To the mark on her cheek. His smile grew.

"Well, well, the empath," he whispered. "God is good." Two dozen heads turned to look at her, and a swarm of muttering filled the air. The crowd parted even further around her, opening her path to the waiting, hulking monster of a man.

To hell with it, thought Jane, I *can take him. So what if he was strong, it hardly mattered.* She had three powers up her sleeve. If this trash-talking idiot wanted to fast-track her ascension, he could be her god-damn guest. He was big, sure, but what did that matter when you were set on fire or electrocuted from a hundred yards away? Some cocky line-backer with an ego ten times the size of his brain—he wouldn't be the first to underestimate her. But he might be the last.

"Step forward, Empath," James said with a fake, mocking bow. He retreated up the steps into the square, facing her the whole time. "Step forward, our newest 'recruit.' " He said the last word laughingly, as if the very concept was a joke.

Jane started to walk forward slowly, watching her steps, her heart beating faster than she would've liked. There were hisses around her—muttered, inaudible threats.

"See who comes to challenge us," crooned James. He was walking backward now, step-by-step, toward the center of the square. "A plagiarist. A parasite." He kept moving backward as Jane ascended the stairs, his eyes never leaving hers. "Here to do old Heydrich proud? Here to prove him right? To finish the job?" There was a rush of hisses and murmur of boos from the Acolytes waiting in the wings. Jane ignored it, staying focused on the Goliath in front of her.

James had reached the opposite end of the platform. He stopped and straightened, rearing up to his full height. A slight tremor ran through Jane's arms—he really was big. But she stayed steady.

He stared her down, still wearing that mocking smile. "Prepare yourself," he said simply. "I am the strongest man alive." He paused and surveyed the attending crowd. His knees bent. He cracked his knuckles, rolled his neck.

A hush fell over the assembled.

"Students," said James Conrad, grinning, "attend your master."

"Three."

"Two."

"One."

"Fight," he whispered. And neither of them moved.

Silence.

Complete and total silence. Jane watched intently, poised, her feet locked, reflexes on a hair trigger. Nothing. He just stood there, smiling. She wasn't used to this—the silence, the stillness. Both just watched, waited, waiting for the other to move.

There was forty feet between them.

One heartbeat.

Two.

Then Jane rolled the coin and rippled her fingers.

Z-Z-Z-Z-Z-Z-Z-Z-Z-ZAP!

The bolt lanced outward, but in the same instant, the giant slammed his hands together, and there was a deafening boom, and the very air around her seemed to explode. She was thrown backward, out over the grass, a ringing reverberation in her chest, blood pouring from her ears.

NO. She fell towards the ground, but a blast of fire pushed her back up, a wild shot but enough to force her to stand, keep her in the ring, crash her onto the hard white stone, and—

He was there. Already above her, across the field in a single bound, his bulk blotting out the sun and he was fast, so fast, already there with his fist raised slamming down into—

NO. She blasted sideward. She didn't even know what—adrenaline and raw instinct—throwing energy out to push her just barely out of the way of his fist as it slammed into the ground. But still the force, the sheer impact sent a shock wave through the stone that rippled out and into her, under her, winding her, launching her up—

She hung there, dizzy, disoriented, trying to regain her bearings, trying to focus, focus. There was still a chance, she had distance, he'd thrown her up and unintentionally away, and she was flying, floating, falling, looking down at his grinning face and—

V-R-R-R-R-O-O-O-O-O-M-M-M-M-M!

Z-Z-Z-Z-Z-Z-Z-Z-Z-Z-ZAP!

Fire and lightning, both hands, straight down, a jagged pillar of death, but he'd already moved, already sidestepped (he was so fast)—and then she saw his smile widen, his knees bend, and the stone crack as he leaped toward her, ten feet in the air—

NO. She tried to turn, pivot, make herself thin, fall faster, move, anything, just get out of the way, because suddenly he was in the air alongside her, blocking her view, a giant, swinging a single, monstrous hand—

"ARGH!"

He'd only nicked her, barely brushed her arm—but that arm was now limp, helpless, screaming with a pain she hadn't felt in years. It was all she could do to turn so that she landed on the other side, crashed heavily on the stone, hearing something pop, feeling something inside her crack. But her arm. Her arm, her arm, her arm. She couldn't move it; it wasn't round the right way. It felt like every bone was splinters. Oh God, the pain, the pain, the pain, the pain—

He landed across the square from her, his feet sending cracks through the arena stone. He was laughing at her; she could hear them all laughing at her. Come on. Come on. Ignore the pain, push through the—

Oh God, her arm, just—

He was coming toward her, slowly, strolling, shouting something, taking his time . . .

"You take powers," the titan roared to the cheers of the watching crowd, his words blurring through her haze, a hearty sneer clear across his face, "you were never meant to have! You pick up tools we"—he gestured to the stadium—"have had a lifetime to master! None of us are here because we were born!" He looked down at her, bleeding on the ground, and there was mirth upon his lips. "Parasite."

And then he blurred. He exploded off the ground, crossing the space between them in a heartbeat, and suddenly the world was falling, because she was rising, a massive hand around her neck.

NO.

She couldn't shake him. She couldn't move. His hands were wrought steel, and they were wrapped around her neck, slowly constricting, and she couldn't breathe, she couldn't breathe—

"You don't belong here." He pulled her in toward him, face-to-huge-black-face, and there was no trace of mercy or kindness in his eyes. "You are weak." And he was right. She was weak, compared to him. Every part of her was weak, breakable, able to be shattered in an instant. She did not have his strength.

But she still had one working arm.

"AAAARRRRRGGGHHH!" she roared, and thrust her fingers up, spread out and open, straight into his mouth, nose, and eyes, lightning arcing from palms. James screamed, spasming, clutching at his face with both hands as she fell, hurtling, tossed across the ring into the—

Ground. The hard white stone rushed out to meet her. She had no time, no strength, no thought with which to react. Her shoulder slammed into stone with all the force he'd thrown her with, then her hips, then her skull. She heard something crack, somethings, all through her—there was a tightness in her chest, a twitching in her mouth, she wanted to get up, but she couldn't, she couldn't move . . .

One eye refused to open, the other looked out helplessly across the ring as her opponent snarled, shaking himself like a Rottweiler, momentarily dazed, his lips drawn across his smoking face. Burns patched his cheeks and nostrils, his eyes bloodshot and furious—and focused squarely on her. He didn't speak—no quips, no taunts, no funny insults. Just moved his feet out, spread his stance wide, faced her right on, dead center, twenty feet across the ring. This time, she saw him raise his arms. This time, she saw him swing his palms together. And this time, she saw it, heard it for a fraction of a second as the very air rent between them, the raw force, the shock wave. She understood, an instant before—

And then an unstoppable power slammed into her and the world went black, and Jane Walker was no more.

* * *

The girl was dead.

She had to be. Dead and gone, swallowed into the abyss. Fragments of her life, slivers of glass and light among the dark, flashed past her fading mind. Hands on her, touching her. A woman in black. A boy she knew once, Matt Callaghan, his face, standing over her, blocking out the light. She imagined her father. A photograph. Someone singing happy birthday. Cold and hot and needles.

And then she woke up.

"Arggh!"

A yelp, muffled by cloth. She couldn't see, she couldn't feel, it was dark, she couldn't move, her hands . . .

Her hands were stiff, her arms held in place by something hard. Her legs too. She tried to move her feet, but they were trapped, equally immobilized. She panted, breathing hard. She felt . . . arggh. She hurt. Everything hurt. Every part of her felt like someone pressing on a bruise. She struggled, tried to break free, but there was something holding her down—she felt weak, paralyzed, her muscles dead and unresponsive to her commands.

Her breathing accelerated, panic blooming in her chest. She tried to think, tried to focus, rise above the delirium and panic smothering her brain. Where was she? Why was it dark? She couldn't think, the blurred world of dreams still entangled with reality.

It was dark. Blue dark. The muffled kind of dark when you're alone in a room but there's light somewhere far away around a thousand corners. No. That didn't make sense. Think. Sit up, shake the thick water from your head. But she couldn't move.

Slowly, in drips and drops, Jane's faculties began to return. She blinked, clearing away the damp film from her eyes as they adjusted to the lack of light. The room she was in was large and open, with high walls and an angled ceiling. In front of her, a row of identical single beds draped in white linen stretched out through the dark in both directions, with another matching row running across five feet further along. Her eyes flicked left and right to find similar beds on either side of her, the immaculate pearl gleam of their sheets trailing off to become orderly lines of ghostly globs floating into the blackness. *So many beds*, she wondered. And all of them empty.

She stared blankly at the bed opposite her for a few seconds before the answer stumbled sleepily from her subconscious. Hospital, she realized. A place to heal the sick. The sick or . . . the injured.

Suddenly, it came back to her. The arena, James Conrad, a fight . . . the fight! She tensed up, straining to rise, to get back, to finish, to win. But then a moment later, reality caught up to her delusions. Jane's head slumped back down onto the pillow, hot shame spreading over her. She'd lost. Terribly. It hadn't even been a fight. It had been a beating. She struggled to raise her head slightly, her eyes wandering down to look at the rest of her body. But there was no body to see—only a giant plaster cast, immobile and unbroken.

God. For an instant, the thought of being locked in, trapped, and vulnerable sent a ripple of panic pulsing through Jane's heart—but that fear quickly faded, giving way to bitter self-loathing. It didn't matter if she couldn't flee or fight, nobody was going to hurt her. She'd been broken, and they'd fixed her. If they'd wanted her dead, they would've simply let her die. The mere fact that she was here in this infirmary, drugged and immobilized hours later, told her how bad her injuries had been. The Legion's healers were the best in the world; these beds were probably barely used. Except when some fresh-faced idiot decided to challenge Morningstar Academy's top recruit.

Stupid, stupid, stupid. She closed her eyes, willing herself to fade away, wishing she'd just die. She was so stupid, stupid to come here, to believe for an instant she could ever be anything but a complete, useless failure. She'd thought she was special, deluded herself into thinking she was strong by beating children at games they didn't want to play. Idiot. Pathetic parasite who could only ever play pale imitations of other people's talents. She wasn't even supposed to be here. She was worthless.

They should've let her die.

Jane lay alone, the darkness still and unmoving around her, the cool air licking at the warm, stuffy plaster, the restless fever of artificial sleep still lingering behind her forehead. She wanted to sleep, but she wasn't tired. Wanted to move but couldn't. More than anything she wanted to leave, to disappear, slink out in the dark when nobody would see her go—when no one was around to smirk and point and laugh. To vanish into the night, another dropout, another failure.

Paralyzed, she lay there as the minutes ticked by—only her, her shame, and the quiet dark.

A muffled sound in the distance, far off and to her left, cut between her thoughts. "Hello?" she tried to utter, but her throat was dry and cracked, the bandages stifling any traces of the word. Her eyes darted over toward where she thought it had come from, but the milky dark only swirled and billowed in its nothingness, throwing conjured phantoms at her fearful mind. "Hello?" she tried to say again, but it was little more than a whisper, caught and sunken between her lips.

For what seemed like hours she watched, tensed, wondering what was out there, if she'd even heard anything, wondering if she was losing her mind.

And then out of the blackness, *he* came.

He emerged from the darkness without a whisper, the only sound of his existence the quiet fall of his boots atop the carpet and the rustle of his cape, the waterfall of molten gold trailing down his back. He moved slowly, his footsteps soft and measured, a figure of almost pure white, a ghost wreathed and touched in shimmering gold—his cape, his boots, his gloves, the sigil on his chest. Against the dead of night, he seemed to faintly glow, a quiet glow, muted by the shadows through which he wandered.

Jane's heart stopped. Her breath caught in her chest. It was the drugs—she was going mad. She blinked furiously, willing her eyes to carve through the gloom, but the figure didn't fade. She wasn't hallucinating. Even here, in the lowlight, drugged and dazed, anyone on Earth would have recognized that face carved from marble, those piercing eyes, that broad chest and golden hair.

Captain Dawn.

Jane didn't know what to do, whether to shout, cry, or pretend to be asleep. She wanted to run, hide, leap, touch, hug him, and shake his hand, but she couldn't. Oh God, she couldn't move at all, stuck here in this plaster, a human papier-mâché. *No. Not like this, please don't let him see me*, she pleaded. But as Captain Dawn moved closer, Jane was suddenly seized with panic that he wouldn't see her, that he'd pass her by, that she was going to miss her one and only chance. *Please let him see me*, she begged. But how could he miss her, she was the only one in the room, she stood out, it was humiliating, but she had to stand out . . .

He was only two beds away now. Her heart racing, her breath trembling, Jane squeezed her eyes shut, desperately pretending to be asleep. She didn't know what she was doing, but she couldn't move and she couldn't think.

For a few seconds, there was only silence, save for the thunderous beating of her heart. And then, from beyond the veil of her fiercely clenched eyelids, someone spoke.

"I know you're awake."

It was a quiet voice, low and softly spoken, but beneath it flowed a hum, this deep, resonating melody—the sound of sunlight washing over rocks. Slowly, tentatively, not daring to hope, Jane opened her eyes.

He was standing at the foot of her bed—a poster come to life, watching her with his hands behind his back, the white and gold of his uniform giving him an inhuman, almost spectral appearance in the darkness. But still real. Still standing there. Still talking. Talking to *her*.

She moved her mouth to speak, but nothing came out.

There was a surreal, billowing pause.

"Are you in pain?" he asked softly. Finally, Jane managed to find her voice.

"N-n-no," she croaked. Her hoarse throat burned around the syllable, but she uttered two more. "C-c-captain."

"Here." He moved around until he was alongside her head, almost beyond her field of view, the white of his suit so close she could almost touch it. There was the soft gurgle of trickling water and if Jane could have moved, she would have jumped. A second later, a golden glove appeared in front of her and something soft pressed on her lips. Cool water ran down her throat, soothing the burn. She coughed, spluttering.

"S-s-sorry," she whispered, but Captain Dawn said nothing, just pressed the cup again gently to her lips. This time she drank more, then greedily. Without a word, the man in white and gold refilled the cup from the pitcher on her nightstand and held it back in place.

"Thank you . . ." Jane murmured, when that cup, too, was empty. Her throat still hurt, and her stomach felt uneasy, but the dry cracks in her mouth were sated and the acidic burning fading in her throat. Captain Dawn merely nodded. He reached behind her head, and there was a soft clink of the cup atop the table, then before Jane could say anything, he simply walked the few steps back to the foot of her bed and stopped, looking down at her.

"Th-th-thank you," she stammered. Again, he just nodded, white and gold against the black, a man made of moonlight. Jane felt her face getting hot. *Say something, anything.* He probably thought she was a moron, the way she kept stuttering, the way she'd . . . Oh God, had she been rude? This was Captain Dawn, he was used to shaking hands with presidents and celebrities and she wasn't, she hadn't . . .

But if the captain was offended by Jane's actions, or if he could sense the panic rolling off her in waves, he didn't show it. He simply stood silently at the foot of her bed, watching her with a blank expression. Long, empty seconds stretched out between them, which Jane's drugged mind screamed at her to fill—but he didn't move or speak. Nor did he seem in any hurry to go. His eyes wandered over her and Jane could tell he was taking in the full extent of her cast.

"I lost," she said finally, stupidly—then regretted the words immediately after she'd said them. They sounded like an excuse, a pathetic excuse, and one that only made her look even weaker in front of the most powerful man in the world.

Dawn said nothing, letting the uncomfortable silence stretch out between them. Even in the cool dark, Jane felt her face growing hotter. A tight ball of shame flowered in her chest, and she found herself wishing she could turn away. She closed her eyes, unable to look at him.

"I . . . I'll leave in the morning," she said quietly. Saying those words, actually speaking them out loud, putting the promise into existence, hurt more than anything she'd had broken.

For a few seconds, the hero didn't respond. Then eventually, through her self-imposed darkness, she heard him ask, "Why?"

Jane hesitated.

"I . . . I lost . . ." She opened her eyes, and tentatively glanced up at him—still standing at the end of her bed. "I'm not strong enough."

"You lost to someone strong," said Captain Dawn. The deep melody of his voice sent shivers down her spine. "That does not make you weak."

Jane didn't know what to say. "But I . . ."

"It was a practice fight," Dawn said simply. His voice was calm and confident, without judgment or impatience, as if he was explaining to a newborn why the leaves danced on the wind. "There will be others.

Some you will win; some you will lose. But they are training. Nothing more."

He looked at her, head tilted very slightly to the side as if pondering some strange puzzle beyond the comprehension of ordinary men. Jane felt his eyes wander toward her bandaged face, to the part of her cheek that was by law left uncovered—already knowing what he was going to find. If she could have turned away, if she could have hidden her shame, she would have.

"I'm sorry," Jane whispered. She averted her eyes.

"Don't be," replied Captain Dawn, surprising her. She looked up at him, standing there at the foot of her bed, arms clasped behind his back, his expression impassive. "You have nothing to be ashamed of."

"I just thought . . ." murmured Jane, "it might . . ."

"Bring back memories?" said Captain Dawn. Even in the low light, she saw a shadow pass across his face, and for the first time his mouth twitched into something that could have been a smile. "My memories are my own. They are not for you to burden yourself with, young one. Nothing you can do or be can alter the past."

"I-I-I didn't mean . . ." she stammered—then stopped. Here, alone, with just them, there was no trace of animosity on his face. "You don't . . . hate me?"

"Why would I hate you?" he asked quietly, as if the question was strange.

"Because . . ." Jane struggled to find the words, not wanting to insult him by pointing out the obvious. Eventually, her medicated mind found them. "Because of . . . what I am . . ."

"You are strong," Captain Dawn said simply. "That is all that matters." And the way he looked at her, without the slightest trace of disapproval or disgust, made Jane believe it.

"I thought . . ." she started, then hesitated—unsure whether she was crossing some sort of line. But the captain made no move to stop her, so Jane pressed on. "I thought you would've hated"—her cheeks flushed—"after . . ."

"No," answered Dawn, saving her from spelling it out. He paused and his eyes grew distant. "I never hated empaths. I never even hated him, to tell you the truth. He was strong. So very, very strong." There was a detachment in the superhero's words, but not in a cold or disinterested way, as if he was speaking through a veil, floating, disconnected from reality. "So much power. So much potential. He was a great man—could have been, if he'd chosen a different path."

He stared off into the darkness for a moment, a ghost of white and gold. Jane marveled at the mourning in his voice. "He killed half a billion people," she reminded him.

"A terrible thing," Captain Dawn agreed. The detachment on his face seemed to fade and he looked back at her. "But one that only someone great could have wrought." He paused. "You do not have to condone an act to see the strength it requires. I respected the strength in him, as I respect the strength in you. You are strong, young one. In your body and your mind. Do not forget that."

A momentary warmth spread through Jane's chest. But then reality sunk back in, and she glanced down at her plastered body.

"I wasn't strong enough," she murmured, ashamed.

"You will be," Dawn said quietly. "Given training. Given time."

"How do you know?" Jane replied. Immediately, she regretted the pettiness, the self-pity in the question. But Captain Dawn remained undeterred, looking down at her as he did with piercing green eyes.

"You have conviction," he answered. "It has brought you this far and it will carry you further, if you allow it."

"I thought . . ." she started, then stopped. The captain raised an inquiring eyebrow, and Jane forced herself to continue. "I thought I was only here because of Matt."

"The clairvoyant?"

"Yes."

"His gift is indeed special," Dawn replied, and his gaze grew vague. "He will be an incredible asset." Then he caught Jane's onlooking eyes and seemed to refocus. "But he merely brought you to my attention. Your achievements, your strength, brought you here."

"Rest, young one." He turned, the gold cape billowing from his shoulders. "Tomorrow is a new day." And then he was gone, fading into the dark, leaving Jane alone, awake, immobilized and trembling.

One of the junior healers came by just after sunrise the next morning to cut Jane free and to check her for anything they'd missed.

"You shouldn't have any lasting injuries," the small, mousy-haired girl, whose name tag said "Editha" assured her, as she removed a thermometer from her white apron and stuck it, not ungently, under Jane's tongue. The reading came back normal. "How would you rate your pain, with one being nothing and ten being the worst pain you've ever experienced?"

"Zero," scowled Jane, who just wanted to get out of there. The small nurse raised an eyebrow, and Jane sighed. "Fine," she relented. "Three."

"I thought so. Lay down and let's see what we can feel here."

Grumbling, Jane rolled over onto her stomach. The healer pulled up Jane's nightshirt and laid her palms on the empath's bare back. "Don't you go taking my powers now." She chuckled, beginning to knead rhythmically into the muscle.

"I don't want your stupid powers," Jane muttered under her breath. But her head was buried into the pillow, so it was doubtful the mousy-haired woman heard. A few seconds later, she began to regret her defensiveness as a feeling of creeping warmth stole out from Editha's hands, melting away the painful bruised knots in Jane's back and shoulders like hot water pouring over ice.

"Arms, arms too," she murmured after a few minutes as the healer prepared to stop. "Arms sore." Even though she couldn't see her face, Jane could have sworn she felt the small woman smirk.

After about ten minutes, Editha had run over every part of Jane's body and evaporated practically all of her pain. "Thank you," conceded Jane, sitting up as she pulled on a new shirt in place of the hospital gown.

"You're welcome," replied the small healer with a knowing smile. Then her satisfaction momentarily wavered. "You . . . didn't actually copy my powers, did you?"

Jane sighed, not even able to muster the energy to be angry at her ignorance. "You'd know if I did."

"Oh," said the medic, smiling normally again. "Good. Just checking."

Dressed back into her normal sweater and jeans, which someone had been kind enough to bring down from her room, Jane made her way out of the infirmary alone, wandering back down the several flights of stairs to the ground level. On her way, she passed several other Acolytes, most of who hissed or swore at her as she walked by—but Jane tried to ignore them. *This was just another test*, she reminded herself, drawing from the conclusion she'd reached last night—another hurdle she had to clear to achieve her goal. If sticks and stones and broken bones couldn't make her leave the Academy, then she wouldn't let words and whispers do it.

She walked through the open doors to the Great Hall holding tightly to her new mindset. A hundred pairs of eyes turned to watch her enter, but nevertheless she continued forward. A quarter of the way up the right side of the room, she saw Matt sitting relatively alone reading a book that looked like it was about horses.

"You're alive," he said without any preamble, turning to look at her as she dropped into the empty space beside him.

"You sound surprised," Jane said shortly.

"You almost got beaten to death like, an hour after we spoke."

"Hour and a half."

"I thought you were going to die."

"Screw you."

"That wasn't an insult," said Matt, rolling his eyes. Jane didn't reply but just made some unintelligible noise somewhere between a grunt and a growl. She glanced around the room—the staring hadn't abated. Matt followed her gaze.

"Ignore them," he muttered, dismissing the onlookers with a wave of his hand.

"I am ignoring them," she snarled.

"Yes," he replied humorlessly. "I can see they're not getting to you at all." Jane crossed her arms and scowled, turning back to face the big sunny windows looking out onto the grounds. Behind her, she could hear the muttering intensifying, punctuated here and there by peals of laughter. She tried to focus on her breathing.

"I'm hungry," she spat after a moment's pause.

"Then get some food, you fool," said Matt, oddly tetchy.

"Screw you," she snapped again.

"You know, that loses some of its impact when you say it, like, every second sentence." They lapsed once more into silence. Finally, Matt looked up at her.

"Do you want *me* to get you some food?" he asked with only a touch of impatience.

"No. I'm fine," she replied, although she still didn't move from the bench.

"Yeah, but you're not eating," said Matt, waving a finger at the empty space on the table in front of her, in contrast to his own plate a few inches away. "You need to eat."

Jane glared at him. As much as she hated it, he was right. She needed to eat, at least to assist her recovery, let alone give her energy for whatever fresh hell she'd be subjected to today. After a few seconds, she stood up and began walking over to the front of the hall. She reached the buffet amid a sea of murmurs and chuckling, feeling every eye in the room drilling into the back of her head. Just ignore it. They didn't matter. She filled up a plate with beans and corn and walked back, breathing slowly. "Ach-loser!" someone behind her sneezed, and an entire table laughed. Just keep walking.

"I need to tell you something," Matt whispered the second she sat down, his horse book seemingly forgotten.

"What?" said Jane, not really listening. She glanced around the room, seeing too many smiles and nudges, too much chortling and whispering.

"It's about the other night. After the ice cream. I got back to my room and—"

Behind her, a commotion was building. There was indistinct calling, shouts of laughter—the wooden screech of the heavy bench being pushed back. Out of the corner of her eye, Jane saw a large shape rising. *Don't turn*, she reminded herself, *don't engage*.

But it was too late.

"LADIES AND GENTLEMEN!"

Even with her back to him, Jane knew that voice. Unable to help herself, she turned, following Matt's eyes as he stopped mid-sentence and turned to look at the front of the hall, where a gigantic dark-skinned man had risen from his table, staring straight at her—his face split into a malicious grin.

"LADIES AND GENTLEMEN, PLEASE!" Anybody else might have stood on the stage to make this announcement, but James Conrad already towered over the rest of the room. He stood, huge and grinning, a full foot above the heads of the smirking crowd around him—and then, as she watched, the strongman held up a glass and gently, with a butterknife squeezed almost comically between two massive fingers, tapped the side.

Ting, ting, ting. The room fell silent.

James's grin widened.

"Ladies and gentlemen," he repeated again, surveying the hall and everyone around him with a broad, sarcastic smile, "good morning." He paused. "Let me ask you a question. Who here knows the name Zephyr?"

A cheer went up around the room, punctuated by the sound of Acolytes whistling and banging their cups on the tables.

"How about the White Queen?" declared Conrad, and this time the cheer was louder, interspersed with scattered whooping. Jane saw Matt's brow furrow, but his skeptical expression went unnoticed among the commotion.

"Captain Dawn," said James, and this time the roar was almost deafening. All throughout the room Acolytes clamored to their feet, clapping, cheering, shouting indiscriminately into a storm of noise that sent a ringing in Jane's ears and a precarious rattling through the windows.

For a few moments, the strongman allowed the noise to continue, but eventually he again raised his massive, plate-sized hands. As if on cue, silence descended on the hall.

"Great names," James said solemnly, "given to great people, right here in this very room." He paused and bowed his head in a respect that vanished as soon he raised it. "Titles that captured the essence of who they were."

There was a smattering of more restrained applause, maybe from the minority of people who didn't get that this wasn't a tribute, and that that wasn't the punchline. James held up his hand and the clapping stopped.

"Giving names has always been a Legion tradition," he declared. "And it's one I'd like to continue." The strongman paused, and with a rush of cold dread Jane felt his eyes fix on her. "Ladies and gentlemen," James announced, raising a powerful fist above the crowd, "a new name! To our newest member!" He raised his hand toward Jane and the entire hall watched as he proclaimed: "Ladies and gentlemen, Acolytes and Ashes, I give you, fresh from her stay in hospital, our very own parasite: LEECH!"

His words rang out, and in an instant they were swallowed up as the entire room erupted, roaring with laughter. Jane's fists clenched in her lap.

The noise drowned out anything she or anyone could have said, but then James held up a lone finger, and the hall again fell silent. "Now, leech," he continued, speaking like a children's storyteller and grinning at the sea of shining faces watching merrily as he spoke, "thoroughly sucks." The hall rang with barks of laughter. "She only ever takes, and she's easily squished." The laughing intensified. "But still, she has one, undeniable talent." James's grin widened, and as the noise around him faded, he looked down at Jane and put a mocking hand over his heart. "And that's to make us thankful." The room fell silent and the strongman paused—then shook his head. "By reminding us all just how worthless we could've been."

"Hey, man—" Matt started to say, but his words were drowned out by James once again thrusting his glass into the air.

"TO LEECH!" he roared, and the hall was filled with shouting and laughter as a hundred Acolytes took up the toast. Jane's face burned, her jaw clenched in place. She could hear the blood rushing through her ears, feel her shoulders shaking. Her eyes never left James's. He smiled at her over the top of his glass and tilted it toward her in a small toast. It took everything she had not to leap up, not to charge him, not to fight right then and there. But that was what he wanted. He wanted her to get angry, to do something stupid. Her nails dug into her palms, the muscles in her hands starting to cramp. Just let it happen, she tried to think, *Just let it go. Just get it over with.*

"Now, James!" cried a new, shrill voice. Jane's head snapped around as its source—a raven-haired girl in her early twenties, as bony and pale as James was dark and meaty—rose to her feet at the other side of James's table. Dressed handsomely in a gray felt overcoat and skin-tight jeans, for a second Jane thought she might actually be getting up to defend her. Then she saw the wicked, sardonic smile on the girl's face, and the pit in her stomach dropped.

"Come now," said the newcomer, her voice refined and rich with sarcasm. She waved openly, one hand on her outstretched hip, a brown leather shoe leaning on the bench. This was a performance—Shakespeare in the park. "Don't be so quick to dismiss our new arrival!"

"Natalia Baroque." James smiled, gesturing to the new speaker. "I, of course, ceded the floor to the Legion's best psychic." The words left his lips with barely restrained glee. He glanced over at Natalia, and there was no doubt in anyone's mind that whatever this was, the two of them were in it together.

"Why, thank you, my dear James," Natalia crooned, and the crowd laughed as she turned to them. "Friends," she said, "come now. It would wrong of us to simply *dismiss* this"—she indicated at Jane—"admittedly mangy individual . . ." The room laughed. "As *completely* useless. Why, what she may lack physically, she may make up for with a cunning mind! What say you, fellow Acolytes? Should we test her, find out what she's made of?"

"YES!" came the roaring reply, which then broke down into squalls of pealing laughter—the loudest of it coming from the lackeys surrounding both the strongman and the psychic. Only a few people out of the hundreds there weren't laughing, including the girl who'd waved to her in the corridor on her first night, who seemed exasperated at the whole thing, and a freckly, curly-haired redhead in a Hawaiian shirt, who was staring off into space as if wishing he was somewhere else. Everyone else was up in arms, banging their cutlery on the table, grinning at her.

Natalia strode out and around the table into the middle of the room, beaming at Jane the whole time. "So, what do you say, darling? Care to see what you're worth? Care to test the mettle of your mind?"

"Jane," Matt whispered warningly, but the girl barely heard him. She only had eyes for that smug pale piece of trash and the garbage chanting behind her. Without even realizing it, she was on her feet. An *oooooooohhhh* went up from the crowd.

"Dear Acolytes, I think she accepts!" proclaimed Natalia.

"Go to hell."

The crowd laughed, but not with her. The psychic tutted.

"So rude, little empath," she said, shaking her head. "A terrible quality."

"Screw you all," Jane snarled. "I'm not letting you in my head."

Natalia smiled, bending low with and expression of mock disappointment. "Oh, but you misunderstand darling. It's just a game—we're all about games here." She turned to the room and the room rang back its resounding agreement. "See?" She smiled at her, showing sharp white teeth. "Just a bit of harmless fun."

"Jane," Matt warned again, louder this time, but Jane wasn't listening. She glared at Natalia, then up at James.

"Leave me alone."

"We'll leave you alone." James smirked, arms crossed. "Just pass this little test and I swear, hand on my heart, *nobody*"—he gestured around the hall, and there were shouts of agreement between fits of laughter— "will bother you ever again."

"Twenty seconds." Natalia smiled. She was tiny next to the rippling mountain of muscle that was James, but somehow that only made her look fiercer, less human. "No, fifteen. Ten. Keep me out for ten seconds, and you'll have earned yourself the respect and admiration"—she said the words with a grand, mocking wave—"of everyone here."

"A true Acolyte," assured James, grinning murder.

"Proved and proper," said Natalia, her dark eyes gleaming.

Jane hesitated. Instinct told her to run, that this was a trap, obviously a trap—but ten seconds? Ten lousy seconds and she'd beat them, ten seconds and she could get them all off her back? Ten seconds. How long was ten seconds? Not that long. All she had to do was clear her mind, hold her breath, endure, for ten measly seconds . . .

"Jane!" Matt cried, but she didn't hear him. She could do it. It was possible. Mental defense had never been her best subject, but if she just thought hard enough, if she concentrated, maybe she could . . .

"Okay," she muttered, and a cheer went out around the room. Natalia's smile widened.

"Okay." The psychic smiled, then her eyes narrowed and her fingers flew to her temple.

Instantly, Jane was gripped by searing, screaming pain. The world around her warped and wafted, twisting sight and smell and sound into a spinning river of silver shards slicing into her skull, burning through her brain. *I am . . .* she tried to think, tried desperately to hold on to, but before she could even finish creating the thought, it was gone, torn away, and she was falling, tumbling down through her memories, her subconscious, every hope and dream, fear and feeling . . .

She wasn't in her body. She wasn't anywhere. She was nothing . . .

She was falling . . .

She was screaming . . .

And then it stopped.

Jane coughed—weak, wet, and sick. She blinked sluggishly, her vision blurry, her head spinning. She was on the floor, cold wood and granules of dirt beneath her hands, beneath her knees. How had she . . .? Where was . . . why?

Her ears rang with delirium, and under that another sound, more distant, more real. Waves of echoing laughter, laughing at . . . at her. She tried to look up, struggled against the wavering dizziness, the rushing, and the ringing—saw a girl in front of her, white-skinned and black-haired, ivory-teethed and ebony-eyed. She was laughing most of all, throwing her sleek head back, grinning from ear to ear. Her vision wavered, the figure split into three—and behind her, high up and far away, the sigil of the Legion and the uniform of Dawn stared down in silent judgment.

The black man and white woman, matching pieces on a chessboard, were speaking.

"Oh . . . ladies and gentlemen . . . come now . . . that's just sad . . ."

Jane tried to focus, tried to force her mind back into place. She heard a small voice say her name, and through blurred eyes saw a familiar hand subtly offered to her right—but Jane snarled and pushed it lurchingly away. She didn't need . . . she tried to move, tried to place one unsteady foot on the ground, but her leg just wavered and wobbled, unable to support her weight.

"Poor little leech." Through the haze, Jane could still hear the psychic speaking, her words rolling through the hall. "It's a sad story really. My heart goes out to her. It really does . . ." Jane strained her neck, pulled her eyes up to see the psychic shaking her head in mock pity.

"Leech, whose middle name is Euphemia"—there was a wave of laughter—"and who slept with a teddy bear until she was fourteen"— more laughter—"has been to *seventeen* schools! At least she thinks she has—she's almost lost count!"

Natalia was turning around now, addressing the crowd of gleeful onlookers. "She has no friends, terrible grades, and—I'm sorry to say—a truly, *truly*, mediocre mind. I'm afraid, James, you might be right." She clicked her tongue in disapproval, then stopped and let out a peal of chortling laughter. "But that's not even the funniest part. You want to know the funniest part?"

The hall jeered. Natalia held her hand to her ear, where a diamond stud sat sparkling.

"I can't hear you," she said, all singsong. "I said, who wants to know the funniest part?!"

Another roar, even louder. Cups banged on tables, feet thumped on floor. So much noise. There was a pounding behind Jane's eyes. She felt like she was going to be sick.

"The funniest part," crowed the psychic, "the funniest part is that she misses her mommy."

Jane's heart clenched in her chest as a derisive "awwwwww" went up around the room.

"Yeah . . ." pouted the girl. "Misses her poor, dead mommy, every day, every night before she goes to sleep. Awwww . . .." Then her face hardened. "Poor woman probably killed herself for having such a useless freak for a daughter."

The room erupted into squalls of laughter, loud and cackling all around her. Blood pounded in Jane's ears. She tried to push herself up, her arms shaking, all strength from them gone. She looked up at the pretty, smiling little girl, and she had never hated anyone more in her life.

"I'll kill you," she whispered, but the girl only laughed.

"Careful, leech," she said with a sneer. "Or I'll make you mess yourself." Jane tried again to rise, only to fall forward again, trembling, onto her hands and knees. Another wave of laughter echoed around the room.

"Ladies and gentlemen, I think she wants some more!" Natalia laughed. Her eyes narrowed to slits and her fingers touched lightly to her temple. "All right then, little parasite. Let's see if we can't go even deeper this time," she whispered.

But then suddenly, a dark shape stepped in front of Jane—and someone else spoke.

"Come on," said a familiar voice. "That's enough."

Matt Callaghan stood, exasperated but resolute, his hands in his pockets, standing—almost passively—between the telepath and Jane.

But standing all the same. The psychic, Natalia Baroque, blinked and stared at Matt like he was crazy. Beside her, the hulking black man James, who up until now had been guffawing stupidly at the ongoing spectacle, glanced at Matt properly for the first time since he'd started this little charade. Matt saw a small shadow of doubt pass over his face.

Sneering, the psychic raised a finely plucked eyebrow.

"Excuse me?"

"Come on." Matt sighed. "She's had enough."

Natalia's head crooked to look at Jane, sweating, swaying, and trembling on the floor, then back at Matt.

"I . . . I think she could use a little more," she said with a smirk, sending a ripple of laughter around the room. Her voice carried the same high, condescending sarcasm that she'd used to speak to Jane and the inflection made Matt want to punch her face in. But he restrained himself and settled for giving the telepath a flat, bored grimace.

"Look," he said, "you got her good, clap-clap, congrats. But that's enough. Leave her be."

"Stay out of this kid," warned muscle-mania. Matt ignored him. Instead, he turned and bent down to help Jane.

"Come on," he whispered. "Let's get out of here." He wrapped an arm around Jane's waist.

"Well, well," Natalia drawled, her cold, imperious voice echoing at Matt from across the room. "Isn't this special. The parasite has a protector." Matt could feel her eyes burning into the back of his head. "Her own knight in shining armor."

Matt kept on ignoring them. With a grunt from both him and Jane, he hoisted the empath to her feet. To hell with the spectacle, he had to get Jane out of here before that woman got back in her head.

"Stop," commanded Natalia.

"Nope," countered Matt.

The psychic's eyes narrowed. "Stop right now, or I'll do to you what I did to her." A sudden hush fell over the hall. Matt's steps slowed to a halt. His grip around Jane loosened.

He was trapped. He couldn't let the psychic get Jane, because Jane knew what he really was—but if this woman broke into his mind, he was equally screwed. He could fight her, maybe, but even . . . even if he won, Matt realized and his stomach sunk, she'd be humiliated. He'd make an enemy of a psychic, and the last thing in the world Matt needed right now was an enemy who was a psychic. A really, really powerful psychic. Matt's swallowed hard, feeling his pulse starting to race.

Run and lose. Fight and lose. Win and lose. And there was no guarantee he could win. Maybe he could. He knew how. But he'd never had to resist a true psychic incursion before, and there were no guarantees— well, his overly correct brain reminded him, short of taking Psy-Block. But it was obviously too late now and besides the very idea was ludicrous, the drug was so ridiculously expensive . . . but at least then, Matt thought ruefully, he'd have been guaranteed to win . . . heck, the threat alone would've been enough to—

And suddenly, in a rush of inspiration, Matt had an idea. A risky, stupid, brilliant idea.

Suddenly, he had a plan.

Matt closed his eyes, took a deep, steadying breath . . . and turned to face Natalia.

"No," he replied. "I don't think you will."

A muttering raced around the room. Out of the corner of his eye, Matt saw Wally watching him, shaking his head, aghast. He ignored his silent warning.

Natalia eyes narrowed to slits, as if unsure whether Matt was joking or insane.

"What did you say to me?" she hissed.

Matt stared back at her, releasing Jane, leaving the empath to lean against one of the tables.

"I said," he repeated, "I don't think you will. In fact"—he took a step forward, his voice rising—"I know you won't." He smiled.

"Listen here, boy, I don't know who you think—" Natalia scowled.

"Oh, boy!" interrupted Matt, in his best impression of this little twat's posh English inflection. Retreat no longer an option, he went on the offensive. "Pish-posh, I do say, madam, oh, harrumph! Tally-ho and a bag of chips." The hall erupted in unexpected laughter. Natalia glanced around in shock, wide-eyed as these people, who had been right behind her a second ago, laughed at *her*. Matt smiled humorlessly and dropped the accent. "Give it up, Mary Poppins. Save yourself the embarrassment."

Natalia leered at him. "Are you an idiot? Do you know who you're talking to?"

"Do you?" He held out a hand to thin air—then twisted it and gave Natalia the finger. "I mean Winters shouted it out to you the other night, but maybe your head's so far up your ass you had trouble hearing. Matt Callaghan," he announced, loud enough for the whole room could hear, and then, with emphasis on every syllable: "Clairvoyant."

The hall fell silent. And twenty feet away, Matt saw the tiniest shadow of doubt flicker across the psychic's face.

"Big word, I know. More than four letters. You might not know it," Matt continued. "Means I see the future."

If looks could kill, Natalia's would've. "I don't care what you are," she snarled, "I can destroy you with a thought." But she didn't move.

"Big talk for a little girl," replied Matt. A vein twitched above Natalia's temple. "Come on then," Matt continued, before his opponent had a chance to speak. He raised an eyebrow. "Go ahead. Twenty bucks says you can't read what color underwear I'm wearing. Without peeking, you saucy minx," he added, sending a ripple of laughter around the room.

The psychic hesitated. Then her expression darkened.

"Fifty," she snapped.

"Two hundred," Matt drawled, rolling his eyes for effect. More gasps. Natalia's eyes bulged, and Matt smiled. "Or higher. I'll go as high as you want. You . . . do know you're betting against a seer, right?" he added with faux concern.

For a moment, the psychic just stared, frozen in place, her face blank.

"Come on, Princess Fussy-Britches," goaded Matt. "It's not like you can't afford it. Look at you, fancy coat and all, you've probably got the cash on you right now." The hall gave another peal of laughter. "Come on. Put your money where your mouth is." He held out his hand and gestured "come here" with his two fingers. "No time limit, no handicap, no nothing. It'll be easy. You can't lose. Who am I?" He spread his arms into a wide shrug at the rhetorical question. "I'm nobody. You're the 'Legion's best psychic,' apparently. There's no way you can lose. I mean, nothing's certain, but hey"—he paused, letting the words hang. A devious grin split over his face—"it's not like one of us can see the future."

His smile held as a murderous expression twisted over Natalia's powdered face—but still, the psychic didn't move. Matt's confidence, his unfounded enthusiasm in the face of Jane's dismantling, was making her hesitate. *What does he know that I don't?* Matt could almost hear her thinking. *Why is he doing this? Why is he so sure of himself?* And that unexplained confidence was triggering concerns and uncertainty, watering little seeds of doubt. Was he bluffing? But why would he bluff in front of all these people when she could so easily call him out? Unless it wasn't a bluff, unless there was something, unless he really could . . .

Over and over and over and over, round and round and round. Matt could practically see the conflict playing out on the psychic's face. He grinned to himself—he wasn't psychic, but he was already inside Natalia's head.

Around the hall, people were starting to call out, shouting for her to do it, egging Natalia on. People were laughing. Someone (possibly

Celeste) was making very genuine chicken noises. Matt watched as Natalia made up her mind, saw the risk of the unknown get outweighed by the looming threat of humiliation in front of her peers.

Exactly as Matt knew it would.

"Fine," hissed Natalia. One single solitary word. And in an instant, her eyes narrowed and her fingers flew to her temple.

But Matt was ready.

I-am-the-very-model-of-a-scientist-Salarian-I've-studied-creatures-Turian-Asari-and-Batarian-I'm-quite-good-at-genetics-as-a-subset-of-biology-because-I-am-an-expert-which-I-know-is-a-tautology-my-xenoscience-studies-range-from . . .

With a staggering crash, Matt felt the psychic's mind slam headfirst into his walls. He felt it but he did not notice it, for his mind was filled only with the same immutable verse, looping over and over again, singular, unassailable.

Urban-to-agrarian-I-am-the-very-model-of-a-scientist-Salarian-I-am-the-very-model-of-a-scientist-Salarian-I've-studied-creatures-Turian-Asari-and-Batarian-I'm-quite-good-at-genetics-as-a-subset-of-biology-because-I-am-an-expert-which . . .

He could feel Natalia pushing, scrabbling, raking mental talons against his barrier, searching for a way through, trying to find some hold or weakness. But every time she managed to pull a piece from the wall, it was so confusing, so bizarre, that the psychic momentarily stopped to examine it, to figure out what the hell she was looking at—by which time the breach had sealed. She was fast—but Matt was home.

I-know-is-a-tautology-my-xenoscience-studies-range-from-urban-to-agrarian-I-am-the-very-model-of-a-scientist-Salarian-I-am-the-very-model-of-a-scientist-Salarian-I've-studied-creatures-Turian-Asari-and-Batarian-I'm-quite-good . . .

Twenty seconds—thirty. Natalia was driving now, pushing against Matt's barrier with all her might, a thousand disparate thoughts—scenes of blood and murder, joy and sadness, Jane and the Legion, sex and sunshine—anything to distract him, anything that might make Matt take the bait and think, even for a moment, of something other than—

At-genetics-as-a-subset-of-biology-because-I-am-an-expert-which-I-know-is-a-tautology-my-xenoscience-studies-range-from-urban-to-

agrarian-I-am-the-very-model-of-a-scientist-Salarian-I-am-the-very-model-of-a-scientist . . .

She pulled back, and back in the real world, Matt could see the psychic panting, sweating, her face contorted with effort and rage. The Grand Hall was silent—every person there watching on with bated breath, blind to the titanic struggle taking place before them.

You'd be cuter if you wore girls' clothes, Matt chanced to think, and Natalia's mind roared and raced at him, straight into—

I-am-a-drystone-waller-all-day-I-drystone-wall-of-all-appalling-callings-drystone-walling's-worst-of-all-I-am-a-drystone-waller-all-day-I-drystone-wall-of-all-appalling-callings-drystone-walling's-worst-of-all-I-am-a-dry . . .

She was getting desperate now, trying to go under and around, trying to cut off Matt's senses from his brain. A clever trick. Most people tended to forget about their unconscious processes. Matt was not most people. He heard Natalia scream in frustration as telepathic blades reaching for the link between his eyes and eyesight met only—

Stone-waller-all-day-I-drystone-wall-of-all-appalling-callings-drystone-walling's-worst-of-all-I-am-a-drystone-waller-all-day-I-drystone-wall-of-all-appalling-callings-drystone-walling's-worst-of-all-I-am-a-drystone-waller . . .

Matt could feel her beginning to tire. Natalia was strong, phenomenally strong, but telepathy wasn't an endurance sport and endless concentration took its toll. She charged again, desperate, a wave of sensory input, slashing wildly, drilling into a dozen separate points. But this attack was scattered, weaker. Matt saw his chance and took it.

ALL-DAY-I-DRYSTONE-WALL-OF-ALL-APPALLING-CALLINGS-DRYSTONE-WALLING'S-WORST-OF-ALL-I-AM-A-DRYSTONE-WALLER-ALL-DAY-I-DRYSTONE-WALL-OF-ALL-LIFE'S-APPALLING-CALLINGS-DRYSTONE-WALLING . . .

Matt pushed out his walls, like forcing a huge breath of air he'd been holding out of his lungs, throwing back Natalia's scrabbling consciousness, a tiny buoy against a wave. The assault wavered, and in reality, Matt could see the apprehension and terror dawning on the psychic's face. He didn't know how long it had been—time flew in patches when you were moving at the speed of thought—but he could hear people muttering, whispering in disbelief at their psychic's beading sweat, pulsing veins and stony, locked-jaw silence.

Again, Natalia pushed, and again Matt threw her back, each assault weaker than the last. A slight raggedness was forming in Matt's chest, and he could feel himself starting to tire—but it was nothing compared to the telepath, who was drenched head-to-toe in perspiration, makeup blotching on her cheeks and thin muscles in her neck twitching irregularly. There was a pause—maybe thirty seconds where one eyed off the other and the other stood perfectly still, waiting. Suddenly, Natalia mentally charged again, but Matt's thoughts lunged, and he rebuffed her like backhanding a jumping cat, and the link between them broke.

The spell shattered. Natalia stumbled forward, her tension suddenly cut. She caught herself after a single step—but it was over. The psychic clutched her hands to her knees, doubled over, the noise of her panting, ragged breathing echoing, the only sound in the entire hall. She looked up at Matt, horrified—and afraid.

Matt smiled.

Without so much as a breath or a brow wipe, he crossed the floor, past the still struggling figure of Jane, over to where the psychic was standing, flanked by her crew of wide-eyed, dumbstruck lackeys—who, it pleased him immensely to see, recoiled ever so slightly at his approach. Even James the giant, with his biceps as thick as Matt's torso, took an almost imperceptible step back.

"Wow-wee," hollered Matt. He slapped Natalia genially on her felt-coated back, causing the psychic to stumble another step forward. "How're you feeling there Nat? Am I boxers or briefs? What's my date of birth?"

The psychic said nothing but just kept staring at the ground. Matt chuckled. "That's what I thought," he said coolly. "Well, a bet's a bet. Two hundred smackeroos, thank you very much." The room was dead quiet—Natalia looked up at Matt with an expression that was one part contempt, four parts afraid, and three parts despairing. Subtly, so no one else could see, Matt threw her a small wink. A frown creased the psychic's face. She gazed questioningly up at Matt and a small tendril of thought made its way across.

What are you?

Trust me, Matt extended, from behind the safety of his walls.

For a moment, Natalia just stared at him—then she withdrew the thought, straightened up, and slowly drew a black leather purse from the pocket of her coat. The hall seemed to hold its breath as she thumbed out ten twenties and passed them silently across.

"Eight, nine, ten," Matt counted under his breath, before pulling out his own wallet and slipping the money inside. "Well done." He looked up and flashed Natalia a smile. The edge of her mind reconnected.

Ask me what I am.

"What are you?" Natalia asked.

"Oh, nothing special." Matt shrugged, grinning at her but speaking to the amassed crowd. "But I am on Psy-Block."

A collective groan went up around the room. Natalia's stunned face blanched, and across the hall Wally Cykes burst out laughing. After a few seconds, James joined him.

"Goddamn it." He chuckled in his deep, booming baritone. He lumbered the two steps beside Natalia and wrapped an enormous hand around her shoulders, shaking the psychic playfully. "You idiot, I was actually worried." He laughed again, and this time most of the people around him joined in. Natalia on the other hand, didn't say anything. She merely looked up at Matt, her face frozen in an expression of confusion and disbelief. *Catch on*, Matt begged.

Their silent exchange went unnoticed by everyone around them, most of whom were shaking their heads in various levels of amusement and returning to their breakfasts. An odd few here and there shot Matt dirty looks but more grinned at him, and a lot of the seniors the psychic had been sitting with were chuckling. Over in the corner, Wally was still laughing hysterically.

"Goddamn Psy-Block," guffawed James, alternating grinning between Matt and the still-slumped Natalia, her hair hanging over her face in loose, disheveled bangs. Matt was quietly glad he found the idea so funny, as opposed to being angry that Matt had "cheated" his friend.

"Hey, I said I'd win," said Matt, throwing up an artificial smirk. "I didn't say why." He clasped Natalia hard on the shoulder, who flinched at his touch. "Pro tip, don't bet against a clairvoyant."

"You're all right, kid." The big man chuckled and held out a gigantic, plate-sized, sausage-fingered hand. "James Conrad. We weren't properly introduced."

"Matt Callaghan," replied Matt, who shook it. "Pleasure."

"Come on, smartass." James grinned. "Let's get some food." He swung his massive shoulders around, still shaking his head merrily at Natalia. "Stop pouting, Nat, no one likes a sore loser."

James started walking away, and Matt followed close behind. As they went, he glanced back at the psychic, who was still standing in the same place, watching Matt go—her face kept blank, a mask to hide her confusion, as the gears slowly turned inside her mind. The shame and animosity that had been there before had vanished, replaced by a slow, subtle creep of understanding, gratitude . . . and maybe still a little fear.

Matt loaded up a plate and sat down among the seniors. "It was actually pretty amazing," he assured them between bites. "I could feel her pushing." He spared a glance at Natalia. *Take heed*, he thought, *and appreciate what I'm doing.* "Didn't even know that was possible, to be honest. She's incredibly strong."

As he spoke, he saw Jane slinking from the hall, unsteady and unnoticed. Matt bit into a slice of orange, watching her leave.

"Leave it to Baroque," said Ed, "to find the one person in the Academy on Psy-Block and try to ream them. Well, besides Captain Dawn," he added, seemingly unable to ignore the technicality.

They were sitting in Ed's favorite computer lab a few hours later, chowing down on a pile of chocolate bars Matt had bought from the vending machine with some of his two hundred dollars, watching on the projector as Ed dominated online *Halo*.

"Yup," muttered Matt, biting into a Kit Kat. "Heads up, rocko."

"I've got him," assured Ed, snapping the blue soldier with the rocket launcher with several clean pistol shots to the forehead. "Wish I could've seen it."

"Start coming to breakfast then."

"Nah." He shifted a little, uncomfortable. "Too many people."

"Wasn't much to see really. Me and her standing there looking at each other for a minute or two."

"I heard closer to ten," said Ed.

"Huh," replied Matt, "didn't feel that long."

They watched in silence for a few minutes while Ed rode around in a ghost on a virtual killing spree.

"Why are you on Psy-Block though?" Ed eventually asked him. "How can you afford it? I thought nobody beside the president and CEOs took it. It's a thousand dollars a pill."

Matt hesitated. "Can you keep a secret?"

Ed head-shotted two enemies with one bullet. "Sure."

"Promise?"

"Yes, promise. I swear on my life."

"I'm not on Psy-Block."

Ed spun around to look at him, so shocked he let a blue player with a plasma pistol take down his entire shield before he regained his senses and no-scoped him.

"You're not on Psy-Block?" Ed whispered. He put down the controller, looking at Matt in disbelief—his team had won.

"Nope," said Matt, not meeting his gaze. He unwrapped another Kit Kat. "Obviously not. Like you said, it's a thousand dollars a pop. Where am I going to get that kind of money?"

"Then what was this morning?"

Matt shrugged. "I genuinely held her off."

Ed swore in disbelief.

"Language," chided Matt. "You're a senior, you're supposed to be setting a good example for us impressionable younglings."

"You kept her out? Just you?!"

"Yup," replied Matt. He snapped the chocolate bar between his fingers. "Wasn't easy. But I'm good at that kind of thing. It was all me."

"Then why did you say you were taking Psy-Block?" said Ed, shaking his head, incredulous. "This is incredible, people should know . . . everyone only thinks you won because you cheated!"

"You're the genius," said Matt, staring at the match stats on the projector screen. "You tell me."

They sat in silence—Matt eating chocolate, Ed just sitting in his desk chair, eyes unfocused, the game forgotten. After a few seconds, Matt decided to spare him the hassle.

"If I'd won straight out, then two things would've happened. First, Natalia would've been humiliated."

"You say that like it's a bad thing," Ed muttered. Matt ignored him. The psychic may have been arrogant, but the genius was missing the point.

"Natalia would've been humiliated," he repeated. "And chomping at the bit for a rematch, every single day, to try and prove to everyone who saw her lose that she's better than some freshman. God knows, she might even try to start something one day when I'm not ready for her— she didn't seem that fussed by Jane's dubious consent."

He paused. "Second, I'd become some bar every psychic in here would be clambering to climb over, some test to pass. I don't need that. Between them and Natalia . . . having to be looking over my shoulder, watching out for an attack, every single day? Nuh-uh. No thanks." He neglected to mention why exactly having psychics continually trying to get inside his head was of particular concern.

Ed looked on dumbfounded. "But Nat must know," he said. "Surely, she must realize you were lying."

"Oh, she knows," Matt assured him. He reached over and lifted the controller from Ed's lap. "That's the point. She knows I won fair and square and she knows I can beat her. But more than that"—he voted to veto the map—"she knows my little lie's the only reason she's not humili-ated in front of the whole Academy. So not only does she, the 'Legion's best psychic,' owe me a big old-fashioned favor, not only do I have her on side for the next, God-knows-how-many years I'm here, but she knows that if she messes with me, at any point . . . Damnit," he muttered, dying to a banshee, "I spill the beans."

Ed was silent. "Jesus," he said eventually, "that's really . . ."

"Smart."

"I was going to say diabolical."

"I'm a clairvoyant, man," said Matt, sticking a digital grenade to an enemy's back. "Planning ahead is the name of the game. Future plays, Eddy, future plays." Matt paused, and his eyes narrowed slightly. "Besides, after what she did to Jane, I don't mind her walking around a little scared."

"Did you see where she went?"

"No," said Matt, and unseen by Ed, his face darkened.

The genius paused. "She's interesting," he said quietly. Matt didn't turn around.

"Yeah?"

"Well, not her personally. But what she represents." Ed glanced over at him, a peculiar look on his face. "You know why she's here, right?"

"To make my life difficult," Matt muttered with little sarcasm. Ed brushed the joke aside.

"Isn't it obvious?" the genius said. "She's Dawn's insurance policy. Last time, an empath decimated the Legion." He paused and his gaze grew distant. "Next time, we'll have one on our side."

Matt didn't know how to respond. He hadn't thought of that. Eventually, Ed just shook his head and turned back to his computer.

"Well, anyway, I'm sure she's grateful—you standing up for her like that."

"Yeah, well," Matt muttered, "I don't think you know Jane."

Knock, knock, knock.

The hollow sound of a fist rapping on wood caused Jane to start. She glanced up at the door to her room but made no move to answer.

Knock, knock, knock.

"Jane, it's me, open up."

Even through the soundproofing, Jane recognized Matt's voice. She scowled to herself, then pushed unsteadily off the ground where she'd been sitting, staggering slightly as the nausea came rushing back up to meet her. Her clammy hand clasped the cool wall for support.

Goddamn psychics.

Knock, knock, knock.

"Jane, I know you're in there, open the damn door!"

"I'm coming!" she snarled. She crossed the length of the small room uneasily. Her legs were still jelly, threatening to give out with every deliberate step, even now, an hour and a half later. Her hand found the handle, and she opened the door to reveal Matt standing there alone, his face inscrutably blank.

"What?" Jane snapped, but she'd barely got the words out before the boy pushed past her into the room, his shoulder bumping her into the wall. For a moment, Jane just stood there, staring at the back of his head, stunned by the physical contact. Any other time, anyone else, she would have reacted, pushed back—but Jane was still drained and groggy from the mind-jacking. And Matt had never laid a finger on her before.

"Close the door," Matt muttered. He stopped in the center of the room and turned around to face her. His face was still completely blank. Jane paused for a moment, then silently did as he asked.

The second the latch caught shut, Matt exploded.

"What were you thinking?!" he shouted, his composure dropped, replaced by an expression of mangled fury. The sudden change caught Jane by surprise. She recoiled slightly, still leaning on the wall for support.

"What are you talking about?" she demanded.

"What am I talking about?!" Matt cried, throwing up his hands in disbelief. "Are you dense?"

"Screw you," Jane snarled.

"Oh no, no, no," Matt snarled back, his teeth bared. "No, screw *you*. I trusted you—I trusted you, and you go and get into a pissing match *with a psychic!*"

Jane felt the blood rushing to her cheeks at the accusation in his voice. "So?"

"So?" cried Matt. "SO? Why did you let her into your head? Are you insane?"

"I was trying to get them to leave me alone!"

"Oh, good job!" Matt sneered, shaking his head and slapping his hands together in a mocking clap. "No, good work, well done. I'm sure they're real scared of you now, you sure showed them!"

"I didn't know she was that strong!" shouted Jane, her own temper beginning to fray.

"SHE'S A PSYCHIC IN THE LEGION!" Matt roared, and for an instant Jane thought he was actually going to hit her—but instead Matt stopped and took a deep, shuddering breath, his eyes clenched shut, silently working his jaw.

"Why do you even care?" Jane snapped before he could gather his words. "It worked out fine for you!"

Matt looked at her, shaking his head in disbelief. "You. Let. Her. In. Your. Head," he whispered.

"I didn't let her anywhere, she—"

"You let her in your head," Matt repeated, his voice low and menacing. "Your head, which contains *my secret!*"

A horrible silence filled the room. Understanding, and the implications that flowed with it, rushed over Jane.

"Your secret," she said quietly.

"Yes, you absolute, unbelievable moron," he growled. "My secret, which I told you, in confidence, which you assured me you wouldn't tell anybody or, I don't know"—his voice rose—"go around throwing yourself at psychics!"

"Oh, I'm so sorry!" yelled Jane, coming off the wall, taking a step toward him. "I'm so sorry I stood up for myself. I'm so sorry I'm trying to survive this place without thinking about how it could affect *you*!"

"Stood up for yourself?!" Matt cried. "You got baited! I warned you, I"—he swore—"warned you, and you went right ahead, because you're a *big girl*, and you've got to show all those *mean bullies* how tough you are, don't you?!"

"What did you want me to do?" she roared in his face.

"WALK AWAY!" he shouted back. "IGNORE THEM! Say 'no, Miss Psychic, I'm not going to fall for your obvious trap . . . I'm going to leave now, go sit on a cactus'!"

"I'm sorry I didn't just take it laying down!"

"You were laying down!" Matt cried. "You were drooling on the goddamn floor!" He threw up his hands. "Are you stupid?! Didn't you think, for one second: Hey, this is one of the most powerful psychics in the world. She's probably pretty good at reading minds! I can't mentally defend myself, like, at all, maybe challenging her is a bad idea! Or do you just not care? Do you not care if I get found out, if I get carted off and cut up for science? Is that it? Are you holding a grudge, have I done something to *wrong you* that I don't know about?"

"She didn't find out!" Jane snarled through clenched teeth.

"But she could have!" replied Matt. "She was right there, in your head, with free reign! You're lucky she stopped when she did—but oh, wait, no, because you were going back for more! If I hadn't stepped in and saved you—"

"Saved me?" Jane cried, not believing her ears.

"Yes, saved you!" shouted Matt. "You remember that; you remember that part, where I had to put *my* ass on the line?"

"I never asked for your help!" she roared.

"Well, you sure needed it!"

"I DON'T NEED ANYTHING!"

"Right!" cried Matt. "No, sorry, clearly, you were all good. You had it under control." He threw up his hands despairingly. "God forbid, I am such a jerk. Really, I should have just done the humane thing and let them keep torturing you." He shook his head, staring at her. "What is wrong with you?"

"What's wrong with me?" Jane started to shout. "I'm not the one with no—"

But before she could say another word Matt slammed into her, his hand over her mouth.

"I swear to God," he snarled. "If you yell it, I will punch you as hard as I can."

Jane's eyes burned. She tore Matt's hand away and shoved him back hard toward the door. "Don't touch me," she hissed.

"Then keep your mouth shut," he snapped.

"I could kill you with one hand tied behind my back," Jane swore.

"I know." Matt glared. "But then they'll kick you out of your precious Legion."

"Go to hell."

"Make me."

"Don't ever touch me again," she told him.

"Don't ever endanger my family," Matt snarled back.

Jane threw up her hands. "Your family?" she cried incredulously. "What the hell did I ever do to your family?"

"If I get found out," he growled, "they'll want my genes. Which means they'll want their genes. Which you would realize if you spent two seconds actually thinking instead of going around picking fights with everyone you met!"

For a second, there was only silence.

"Get out," Jane finally whispered. She shoved him back further. "Get out, go be with your new friends who think you're so clever and cool."

"My . . .? You know what?" Matt cried incredulously, letting himself be pushed out into the hallway. "Maybe I will! Maybe it'd be nice to hang around someone who's not a COMPLETE AND TOTAL PSYCHOPATH!"

"Go to hell," Jane swore again, and slammed the door in his face.

FLYING HIGH

"The Effects of Mood and Mind-Altering Substances
on Superhuman Abilities"
Extract, Transcript, Congressional Hearing, August 1974

Committee: Senator Arthur Conway (R)
Conway: . . . the impact of alcohol . . . remains one of the biggest concerns to this investigation, especially in light of the number of lives lost and the scale of property damage during the period after the Aurora Nirvanas—

Floor: Professor Jeffery Morrison
Morrison: You are referring to the "Year of Chaos"?
Conway: I believe that's the colloquial term, yes.
Morrison: That period was an outlier in terms of superhuman history—the world had changed, everyone was still coming to terms with it. I would attribute the death and destruction to instability, coupled with a certain degree of ignorance that I believe is no longer applicable.
Conway: And what makes you so certain?
Morrison: Well, Senator, at the risk of invoking slightly . . . Darwinian theories . . .
Conway: We're all adults, Professor, there's no need to be coy.
Morrison: Yes, Senator, well, to put not too fine a point on it, during the Year of Chaos many less . . . thoughtful citizens, finding themselves endowed with superpowers, engaged in, shall we say, less than intelligent behavior. [Pause for gallery laughter] This, coupled with the high rates of capital punishment our—at the time—woefully unequipped justice system

was forced to doll out, seems to have somewhat "pruned the tree," evolutionarily speaking.

Conway: You're saying we've gotten smarter?

Morrison: Not individually no, but as a society yes. Through the efforts of those with less foresight in removing themselves from the gene pool. [Pause for gallery laughter]

Committee: Congresswoman Ruth Fines (D)

Fines: As fascinating as that may be, Professor Morrison, it does not answer the question of whether the emergency restrictions placed by Congress on intoxicants should continue. Notwithstanding the fierce opposition these prohibitions have invoked from our constituents—

Conway: [Laughing] I've never seen them so united in my life—who knew all we needed to do was ban beer? [Pause for gallery laughter]

Fines: Yes, thank you, Senator Conway. The near-universal opposition notwithstanding, the question remains: Is it safe for we, a superhuman society, to allow the sale of mind-altering chemicals?

Floor: Professor Elizabeth Tsang

Tsang: I believe I can answer that, Congresswoman.

Fines: Professor Tsang, please.

Tsang: [Pause for arrangement of notes] Although research into the exact mechanisms behind superhuman abilities remains in its infancy, one thing our tests have concluded is the direct causal link between activation and sentient consciousness."

Fines: In layman's terms, Professor Tsang.

Tsang: In layman's terms, Congresswoman, our powers are linked to our thoughts—our clear and conscious thoughts, not our reactions or unconscious urges.

Fines: Continue.

Tsang: It's why you never hear of a pyromancer burning down their house when they have a bad dream, or someone with superstrength breaking their bed while they sleep—they lack the conscious thought which our tests have shown our powers need to activate. Indeed, there are some individuals born with severe mental handicaps or trapped in persistent vegetative comas who have never demonstrated any kind of ability, although we believe the potential is still there, genetically.

Conway: What does this have to do with drink and drugs?

Tsang: Everything, Senator. If abilities require a clear and conscious mind, then substances that impair clear thinking impair those abilities. Essentially, an individual's level of intoxication is inversely proportional to the accessibility of their powers.

Committee: Senator Julianne Lowe (R)

Lowe: So you're suggesting the ban be lifted?

Floor: Mr. Martin Weltman

Weltman: If I may, Senator. The Treasury Review Commission has, in conjunction with the research provided by Professors Morrison and Tsang and their associates, analyzed the available data and concluded that the sale of alcohol is feasible, provided those sales attach sufficient duties to pay for increased insurance premiums, police, and public works programs.

Conway: Taxes?

Weltman: Excises, yes, both to moderate consumption through economic forces and to fund the state's ability to cope with the inevitable . . . incidents.

Fines: What about marijuana?

Lowe: Tell me we're not seriously considering this.

Tsang: Actually, Senator, all our tests have demonstrated that marijuana poses a significantly lower risk in terms of aggressive or antisocial behavior. Even putting aside THC's generally positive mood-altering affects, the drug also seems to weaken concentration to the point where the danger posed by a user's powers is essentially negligible. In our assessment, alcohol poses a substantially greater risk.

Weltman: Sale of regulated marijuana to adults, with proper oversight, could provide a significant source of state revenue at it would seem very little public cost.

Fines: Interesting. Could be hard to get through Congress.

Conway: At least it might provide a silver lining for the overpriced beer.

Matt didn't see Jane for the rest of the week. He didn't know if she was avoiding him or if she was busy training and to be honest, if it wasn't for the fact that she was walking around with his secret in her head, he wouldn't have cared. But the continued liability she and her pride posed meant he had to, somewhat ruefully, keep tabs on her. At least, that's how it was initially. By the time the weekend came around, Matt's anger at Jane over the whole psychic situation had burned out, and he began to view her continued absence as something of a shame.

While it might have been a stretch to say he *enjoyed* Jane's company, she was at least vaguely interesting to be around—and, as the days dragged by, Matt realized with some annoyance that somehow, unintentionally, the girl had managed to invoke in him a sense of begrudging loyalty. Perhaps it was their shared secret or simply that, out of all the strangers here, he'd known her first. Maybe it was finder's sympathy, like one might feel if they had been walking along one day and come across a particularly lost and stupid goat. Realistically, Matt knew he should ignore her and concentrate on getting expelled, but since his day-to-day life at Morningstar was completely devoid of structure, the (perhaps boredom-induced) loyalty just sort of . . . lingered.

Although Matt was now determined to get kicked out of the Academy, the best method for this proved elusive. He tried showing up late to class, then drunk to class, then not showing up to class at all, then not showing up to all his classes. Nothing worked. There were no warning letters, no penalties, no strikes or suspensions—all he got were ad hoc meetings with Daniel Winters and Hillary Cross, who encouraged him, in alternating levels of hostility, to be more studious. Sure, whispers were now going around that Matt was some kind of rogue maverick clairvoyant who kicked ass, saw the future, and played by nobody's rules, but that wasn't actually helpful because Matt didn't want people to think he was cool—he wanted to be expelled.

Another problem was that without classes, Matt simply had nothing to do. He had no homework, no assignments, no chores, no job to work at, no family to care for, no idiot friends to protect. Even his twice-daily mental exercises—and thank God for those—no longer served as time sinks since Matt had started doing them during his daily meditation with Selwyn, which he continued so as not to appear intentionally delinquent, figuring that if he was going to be sitting doing nothing with his eyes closed anyway, he may as well make the most of it. So that had killed two birds with one stone, but now his metaphorical life-bush was overflowing with time worms and he had no task birds left to eat them all. Even playing video games with Ed, who was fast becoming his main companion, got old after a while—and besides, the genius actually had work he was supposed to be doing. There were only so many hours in a day and so many days in a week that Matt could spend eating, gaming, browsing the Internet, or watching other Acolytes do things before he started to lose his mind.

On the upside, Matt's shenanigans in the Grand Hall with Psy-Block had worked about as well as he could've hoped. While there was still the odd malcontent who liked to grumble that Matt had cheated Natalia, most Acolytes seemed to appreciate the humor of his victory, and suddenly Matt found himself not only known but liked. He was hailed in the corridors, chatted with in the hall, and invited to watch the various training exercises open for viewing, all of which Matt seized upon to pass his vast swathes of free time. Wally, in particular, soon became something of a friendly acquaintance, regularly inviting Matt to join him and the other seniors at their table (which Matt understood was some kind of unofficial honor) and staying to chat and exchange stories long after everyone else had gone.

A perpetually relaxed and easygoing guy, Walter Cykes, the Legion's "second-best psychic," was as different from his first psychic "superior" as his unruly curls and never-ending parade of Hawaiian shirts was to Natalia's overgroomed locks and Milan-fashion-week wardrobe. Wally was a happy, laughing daydreamer who didn't seem all that interested in training, or really doing much other than lounging around and shooting the breeze. The fact that he was even at the Academy, let alone their "second-best psychic," was to Matt a continual source of surprise.

"Eh, I do what I do," Wally replied disinterestedly whenever Matt broached the subject. Slowly, Matt began to suspect that the redheaded psychic might be something of a prodigy, harboring phenomenal natural power—which would have been disconcerting had the short freckly carrot top been anybody else, but as it was it just made Wally's nonchalance even more endearing.

Wally's company, and Matt's presence at the seniors' table, also brought him into repeated contact with Giselle—something Matt had initially been excited about, but which had quickly developed into a slightly disheartening realization. Based off their first few interactions—where Giselle had smiled at him, laughed at his jokes, and touched his arm occasionally with her flawless, delicate hands—Matt had thought that maybe the gorgeous speedster girl had a thing for him. But that notion quickly dissipated once Matt realized that Giselle wasn't being especially nice to him but was just especially nice. She was always laughing, always smiling, hugging girls, and complimenting boys—an irrepressible ray of light and optimism universally beloved and blindly crushed on (by conservative estimates) by at least two-thirds of the Acolytes.

It was little wonder, Matt realized, as he watched her blur around the hall one morning with a plate in each hand. Giselle had everything: looks, talent, intelligence, success, great clothes. Of course, she was nice to everyone; she'd never been treated any differently. *What a terrible quality*, he mused sarcastically—although it did ironically make it almost impossible to tell if she genuinely liked someone, either romantically or otherwise.

This paradox seemed particularly lost on James Conrad, who Matt quickly figured out was something of the big man on campus, in several senses of the term. James, according to the gossip-loving Wally, had been amorously pursuing Giselle Pixus to no avail for years, and, it seemed, without ever taking the hint. Not that James himself was lacking in feminine attention—any man who spent several hours a day lifting impossibly heavy weights would always have admirers. And he wasn't a complete meat-headed gorilla, either, Matt came to realize—the strongman had a brain between his ears, and it functioned, although perhaps not as exceptionally as every other muscle in his body. Matt still bore him some lingering resentment over him putting Jane in the hospital, but the longer he observed the black colossus in action, the less he thought that his violence in the arena was necessarily indicative of his true personality. James, he learned, was an only child, and pushed hard by his parents from early on—a recipe that, combined with good genetics and raw talent, meant he had pretty much always been destined to star in either the Legion or the Olympics. He wasn't a bad person, Matt thought, just someone with a lot of gifts who'd spent their entire life being very gifted.

But all his new friends had their own lives, and as much as Matt enjoyed spending time with them, in the end it wasn't enough. So, Matt increasingly found himself—once he'd prepared for the next biweekly clairvoyancy test—wandering aimlessly through Morningstar's grounds and the surrounding countryside.

"I need a hobby," he complained to Ed one night over *Super Smash Brothers* and bowls of spaghetti Bolognese. He pressed clumsily at the jump button with his left hand while his right operated the fork—the fact that Ed was going to carry their partnership both predetermined and completely beyond Matt's control.

"You could start doing peoples' futures again," Ed suggested without looking over. He called down a well-timed thunder and blasted both level nine enemies off the screen.

"Nah," replied Matt. He slurped a particularly saucy string of spaghetti before guiding the subject away from his "clairvoyancy." "I was thinking like woodwork."

"Woodwork?"

"Yeah, man, make a cool chair or something."

Ed's polite silence told him all he needed to know about that idea.

"I'm just spit balling," Matt grumbled. He looked over at the genius. "What do you do in your spare time?"

"Uh . . . play games?" said Ed, doing exactly that.

"Well, all right, what do you do when you're not playing games then."

"I have . . . projects," Ed confessed reluctantly. Up until now, he had been very coy about discussing his work. Matt had never pressed him on it, but it did pique his curiosity.

"Projects."

"Yeah. Projects."

"Anything cool? Anything I can help with?" asked Matt, trying not to sound too desperate.

Ed shifted uncomfortably, obviously reluctant to give an outright no. "I don't know, it's all kind of . . . you know, sitting in front of a computer . . . you don't really want to . . ." He trailed off.

"Come on, man, there must be something."

"Well . . . I mean . . . do you know much about gene sequencing?"

"I probably know how to spell it?"

Ed grimaced. "Sorry."

Matt sighed. "It's all right," he conceded. "I get it. Genius stuff."

"Genius stuff," Ed confirmed, his eyes back on the screen.

The highlight of Matt's weeks were the calls from his family—hearing Sarah talk about her day, listening to his parents worry about him, having Jonas begrudgingly forced to share more than monosyllabic grunts.

They'd made noises initially about using a psychic to facilitate a group long-distance mind-call, but Matt for obvious reasons had waved that suggestion away, so they'd just stuck to phone. After about the first week though, these calls started to drop in frequency; the novelty of him being away obviously starting to wear off, especially considering he never had any news. His Northridge friends, too, were becoming more sporadic in their communications. For the first few days, they'd texted frequently. But as their lives began filling with assessments, exams, and drama he was no longer a part of, their replies began to shorten and slow. Matt couldn't really blame them—it must have been pretty boring repeatedly hearing how he was sitting around essentially twiddling his thumbs.

Maybe I should take up substance abuse, Matt thought half-heartedly, lying on his bed that Friday night, shooting aimlessly in *Bubble Spinner*. He'd heard good things about drug addiction. Well, not *good* things, but definitely *things*. It sounded like a very involving hobby that could definitely get you expelled. He sighed as his game ended not even remotely close to his high score.

God, he needed a drink. He flicked idly over to Taylor's latest update on the house party on Saturday that was supposedly going to be wild—a message Matt had been thus far too bummed at his own lack of parties to respond to. As far as college dorms went, this place was ridiculously tame. Nobody partied at Morningstar.

Suddenly, alone in his room, Matt's eyes widened, and he sat bolt upright.

Wait a minute, he thought, *that was it—nobody partied at Morningstar*. Nobody partied at Morningstar *yet*.

Alone in his room, with a burst of inspiration, Matt realized he'd been going about his delinquency all wrong. His actions weren't "bad" enough on their own to justify expulsion, because a "bad" person could be overlooked—but a bad influence, bringing down the whole team, corrupting those around them, weakening the entire Academy . . .

Matt leaped out of bed, snatched up a towel and raced into the shower for a quick wash and to remove his two-day-old stubble, emerging five minutes later clean, clear, and feeling fresh. He pulled on his best jeans and coolest T-shirt, then ran out of the door and down the hallway, dialing the number of a very particular someone.

Will met him in the foyer.

"So, where do you need to go?" the teleporter asked without any fore-play. They walked out the large wooden front doors side by side and into the brisk dusk air of the grounds.

"Right here," Matt replied, showing him a long-saved message on his phone as they strode purposely through the freshly cut grass. "Is that going to be a problem?"

Will gazed at the coordinates. "Shouldn't be. My paperwork's in order." He scrunched up his face as if performing mental calculations. "Yeah. I got it. No sweat."

"Awesome," said Matt, trying to suppress a grin. "Five bucks all right?"

"Heck, man, I've got nothing else on, you know I'll do it for free. Sorta my job."

"Shh-shh-shh-shh-shh," shushed Matt, cupping the other man's cheek with one hand and placing a crisp fiver in his pocket with the other. "Don't fight it."

"I'm not," Will said with a laugh, pushing Matt's hand away. Then he added, "You know your neck's bleeding, right?"

"Oh, for crying out—" Matt grumbled, dabbing at where Will was pointing and pulling his fingertips away to view the small speckle of blood. "Razors. Remind me to get some better razors."

They'd reached the edge of the forest, which marked approximately where Morningstar's Disruptance™ Anti-Teleportation security extended to. Matt gripped Will's arm.

"And a one-two-three," Will whistled. There was a lurch, rush-ing darkness and pressure all around them. After a second or two, it stopped, and Matt opened his eyes to find them standing in the middle of a cobblestone street full of single-story, brightly colored, slightly run-down houses.

"Wow that was . . . really fast," said Matt, looking around in mild amazement at exactly where he'd wanted to go. The teleporters at North-ridge had always taken at least ten minutes to line up a long-distance jump and—even then—had routinely ended up a mile off target.

"What do you think I practice all day?" Will chuckled, not even sweating. He glanced up at the open doorway in front of them and the neon blue lettering above it, seemingly unfazed by the smell of rotten eggs which for some reason always accompanied teleportation.

"*Licorería?*" he read aloud with a slightly derisive snort, seemingly unimpressed by the second flickering "r" in the sign. "Matt, why are we at a Mexican liquor store?"

"Be right back," Matt replied without a backward glance, walking inside before the teleporter could ask any more questions. He moved purposefully, his shoes scuffing across the dull wooden floorboards as his eye adjusted to the irregular lighting and gleam of walls of bottles. To his right, a round, swarthy face above a rough-hewn white cotton shirt looked up at him as he entered.

"*Hola*, Mauricio," Matt hollered at the squat, balding man behind the counter.

"*Hola*, Señor Calejandro," Mauricio replied, turning back to the tiny TV screen he'd been watching, easily the brightest thing in the room. He made no further move to acknowledge Matt's existence as the American moved between the shelves, picking out bottles and cartons with the eye of a seasoned inebriant. Matt's math was good, and he'd already checked the exchange rate, so he had a fairly good idea what he was up for when he finally brought his collection to the counter.

"*Eso también, por favor,*" he told Mauricio, who'd already started dutifully arranging Matt's purchases in a cardboard box. He pointed to the packets of Purple Dragon on the shelf behind him. "*Tres.*" The shopkeeper grunted and added three packets of cannabis to the pile.

"*¿Dólares americanos?*" Matt checked, just to be polite. His Spanish was appalling, probably because he'd never practiced with anyone besides his dog, but since he'd only learned it for this exact purpose, it did the trick.

"*Sí, por supuesto.*" Mauricio shrugged. He never had any problems taking American money before. He glanced down and tapped on a calculator. "*Ciento noventa y nueve setenta y cinco.*"

"*Gracias,*" replied Matt, wincing internally but reminding himself that really Natalia was paying for everything. He handed the two hundred over to the Mexican, stuck the weed in his front pocket, and grasped the box full of alcohol with both hands, not bothering about the change.

"*Hasta luego*, Mauricio."

"*Adiós*, Señor Calejandro," said Mauricio, already turned back to his soaps.

Will was still waiting for him outside with an expression of some concern.

"Hold this," Matt instructed before the teleporter could get a word out, handing Will the box. The older guy glanced down.

"What're these drinks for?" he asked, half-skeptical, half-nervous.

"I'm building a drink fort," Matt replied sarcastically. Will just looked at him. Matt shook his head in despair. "For drinking. Drinks for drinking. Come on, home, Jeeves." He gripped Will's arm, which was locked precariously around the booze box as though it was filled with snakes, and gazed up expectantly. For a moment, the teleporter looked like he might protest, but the confidence and resolute calm of Matt's expression seemed to put him off. Will made a face, and suddenly there was a rush of familiar teleporting sensation. Before Matt could worry too much about what would happen if they dropped the booze box mid-jump, the pressure around him ceased and he opened his eyes to see the foothills of the Academy.

"Nice," complimented Matt. He reached over and gingerly relieved Will of the alcohol. "Thanks."

"Hold on," said Will, finally finding his voice though it stumbled slightly. "Aren't you underage?"

"Not in Mexico," Matt corrected.

"Yeah but—"

"You're the one who brought it into the country," Matt said with a shrug. Technically, he was right. "You're over twenty-one."

"But I—"

"Come on," said Matt, rolling his eyes overdramatically. "It's Friday. Relax a little." He started up the hill. "It's just a few drinks."

"I don't know, man," stammered Will, hurrying to follow, glancing nervously around them as though afraid some authority figure might materialize out of the night. "We don't really dr—"

"Shh-shh-shh-shh-shh." Matt reassured him again, although with no free hands this time. "No doubts now, only drinks. Let's just get this to the pavilion."

The pavilion was a wooden outdoor gazebo someone had erected on Morningstar's east side for God-knows-what purpose near some training trenches and storage sheds. It wasn't ideal, but it was probably better than drinking in a ditch. They walked there in silence, Matt humming idly to himself. Upon arriving, he placed the box down on one of the pavilion's wooden slat seats.

"Here you go, man, want a brew?" asked Matt. It felt a bit weird offering as if he was the one with seniority here, almost bossing the older Acolyte around. But for some reason, the presence of intoxicants imbued Matt with authority. Will shifted on his heels, looking like a big kid who'd been caught doing something naughty.

"Man, I'm not sure, I don't really—"

"One drink, man, come on," said Matt. He shot the teleporter a friendly, reassuring smile. "It's not illegal. Just have one drink, and see how you feel." Will hesitated for a moment, but in the end, the combination of Matt's easygoing demeanor and subtly crafted peer pressure won the day.

"Okay," he replied with a nervous smile. "Just let me go change and I'll come right back."

"Bring anybody you want!" Matt called after him as Will's figure hurried back toward the Academy. He pulled out his phone and dialed.

"Hello?" the reply came after two rings.

"Ed, do you have speakers?"

"Ah, yeah, definitely," Ed's voice replied. "What do you need?"

"Can you bring them down to the pavilion?"

"Uh, sure, I could . . . I mean I'd have to disconnect and . . . It would probably take a trip or two . . ."

"Excellent, man, bring them down. Also, I need a cooler."

"Uh, I don't have one on me."

"Ed, you're a genius, work with me here. Speakers, cooler."

"Um . . ."

"Good, man." Matt hung up and started texting Wally.

Come pavilion emergency need help

Half a minute later, his phone was lighting up.

"Matt it's me, what's going on?!"

"Wally, thank God you called. Come quick. I've got all this weed and I don't know what to do with it. Bring as many people as you can."

*　*　*

Jane stared bleary-eyed at the words laid out in front of her.

... but to inextricably tie the demonstration of what is widely defined as supervillainous ambition or action to a single psychological or experiential characteristic is not only to fallaciously equate properties that have never been conclusively linked, but to condense a broad spectrum of...

She read the same words four times over before finally realizing none of it was sinking in. Jane let out a low groan—the only sound in her dim, stuffy room besides the faint buzzing of the desk lamp—and slumped her head onto the textbook. Come on, she berated herself. She propped her head up on her arm and shifted forty-five degrees in her plastic chair.

... megalomaniacal ambitions undeniably demonstrated as a correlative element, but have not yet been proved causal (Parker et al., 1995); presenting an inherent problem for psychological profiling...

She closed her eyes and rubbed her temples, the inside of her head feeling hot and heavy. Oh *God*. Why couldn't these stupid people just speak English? She looked across at her notes, which so far were just a squiggly doodle she'd made in the margin. *Ugh*, she swore to herself, putting her head in her hands. None of this made any goddamn sense. She was never going to pass.

Someone was playing music off in the distance—she could hear the faint hum of it coming ever so slightly through the window. Jane gritted her teeth, wishing they would shut the hell up. The tiny noise gnawed at her concentration. She blinked hard and stared down again at the words drably blanketing the textbook.

... genuine beneficence, or a belief in such; or perhaps a fundamental disconnect with structural elements of society and a desire for baseline cultural reform or revolution, with historical disregard...

Ugghhhhh... Almost against her will, Jane's eyes flicked up to the number in the corner of the page: 76. Jesus, she'd barely read five pages. She thumbed through the chapter, then internally groaned—it went on until page 132. And then there were two more for this . . . *Ugggghhhhhhhhhhhhhhhhhhh*. Jane ran her hands through her hair, the words swimming before her eyes.

It was hopeless. She was never going to pass.

"Pass, man, come on," said Matt, squinting one eye unnecessarily as Wally took another drag on the joint. "It's puff, puff, pass." He paused, then added, "Dick."

Wally let out a long column of smoke, leaning back on the pavilion's wooden railings.

"Maaaaan . . ." He sighed. "Negativity, man, you've got to . . . you know, we all should . . ."

Beside him, Giselle cackled with laughter, the sound echoing through to join the happy hum of voices and the beats of the stereo pumping music in the background. They'd lucked out, it was a warm night, and a generally awesome time to be out . . . outside? Outside.

"Oh-my-god-you-guys-why-do-they-call-them-fingers-if-you-never-even-see-them-fing-oh-wait-a-second," she blurted. The speedster held up her hand in front of her face and vibrated it so fast it blurred out of existence. "There-they-go-look." She stopped vibrating and broke down into fitful giggling.

"Giselle, you're speaking too fast," wheezed Wally, coughing up more smoke.

"You sound like a chipmunk," confirmed Matt, taking another sip of vodka and lemonade. Giselle doubled over with laughter.

"I-i-is she okay?" Ed asked, glancing over nervously from his spot on the bench in the corner. He was still awkwardly clutching his first beer, his eyes flicking up and down at Giselle whenever he thought she wasn't looking. Matt breathed in a deep, enjoyable breath of night air and smiled a slow smile at him.

"Ed, man, relax, she's cool, we're all cool, she just . . . drink your beer, man, come on."

"No, I-I-I mean, it's all right . . . I don't . . . I don't really like the taste . . ."

Matt leaned forward and looked at the genius, the world wobbling slightly. "Ed, it's beer. Nobody really likes the taste." Behind him, a group of girls were laughing at something, and the next song on his iPod playlist started. Goddamn Backstreet Boys. "Everybody pretends to, but really it's . . . it tastes like dirt, you know, gross water dirt. You don't drink it for the taste. You just . . . you know? It's cheap."

"It's a conspiracy, man . . ." Wally breathed to his right.

"Hey, hey, you guys," James Conrad called from down over on the lawn, already halfway through his second bottle of vodka. (He'd brought five, Will having jumped him and a few others back to Mexico.) "Do you think I can . . . ? Do you think I can lift the pavilion? I can lift the pavilion, watch." Several more junior Acolytes behind him, most of them girls, cheered him on.

"No, James, relax, man, don't lift the pavilion," said Wally, clutching the edge of his seat.

"Please don't lift the pavilion."

"Yes, come on, James, believe, you can definitely lift the pavilion," encouraged Matt.

"No, it's cool guys, I've got this. I can totally lift it. Watch, I'll—"

"Big-boy-muscle-man-big-boy-muscles-going-to-lift-things-so-strong-ha-ha-ha-ha-ha."

"Giselle, I can't understand a goddamn word you're—"

"I'm going to do it, watch, here we go, one two thr—"

Matt lurched to the side as the noise of the party was punctuated by the sound of wrenching earth and splintering wood.

"James, no stop, what're you . . . ?"

"Argh!"

"Do it! Throw it, you—"

"Oh my God, you idiot, you're breaking the—"

"Put us down!"

The was a crash and the right side of the significantly worse-for-wear wooden structure and its uprooted foundations crashed back onto the ground, spilling Matt's drink all over his pants.

"Aw, man, come on, I . . . waste . . ."

"See, guys," James announced proudly. "I told you, I told you I could do it, I"—he let out a loud belch that Matt swore physically impacted Morningstar's walls—"I did it. I lifted the pavilion."

"Only half of it," Ed muttered under his breath, but nobody seemed to hear him. In the confusion, Wally had fallen flat onto the wooden gazebo floor and was now struggling to get back up.

"Aw, man," Matt complained, looking down at him. "Did you drop the joint?"

"I don't . . ." replied Wally, struggling. "Hold on, let me just . . ."

"Is . . . it . . . better . . . when . . . I . . . talk . . . like . . . this?" slurred Giselle in slow motion, who'd somehow completely avoided being upended and was still in her seat, making funny faces at the air and then laughing hysterically.

"No, that's worse."

"Significantly worse."

"Haters."

"Matt, we're out of ice!" a girl called from over near the speakers.

"Ah, heck." Matt staggered to his feet, feeling a little seasick from a combination of beer, Purple Dragon, and James's magical pavilion ride. He clambered down the gazebo steps with some help from the railing and meandered his way through the small groups of people clustered here and there. It wasn't, like, the biggest party ever, but everyone who mattered was here and they'd all brought a few randoms who seemed cool and, you know—he hiccupped—this was good, he was having a good time, this should definitely get him expelled.

He managed to pass behind James, who was trying to flex and bust out of his shirt for his admirers, without being pulled into another one of the strongman's bear hugs (drunk James was very affectionate) and lurched over to the cooler beside the speakers.

"Can we"—hiccup—"excuse me, can we, can someone make more?"

Becky Sandstrom, a friend of Celeste's who could fly, shook her head. "There're no cryomen . . . cryomin . . . ice people." Beside her, Celeste, who appeared to have unconsciously sprouted antlers, nodded in reindeering agreement.

"Uuuuuugggghhh," groaned Matt, rubbing his face, trying to think of a solution to this insurmountable problem. Celeste turned to her friend.

"Becky, can you um, can you fly, to like the gas station, like, they'd have—" But Becky was already shaking her head.

"Don't drink and fly," she recited. "Don't drink and fly."

"You're so responsible," Celeste complimented.

"No you're so . . . you're so talented, look at your deer horns!"

"Deer horns!" howled Celeste, and they both broke down laughing.

"Uggggggghhhhhh," Matt moaned again. "Why doesn't this place have ice people?"

"I think it's the White Queen," answered Becky, putting her hands on her hips. "I don't think, you know, anybody wants to try and live up to that, you know? Too much pressure."

"I'd feel so nervous."

"I know, right? It's like, oh my God, the shoes to fill, I couldn't even."

"What about . . . where's Will?"

Matt rubbed his eyes. "He's passed out."

"He had like three beers!"

"Nah, he and James were doing shots."

"Oh, damn."

"Right?" Matt blinked hard, trying to clear his head. "It's all right, we can still . . . Giselle can . . ." That was only a temporary solution though, he thought, Giselle couldn't carry that much ice . . . and then Matt's thoughts stopped dead in his tracks because he'd just remembered something.

"Giselle!" he shouted, and before he could blink the speedster had zoomed over to him in a blurry zigzag and was leaning her head on his shoulder.

"Maaaaaatttt," she mimicked. He looked down at her, his vision slightly watery.

"I need you to go get someone."

Knock. Knock. Knock. Knock-knock-knock-knock-knock-knock-knock-knock-knock-knock.

"Christ I'm coming!" shouted Jane, getting up out of her chair. She had no idea who the hell that was supposed to be—probably Matt again, the jerk, knocking slow like a moron. But she wasn't sure who the second person was, the person rapping on her door like a woodpecker.

She swung her door open, her face already set into a scowl, but to her surprise it wasn't Matt but the beautiful Eurasian girl from down the hall she'd seen on her first night at Morningstar, standing there, looking dazed and weaving ever so slightly on the spot.

"Um . . . hi?" Jane said skeptically, having no idea what this was about.

"Hiiiii," said the tall girl with the face like a model. "Hiiii."

"Hi," Jane repeated coldly.

The girl smiled warmly at her and Jane noticed her unusually wide pupils. "Do you want . . . can you please . . . ?" She hiccupped. "We're having a party."

"So?" said Jane.

"Sooooo . . . you . . . should . . . coooooommme," the girl pleaded, twisting her feet. She made as if to reach out and put her hand on Jane's shoulder but halfway through seemed to realize the problem with that gesture and pulled her arm back.

Jane could recognize an obvious trap to lure her somewhere and beat her up when she saw it. "I'm studying."

"Booooo," booed the girl, squishing her elegant face into mock disappointment. "No . . . you . . . should . . . coooommme!"

"No."

"Come . . . on . . . come . . . partyyyyyyy!"

"Go away," Jane snapped, closing the door in her face.

"Jaaaaaannnnnnne," came a muffled voice.

Knock, knock, knock, knock, knock.

"Go away!" she shouted. "I'm not opening this door!" The knocking stopped and then when silence elicited no further response on Jane's behalf there was a sigh and the sound of rushing air. Jane scowled to herself and sat back down with her textbook, trying to ignore the sounds of distant merriment.

"I don't think she's coming," informed Giselle, reappearing at Matt's side in a blast of wind and admirably only stumbling a step or two. "She's study . . . *hic* . . . studying."

"Ugh," groaned Matt, rubbing the bridge between his eyes. He thought something like this might happen. He rested his elbows on his knees, considered his options, the gazebo bench hard against his butt. Okay—they were going to have to go for a riskier play.

"Wally," he muttered, shaking the psychic by the shoulder as he sat there, peaceful and silent, looking up at the stars. "Roll another joint. I'm going to need to get really, really high."

Then he turned to the throng of people scattered in dribs and drabs around the speakers and, in particular, the gigantic figure who was almost invisible against the darkness.

"James!" he shouted. "How's your juggling?"

. . . the manifestation of which is almost incidental to the trauma, but which is not by itself indicative . . .

Jane gritted her teeth and tried to concentrate on the words in front of her. She swore it was like that stupid music was getting louder every second. Soundproofed rooms my ass, she'd . . .

"Aaaaahhh, Jane!" a muffled voice suddenly cried to her right. Jane started and spun around, looking for the attacker, but there was nobody there.

Her eyes narrowed. Maybe she was hearing things. She turned suspiciously back to her textbook.

"Jane!" came the voice again, hurtling soft to loud to soft again like the shouter was speeding past her on a freeway. She twisted in her seat in time to catch a glimpse of brown hair falling down out of view of her window. She rose and apprehensively approached the glass, fists clenched, ready to fight.

"JANE!" shouted Matt, suddenly appearing on the other side of the glass, suspended in the air for half a second before plummeting back down. Jane blinked. What the hell was—

"JANE, OPEN THE—" yelled Matt before he was gone, fallen down the three stories between her window and the ground. And then he was back up again. "JANE, OPEN THE WINDOW!"

Jane did no such thing. Instead, she pressed her face against the glass and peered down at the base of Morningstar's walls. There was a small crowd of people gathered down around a single speaker blasting some top forty pop trash, most of whom Jane didn't recognize. In the middle of them stood the hulking figure of James Conrad, who waved at her with one hand and caught Matt's tumbling body with the other. Then he tossed him up again.

"JANE, PLEASE I—" Matt managed to get out before gravity took its toll. Jane rolled her eyes.

"Come on, Jane, just—" Whoosh, back down.

"This isn't really—" Arms and legs flailing everywhere.

"Open the wind—" He was upside-down this time.

"Please, Jane, come—"

In spite of herself, a small smile managed to worm its way across Jane's face. She quickly wriggled her jaw, trying to make it go away before Matt saw. Not that he could've, Jane thought as his flailing body tumbled legs over head once more up and then back down again. She sighed, took a deep breath, and then against her better judgment unlatched the window.

"What?" she asked on his next flight up.

"Let me in, I need to . . . oop," he said, plummeting back down.

"What do you want?" she demanded, although the sight of him tumbling stupidly though the air made it hard not to laugh.

"Grab me, Jane, I—" Matt cried, holding out his hands. The girl rolled her eyes. The next time he came up, she reached out, grabbed hold of his chest, and pulled him through the window.

"Oof. Thanks." Matt heaved his front half in, his hands clasping the windowsill, his legs still dangling precariously over the abyss. He struggled for a few seconds and then pulled himself through, tumbling onto the floor where he lay on his back, breathing heavily. Jane stood with her hands on her hips, looking down at him.

"I think I'm going to puke," he whispered, staring up at the ceiling.

"Not in my room you're not," she growled. "I will throw you right back out."

He blinked. "You're really strong."

"I know."

Matt closed his eyes. "Jane," he murmured. "Jane."

"What?" she said. She could smell the alcohol on him from here.

"You didn't want to come to the party."

"No."

"So . . ." He hesitated. "So, I brought the party to you."

Jane cocked an eyebrow. "You mean you or that stupid speaker you've got blaring outside my window?"

"Matt's party delivery service," whispered Matt.

"Leave me alone. I don't want your stupid party."

Matt closed his eyes and ignored her. "Come to the party."

"Seriously."

"Come to the party, Jane."

"Why?"

Matt hesitated, then stared up at her with the expression of a guilty puppy. "We need ice."

Her eyes narrowed. "I'm throwing you back out."

"No! Jane! Wait!" Matt shook his head, holding out his hand for her to stop. Slowly, he propped himself up so that he was sitting upright, his head resting on the window frame. "Jane, listen. I'm sorry. I'm sorry about the other day, I'm sorry I got mad, I was just—"

"A jerk?" she finished, standing in front of him, her arms crossed.

"Yes. No. I don't know. I was scared Jane, I was . . ." His voice trailed off and grew soft. "I was just so scared someone was going to find out."

He looked up at her, his eyes wet and pleading. Jane didn't know how to respond.

Finally, she sighed and dropped back down into her desk chair. "It's fine. You . . . you were right. I was stupid." She paused and stared off behind him, out the window. "I shouldn't have done it. I let them get to me."

"They're not—" Matt started, then he burped. Jane made a face. "Sorry. They're not bad people."

She gave a small sarcastic laugh and stared down at him wearily. "They don't hate you."

"Yeah, but . . . but they don't have to hate you either. They don't . . ." He blinked and shook his head slightly like a dog trying to shake water from its ears. "Give them a chance."

"They hate me. They mock me. They tried to kill me. Why the hell should I have to prove myself to them?"

"I know; it's not fair," agreed Matt. He put a hand on the window-sill and tried to stand, then thought better of it. "You shouldn't . . . it shouldn't be on you to . . . to do that." He hiccupped. "But it is. It's just the way things are. And you can cry and moan about it"—Jane's eyes narrowed, but Matt didn't seem to notice—"about how. . . *hic* . . . unfair it is, but that won't change reality, that won't . . . *hic* . . . make anything better."

Jane was silent.

"Just . . . come down to the party," the boy pleaded. "Make the ice. Talk to them a-a-and laugh and h-h-have a drink"—he burped again— "and sh-sh-show them you're still human."

"I thought the only human one was you," Jane replied quietly. Matt put a finger over his lips and made a *shush*-ing noise, though he did so with a slight, crooked smile. In spite of herself, Jane felt herself smiling back.

"Fine," she conceded, "so are we going out the window?" Matt blanched.

"Please no. Stairs are good." Matt put one hand on the windowsill and one hand onto her bed and tried to push himself into standing. He failed miserably.

"Come on," Jane muttered. She wrapped her arms around his chest and pulled him to his feet.

"H-u-u-u-g-g-g-s-s-s . . ." said Matt, swaying slightly.

"Kill yourself," said Jane, letting go.

"You're . . . nice. You're a sweet . . . *hic* . . . sweetheart. Deep down inside."

Jane struggled not to smile. It was hard to be angry at someone this pathetic. "No, I'm not. I'm a mean old lady." She led him toward the door. "Now let's go to this stupid party."

Matt was welcomed back with cheers and open arms, and Jane with awkward silence. But to his credit, even through his heavy intoxication, Matt never left her side. Jane filled up the cooler with ice, beside which Ed had already replaced the speakers in their original position—and reluctantly, people began moving forward to get cold drinks. His hand on her arm, not un-gently, Matt then led Jane over to the gazebo—they sat. Matt grabbed another beer, and Jane declined the one he offered her.

"I don't drink," she told him stiffly. Matt just shrugged and offered her a joint instead. Jane hesitated.

"I've never really tried . . ." she started, but Matt brushed her concerns away.

"It's fine," he assured her. "Trust me. It'll help you relax. Just try a little. If you don't like it, don't have any more."

He passed her the reefer. She looked at it warily.

"Trust me," he repeated, smiling. And then after a few seconds, Jane sighed—because she supposed she had to, didn't she, in this situation? He'd trusted her. And, she supposed, it was legal.

She flickered a small flame from her index finger, lit the tip of the joint and inhaled, then coughed.

"Ugh," she complained. She went to pass it back to him, but Matt shook his head. "I think I should probably go easy for a while," he murmured, rolling his head back and staring up at the sky.

So, they sat there, in silence and idle talk, in the warm night air and the soothing rhythm of the music, under the gazebo's hanging lights. Jane drew another puff, here and there. And then slowly, the world changed.

People came to join them—to sit, to pass around the joint, to talk, at first with Matt but eventually with her too. First came a freckly redhead named Wally, who smoked like a professional and called her by her name. She panicked slightly when he told her he was a psychic and looked at Matt for danger—but Matt just shook his head and smiled. They talked about swimming, of all things, though Jane couldn't recall quite how and why. Then came the speedster girl, who smiled at her with perfect teeth and actually went to shake her hand—only to stop again halfway, an uncomfortable expression seeping across her face, as if unsure what to do. Matt looked up from his nap, laughed, and rolled his eyes.

"You'll know if she takes your power," he told her, "and she'll go to jail." Then he blinked, sat up and apparently felt the need to inform everyone else about this. "YOU'LL KNOW IF SHE TAKES YOUR POWER—" he shouted to the crowd over the top of the music.

"And she'll go to jail!" chimed in Wally. Jane pinched the bridge of her nose.

"Thank you," she muttered, humiliated. "Thanks for that. I needed the attention." But to her surprise, her despairing made the speedster girl laugh and she held out her hand again, for real this time. Jane warily, disbelievingly, shook it, feeling the girl's speed pulsing, light and bright beneath her skin. They started to talk. Her name was Giselle.

Matt's friend Ed was next. Or rather, he'd sort of been there the whole time, just sitting in the corner of the pavilion nursing a beer, not really joining in the conversation. He pulled up deliberately alongside her and flashed Jane a shy smile. He held out his hand.

"Edward Rakowski. Genius."

"Jane Walker. Empath." They both laughed at a joke that that wasn't immediately obvious. Jane glanced down at his hand, where they'd just touched. He felt like a mountaintop sunk deep beneath the ocean.

"You're not worried?"

"No." He smiled, rocking forward on the bench and crossing his feet. "To tell the truth, I'd be interested to see what'd happen. To hear what becoming smart was like."

"Thanks." She chuckled, not taking offense.

Ed looked aghast at what he'd just said. "S-s-s-orry," he stammered. "I didn't mean . . ."

"I don't care," she assured him. The tangle-haired little man looked relieved.

"I've always wondered what it would feel like," he continued, looking at her cheek with genuine curiosity, "to have your intellect expand. We spend our entire lives trapped inside our own minds, with perceptibly the same capacity for thought . . ." He pondered. "We only know what we perceive, everything filtered through our brains. Would feeling our brain's ability change be terrifying or incredible?"

"Oh God, Ed, please, I'm too high for this," Matt murmured, head back and forearm over his eyes, apparently listening.

Not long after that, there strode over a figure that made her genuinely flinch, the gigantic James Conrad—coming to grab Matt's empties, which he was crushing against his forehead. Jane stared apprehensively at him, and he glowered back at her, but Matt just shook his head and introduced them to each other as if they were meeting for the first time.

"Thanks for the ice," James said begrudgingly.

"Thanks for not throwing Matt through my window," she admitted, working hard not to clench her teeth.

"I'm a pretty good shot," he confessed—and that seemed to be enough. Neither of them really apologized to the other—that wasn't on the cards—but they sat peacefully in close proximity, James talking mainly to Matt and the beautiful Giselle. Eventually, though, he and Jane exchanged a few small words.

"I was harsh on you," he muttered quietly, leaning over, the others momentarily engaged. "I know. But that's just the way it goes here."

Jane didn't say anything. She would have given a small nod of understanding, but she couldn't help but feel like that would have come across like she was fine with it all, which she wasn't. James continued on regardless.

"I'm a senior. *The* senior," he told her, keeping his voice low. "I've got to be tough." He paused and looked at her, a strange glimmer in his eyes. "We have to be the best."

"I know," Jane acknowledged.

"The hotter the flame, the stronger the steel. We're forging a new *Legion*." He quietly stressed the last word. "If I don't push people . . . When the time comes, we need to be worthy."

"I know," Jane said simply, and that was all of that.

Time passed. The music mellowed. People said their goodbyes and began weaving their way back toward the Academy. Wally got up to help Will, the teleporter who Jane remembered had brought them here, up off the grass where he'd been snoring peacefully for some time—they were gone for fifteen minutes or so while the psychic helped him stagger back to his room before Wally returned to the pavilion to sit and smoke some more. Shortly after, James, too, began making noises about leaving, glancing across at Giselle every time he said it. But the speedster never seemed to pick up what the strongman was putting down, and so he lingered, continuing to steadily drink his way through an almost inhuman amount of vodka.

"Giselle!" yelled a girl in the night, who seemed to have sprouted wings. "Come play!" Giselle laughed, and with a round of hugs and kisses on the cheek for everyone in the gazebo ran off into the dark to throw and catch a Frisbee. With her gone, James took only a few minutes to grumble to himself before leaving alone, albeit for the ten seconds it took for another giggling Acolyte girl to seemingly materialize on his arm.

"Man pulls like a magnet," Matt murmured as James's giant back disappeared into the darkness.

"But not who he wants to," Wally said softly, gazing over at the Frisbee game and Giselle's laughing, blurring form. Matt chuckled and Jane sat silent, watching the fireflies. Only Ed, sitting by himself in his corner, looked unhappy for some reason.

They kept on talking while things died down. Eventually, the party was over. The last guests left, Ed turned off the music, and they all for some reason—probably because the wooden benches hurt your butt after a while—ended up sitting on the grass.

"This was nice," murmured Wally. He drew long and deep on the joint they were smoking—Jane had lost count what number this was—then exhaled, slow and satisfied. He passed across to Ed, who pinched it awkwardly between his thumb and forefinger like a piece of moldy cheese. "We should do this more often."

"Yeah, man," said Matt, laying on the grass, his hands behind his head. "Definitely. All the time." They lapsed into peaceful silence.

Eventually, Wally turned to Jane. "I'm sorry about what happened with Nat," he said. "I told her not to, but . . ."

Jane shook her head. "It happened. I'm fine. Move on." She sighed and looked up at the lights of Morningstar, glowing off in the distance. "I just wish I could've . . ." she trailed off.

"Won?" asked Wally, smiling. Jane nodded. The psychic shook his head.

"It would've taken an extraordinary mind to repel Natalia Baroque."

"Lucky I had Psy-Block," Matt's voice murmured up from the ground, his eyes closed.

"Exactly," agreed Wally. He took the joint back from Ed, who didn't seem to have any idea what to do with it, and took another draw. "She's really powerful."

"And my mental defense sucks," Jane admitted. Wally handed her the joint, and she took another funny-tasting puff. The psychic gazed at her with an odd look on his face.

"Do you want it not to?" he said finally. Jane looked at him.

"What do you mean?"

"If you're no good. Do you want me to help you?"

The redhead seemed genuine, but still she shifted uncomfortably. "I . . . I'm all right."

"What're we talking about?" said Giselle, reappearing in a rush of air cross-legged by Wally's side, breathless but beaming.

"Jane's too good for anyone's help," Matt murmured, not looking up. "Ow," he added as Jane thumped him on the chest.

"Shut up," she countered, scowling. Maybe it was just the marijuana, but his insult gave her a genuine pang.

"You always hit me."

"You always deserve it."

"That's victim-blaming."

"Whatever." She turned back to Wally, struggling to find the right words. "I just . . . I don't want to . . . it's fine. Really. Thank you. But I don't . . . you don't need to."

"You're in the Legion," said Giselle, and to Jane's surprise the words were straightforward, without sarcasm or disgust. Jane looked up from the piece of grass she'd been picking at to find the speedster looking directly at her. "We're a team. All of us. Just like the old days."

"The good old days," Wally echoed.

"None of us are perfect. None of us can go it alone." She reached across and placed her hand on Jane's lap. "Let us help you."

"I don't . . . I mean you can't . . . I can't . . ."

"Let us try," said Wally, and the two of them smiled. Jane looked from one to the other, not knowing how or what to say. Her throat felt tight.

"I'll help too," piped up Ed, joining in ineffectually. "You know, if you want."

Giselle laughed and leaned over and pecked him on the cheek. "You're excellent, Ed." The genius's face turned bright red where her lips had brushed.

"Screw you all, nobody's helping me," Matt muttered from the ground, and everyone laughed.

"Come on," said Giselle, standing up and pulling Wally to his feet. "We should get to bed."

"Carry me," begged the psychic. "Darling. Please. It's so far."

"Oh my God, Wal, you're so lazy."

"But you love me."

"You're right. I love you." She bent down and with surprising strength slung the pudgy psychic over her shoulder. "Work, work, work," she faux-moaned—then she winked at the three of them and vanished into the night. Ed watched her blur disappear into the darkness with a mournful look on his face.

"I better get going too," he said quietly.

"No, stay," whispered Matt. "It's nice out."

"No," said Ed, shaking his head. "I think I . . . I think I'll go. I need to . . . I've got things I should be doing."

He climbed to his feet and walked away slowly toward Morningstar with his hands in his pockets.

"Can never tell if he's serious," Matt muttered. "Or if that just means he's going to play games."

"Who knows," said Jane, laying down beside him. Half-asleep, his eyes still closed, Matt snuggled into her armpit.

"You're warm."

"I'm a pyro."

"Oh yeah." Matt paused, considering. "But you're a cryo too." He yawned and shuffled his hands between his thighs. "Would think they'd cancel each other out."

"Apparently not," Jane said with a smile.

"Apparently not," Matt murmured.

And so, they lay there, the empath and the human, alone on the grass in the warm autumn air. They lay there in peace and silence, him asleep, her looking up at the stars, until the first rays of sunlight peaked over the horizon. Then Matt awoke, and together they faced the coming dawn.

THE HUNTED

"Super Salaries: The Top Ten Most Employable Powers"
Forbes Magazine, January 1995

From those able to move mountains to those able to move us, Forbes lists the top ten powers most capable of paying off a mortgage.

#10 Telepath: With its prevalence and the legitimate concerns surrounding its use, it's easy to forget how important telepathy is to modern society. From psychologists and emergency workers to police and in-house security, telepaths can attract a larger salary than their non-telepathic colleagues for the application of their mental skills—and while it's arguably the need for protection from other telepaths driving much of this, the reality of the wage gap remains unchanged. Telepaths at the top of their field have a broad range of opportunities and despite strict penalties against improper conduct (as well as the rise of Psy-Block and anti-paths in the corporate arena), their ability remains one of the most consistently valuable in the business world.

#9 Long-Range Teleporter: Not to be confused with their short-range counterparts who can jump almost instantly but are limited by their field of vision, long-range teleporters turn what would have been an eighteen-hour flight into five minutes of concentration and sulfur (not including passport and immigration control). Although, of course, subject to strict customs obligations, professional LRTs can make big bucks ferrying wealthy clients, for whom time is more valuable than money, to various locations around the world, and quickly rack up a stack of fares and perks—so long as they hold their concentration and don't accidentally jump their passengers' luggage inside a volcano.

#8 Healer: An apple a day may keep the doctor away, but a qualified doctor with healing abilities can keep themselves in no shortage of cash. As the backbone of the health-care system, healers need not be med-school trained to make a living, but those who go the extra mile by getting a "traditional" medical education will find themselves consistently in the country's highest income brackets. In addition to the public sector, qualified healers can also find lucrative employment in private practice or as support staff and are arguably the most change-proof professionals on Earth. After all, there's no end in sight for sickness, injury and the human condition.

#7 Replicator: While not prevalent in the white-collar world, those able to create multiple copies of themselves can nevertheless find great success in a variety of noncorporate ventures. Popularized in mainland China, the idea of one-man/multiple-men construction crews is gaining traction within the United States and Europe, with property developers warming to the notion of only paying one (large) wage to a sufficiently skilled contractor. Likewise, synchronized factory workers, mining teams, and clean-up crews offer replicators potential avenues for fast, easy money, despite union protests—not to mention the surging popularity of replicator dance, singing and sports "groups," which can reward talented individuals (and the ability to be in several places at once) with fame, fortune, and sold-out concerts.

#6 Terramancer: As growth in the Asian economies booms and the Africa Restoration Project gains steam, the worldwide demand for iron ore and other raw materials continues to surge, leading to a (sometimes literal) gold rush throughout parts of Australia, South America, and the Middle East. With exceptional profits on the table, even unskilled earthmovers have the potential to make megabucks shifting rocks for those companies in the resource sector willing to pay maximum wage to keep their product flowing. As Mike Rowe says, it's a dirty job, but someone's got to do it—and if they're willing to work hard and travel far that someone could easily be earning six figures straight out of high school.

#5 Genius: Steve Jobs once stated that "humanity moves forward because geniuses tug on the leash"—a sentiment not lost on corporate America. At the forefront of development in everything from technology to marketing, those gifted with superhuman intelligence can single-handedly create innovations that revolutionize an industry—and be paid handsomely for it. With low numbers and a presence in every breakout company of the last three decades, geniuses are widely regarded as the "golden geese" of the business world. Though, as in fable, they are not without their problems, including a propensity toward estrangement, irrationality, and mental illness, properly looked after, geniuses can be an invaluable asset to businesses, humanity and their own wallets.

#4 Antipath: The rarest entrant on the list, anti-telepathy, colloquially known as "antipathy," is an emergent and littleunderstood ability that has in the approximately fifteen years since its discovery become a status symbol within the corporate world. Normally unannounced and understated, an antipath can attract a pay check many times the size of their colleagues'—an exorbitant salary, but pennies compared to the billions in company secrets they can safeguard from wandering telepathic minds. The fierce competition between private and government sectors for the few antipaths on offer means that anyone who finds themselves with this ability has their pick of employers and is unlikely to be going hungry anytime soon.

#3 Neutralizer: Being a relatively rare power, neutralizers are sitting pretty on the "supply" side of supply and demand, watching with expanding bank accounts as demand for their services continues to grow. In addition to established positions within law enforcement and correctional fields, neutralizer security is fast becoming a must have for any responsible organization keen to safeguard against troublemakers (and keep their insurance premiums down). Indeed, perhaps the only complaint a neutralizer could possibly have about having an ability sought after by everyone from the Department of Defense to festival planners is the sheer amount of sitting involved—sitting on planes, in courtrooms, at baseball games, endlessly waiting to suppress the powers of anyone using them where they're not supposed to.

#2 Technopath: Don't you hate it when your computer stops working and you don't know why? Don't you wish that for once you could just tell technology to work and it'd do it? Well, apparently, so does everyone, which is why tech-nopaths, with their ability to talk to machines and make machines talk back, are in such incredible demand. From programming and website design to troubleshooting and network security, technopaths are the people who keep the Information Age running—and at a far faster pace than would be other-wise possible. Modeling by MIT has estimated that the combined efforts of technopaths and the superintelligent has already accelerated technological development by decades—a fact regularly reflected in a technopath's salary.

#1 Speedster: What do you call an employee who can do five times the work in one quarter of the time? Invaluable, desirable, and exceptionally well paid. Yes, despite the expansion of the Internet and personal computing giv-ing technopaths a leg up, the old adage that efficiency is the heart of good business continues to hold true, making superspeed once again the most valuable power a person can be born with. To add insult to injury, unlike the speedsters of yesteryear, the modern supersonic worker has at their disposal a range of products tailor-made to maximize the advantages of their speed, from friction-proof corporate-wear to Kinetic™ computers capable of keeping up with their blistering WPMs. Parents, watch your children—if they start moving faster than you can see, you may be looking at early retirement.

#0 (Honorable Mention) Captain Dawn: While technically an ability that has garnered him great success, it seemed slightly unfair to include Captain Dawn's phenomenal power of unlimited energy when considering powers that would give our readers an edge in today's job market. However, it is worth noting that through merchandizing, donations, and creative rights, the power of Dawn has netted Captain Dawn several billion dollars—which he has, of course, put toward the rebuilding of the Legion of Heroes, charitable causes, and the continued safety of the world.

"I'm seeing a child. Young on the outside, old on the inside. He's troubled."

From the other side of the desk, he heard Cross's pen quietly *scritch-scratch* across the paper.

"What do they look like?" she demanded.

"Blond," Matt stated. "White. A little boy. Blue eyes."

His head still down, Matt opened his eyelids just a fraction, watching Cross's face for any trace of recognition.

There was none. Cross just looked irritated. "Tell me what he's connected to," she ordered. "Give me a specific place or time."

Matt shook his head, his eyes still closed. He heard Cross make that little *tch*-ing noise she made when she was annoyed.

"Is he related to the priest you identified last time?" she pressed. "The one where there's, quote, 'deception laying inside'?"

"I don't know," replied Matt, not needing to fake the exasperation in his voice. She'd taken to asking questions in their last few tests, which did not bode well.

"Hmm-hmm," muttered Cross. She poked a hard full stop in her paper. "And this priest, any more on him? What does he look like?"

"Like a priest," said Matt, rolling his eyes. "Older. Gray hair. Not as much of it as there used to be."

"Uh-huh," Cross muttered, sounding dissatisfied. Her pen scratched a small note and she looked up at him. "And that's it?"

"That's it," Matt said impertinently.

An uncomfortable silence stretched across the small room.

"You know what I think?" said Cross, and it was abundantly clear that he was going to find out. "You know why I think we don't seem to be getting anywhere?"

Matt felt a sudden rush of fear.

"Why?" he asked, trying to control his heart rate.

"I think you're lazy." Cross scowled and Matt struggled not to let loose a sigh of relief. "I think you're lazy, and I think you're not putting in the effort befitting your gifts."

Matt folded his arms, acting defensive. "Well, maybe I'm sick of these stupid tests," he snapped, doing his best to sound brattish. He'd spent the morning watching online videos of delinquent children forced to live in the wilderness and was working on mimicking their belligerence. "Maybe you suck, maybe you should learn how to do your job."

Cross's eyes narrowed, and for a moment the room fell unnaturally quiet as the stumpy woman's skin began glowing. Then the glow faded, and she drew a long breath between her teeth.

"Let's press on, shall we?" she said, with meticulously forced calm. She turned a sheet over on her clipboard and gave a small, amicable nod. "This prediction here. That something terrible will afflict Detroit." Cross looked up at him with what could have been an attempt at a placating smile. "Anything further on that?"

"No," Matt answered, who truthfully hadn't, but nevertheless felt safe to predict that something at some point would go wrong with that crappy place. The corners of Cross's mouth twitched.

"Okay," she murmured, closing her eyes and rubbing her temple with a short finger. The red was coming off her manicure. "Okay. Matt, I'm trying to help you, but you need to work with me. I really need you to focus."

Despite his position, Matt couldn't help feeling a little sorry for the beleaguered Ashes woman. Throughout all their testing, the most specific visions he'd managed to give her had been "I see a man in a white shirt" or "I see the color brown." A part of him wanted to keep it at that, to keep being so vague in his predictions that the Academy decided he wasn't any use after all and kicked him out. But unfortunately, that course of action carried with it the risk of going too far—of Cross or someone else coming to suspect that maybe, just maybe, he actually wasn't a clairvoyant at all. Having already survived one close call and unable to forget the child's warning to "stay hidden," that was a risk Matt simply couldn't stomach.

And so, almost regretfully, he had started making plans.

"All I see is wings," he announced. Cross's eyes shot open.

"Wings?" she demanded. "What wings?"

"I don't know." Matt shrugged, looking genuinely indifferent. "It's not, like, a serious thing. I just see wings. Black wings. I don't get it any more than you do."

Cross looked curious, but nevertheless sighed after it became apparent that nothing more was going to be forthcoming. "Very well, Mr. Callaghan, that'll be all," she said, waving him away. "We'll break for lunch." Matt stood, and after gathering the papers she had scattered across the desk and tucking the clipboard under her arm, Cross joined him.

They moved through the halls and down the central stairs in silence—the lack of talk between them the awkward kind that arose between a teacher and pupil with not that much in common. As they made their way toward the hall however, their silence was overrun by the sound of commotion. Cross glanced, furrow-browed, at Matt.

"What's going on?" she demanded of an Acolyte, a Sri Lankan girl who was laughing her way through a half-jog out the double doors.

"It's a bird." She laughed. "A stupid crow somehow got in through the windows. It's flying around screeching at everyone." Her face was a beacon of mirth. "I'm going to get Becky. Hopefully, she can catch it." She walked off, still chuckling.

Cross's face paled, and she threw a wide-eyed glance at Matt, who shrugged. Slowly, the stocky Ashes woman pushed open one of the hall doors and stuck her short blond head inside—where, indeed, a wild and very disgruntled crow was making its displeasure at its current situation decidedly known. Cross stared at the crow, squawking and flapping between the rafters. Then slowly, like clockwork, she turned back to Matt, who was standing nonplussed beside her and who she'd been sitting with for the last half hour—and therefore couldn't possibly have been involved.

"Wings," she whispered, gazing at him with shaking eyes. "Black wings."

Operation Tranquil Seagull was not Matt's most elegant plan, but it was special in that it required a partner. A partner, a backpack, a bottle of cough medicine, a bag of French fries, and considerable patience. And it had all come to Matt through the power of procrastination.

As the days grew shorter and the cool winds of autumn shifted into drizzling miserable rains, which cast a gloom over everyone's morning activities and spackled anyone who went outside with mud, Matt's life at Morningstar Academy settled into a kind of eclectic routine. He'd sleep in in the mornings, then get up around ten and meander down into the Grand Hall for a late breakfast, which sometimes turned into an early lunch. Around midday, he'd wander up to the cushion room to sit with Selwyn—who, Matt was pleased to note, showed no signs of moving toward requiring any kind of tangible results—and then after an hour or two of silence thank the bald projectionist for his "help" and go off to spend the afternoon doing what was now his primary activity—messing around.

Driven by boredom, Matt Callaghan had transformed the burden of having too much free time into a reservoir of hours in which to up-skill himself—a fanciful term that here meant "start a bunch of useless hobbies." One of these, completely on a whim, was bird-watching, and it was here that Operation Tranquil Seagull came to life.

Matt knew, for a fact, that Cross was starting to get irritated at his lack of trackable progress. He'd made predictions, yes—but he hadn't stated when or where they'd be occurring, and so they were all hard to quantify. In principle, Matt knew Cross understood this, but in practice he could sense the Ashes woman getting impatient. In order to avoid suspicion, he knew he needed a genuine prediction. Cross needed a tangible result.

And so, Matt got to work.

Many of his plans were long cons. The vision of the deception-riddled priest (who could be either losing his faith or finding something worse), Detroit suffering literally any negative event and his prediction that a US Senator would cheat on his wife were all just a matter of time, but Matt didn't trust them to be enough on their own, so he'd started scheming closer to home.

His first trick was simple. The NyQuil Cold & Flu Nighttime Relief went in the chips; the chips went in the bird; the bird went in the backpack. And then the backpack went to Jane.

"I hate you," she told him, heaving the bag of unconscious crow over her shoulder as discreetly as possible, looking thoroughly uncomfortable.

"You're the best," he assured her. He gave the empath an enthusiastic double thumbs-up, which he toned down somewhat as a pair of Acolytes walked past. "Remember, nice and subtle. Bag open. Bird under the table. When you start to feel it move, that's your cue to leave."

"I hate you," Jane reiterated. But nevertheless, his plan went off without a hitch. Cross had her prediction—and Matt had an alibi.

Matt's hobbies, however, were not restricted to drugging unsuspecting wildlife. In his abundance of time, the so-called clairvoyant went on nature walks, searching for edible native plants to pick and boil into teas. He had Ed set up a personal computer and makeshift DJ equipment in his room and started working on making his own remixes and music sets. He requisitioned canvases, paints, pencils, and clay under the guise of "better expressing" his "clairvoyant visions" and began teaching himself to draw, sculpt, and paint—a fruitless venture, it turned out, as Matt had literally zero artistic talent and his hideous creations all ended up being gifted to the ranges for target practice.

He exercised, going for runs around the grounds, and lifting weights in the Academy gym, which earned him enthusiastic encouragement from James and permanent envy at how much the senior could bench. He mastered the art of the Rubik's Cube, learned how to knit, and even tried his hand at computer coding—although that last one he gave up after Ed informed him (somewhat snobbish and narrow-mindedly, in Matt's opinion) that a window full of two hundred identical Exit buttons where only one of them actually closed the program was not, in fact, a "real" game.

Ed was fast becoming Matt's best friend at the Academy—a real friend, the type of guy who'd try your nettle tea and then tell the infirmary nurse that his vomiting was due to a "virus." The genius was funny, easy-going, slightly cynical, and unpretentious—something that couldn't be said for a lot of other Acolytes. Almost without meaning to, the pair began hanging out more and more, gaming together or with Matt just playing single player while Ed worked on whatever he was doing. Ed's mind, far outpacing his own, did tend to veer into moods and tangents that Matt struggled to follow, sometimes plunging into lingering, incomprehensible unhappiness—but these always seemed to pass and Matt genuinely felt like his presence helped them do so. Ed had actually been a bit more social since the night of the party, and although he still rarely left his computer nest, Matt at least managed to badger him into getting some fresh air or having a public meal every once in a while.

Outside of his growing range of hobbies and the hours he spent with Ed, Matt had also unexpectedly fallen into the role of illicit Acolyte activity organizer—a role he hadn't necessarily anticipated, but which he nevertheless enthusiastically embraced in his ongoing and ever-increasing efforts to be expelled. Every day Matt lingered increased the chances of Cross figuring out his true identity, and so when people he barely knew came up to him in the corridors asking (with the kind of giddy nervousness Matt would have associated with children sneaking cookies) the finer points of delinquency, Matt was only too glad to openly and loudly point them in the right, morally wrong, direction.

Matt did find it a bit weird that they needed him to do this—they were, as Jane had said, all adults—but it seemed that many Acolytes, coming from uncompromising backgrounds, still needed someone to tell them that it was alright to relax and occasionally have a good time. He was that person—apparently—and so almost without trying, Matt found himself as the Academy's unofficial party liaison—telling Acolytes which booze to buy, arranging impromptu gatherings and explaining that, arguably, you weren't really committing a crime if you didn't get caught.

Any day now, Matt thought as he directed three Acolyte girls to the fact that three Acolyte boys had acquired two cases of beer for the coming Saturday, after selling them a box of fireworks and subtly dropping the little-known fact that mixing Styrofoam with gasoline-made napalm. Surely, the administration would get fed up soon.

While Matt was busy wasting his life and corrupting her peers, Jane was training harder than she'd ever trained before. This had its positives and negatives. On the one hand, the physical exertion was enormous. Every day, she collapsed into bed with aching joints, burning muscles, and more than once untreated wounds that she was just too tired to get fixed. In each session, the Academy's trainers pushed her mercilessly, indifferent to what she could do or what she'd already done. She blasted through collapsing tunnels, ran laps through a self-contained hurricane, performed push-ups, sit-ups, and pull-ups while enduring psychic assault. That last one Jane especially hated—although none of the telepaths assigned to assault her during training ever properly invaded her mind, they all broke down her defenses laughably easily and many (with the exception of Natalia, who for some reason seemed wary) clearly relished beating her.

On the other hand, Jane could feel herself improving—and seeing progress was exhilarating. Her barriers of fire, ice, and lightning no longer wavered after the first thirty seconds, her pain tolerance was through the roof, and she was—almost—able to confidently hover. Her muscles, already strong, were becoming bands of iron—helped, no doubt, by the fact that she was actually eating properly now. Jane was still wary of the hall, especially during peak times when it filled with crowds who stared at her with open contempt. In theory she knew the Ashes' commandment prevented anything worse than staring, but in reality, even among budding heroes, rules only restrained resentment for so long. However, Jane soon found her caution ruffled by the ongoing presence of Giselle Pixus, who had seemingly decided—without the empath's input or consent—that they were going to be friends.

The first time Giselle had asked Jane to sit with her, she'd been too stunned to say no. The second time, she'd tried to argue and lost. The third time, Jane had simply started walking away, but before she could blink there'd been a rush of wind and suddenly she'd found herself sitting on a bench on the other side of the hall with Giselle chatting animatedly away beside her as if nothing had happened. After times four and five had the same outcome, Jane resigned herself to the speedster getting her way.

At first, Giselle's presence and the presence of the droves of people who flocked to her made Jane incredibly wary, and she held firmly to the belief that at any moment Giselle's "friendship" would be revealed as the elaborate prank it logically had to be. But as the days passed and no ambush came, Jane reluctantly had to consider the uncomfortable possibility that this pretty, popular girl was genuinely trying to be nice to her—an idea she approached with the same enthusiasm one might approach suspiciously old meat.

It wasn't that Giselle wasn't fun to be around—on the contrary, she was amazing. That was the problem. Giselle was gorgeous, bubbly, affectionate, and funny, and never seemed to wear the same outfit twice. And all those things were so incomprehensible to Jane, who had spent most of the last decade without any meaningful female interaction, that the speedster may as well have been an actual alien. Day after day, Jane found herself sitting beside her half hypnotized, staring at this beautiful, elegant creature as Giselle talked about makeup, politics, boys, and a thousand other topics on which the empath had nothing to contribute—and all while somehow, impossibly, not trying to extricate itself from her presence. One morning, without warning, Giselle even braided Jane's hair.

But it wasn't just at meals. Although running an incredibly tight schedule and seemingly involved in everything Morningstar Academy had to offer, Giselle's assistance to Jane quickly grew unrelenting. She talked her through lecture concepts, ran over tips and tricks enemies with various powers might pull, and in particular, drilled Jane on combat theory, lecturing extensively about how the empath was fighting defensively—an assertion that initially rankled Jane to no end—and needed to concentrate on dictating the terms of her battles. She then demonstrated this concept in practice fights that, although arguably educational, were also universally humiliating. The speedster moved so fast and so without warning that by the time Jane knew they were fighting she was already dazed, confused, and defeated on the ground. Giselle Pixus looked like a cheerleader and hit like a linebacker, and Jane couldn't help wondering if the former was partially to disguise the latter.

True to his word, Wally Cykes had also been helping Jane. The red-haired psychic had appeared out of nowhere one morning as she'd been filling up a plate at the buffet and reiterated his offer from the party. "You're no good to anyone if you crumple the first time a telepath touches you," he'd insisted. Initially, Jane had wanted to argue, but then she'd remembered how upset Matt had been at the thought of her mind exposing his secret, so she'd agreed and they'd started meeting, once every Saturday in an unused classroom. Unlike combat with Giselle, however, mental defense did not come naturally to Jane—or at all.

"Nope," came Wally's ethereal voice. Once again, he brushed aside her ramshackle defenses with a single sweeping thought. "No good."

"Urgh!" swore Jane. She opened her eyes, feeling his billowing presence, the engulfing summer storm cloud, retreating away from her exposed mind. It was their fourth session, the fourth Saturday in a row that the empath had failed miserably to keep out the psychic. She let out a flurry of swear words that would have offended an ex-convict.

"You got distracted," said Wally, not unkindly. "You panicked."

"Of course. I goddamn panicked," she snapped. "Greatest psychic in the goddamn world going through my head, what would you . . . URGH!" She wrung her hands together, shudder-shaking her arms, trying to throw off the wretched, sickening feeling of someone scraping inside your mind.

"Mental defense is about discipline," Wally stated calmly. "Concentration."

"I know," she replied, shaking her head like it was full of spiders. "I know. I know. I know."

"It's okay," he assured her. "Focus on your breathing."

"Why does it have to be breathing?" Jane spat, petty, annoyed, and angry at herself for sounding petty and annoyed. "Why can't I think about something else?"

"You can think about whatever you want," Wally replied with a shrug. "Controlled breathing just helps you stay calm. And it's easiest for most people to concentrate on something about themselves."

"Why?" asked Jane, still angry and shaky, mostly just talking to delay their next bout. "Why is that easier?"

"I assume it's because most of us are self-obsessed," Wally mused. "Why? Don't you like thinking about yourself?"

"I don't know," Jane replied through gritted teeth. "I'm fine. Whatever."

"Hmm," said Wally, looking unconvinced. "Maybe that's the problem. Maybe you need to do a little soul searching. Come to terms with yourself. Figure out who you really are."

Stupid idea, thought Jane as she readied her mind. Pointless. She knew who she was.

"You're an idiot," Matt said politely, pointing out the spot on her take-home assignment where she'd mislabeled the skeleton's anatomy with the tip of his pencil. "In what universe is the tibia in the arm?"

"Shut up," Jane snapped, though not particularly harshly. "I knew it was one of the limb bones."

"I don't know if Professor Lun gives marks for half-answers."

They were in his room, Jane having brought her chair around so they could sit side by side at his desk. Theoretical work not being her strong suit, Jane found it helpful to bounce her answers off someone and despite not attending the lectures Matt was happy to be a sounding board.

"I don't get why I have to know first aid," she said, sighing and running her hands through her hair. Her tattoo was itchy today. Matt raised an eyebrow at her and after a moment she relented. "All right, I get *why* I have to know, it's just—"

"A lot to take in," Matt finished for her. He was leaning back in his seat, thumbing through her criminal psychology reading. "I can't make heads or tails of this."

"Well, maybe if you came to class . . ."

"Expelled, remember? Besides, why do I need to know how crazy evil people think? Will it help me run away better?"

"Maybe you could outsmart them." Jane smirked, erasing the incorrect answer and writing "ulna."

"I'll leave that to the smart people," said Matt.

"It's better than sitting around playing with songs."

"What is? Outsmarting people?"

"No, going to lectures."

"That's only because you haven't heard my latest mix," Matt said, putting down her assignment and turning enthusiastically to his computer. "Do you want to hear it?"

"No," Jane replied with genuine disinterest. Matt looked a little crestfallen. She sighed.

"Okay, fine, play your stupid song. God, I cannot believe you're an Acolyte."

"Well, it's not my fault." Matt scowled. He moused over to the DJ program, then paused, and muttered darkly, "Though we know whose it is."

After they'd made up at the party, Matt had filled Jane in on his visit from the mysterious child. Beyond Matt slowly descending into lunacy, neither of them had been able to brainstorm an explanation for the boy, or how he'd managed to get in and out of Matt's room. Matt's mental defense was too good for it to have been a psychic projection, and Jane had been quick to point out that Morningstar's security systems prevented anyone teleporting or phase walking through the walls.

"Cross didn't bite then?"

"Not an inch." Matt sighed. They'd come up with the idea of dropping a reference to the kid to Cross to see if somehow she'd been responsible, but the hint had got them nothing. "And I would've noticed something. She's not half as subtle as she thinks she is."

"It just doesn't make sense," Jane said for about the millionth time. "If it's a prank, it's not funny. If it's a test, what's it testing? And if it's seriously a warning—"

"Then why be so obtuse?" Matt added wearily, for what felt like the millionth time. "Why not say who's supposed to be dying or what I'm meant to be hiding from?"

"Exactly."

Matt shook his head. They'd been around these circles enough to carve tracks in his brain. But with no further sign of the blue-eyed boy and no more clues about his meaning, all they could do with his words was worry.

"Don't worry. Be happy now."

"Do, do-do-dodaloo, do-da-do-da-dodaloo," Matt whistled. He turned the corner of the third-floor hallway toward his meditation class, enjoying the morning sunlight as the upbeat sounds of Bob Marley played in his ear.

"Selwyn!" he called out as he reached the closed door. "Stop space-walking, you big, beautiful bastard. I've brought doughnuts." He balanced the box precariously on one hand while he fumbled with the doorknob. "Some new place the chef passed when he was shopping. He's got boxes of them."

The knob turned. Matt pushed open the door and stepped through. "Apparently, it's a franchise, you have to taste this, they're completely coated in—"

Matt looked up and the words died on his lips. He stopped moving. "Sugar . . ."

Selwyn was not in the room. But the room was not empty. The pillows, the candles, all the trappings of their meditations had been pushed haphazardly against the walls. And there, in the emptiness, standing side by side in quiet, serious conversation stood three solemn, menacing figures.

Winters, Cross, and Natalia Baroque.

Matt's heart leaped to his throat. "Um, hi," he managed, trying not to stutter. "What, um, what're you guys doing here? Do I"—he looked weakly back at the door—"um, have the wrong room?"

"Come inside, Mr. Callaghan," Cross said with a weary sigh. Daniel Winters's face was blank. Natalia looked at the ground. "And shut the door."

Matt gulped. Slowly, as if his limbs were draped with lead, he turned and closed the door behind him. The sound of the outside world faded into a distant, inaudible hum.

"What's . . . ah, what's going on?" he asked them, taking a single, nervous step forward. Without thinking, he clutched the doughnuts closer to his chest. "I . . . is everything all right?"

"A fact has come to our attention," said Cross, and her eyes flicked first to Winters then Natalia. The former turned his back to them with a slow, resigned sigh, and gazed through the full-length windows out into the grounds. "A fact that involves you."

Matt stopped breathing. Without thinking, his eyes raced to Natalia. The psychic didn't look up. Matt's knees weakened. His back slumped.

"No," he whispered.

"Yes," Cross said simply, and then she sighed and beckoned with a short, stubby hand. "Come. The other two are almost here."

"Other two?" Matt asked, but the words had barely left his mouth before there was a knocking on the door causing him to start, his hands clutching creases in the doughnut box. "Come in," called Cross, and Matt watched in horror as the door opened and James and Giselle entered. The former's face was a mask of displeasure, as if he'd been asked to put down a puppy, and the latter was bereft of her usual bubbliness. Matt's hand instinctively raised to greet them but stopped halfway. Neither one was meeting his eyes.

Oh God. Matt's head whipped back around to look at Natalia, who was still staring at the floorboards. James's and Giselle's footsteps drew closer and suddenly Matt felt the pieces clicking into place. Cross, his assessor, and Winters, the authority. A strongman to restrain him. A speedster to catch him if he runs. And the psychic who had been in his head.

"No," he whispered again.

Silently, James and Giselle trudged to stand with Cross and Natalia, while Winters remained staring out the window. As they passed, the speedster threw Matt a small, sad smile, and the giant clapped him gently on the shoulder.

Matt gulped, feeling sweat beginning to bead across his forehead. "Hey," he managed weakly. "Hi. Why's . . . why's everyone looking so down? Is this an intervention? Did someone die?"

"The door, Ms. Pixus," Cross said with a sigh. Giselle nodded, there was a rush of wind, and suddenly Matt's only avenue of escape was cut off.

Oh God.

"Thank you for coming," Cross said heavily. She looked from James to Giselle and finally Natalia. "And I apologize for the disruption, Mr. Callaghan, and for the ambush. But it was necessary, I think, to do this discreetly. To not cause undue confusion or alarm."

She paused and looked at Matt. For what felt like an eternity, the six of them just stood there, beneath the high paisley ceiling, light streaming onto the sea-blue shelves from the beautiful world outside. Matt's heart hammered in his chest, and he fought desperately to keep his mind focused even as he felt his breathing quicken, his fingernails digging into his palms.

Finally, Cross's voice broke the silence.

"We've got another one," she said in a final, revelatory tone. All around the room, the Legion members deflated with various muttered curses or sighs. James shook his head. Giselle massaged her temples and closed her eyes. Natalia let out a tiny groan.

Matt stood stock-still. "What?" he asked, the words crawling from his mouth, bone dry. "Another what?"

At first, no one answered. Then after a few moments, Daniel Winters sighed, and he turned from starting out the window to look directly at Matt.

"Matt," he said, "I'm sorry to have to do this. Believe me, if there was any other way, I'd take it. But our hands are tied."

There was a ringing in Matt's ears. The room around him seemed to swim, and all he could see was Daniel Winter's smooth, inscrutable face, his clear gray eyes.

Winters looked away. "We've found another one," he said, turning to James and Giselle. "In Albania. A rural area, up in the mountains. An area called Buzahishtë."

Oh God, they—wait, what? Albania?

Suddenly, the world came screeching back into focus. The surreal sensation surrounding Matt shattered, and the panic that been coursing through his veins a second earlier pivoted to monumental trepidatious confusion.

"Excuse me," he asked, his eyebrows furrowing. "Sorry. What? What's a Buzahishtë? What about Albania?"

None of the other Acolytes answered. Giselle kept rubbing her temples, and James merely shuffled in place, avoiding his gaze. Winters and Cross exchanged glances.

"Mr. Callaghan," said Cross, and she straightened as she said it, obviously trying to keep some appearance of self-assurance and authority. "An issue has arisen. An issue in which the Legion"—she said the last part with only a trace of bitterness—"requires your help."

"Why?" said Matt, suddenly wary for a whole different set of reasons than he was ten seconds ago. "What? What do you want me to do?" Unconsciously, he took a step back. "What's in Albania?"

"Not *what*," Cross replied, folding her arms tightly across her chest. "Who." She glanced at Winters, whose face remained inscrutable.

"We've found another clairvoyant."

* * *

"The target's name is unknown."

They stood there in the concrete bunker: James, Giselle, Natalia, Cross, Winters, and Will—the four Acolytes standing at attention, Cross and Winters standing opposite. The blonde woman watched on silently as the director addressed the assembled line.

"She is approximately five-eight," he declared. "A hundred and fifty pounds. Hair, brown, though that may be dyed. Complexion, Mediterranean, though that may be tanned. You will each be given a briefing"—as he said this, he nodded to Cross, who approached and began handing them each a thin manilla folder—"containing a photograph, taken eight days ago from a security camera. This is the target's last known image. She may or may not look like this. She may or may not be wearing prosthetics."

If any of the other Acolytes found this surreal, none of them showed it. James, standing at his full height, responded only with a wordless grunt as Cross handed him the folder. Giselle gave a small, polite nod. Natalia, her eyes unfocused, barely seemed to register Cross passing her field of vision, and Will the teleporter, who'd arrived last, simply kept staring straight ahead. Only Matt, slumped like some sort of lumpy growth at the end of this lean, regimented line, showed any sort of emotion, his clammy face alternating between shock, nausea, and despair.

They were in the armory: a gray little nugget of a bunker Matt hadn't even noticed was built into the backside of the Academy until they'd lead him straight down its concrete steps. Looking like nothing so much as a fallout shelter from the outside, inside, the armory's walls were lined with rows upon rows of crimson-and-gold body armor, not to mention guns, riot shields, and dozens of other bizarre and deadly looking implements that Matt could only assume were used for bringing peace and security violently to someone's face. Between these walls, where they all now stood, the other Acolytes had donned this mostly maroon armor. Each set seemed slightly different. James's armor consisted of plates an inch thick and was cut vest-shaped to leave his enormous arms free, while Giselle's seemed to be made of a different material than the others', a thin frictionless weave. Natalia's suit had black highlights and a silhouette of a crow painted on it, while Will's armor lacked gloves. Standing strong and tall, their shoulders straight and their hands clasped behind their backs, the four Acolytes of the Legion looked every bit the lethal superhuman vanguard they were supposed to be. Matt, on the other hand, who was stuck wearing colorless junior's armor, looked like an amateur cosplayer who compensated for being fat and ugly by over-spending wildly on materials.

"Eight days ago," Winters continued as Cross handed Matt his folder, her eyes meeting his with only the briefest flash of displeasure, "a bank in Switzerland was robbed. The thief used no powers or weapons of any kind. They simply walked in at the exact moment a change of guard coincided with a teller going into early labor, strolled through second-wide gaps in complex, multilayered security, and walked out unchallenged with half a million dollars."

Winters held up a photo. "This robbery," he stated, showing a black-and-white still of the woman casually carrying a duffel bag, "is the latest in a string of thefts across central and southern Europe. All of them involved one person and no clear use of powers. All of them were executed so flawlessly that it took weeks for the theft to be discovered. And none of them returned any clear photographs or surveillance footage of the perpetrator, as if the person responsible knew exactly where the cameras would be pointed and when."

Winters paused and bore his gaze down on each of them in turn. "Until now."

The director began to pace, slowly. "Local sources and our own investigations have tracked this woman to a small property in rural Albania. Mr. Herd will teleport you in half a mile from the site. From there, you will approach on foot. Your mission is to make contact, nothing more. I want a conversation, not hostilities."

Winters paused. "The modus operandi of these robberies makes it almost certain that this woman is a clairvoyant. This means that she knows the camera saw her. This means she knows that we're coming." He stopped pacing, and turned to fix his gaze directly on Matt. "But what she might not know is that for once, she won't be the only one who can see the future."

It was all Matt could do to not throw up. Winters appeared not to notice.

"Mr. Callaghan," he said, "Matt. I cannot overstate how vital you are to this mission. For the past ten years, it has been one of Captain Dawn's highest priority to locate a clairvoyant." Winters's mouth twitched. "You can imagine why. For years, we were unable to engage one clairvoyant—now, maybe, we can recruit two."

"I . . ." stammered Matt, "I don't . . ." The words wouldn't come out. It felt like he was boiling alive in this stupid armor.

Winters took a step forward and placed a firm hand on Matt's shoulder, fixing him with that kind, moviestar smile. It was probably meant to be supportive, but the gesture reminded Matt of nothing so much as the look the *Star Trek* captain gives the nameless red-shirt crewmen before they're sent off to an alien planet to die. "It's okay to be nervous," Winters reassured him. "I know this might be earlier than you expected. But I need you to search inside yourself and see what this clairvoyant's doing before she does it. What we need to do to speak to her. That's all we want. Just to talk."

His voice grew softer. "Think, Matt," he said, almost whispering, so focused it was practically intimate. "Think. What do we need to do? What is our pathway? What do you need?"

"Jane," Matt blurted out immediately and without thinking. "Jane. Help."

"Miss Walker?" The director's face frowned and he and Cross exchanged looks. "I don't know if she's . . ." He glanced at the other Acolytes; Natalia and Will scowled, but Giselle gave a small nod. Winters's eyes turned to James, standing at the other end of the line. The strongman just shrugged.

"His call," said James, "if there's trust, there's trust."

"She's useful," Giselle quickly added beside him. Winters looked at her, though Giselle kept her eyes focused forward. "Wouldn't hurt to have three extra powers in the toolbox."

The director considered for a moment. "Fine," he relented. "The whole point of this is to listen to our clairvoyant. Miss Pixus, retrieve Miss Walker. Brief her on the way over. Discreetly." He turned back to those assembled as Giselle disappeared in a blur. "Everyone else, you know the drill. Check your gear. You move out in five."

Help, Matt whimpered internally.

They took a tunnel out beneath Academy grounds and teleported once they were beyond range of the Distruptances. The six of them appeared on a hillside in the night air, gathered in a circle around Will, each with a hand on his arm, chest or back. The moon shone bright overhead, and a cool breeze rustled a sea of long, calf-high grass. Matt immediately needed to hurl.

"Huhgluh," he heaved, pushing away from the teleporter and doubling over. Nothing came out. Matt paused, his stomach continuing to churn, and tried one or two more half-hearted dry retches. A moment later, he felt a hand gently patting him on the back.

"Hey, man," came Will's voice, concerned. "Sorry. You all right?"

"Yep," Matt whispered, though his voice and legs kept wobbling. "All good. Fine." Out of the corner of his eye, he saw Jane similarly bent down and breathing heavily in the darkness, although she, too, had managed to hold down her lunch. Giselle had gone to stand beside her and was gently rubbing her back, murmuring soft words of reassurance and concern. Beside them, James stared out over the moonlit countryside, seemingly oblivious.

"How far we out?" he asked. "Are we alone?" He glanced down at Natalia, standing glumly at his side. "Nat?"

The psychic pressed a finger to her temple, and Matt involuntarily felt his insides clench. There was no rush of psychic assault however, and Natalia opened her eyes a moment later.

"No blips for two miles," she stated, dropping her hand and glancing up at James. The strongman nodded. Beside him, Matt felt Will stiffen.

"I got us on point," he said, turning to scowl at Natalia as Matt straightened up. "We're a half mile out, just like Winters asked."

"Who's saying we're not?" Natalia glowered. Her black hair was tied up in a bun, which combined with her sallow, angular face and sour expression gave the impression of a habitually disgruntled librarian.

"Well, you're implying I'm—"

"Enough," James groaned. "God, it's the same dumb argument every time. Let it go."

"I'm good," protested Jane, shooing Giselle's hand away and standing back upright. "I'm good, let's do it, let's go." Like Matt, the well-worn body armor she'd been put in was white-gray and colorless, making the pair of them stand out next to the four sleek senior Acolytes like lone teeth against crimson gums. Unlike Matt however, Jane's armor actually looked like it fit her, or at the very least her physique was sufficiently tall and athletic that she didn't look like a child playing dressup.

To Matt's surprise however, Jane's proclamation of readiness was not echoed by anyone else. On the contrary, and to Matt's slight confusion, far from being excited, serious or "mission-ready," the rest of the Acolytes just looked kind of . . . glum?

James sighed and rubbed the back of his head. "Giselle, can you grab some firewood?"

"Copy, copy."

"Thanks." He glanced over at Matt as Giselle vanished, the rush of air from her departure barely rising above the wind sweeping over the hillside. "Sit down, kid," the strongman told him. He began patting a circle flat on the ground with his enormous hands. "Get comfortable."

"Wait," said Jane. She walked over as Natalia and Will spread out around James's circle, the psychic standing with her arms crossed, the teleporter sitting atop the grass. "What's going on?" She flinched slightly as Giselle returned, her arms laden with sticks, which the speedster began wordlessly arranging into a pointed stack. "Why do we need a fire? Shouldn't we strike quickly? What about the element of surprise?"

Natalia muttered something inaudible under her breath. Across from her, Will laughed bitterly, his arms crossed over his chest.

"First rule of hunting clairvoyants, Empath," he said, not sparing Jane any eye contact, "there are only bad surprises."

James just shook his head and kept patting down the grass.

"Just light the fire," he said, sounding more resigned than annoyed. Jane's mouth moved as if to protest and she glanced over at Matt, who was struggling to articulate anything as his stomach veered between confusion, helplessness, and terror. Eventually, grumbling, she gave up and flicked a quick stream of fire from her hands. The sticks ignited, crackling happily in the center of the depression, and a thin trail of smoke began drifting along with the breeze.

"Good," said James. He leaned down into sitting, the plates of his armor squeaking beneath his bulk. "Now pop a squat. There's some stuff we have to cover."

"What about the mission?" Jane protested, pointing her hand toward the rising hill. "What about the—"

"Oh my God, shut up," growled Natalia, pinching between her eyes. "This is not about you, you stupid dumb—"

"Screw you, you piece of—"

"Shut up," demanded James, scowling at them. "Both of you." Natalia fell silent, though she continued to stare at Jane with obvious venom. The gigantic man glared. "Empath, sit down."

For a few moments Jane remained standing, grumbling under her breath, but eventually under the group's withering gaze she dropped to the ground, shuffling into a cross-legged glower to Matt's right. Matt, for his part, was still completely dazed, feeling like he was sleepwalking through some surreal waking dream. Slowly though, from beneath the waves of adrenaline, his brain began sifting through everything that had been said.

"Wait," he said hoarsely, raising his head to look at Will. "What do you mean 'the first rule of hunting clairvoyants'?" He turned to James, the giant's face lit by the fire's cracking shadows. "And back at the mansion, Winters said they'd found 'another one.' " Matt looked around at his classmates, who were all avoiding his eyes. "Have you guys hunted clairvoyants *before*?"

"You're the seer," muttered Natalia.

"Nat," James grunted, though again more placating than annoyed. He turned back to Matt and sat up a little straighter in the firelight. "You're right. This isn't the first clairvoyant we've gone after. And the others . . . well . . . they went . . ."

"Bad," finished Will. He didn't meet Matt's eyes, staring directly into the fire. "They went bad."

"Bad," agreed James. He sighed and leaned back on his massive hands, pushing divots into the ground. A few moments passed as James gazed up at the night sky and Matt stared at him with concerned incredulity, before eventually the strongman shook his head and spoke.

"All right, so, the thing you have to know is," James began, sounding like someone's boss explaining why they weren't getting a raise, "the Legion's been hearing rumors about clairvoyants for decades. Least according to Farrington anyway."

"Farrington?" Matt asked. "Who's—"

"Chuck Farrington," said James. "Ashes. The fire guy?" Matt just stared blankly. Beside him, Jane spat out a little huff of disbelief. James waved a brief, indifferent hand. "Doesn't matter. Anyway, after the Black Death, well, obviously they're pretty keen to find one, so the Ashes keep their ears to the ground. Finally, a lead pops up, and they send Winters to check it out." He gestured at Matt. "You know, meet and greet. You want to join our clubhouse. That sort of thing."

"Right," said Matt, having himself been met and greeted.

"Right. So, Winters finds this guy," James continued, and in the flickering firelight, Matt could almost see images of the story dancing in the flames. "Up in the Appalachian Mountains, border of West Virginia, small little cabin somewhere in the woods. Winters flies down, usual immaculate self, says hi to the guy, guy says hi back, they shake hands, and then Winters has a perfectly pleasant conversation about who he is, what he wants, and how great it is to join the Legion. The guy says yes, sir, thank you, sir, that all sounds great, won't you come inside for a bite, have a coffeepot on the stove, now just wait there a moment, I need to step out back. Next thing you know, Winters hears this *krrrrsh-krrrrsh-KRAK*"—James slapped his hands together and both Matt and Jane jumped—"and suddenly the whole cabin's full of smoke." He paused and looked between the two of them. "Winters races around back to find the man with one hand clasped either side of a generator, body and soul fried completely effin' black."

"What?" Matt whispered. James grimaced as the other Acolytes around the campfire averted their eyes.

"Yep. Electrocuted himself. Couldn't be more dead if he tried. Winters said it was the worst thing he ever saw, and all the more horrifying because half a minute ago this guy had been all politeness and smiles. Smelled something fierce too, apparently."

Across the campfire, Giselle clutched her legs to her chest, looking decidedly sick.

"I don't understand," said Matt. "Why did he . . . ?"

"Good question," James answered. "Winters, well, he was obviously pretty shook up, but he chalked it up to that one dude being a crazy person and tried to move on. Anyway, a year or two later, another rumor pans out, so Winters goes again—this time brings Cross along for, what"—he looked at Will—"comfort?"

"Moral support," said the teleporter.

"Moral support. Anyway, they find this next lady, what was she, Indian?"

"Tamil," corrected Giselle, still looking uncomfortable.

"Tamil. Right. Well, this nice little eighty-something-year-old grandma, I don't think they ever properly established her name, she's been giving predictions to people for a while there in a little lone house up in the hills, so Cross and Winters go to see her, and about ten feet out from her house, they start smelling gas."

"Oh no," whispered Matt.

"Oh yes," James replied, his voice torn between incensed, incredulous, and grave. "Little old lady fire-balled herself so bad it took a week to identify her remains. But you know the crazy part?" He leaned in toward Matt and Jane. "She waved at them beforehand. Stuck her head out the window and waved at them a big gummy smile, then flicked a lighter and blew herself up. Cross and Winters saw the whole damn thing."

"But why?" said Jane, visibly confused. "Why would she . . . ?"

James held up his hand. "No. See, it's not just her. Not just him neither. All of them, every single one. There's been what, six over the years? Seven? I lose count." He shook his head. "Next one after Sri Lanka, Winters took Natalia. Guess the plan was to sniff out crazy ahead of time. How'd that go, Nat?"

"Claymore," the psychic said glumly.

"Claymore," confirmed James. "Military-grade goddamn antipersonnel mine, which I don't even know how you find on a sheep farm in Scotland, but damn if he didn't set it up right inside the barn door."

"I reached out to him," explained Natalia, leaning toward Matt, clearly feeling the need to elaborate. "We were about half a mile away. That's what's"—she swore— "insane. I was chatting to him as we walked, barely brushed his mind. He was perfectly happy. Perfectly calm."

"Tell them the conversation," James encouraged. Natalia sighed, cleared her throat and began miming out two people talking.

"Hello, sir? My name's Natalia Baroque. I'm sorry to bother you, but—"

"Natalia! Good morning! Lovely ta meet ya. Beautiful weather we're having!"

"It is, sir, if we could have just a moment of your time—"

"Aye, sorry, lass, not today. But if innae too much of a bother, I'd be ever so grateful if ya could round up the sheep afterwards."

"I . . . what? After what?"

"They spook at loud noises, I'm afraid, and three spritelier ones'll clear the fence right smart—daft buggers be halfway ta Glasgow this time tommora if ya dinnae stoppem."

"I'm sorry, loud noises? What do you—"

"Don't fret, love. This innet your fault."

The psychic paused and puffed out her cheeks. "Boom. No hesitation. Took out half the sodding barn." Matt gaped at her, and the psychic shook her head. "Bloody awful."

"He was right too," James added, ruefully chipper. "After the explosion, the sheep freaked out. Three of them made a break for it. Winters had to spend twenty minutes flying around trying to catch 'em."

"The thing is," Natalia interjected, cutting over James's words, "he wasn't crazy. He wasn't scared. He just . . . killed himself." She shivered. "Like it was the most normal thing in the world."

A horrible silence spread out around the campfire.

"Well," James continued eventually, reaching up to pat Natalia gingerly on the arm. "After that, Winters starts going in heavy, 'cause, man, he is *freaked out.* 'Course, the Legion's not re-formed yet, and they're not technically supposed to be doing missions so it's all on the hush-hush—but he's got me, Will, Nat, and Giselle as backup, and he has us going in armored and . . . well . . ."

James trailed off, then shook his head. "Look," he said. "Don't get me wrong. I ain't a stranger to violence. I've given it and I've taken it and I ain't queasy. But these clairvoyants, man, goddamn, they are a creative bunch." He threw a dark, humorless look at Giselle. "Remember that one guy who dropped an anvil on himself then fell in a vat of acid?"

"Please don't," the speedster murmured, not looking up.

"And there was that other one, this crazy guy—you won't believe this—rigged like fourteen shotguns, all in this one tiny cabin, could barely freaking move," James continued, powering obliviously on. "All pointed at different angles, all tied up on a single string. Craziest, most *Home Alone* thing I have ever seen in my entire goddamn life. Pulled it right as we walked in the door."

"Oh God, can we not?" moaned Giselle.

"This is making me feel, um, somewhat concerned," said Matt, in what was possibly the understatement of the decade.

"Yo, James," Will piped up, ignoring Matt's distress. "Remember the woodchipper?"

"Son, I ain't gonna be able to forget the woodchipper until the day I mercifully die."

"What the hell?" breathed Jane. Matt stared at James in mute, aghast agreement. The strongman just shook his head.

"That's just it, man. Nobody knows. No one's got the faintest clue. It's not like we're going there to assault these folks, cause 'em any kind of harm, not in the slightest. Legit, all we want to do is talk. But like clockwork, every time we do, they just . . . kill themselves."

James paused. In the flickering firelight, his expression grew dark. "Makes you wonder," he murmured, "makes you wonder what they're seeing. What fate was in store for them that they'd rather die than even talking to the Legion."

Death stalks Morningstar, whispered in the back of Matt's skull. And despite the warmth of the fire, he shuddered.

For a moment, nobody said anything. Then James piqued back up, sounding much cheerier.

"'Least, that was what everyone was thinking, right before you came along. I gotta say, man, that was a goddamn relief. Like"—the strongman raised a hand and began counting off his sausage-sized fingers—"you were on the register. You lived in a normal home. You weren't a crazy person. And you didn't immediately try and off yourself the minute Winters walked up. I don't know. I, for one, found that very comforting." He smiled genially around the group with a false sort of positivity that was in no way reciprocated.

Implications—horrible, horrible implications—rampaged through Matt's mind. Eventually, he managed to cobble together some words.

"But this one," he managed to stammer, "this clairvoyant. She . . . she walked in front of the camera. She must've known it would see her, and that we'd see it, and that we'd find her . . . so maybe . . . she . . ."

But James shook his massive head. "Nuh-uh. Sorry. That's the pattern too. See, it's never easy to find these folks. Not one of them lives anywhere populated, and none of them are registered. If we try to ID them, it comes back fake. They all live off the grid—waaaay off the grid. Except for when they don't."

He kneaded his giant hands slowly into the dirt. "The year or so leading up to finding one of these guys, the Legion starts hearing 'bout these crazy thefts. It's like the one Winters told you about. You seen that movie *Groundhog Day*?" He paused, and when Matt didn't respond, powered on regardless. "Remember that bit where the guy just walks over and lifts money out of the armored car because he knows exactly what's going to happen? It's exactly like that. These dudes, these clairvoyants, they just walk in, flawless, impeccable timing, take whatever they want, and walk out. Security is helpless; the cameras never see them—never get more than a glimpse or the top of a head through a smudge on a lens or something. Until they want them to. Until one day they go to a bank, walk out with a sack full o' money, turn to the camera, and just . . . smile."

James shook his head again and fell silent. After a few moments, Giselle picked up where he'd left off.

"They don't just steal money either," she told them. Her lips twitched into a grimace. "Factories, tech companies, military facilities—and that's just the stuff we know about. Half the time, it's not reported. Half the time, we're not even sure it's them. And half the time, whoever it is that's been stolen from doesn't figure out they've even been robbed until weeks afterward. It's so seamless."

"And a lot of it doesn't make sense either," piped up Will. "Like the shotgun guy, we think he might've hit a medical lab, some high-tech place, and made off with some . . . what, regenerative cream?"

"Serum," Natalia corrected, rolling her eyes.

"Serum, whatever." Will scowled. "Doesn't really matter, because two months later, he blew himself to bits. That's what I'm saying. Like, why bother? Even if it works, and who knows if it did, what's the point of stealing, like, high-tech bedsore medicine if you're going to kill yourself in two freaking months?"

"Ain't no cream in the world fixing fourteen shotguns," James agreed.

"Serum!" snapped Natalia.

"And we never find it," Giselle continued, ignoring the others. "Not the money, not anything we think they stole, none of it. They never make anything; they never buy anything. There just doesn't seem to be any point."

A long silence stretched out across the hillside. The fire was starting to burn low. Beside him, Jane turned slowly toward Matt, her features carefully arranged in discreet, horrified panic.

"So," she said, her voice unusually high, "then . . . um . . . what's the plan?"

James grinned at Giselle and cracked his knuckles. "This time," he told them, "it'll be different. We've turned a corner, I can feel it.

We've got a clairvoyant with us now, a good one, and this time we can follow your lead. Any traps, anything like that, you'll see it coming. And when you get close enough, maybe, just maybe you can see what's got these other clairvoyants so messed up and you can get through to them, help them see we're not the bad guys, convince them to talk."

"Or alternatively," Natalia posited dryly, "you'll also see what's causing them to lose their minds and you'll go psycho and kill yourself."

"No, you won't." Giselle scowled, staring daggers at the psychic. "That's not going to happen. Matt, the minute you start feeling anything's wrong, okay, you just yell as loud as you can, and I'll come get you out of there. There's nothing so bad that can happen that we can't talk about it, and that we can't work through as a team. Okay?" She leaned over and squeezed his hand. "I promise. We'll get through this. Whatever it is you see."

Will and James nodded in agreement. Natalia just rolled her eyes. Slowly, Matt turned to look at Jane sitting beside him, and the pair stared at each other with wide, terrified eyes.

"Ahhhhhhhhhhh . . ."

"I'm-gonna-die-I'm-gonna-die-I'm-gonna-die-I'm-gonna-die-I'm-gonna—"

"Will you shut up!" Jane hissed.

It was still night. They were crouched in the mud at the edge of a small patch of forest, pressed side by side against a gray deciduous beech. Above, the sky spread in a swirling violet dome over the valley, the moon's light shining down between occasional wisps of cloud, illuminating the ruined property below. Nothing stirred. The farmstead, or what had once been a farmstead, was long-since abandoned, a maze of crumbling bricks and rotting stockades, dark single-story cottages with collapsed roofs and fallen drystone walls. Long grass grew up around shadowed doorways, and creepers twisted silently through paneless windows into the darkness beyond. Somewhere inside, apparently, was the clairvoyant, but from here there was no sign of her—no light, no movement, no noise. The cold night air was silent, save for crickets calling from the undergrowth, the occasional hooting of an owl, and . . .

"I'm-gonna-die-I'm-gonna-die-I'm-gonna-die-I'm-gonna-die-I'm-gonna—"

"Shhhhh!"

It was just the two of them. After James had finished his enlightening but thoroughly unsettling explanation, the Acolytes had set out toward their target with Matt and Jane exchanging frantic panicked sign language in the rear. A few hundred feet out, at a small grove of crooked beech trees, they'd stopped, and at Matt's insistence he and Jane had gone on ahead for the sake of "reconnaissance." Then, once he'd made sure that they were far enough away that no one could hear them, Matt had allowed himself the indulgence of freaking out.

"I'm-gonna-die-I'm-gonna-die-I'm-gonna—"

A sudden, stinging pain rang out across Matt's cheek, causing him to recoil, cowering and clutching defensively at his face. Jane raised her hand for a second slap.

"Ow!" he whispered, glaring at her. The empath glared right back. "Don't!"

"Calm. Down," she snarled, leaning close, her eyes wild. Beneath mottled shadows and moonlight, the angles of her face turned inhuman and deranged. "Get. Yourself. Together."

"I am allowed to freak out!" Matt hissed furiously. Nevertheless, he sunk back down into seething, terrified silence. They stared out over the ruins.

"What are we going to do?" Jane asked after a minute or two. She kept her voice level but seemed unable to stop intertwining her fingers, her jaw clenched.

"Jesus freaking Christ, Jane, what a pertinent question," said Matt, unable to help himself. Now that he'd found his voice, the words tumbled out in an unstoppable torrent. "Really glad I brought you here to penetrate into the central logistical conundrum!"

"Matt."

"Sorry. Sorry!" Matt forced himself to take a deep, shuddering breath. He ran his hands, shaking, through his clammy, sweaty hair. "Okay. Okay. This is bad."

"You think?"

"Yes, I do. I do think. Okay. Okay." Matt closed his eyes, feeling like his heart was trying to beat itself out of his rib cage. If he had been standing, he would have started to pace, but as the two of them were trying to be stealth-like, crouched uncomfortably against the tree, he settled for rocking back and forth on the spot.

Jane shook her head, her face pale in the moonlight.

"You've got to call it," she murmured.

"What?"

"You've got to call it. Give up, before this goes any further. Tell them the truth about what you are."

"Are you insane?" Matt hissed, turning on her completely. "I can't do that, I'll—"

"You are not a clairvoyant!" Jane hissed back, cutting him off. "Were you listening? Did you hear all that back there?! They think you're an actual clairvoyant! Like these actual clairvoyants! Who are actually killing themselves, horribly, rather than letting the Legion talk to them!"

She took a deep breath and rubbed her temples, clearly working hard to steady her voice. "Look," she said, "I have gone along with this so far, and I have kept my stupid mouth shut, but this is not a goddamn game anymore. This is not freaking crows in backpacks. This is real"— she chained together several violent swear words—"danger! People have actually died! You've got to come clean! You can't keep lying!"

"Absolutely not," Matt said, vehemently shaking his head. "No goddamn way. Have you lost your mind? What about the child? Have you forgotten what he said?"

Jane paused. "Stay hidden or the world ends," she conceded.

"Exactly," said Matt. "This has to be what he's talking about."

"And you believe him?"

"Well, I don't know!" Matt turned toward the farmstead then looked back helplessly at Jane. "I don't want to end the world!"

For a moment, the empath looked like she was preparing a derogatory retort, but eventually settled for just shaking her head. "This is insane," she muttered.

"I know," said Matt. He forced himself to take a deep breath. "Okay. Look, I agree, this is less than ideal. Let's . . . let's just see if there's actually anyone down there. Maybe it's a dead end. Maybe this will all sort itself out."

Jane murmured something under her breath, but nevertheless begrudgingly got to her feet and likewise pulled Matt into standing.

Crouching low, the two of them began a slow, cautious descent down the hill.

"Wait," said Jane, barely a minute later as they approached the outer edges of the ruins, a line of rotting wooden fence posts. Her eyes narrowed and she stepped forward, reaching out blindly into the night air with searching, wary fingertips. After a moment or two, she stopped short, clearly having found something. Matt squinted to try and see.

"Is that—"

"Wire. Yep. Get behind me." She spread one hand and a thin shield of fire flared between them and the posts. "Back up." They retreated several steps up the hill, then with the flaming shield still active Jane raised her other hand and conjured a small, jagged ball of loose ice. Gingerly, she lobbed the ball at the wire, strung almost invisibly between fence posts. Matt cringed and plugged his ears, waiting for an explosion, but instead the ice just sailed in a low arc, hit the wire and cut cleanly in half, falling to the ground with a soft hiss of slush.

"Trap," Jane grunted. Matt looked up at her.

"Trip wire?"

"No. Line's tense. Trap's not for us." She lowered her hand and the fire shield snuffed out.

"Who's it for?"

"Giselle," Jane muttered darkly. She looked back at Matt. "Piano wire. It's a ghetto anti-speedster trick. Difficult to see when they're running and if they go through it—"

"Sliced like a deli sandwich." Matt grimaced and swallowed. "Guess that answers whether they know we're coming or not."

"Guess it does." Jane paused. "Want to keep going?"

"Do we have a choice?" Matt replied.

"I mean, you could go back and tell them you foresee disaster or something. Get everyone to leave."

Matt grimaced. "Raises too many questions. Besides, I don't know if 'disaster' will be enough. Were you listening back there? This is like the seventh time the Legion's found a clairvoyant. Every one of them has been a"—he swore—"disaster, and here they are again, un-de-freaking-terred." He shook his head. "Cross is already getting suspicious. I've been making vague predictions for weeks, if I bail on this with something hazy, she'll crucify me."

"Still though." Jane frowned. "Aren't they supposed to be listening to you?"

"Sure," said Matt. "People love listening, right up until you tell them they can't do something they want to."

Jane made a face. "So, through the piano wire then."

"Yep." Matt pointed to the rotting fence posts. "Guessing it's glued to that?"

"Or tied or wedged somehow."

"Great. Burn it. If and when I scream very loudly, I want Giselle to be able to run in and rescue us."

"Sounds good." Jane stepped warily forward and incinerated the fence posts, and in the light of the moon Matt saw something thin and silvery fall to the ground.

Slowly, steadily, they continued onward, passing cautiously through the fence line, keeping their eyes open for additional surprises. This time, as they advanced toward the farmstead, it was Matt who spotted the trap.

"There," he said, pointing at a gap between two walls that might have once been an alleyway. "Right there, look, there's a gap in the grass. The earth's been dug up."

"I see it," confirmed Jane, and again she drew the two of them back, raising the fire shield. She knelt and placed her other palm on the ground, and a thick trail of frost began snaking out across the mud. The ice continued to spread and thicken, and sure enough, when it reached the section of dug-up earth there was a sudden *boom*, and Matt felt a rush of force.

"Land mine?" he asked, straightening up.

"Land mine," Jane confirmed. They exchanged a look. "Low-yield. Probably homemade."

"That's reassuring."

"Thoughts?"

"Retreat. Retreat and ponder our options." They withdrew back up the hill, Jane scanning around suspiciously at the geography, Matt sticking close to her side. They'd almost gotten to the edge of the beech grove when Jane touched a finger to her head.

"It's Natalia," she informed him. "She's linking me up to the rest of them." A pause. "James is asking if we're all right. They heard the boom."

"Tell them we're fine. Tell them what we've found. I need a minute or two to think."

Jane nodded, put her finger to her temple, and scrunched up her eyes. "Natalia says she can sense someone in the ruins," she told him, dropping her hand with a scowl. "Now that she's looking for them. Can't pin down an exact location though. Apparently, they're using Psy-Block. 'The legitimate thing,' she says." Jane smirked. "Wonder who that's directed at."

"Great," Matt muttered. "Another amazing coincidence." He clenched and unclenched his hands, his fingers stiff and freezing despite the uncomfortable heat in his chest. "So, we can be fairly certain they know we're coming. And their attitude toward guests."

Jane paused, staring at him. "What do we do? How do we get out of this?"

For a moment, it was all Matt could do not to panic—to run, screaming, as far away from this haunted-looking place as fast as his stumpy legs could carry him, find a nice pile of sand, and bury his head in it. Eventually though, the worry on Jane's face as well as her seemingly unconscious iron grip on his arm forced him to slow his breathing and try vainly to reassert some measure of control.

"Okay," he muttered. He sucked a few long breaths between his teeth. "Think. Let me think. I'm thinking."

A moment passed.

"Well?"

"Shut up!" he hissed. "I'm still . . . Okay. All right." He took a deep breath and forced himself to stand up straight, peering out over the darkened farmland beyond.

"It seems fair to say this is a real clairvoyant," he said.

"Agreed."

"Gathering from all the evidence Winters found, plus the traps being tailored for each of us."

"Are they?" Jane sounded skeptical. Matt nodded.

"You said it yourself. The piano wire's meant for Giselle. And the land mines, they might not go off fast enough if she ran over them, but they sure as hell would if James came stomping through. Strength's not much use against explosives."

"Plus the Psy-Block."

"Plus the Psy-Block," Matt agreed. "And I'm betting if Will tried to jump in there, he'd find a Disruptance blocking him too. Whoever this woman is, she's tailor-made traps for each of the other four."

"Agreed."

"Which means either she's got insider knowledge—"

"Seems unlikely."

"Or she's a clairvoyant."

"A real clairvoyant," Jane added.

"Thank you," Matt glared at her in the dark. "Yes, a real clairvoyant. And if she really is a real clairvoyant, then she knows we're coming."

"Right."

"And she knows we know that she knows that we're coming."

"Got it."

"And she knows we know she knows that we know that she knows that we're coming"—he waved around his hand—"ad infinitum. Right?"

"Uh . . . right?"

"Right. Which raises a whole lot of very difficult philosophical questions," Matt continued, furrowing his brow. "Like if she knows what's going to happen, can she stop it? Can we stop it? Is there even such a thing as free will? Is our entire existence predetermined?"

"Um . . . I don't know," replied Jane, her face paling.

Matt shook his head like a dog trying to clear water from its ears. "No. It's irrelevant. We can't get bogged down in philosophy. It is what it is, time is what it is, the future remains to be written. Or it doesn't. It doesn't matter. Either way, we still feel like we've got a choice."

"Right," confirmed Jane, sounding semi-back on board.

Matt screwed up his eyes, trying to think. "This lady walked in front of the camera knowing the Legion would come here. And if she knew that'd happen, then she knew they'd send me to try and talk to her. And if she knew that, and she didn't leave, that means either she wanted it, or she doesn't care."

"Right," said Jane, "except for the land mines."

"The land mines, yes. Those indicate a pretty strong preference for being left alone."

"And they might not have just been for James either. They could blow you up."

"Yes," Matt conceded. Then a moment later he said, "No," contradicting himself. "They couldn't. Because think about it. If they knew I was coming, then they knew you were coming. And they knew you could clear the land mines with your ground icy thing."

"Really?"

"Yeah," said Matt, suddenly bizarrely certain. "Think about it. You're a counter to all the traps. Your fire burns whatever's holding the piano wire. And you can roll the ice forward from a safe distance, clear a path through the mines."

"Which means . . ."

"Which means you're meant to come with me," Matt murmured. He ran his hands again through his hair. "You, not any of the others."

"Are you sure?" said Jane. "What if I'm supposed to clear a path, and *then* we come in with the others? All together?"

Matt made a face. "No, because then . . ." He hesitated, chewing his lip. "If we were just going to clear them all and come in anyway, why put any traps to begin with?" Thoughts came rapidly and unbidden. "It's like . . . the traps aren't actually *traps*, you know? They're not supposed to be. The clairvoyant's trying to tell us how to approach her, we . . . we're square pegs. They're square holes."

Jane's face was pained. "Are you sure?"

"No," Matt muttered, "not at all." He turned to her. "But it's the only thing that makes sense."

"None of this makes sense," Jane lamented. Matt ignored her.

"Think about it. They knew I was going to be here. They knew I'd bring you. They knew what powers you have and they knew"—he swallowed—"they knew what I can do. That I can't go back empty-handed. So, either this is all some huge trap—"

"Definitely likely."

"Or somebody wants me in that house." The pair fell silent. Matt looked at Jane. "We've got to go."

"Are you sure?"

"No. Not in any way, shape, or form. But what other choice do we have? I can't leave. And I can't send Giselle or James in first, they'll get killed. Besides, I've just got a feeling. Occam's Razor." He glanced at Jane as she gave him a puzzled look. "Simple solutions. If this clairvoyant wanted me dead, all she needed to do was put a land mine exactly where she knew I'd land when we teleported. She didn't do that, so she mustn't *want* to do that." He glanced over at the farmstead. "Which means I need to talk to her."

For a few moments, Jane just stared at him. "My head hurts," she admitted. Matt distractedly waved her concerns away.

"Mine too. It doesn't matter. I have no idea what I'm doing. Nobody has any idea what they're doing. I feel like I'm going insane. Please don't let me die?"

"I'll goddamn try. We doing this?"

"Oh God, I think so." He groaned. "Jesus Christ. What am I doing? Why is this happening? Why couldn't I just stay home?"

"You lie too well."

"Thanks. I think. Oh God, this is a bad dream. This isn't happening." He shook his hands and fingers, sucking in deep, shaky breaths.

"You got this? You good? Want to freak out a bit more?"

"No. Yes. Maybe just a little." Matt took a deep breath and closed his eyes, trying to find his mental center. "Okay. Okay. Let's do this."

"Let me go first. I'll ice it."

They set back off down the hill, Jane in the lead, Matt following closely behind, keeping his left hand warily on her right shoulder. Once they passed the line of broken fence posts, the empath conjured a thick ball of ice the height of a car tire, which she sent rolling at a steady pace some hundred feet ahead. The pair continued, if possible, even more slowly this time, and Matt found himself struggling not to jump at the slightest movement or sound.

They reached the edge of the farmyard, collapsed brick walls and wooden palings that, at some point, might have herded stock. They ducked underneath some piano wire, which Jane incinerated, and a few seconds later a hundred feet away the ice ball exploded. Jane waved her hands silently to conjure another one, and the pair advanced into the ruins.

All around them, debris loomed—lines of stones and walls of crumbling bricks, buildings only marginally taller than Matt with purposes as long-lost as their roofs. Some were flecked with peeling paint, others rusted and bare; weeds grew out between cracks in the brick, and many of the walls were pockmarked with fist-sized gaps, blank, stony eyes through which stared only darkness. Every step they took drew them deeper in, until it seemed like the whole world was this looming, crumbling maze, this rural rabbit warren of stone and rot. Ahead, the ice ball turned around a corner, and there was another explosion, and the side of the building ahead of them collapsed. Matt's heart pounded in his chest.

"Wait," said Jane abruptly. She came to a stop, causing Matt to almost run into her. She turned to him, her brows furrowed.

"What the hell are we doing?" she asked as they stood between the walls of two ruined houses.

"Trying to find a clairvoyant?" Matt answered. Jane's face scrunched into a dissatisfied scowl.

"No," she replied. "I mean what am I doing? Why the hell am I letting you come along?"

"What?"

"You're a civilian," Jane said, and then evidently realized that she thought that was insulting because she immediately added, "I mean not *technically*, not like a civilian-civilian, but still, you don't have any powers. You shouldn't be anywhere near this."

"Shouldn't I?" Matt asked, a little perplexed.

"No." Jane scowled and shook her head as if she had just woken up. "God, what the hell am I doing? I should've swept this whole place. Clear then advance. That's what they taught us in VIP extraction."

"Glad you think I'm very important," said Matt. Jane rolled her eyes.

"Stay there," she commanded, rising abruptly into the air on a pillar of fire. "Don't go anywhere. Don't step anywhere. Don't go walking on anything. I can scout out the area, see if I can see anyone, and clear out the mines."

"Wait—" Matt started to protest, but before he could say anything Jane was off, rocketing from wall to wall like she had jetpacks on her feet. There was a crack of ice and a distant, dusty boom, and then the light of Jane's fire powers began receding into the distance. Alone in the darkness, Matt watched her go.

"Wait," he whispered ineffectually, the words falling hoarse from his lips. He glanced nervously at his surroundings, the crumbling walls and skulking shadows looming precariously all around. Matt drew a deep breath, willing his hands not to shake.

"Horror movie," he muttered, more to himself than anybody. "Never seen one single freaking horror movie in her entire goddamn life . . . yeah just split up, go on . . . don't mind me, I'll just wait . . . alone . . ."

Matt breathed deep, trying to keep his thoughts from spiraling wildly. He looked up at the stars, focusing on the patterns, trying to see if there were any he could recognize. Astronomy. That was a stupid hobby he could take up when he got back to the Academy if he actually survived. Maybe he could tie it into astrology, traditional stupid future-telling stuff. Maybe Ed could order him a telescope. Breathe. Just breathe. The air smelled of damp and dirt and despite the nighttime cold sweat beaded on Matt's brow.

It made sense, he tried to reassure himself, what Jane was doing made sense. This would save them wandering around blindly, and heck, half the buildings here didn't have roofs—maybe she could spot the clairvoyant from the sky. There had to be some signal right? Some light or sign of life? Clairvoyant or no, she was still a person—still had a normal person's needs. She was just better at anticipating them. At anticipating everything. Perfectly.

Suddenly, Matt realized his mistake.

"JANE!" he began to cry—but before the words could come out, there was a snap, a rush, and a rumbling, and the ground beneath Matt opened into a blackened pit, and he tumbled down into darkness.

THE CHAIN OF SACRIFICE

"Light thinks it travels faster than anything, but it is wrong. No matter how fast light travels, it finds the darkness has always got there first, and is waiting for it."

—Terry Pratchett, *Reaper Man*, 1991

Through darkness and dust Matt fell. He plummeted, turning, his shoulder colliding with something hard, and then suddenly he was rolling blindly, tumbling down a slope. His arms curled around his head and his legs clutched to his chest and he braced himself for pain or death or worse—

And then abruptly he felt himself hit solid ground and with a sudden *oof* he stopped.

Darkness. Complete and utter darkness.

"Hhhhhggggg . . ." The breath came painfully, through reluctant, shaking lungs, but to Matt's everlasting relief it did eventually come. He lay there in the blackness for a few moments, waiting for his breathing to recover, completely unable to see, feeling like he'd just gone three rounds with a flight of stairs.

Get up, a dull, distant part of his consciousness thought, *get out*. Slowly, blearily, Matt attempted to comply.

His hands scraped around the ground, fingertips trembling, finding nothing but dirt. Slowly, Matt tested one leg, then the other, and with a winded groan rolled over to his stomach. He reached out until his fingers found solid rock and with an almighty effort pulled himself to standing. The darkness swam as he stood upright, lurching and spinning, and

Matt clutched the wall for balance, tasting dirt on his tongue. It was still completely black.

Okay, he whispered to himself, cold, petrified, alone. *Okay. Breathe.* He was alive and relatively unharmed. Was he? In a sudden rush of panic, Matt fumbled up and down his body, patting over himself for hints of broken bones. A few things ached but nothing screamed. He let out a sigh of relief. Okay. Good. Now think. He'd clearly fallen down something, some hole in the earth, though obviously not too far, because he'd been banged about but not broken. He'd rolled down some sort of slope. That meant there was probably—

Groping blindly in the darkness, Matt's fingers traced clumsily in random directions across the wall. Sure enough, within a few seconds, his left hand turned a corner, and Matt found himself gingerly patting an earthen incline. He moved both hands and put his palms to it, trying to judge the degree. If zero was flat and ninety was a right angle this was . . . steep. Damn. Matt's hands slid up the slope. Nope. No way was he getting back up that. Not with who knows how much space ahead, and nothing to grab or hold on to.

Okay. Okay. Just breathe, he reassured himself. You're a little bit underground. That's fine. Worse things have happened to better people. Jane was nearby. She'd probably heard the commotion, and even if she hadn't, sooner or later the others would figure out he was gone. They could get, like, sniffer dogs or something. Or terramancers. Celeste as a bloodhound. They could find him. It'd be fine.

Stay put, Matt told himself. *Don't do anything stupid and you'll be absolutely fine.*

A soft scrape of wood creaked out from the darkness.

"Hello?" Matt called instinctively, before his hands jumped to his throat. Oh no. His gaze raced around wildly for the source of the sound, heart hammering in his chest. Nothing. He could see nothing.

"Hello?" he whispered, the words barely coming out. Fear, cold and clotting, rose thick inside his chest.

I've seen this movie, came the unbidden, terrified thought.

Wait. Wait, no, his phone! Matt's hands scrambled to his pockets, fumbling for the—yes! Trembling, his arm reached out, and a beam of neon light cut straight into the darkness.

Right into the face of an old, hook-nosed woman.

"ARGH!" Matt screamed. He jerked backward, his feet snagging on uneven ground, sending him lurching into a fall. His hands flayed wildly, and it was only by chance that he caught himself, barely, fingers scrabbling against the rock. The phone fell from his grasp and landed face down in the dirt, its light fading to a tiny square creeping feebly around the edges. Matt swayed in the barely illuminated darkness, heart hammering.

Across the room, the woman let out a low, soft chuckle.

"Come now," she murmured. "No need for all that."

Matt recoiled upward, the back of his armor scraping rough against the wall. Faintly, distantly, he was aware that one of his hands was bleeding, but his screaming mind barely noticed. He stood there, frozen in place, as among a tomb of earth and darkness, the old woman turned away.

"Better light, I think," she said, and there was a hint of merriment in her voice. Her weathered hands reached over to the gray wooden table in front of her, her fingers tracing the curves of a small gas lantern. There was a *click*, and in an instant the room was set to dancing with a flickering orange glow.

Room. They were in a room. Matt's hands shook, his mind struggling to take in the details. It was earthen and square, barely ten feet high and maybe that again across. The walls were cut from earth; the ceiling was cut from earth. The floor had some gray cobblestones laid into it, wide and flat and thin, but dirt still showed between them. Along the sides rotted a few dark timber shelves, and in the center was the wooden table where the old woman sat. A wooden bench was pressed against the far wall, and as Matt's eyes swept the room, the woman rose with her back to him and shuffled toward it, reaching for a small copper kettle atop a pine green camping stove.

"Are you hurt?" she asked. She didn't seem as small now that she was standing, and in the dancing shadows Matt's mad eyes thought they saw streaks of black still peppered through her gray and wispy hair. She had on a simple brown, floor-length dress, an overcoat, and a knitted scarlet shawl, which draped loose around her shoulders as she bent and clicked the stove's igniter. After a few seconds, the flames ignited and the kettle began to boil. "We thought the armor would take most of the hit, and if not, well, the Legion's healers . . . very skilled. Still . . ." She paused and cast a glance back at Matt, still frozen against the wall. "I do hope you're all right."

The woman turned away from him and shuffled toward the nearby shelf, picking two porcelain mugs out with slow, deliberate movements. Somewhere far above them, there was a distant boom and the ceiling marginally rattled. *The mines*, Matt thought sluggishly. This all felt like a dream. He could barely move.

"I . . . you . . . where is . . . how . . . ?"

"A trapdoor," the woman in the shawl said simply, turning back toward the bench, a mug in either hand. "Rather clever design. Slides right beneath the mud. Took some fiddling to get right. But it should keep young Miss Walker busy, bless her soul."

"You know . . . Jane?"

"Oh yes. Know all about her. And you. Wonderful, the both of you."

Matt stared at her, not knowing what to say. The woman appeared not to notice, humming contentedly to herself as she pried open a duck-patterned tin and spooned something pungent into the cups. She was hunched over, Matt noticed, hair dangling free across her face, and her skin was leathered and worn. Yet she lacked the frailty and wizening of age, and by Matt's estimate was younger than his initial impression, maybe fifty-five, maybe sixty. Reluctantly, Matt forced his gaze around the rest of the room. The shelves, those that weren't broken, were sparsely laden with tins and bowls, lone dusty cans, the odd cup and saucer. And the far wall, the one the bench was up against, was different from the others somehow. The left side—it wasn't even. It looked like a pile of rocks, collapsed over something. The bottom of a staircase. Matt craned his neck. As he did, he spied the edge of something at the woman's feet, something flat and white, something familiar. A pillow. A camping mat.

"How long have you been here?" he murmured.

"Long enough," said the woman, calm and unperturbed. Steam wailed from the kettle's spout, and she lifted it off the camping stove and poured a slow stream of boiling water into both cups.

"Here," she said kindly. She turned around and shuffled forward, back toward the front end of the table, her face hidden in shadows by the orange light. Matt's eyes lingered on the camping bed, his thoughts churning. "Pomegranate. Good for the nerves, I think, when one has had a fall." She held out a cup. Matt stared at her, her lank-hanging hair and shadowed face. In the lamplight, the corners of the woman's mouth twitched, and in the distance, there came another thudding boom.

"It's not poisoned, dear boy. I've no means nor cause to hurt you. Come. Sit. Drink with me. I promise, by the time my cup is empty, you'll be back in safer hands." She patted the space on the wooden bench beside her, but Matt stood frozen, unable to move. The old woman sighed.

"He said you probably wouldn't. Ah well. All one can do is try."

"Where are we?" Matt forced himself to ask. He took a slow half-step backward. "What is this place?"

The woman waved an idle hand around. "What, this? A meat cellar, at some point. A few hundred years ago. Buried by a landslide some great eons past, but perfect for our purpose. Took us some time to clear, I'll have you know. There were a few dried sausages in here that sure weren't fit for eating."

Matt's eyes traced around the room, the collapsing furniture, the cave-in. "But you can't . . ." he tried to say, but the words didn't want to come out. He clenched his eyes closed, trying desperately to control his breathing, to fight the billowing, rippling fear. He opened his eyes and found himself staring straight at the ground. His phone was still laying there, facedown. Matt bent to pick it up, then quickly jerked back upright. The woman hadn't moved.

Matt drew a deep, shuddering breath. "What is this?" he muttered. He looked up at her, bloodied hands balled into fists. "Where am I? What's going on? How'd you get trapped like this? Who *are* you?"

"This is a conversation," the woman answered, simply and clearly, her hands wrapped around her tea. "You are ten feet below ground in rural Buzahishtë, Albania. I brought you here so I could talk to you, briefly, free from interference. My name is Cassandra Atropos. And I am not trapped here, Matt Callaghan; I am waiting, as I think you know. For we have much to discuss." The ceiling rattled with another distant boom, setting the porcelain to chatter, and the woman glanced ever so slightly up. "And precious little time."

A long, deafening silence stretched out into the cold, dark air. The woman drew a long sip of her tea, trails of steam wisping around her nose. Matt's heart pounded in his chest, a ringing in his ears, his head swimming and light.

"You're the clairvoyant," he whispered.

The old lady laughed. "No more than you, dear one. None of us are. There's no such thing as clairvoyants."

She chuckled. Matt's brow furrowed.

"You knew where I was going to go," he said. "Knew who I was going to be with. Know about Jane. How are you not clairvoyant?"

"All true," said Cassandra, blowing steam off her mug. "But appearances can be deceiving. That's the crux of a lot of this." Matt stared at her.

"If you're not clairvoyant," he asked, "then how'd you do all this? How'd you rob that bank?"

"Simple," the woman replied. "I saw the future."

"You saw the future," Matt said flatly. "But you're not clairvoyant."

"No," said the woman, "because I did not *see* the future. I was shown it."

"Right," Matt said warily. "By whom?"

"By the Weaver," she replied simply. "The Watcher, the One Who Walks through Walls."

"And who is that?" Matt asked.

"My master," the woman answered. "My teacher. My friend."

She let out a long, contented sigh, her bony hand stirring her tea. "Let me elaborate. Seven years, three months, and eight days ago, I was sitting in a locked room in an Athenian psychiatric ward. Depressed, you see. Isolated. Couldn't handle all the noise." She tapped the side of her head with a bony knuckle. "I wanted to kill myself. I was going to kill myself, had figured a way to do it and everything, with a little creativity, padded cell be damned." Cassandra sighed again. "It's amazing what the human mind can come up with when you really set it a challenge. Anyway," she continued, completely nonchalant, waving away talk of her own suicide like gnats in the night air. "I'm sitting there, thinking this was it, about to do the deed, when all of a sudden *he* appeared." A laugh, a pearling, joyous sound, pealed from her throat. "My word, it was such a fright. I thought for certain I was losing it, that my mind was playing a final, twisted trick. But then he didn't go anywhere, and I realized it wasn't a hallucination, and he asked me very nicely, in his kind and lovely way, if, as I was going to die anyway, I wouldn't mind doing some *good*." She shook her head at that last word, smiling and clicking her tongue. "I have to say, it was one of the more remarkable conversations I've had in my lifetime. You don't often get someone who looks like that talking you out of suicide, let alone showing you the universe. Or at least a part of it. At first."

She tilted her head, gazing wistfully up at the wall. "He showed me the truth. The strings, the web, his long game. What could be my part of it. My purpose. My destiny. And once I had seen that"—her voice dropped to a whisper—"I didn't need to see any more."

And as she spoke, she turned so that her head caught the light, and with a rush of curdling horror Matt realized that where her eyes should be were two empty, blackened pits.

"Oh God," he whispered.

Boom.

Twenty feet below her, Jane's ball of ice exploded another land mine, sending shock waves through the earth and nearby walls. The fire beneath Jane's feet flickered, and for an instant, she dropped before catching herself. Jane grimaced, hovering precariously. She wasn't yet good at this.

Her eyes found a nearby drywall and she descended, landing in a wobble on the unsteady outcrop of rock. Jane's arms spun to regain her balance, and then she steadied and surveyed her surroundings. The ruins were quiet. She'd done a full lap of the farmstead, a zigzagging aerial reconnaissance, and was reasonably confident she'd got a look inside each of the decrepit structures. None of them held anything interesting—indeed, the entire place looked like it hadn't been inhabited by anything bigger than a field mouse since long before she was born. Yet there was obviously someone here, from the sheer concentration of land mines and wire traps. It just didn't make sense, otherwise, unless somebody really hated wandering cows.

Jane chewed her lip, feeling a growing sense of concern. What was the point of all these booby traps if there was nothing here worth protecting? Had the clairvoyant moved? Was it all just misdirection? A colossal waste of their time? Her eyes scanned out over the ruins, searching for movement. A cool breeze flicked over Jane's ears and in the dark her mouth twitched into a frown.

She needed to reconvene. With Matt at least, the others maybe, though she wasn't sure she'd cleared all the traps. Still frowning, Jane turned back toward where she'd left the faux clairvoyant and leaped from wall to wall with short, controlled bursts.

Wait. Her eyes focused as she approached the edge of the farmstead, the darkened corner between buildings where she'd last seen Matt. Wait. She leaped from a rooftop and landed skidding in the mud, her heartbeat accelerating. There was no one there. She'd sworn this was . . . Jane spun around wildly, eyes snapping from broken wall to broken wall. This was right where she'd left him, she was sure of it, unless . . . had she got confused? Maybe in the darkness she'd gotten turned around, got the wrong patch of ruins, but she thought . . . she thought . . .

"Matt!" Jane cried out, searching in the shadows, turning rapidly around. Panic rose in her chest and she jumped into the air, flames streaming from her hands. "MATT!"

Ten feet below ground, in a tomb of earth and darkness, Matt Callaghan stared into the twin pits of the seer's gouged-out eyes and felt true, curdling fear.

"Oh God," he whispered.

"No, not yet," the woman replied calmly. "Not for another few months." She paused, turning her head away, and the scars around her empty eye sockets were once again swallowed by the darkness. "I'm sorry, dear one. I forget how this must seem to you, how distressing all this"—she gestured vaguely at her face—"must be. I'm sorry. If there was another way, we would've taken it. I would have."

"How . . ." Matt whispered. The words could barely claw their way out from his throat. "How did . . . ?"

"I did it myself," she replied matter-of-factly, as though the topic of her gouging out her own eyeballs was a disappointing tennis score. "Not long after he came to me. Helped me focus, you see. Too much interference. Too many distractions from the tapestry."

"You . . . you . . ." Matt felt his head grow lighter, his breaths starting to come quick. "You're insane," he whispered. The old woman smiled.

"No, my dear boy, sadly, I am not. I am, however, doomed, in about"—she gingerly lowered the tip of her ring finger into the liquid she was drinking—"three-quarters of a teacup. But that is entirely another matter."

A surreal lightness snapped at the edge of Matt's vision. He shook his head. "What do you want from me?" he asked. But the old woman only smiled.

"I want nothing from you, dear one. Nothing more than what you're already going to do." And to Matt's utter shock, although her smile never wavered, a shining tear leaked down her cheek. "I'm so sorry it has to be like this. For the pain you're going to go through. We both are."

Matt's stomach churned. "I thought you said—"

"Oh, not now," the old woman said dismissively with another wave of her hand. She leaned down and gently blew across the tea. "Not me, no. I'd never hurt you. Even if I wanted to, he'd never let me. Gods above."

"What do you mean?" Matt demanded, gritting his teeth. "What you talking about? Who's 'he'? What the hell is going on?"

"What's going on, Matthew Callaghan, and I'll mind you watch your profanity, is a distraction. All of this is . . . All of us are . . . One tantalizing distraction after another, shadow after shadow for him to chase, and before you know it, it's been a year if it's been a decade. But it's all over now. I'm to be the last. He has stalled him for as long as he can, but he's getting impatient, and there's no pushing sand back up the hourglass. He has you in his sights now, and you're ready, as ready as you can be. You have a part to play, Matt Callaghan, as do we all, and if we don't rightly play it, we will all horribly die."

Silence.

Matt squeezed his eyes shut a second, trying to draw sense from the gibberish, feeling like his brain was on fire. "You keep saying 'he.' He said this. He appeared to you. Who?" Matt hesitated for a long moment, reluctant to articulate his next thought. "Jesus?"

For the first time since he'd gotten down there, the old woman erupted in a loud, booming laugh. She shook her head.

"No, dear boy. Nothing so theological. He's not a god. At least so he insists." For some reason, this caused her mouth to crease with a knowing smirk. "Although one could argue it's genetic."

"Right," said Matt, his heart hammering, still not understanding a word. "So, uh, who is he?"

"Ah, it's not quite time for that," the woman said simply, taking another sip of her tea. "You'll figure it out. Eventually. Just know this." Her head turned and she looked at him directly. "He loves you. Both of you. So much." Her trembling hands put down her mug and her voice stretched out, warm and melodic into the dark. "You wouldn't know it to look at him, but he does. He's so full of love. And he wouldn't do this, any of this, if there was any other way."

Another rumble. Another mine.

"Why isn't he here then?" Matt asked. His mind swam but he pushed forward, trying to get something, anything, leaning into the delusions. "This person, whoever he is. Who wants to talk, who loves me so much. Why isn't he talking to me himself?"

The woman's face scowled. "Him." Her head tilted toward the ceiling, to the single lightbulb flickering overhead. "That abomination. That coward. He's above us right now. Watching. Pah." She spat with surprising violence on the ground. "Let him scramble, let him rage. These walls are lead-lined. He'll get nothing, traitor, nor step into my mind."

"Wait who?" said Matt. "What? Is, is this a different person? Who are we talking about now?"

"He who I shall not honor naming. That would-be king, that murderer, consumed by greed and fear. Weak little boy, pale and heartless as your forebears, I've seen the truth. So terrified of failure, so far come, so much to lose. Biding his precious time." The woman snarled. "He frets and skulks and plots. Tyrant. Terrified, now that he is within reach, so close to the precipice, this socalled conqueror. This boy who would be king." She turned to Matt, her empty eyes gleaming. "How can he know who's coming for him? What's a king to a god? What's a god to a nonbeliever?"

The old woman shook her head, as if any of this made sense. "But one cannot be too cautious. He's watching you, closely, and though he can slip here and there unnoticed when his attention is turned, he cannot risk him ever finding out. It would change everything, you know? Forget his pursuit of you. Ha!" The sudden bark of laughter made Matt jump. "The horror he'd unleash if he got even a whiff of his power. It's hard to know how far a mind reaches. And nothing moves faster than thought."

She sighed, idly stirring the remnants of her tea. "Hence, me. Hence, you, wonderful boy. An air gap, if you will, to protect that separation." And then she smiled at him, and to Matt's horror and disbelief, the next words she spoke were not sound, but thought.

We all know your mind's like a trap.

"Gah!" Matt recoiled, throwing his hands up, barriers scrambling wildly. He breathed heavily, his eyes wide. "You're . . . you're . . ."

"Not a clairvoyant." Cassandra smiled. "Like I said. None of us were."

"Then what were you?"

"Conduits. Distractions. All a very specific demographic. All willing to buy you more time."

Up above, there came the sound of more booms, the vibrations shaking dust from the earthen ceiling, closer and closer, still so far away. Matt's heart hammered in his chest. "Time for what?"

And in the flickering lamplight, the old woman beamed.

"Time to win," she said simply. Then in a single, fluid movement, she rose and flung open her gown, revealing the explosives wired beneath.

"HOLY FU—"

Matt yelped, stumbled, scrambling back, his armor slamming into the wall. He turned, spinning, scrambling desperately for an exit, but there was nowhere to go, no way out. He turned back to Cassandra.

"Please," he begged her. "Please. You don't have to do this. Whatever it is you're going through, whoever you think is after you, we can fix it, I can help!"

"My darling boy," she said, smiling softly and staring at him with empty eyes. "All I am going through is time, and I have already gone far beyond my allocated amount. And as for who is after me, well, this is how I beat him."

Matt stared at her, heart fluttering in his throat. "You said you wouldn't hurt me," he whispered.

"I won't."

"You said I had a part to play!"

"You do."

"Why then? What am I supposed to do? Why did you bring me here? Why are you doing this?!"

"Why?" said Cassandra, and she raised the detonator in her hand. "Why? Because next month's winning lottery numbers are four, seven, thirteen, eighteen, twenty-one, twenty-six, thirty-two, and three. Because love is more powerful than hate. Because true souls can disagree on the color of a garden. Because you are human. And because he has waited a long, long time to save you, and it is my privilege to call him my friend."

Another boom, the loudest one yet. The wooden shelves clattered against the walls. The old woman smiled.

"It's almost time. He's getting impatient. He'd come down on us in about eighty more seconds, but thankfully she'll get there first." The old woman smiled. "Take care of her, Matt Callaghan. Even when it's not easy."

"I don't understand," whispered Matt. There were sounds now, a thudding, getting closer. The walls seemed to close around. "Please. Please don't do this. Please."

"Ten," Cassandra whispered, "nine."

Matt ran. He sprinted, ducking under the woman's outstretched arms, barreling past the table to the other side of the room. Cassandra didn't move.

"Eight. Seven."

He dove, hands and knees, clawing at the rockfall, the staircase, the passageway blocked. He scrambled, furiously, his fingers drawing blood. But the rocks wouldn't move.

"HELP!" he screamed. "HELP!"

"Six."

Matt leaped to his feet, heart hammering, eyes flying around the room, looking for something, anything—

"Five."

The table. He raced forward, heaving it up with a wordless cry, pulling it on its side, as above him there came another boom, and he was dragging it—

"Four."

Dragging it backward, away from her, still standing there with her back to him, with her horrific empty eyes, as far as he could go, as far as he could manage—

"Three."

Until his foot stumbled on the bottom of the staircase and he cowered, leaning desperately into the wood, his eyes clenched shut—

"Two."

There was another shuddering boom and the air around Matt grew hot. Suddenly, there was a wave of force, a roar from behind him, and a hand wrenched Matt back.

Cassandra's head turned. Her scarred face gazed down at Matt and the figure standing between them. Her finger hovered on the detonator. The world began to darken.

And for the briefest moment, Cassandra's mouth twitched into a crooked smile.

"One," she whispered.

And then she pressed the button.

BOOOOOOOOOOOOOOOOOOOOMMMMMMMMM!

The world trembled.

Trembled, shook, shuddered, and roared with a fury Jane Walker had never known. Here, underground, in this prison of stone, there was nowhere for the fire and force to go other than out, other than forward. It surrounded her, enveloping her, enveloping both of them—and it was all she could do to hold.

Hold.

She'd felt it. The explosions sounding different, the ground around the mines making more of an echo the closer she got to where Matt had stood. She'd saw it, landed in the empty ruin nearby, seen a collapsed wall hiding a staircase covered in rock. And then she'd heard it—the cry for help. And she'd known.

Her hands searing ablaze, Jane Walker had burned through ten feet of crumbling rock to find Matt Callaghan cowering behind a table, and a suicide bomber ready to explode.

And in that single, hanging instant, she'd felt something she'd never felt before rise in her chest, and she had known without thinking what to do.

Jane lunged forward, one hand grabbing Matt by his breastplate and pulling him behind her, one hand outstretched, streaming fire. All around them, unbidden, thick packs of ice rose from the ground, covering them, pressing down. Jane crouched over Matt and let out a wordless roar. And as her voice rose, the world exploded, with noise, with force, with all-consuming sound, and fire whipped around them like a hurricane, writhing, burning, a vortex born from hell.

But she would not let it take her. And she would not let him die.

BOOOOOOOOOOOOOOOOOOOOMMMMMMMMM!

Force slammed into her and the ice cracked, her legs buckling, her arm staggered. Fire slammed into fire, heat searing her fingertips, and all around them the explosion howled, burning, mindless against its confines, swallowing air, earth, and wall. Death came in a wave of flame, and she forced it back with soundless fury, every muscle tensed, blood spinning on her tongue.

YIELD! she cried, and it was not a word but a thought, a primal, burning drive. She pushed, screaming against the impossible, as the world around them blazed with blinding, howling will.

The fire came to claim them, and it was all she could do to hold.

Hold.

And then, in a moment, it passed.

The light faded. The sound stopped. Jane's chest sagged and her arm drooped, and she slumped to all fours. In front of them, the flames of the explosion splayed up into the ceiling, the corners and far wall, washing fruitlessly against the rock, flickering, dying. Suddenly, the room was empty, eviscerated, cleansed of all but the smell of ash. Heat radiated from blackened walls. Of the woman, the explosives, everything that had once been inside, there remained no evidence. Jane's ears rang and her vision swam, and when she tried to breathe, hot smoke coughed from her lungs.

"Jane?"

The empath turned to look behind her, let her legs and arms drop. She half-fell, half-rolled to face away from the destruction, sitting one leg crooked like a clumsy child. Her hands touched hot dirt, and she had to blink to draw the blur from her eyes.

There, behind her, singed but unscathed, looking up at her with frightened awe, was Matt.

"Jane."

For a moment, they just sat there, looking at each other. Jane's ears were ringing, and she couldn't quite see straight. Matt's armor was covered in soot, and there were burns on his fingers and cheeks. The ends of his hair were still slightly on fire. Neither seemed to notice.

Jane opened her mouth to say something, only to erupt in a fit of ashen coughs. She retched and spat out a chunk of something black.

"You all right?" she managed finally. Matt nodded, dazed, staring at her. Jane's shoulders slumped, and she let out a relieved, rasping sigh. She closed her eyes and leaned back on her hands.

And then suddenly in the darkness, she heard a sobbing shuffle of movement and felt two arms wrap tight around her chest. A face pressed into her neck, and she felt a vast stretch of humanity.

"Thank you," Matt whispered. And after a moment, though it was probably just the shell shock, Jane unexpectedly hugged him back.

"Jesus Christ," muttered Jane.

They were alone, sitting on a low drystone wall in the middle of the farmstead; Jane occasionally coughing, Matt prodding tenderly at his burns. Neither was saying much. After their long, near-death-fueled hug had ended, Matt and Jane had pulled apart, and the empath had resolutely blasted a path for them back up through the shattered rock. The west half of the basement had collapsed not long after, weakened by the explosion, but by that point they were long out. James Conrad and Natalia were down there now, the former clearing away the rubble, the latter looking for clues. Neither were likely to find anything.

The others had arrived, of course, not long after Matt and Jane had pulled themselves to safety. After hearing the repeated explosions and Natalia sensing Jane's sudden, distant panic, they'd come charging down—unharmed, thankfully, since Jane luckily seemed to have cleared most of the traps. They'd been warned now though, and were cautious only to tread where Jane had already been. None of the other Acolytes had stayed put for long. James and Natalia were down in the cellar; Will and Giselle had teleported off to get a healer. And some water, Jane had requested, for her parched and ashen throat.

They'd be back soon. Alone in starlit darkness, in an ancient, ruined home, Matt Callaghan and Jane Walker sat burned, bruised, and bloodied, and knew without saying a single sentence that now was their window to talk.

"What the hell just happened?"

"I don't know," Matt said quietly. A thin trickle of blood lay drying beneath his ears and a patch of his hair was singed. "I don't know."

Jane glanced at him, her soot-stained face twisting in a grimace. "I'm sorry I left you."

"You didn't know." Matt shook his head. "And I don't think it would've mattered. This was all set up."

They lapsed into dark, starlit silence.

"What did she want?" Jane asked.

"I don't know," Matt answered truthfully. He leaned forward, resting his hands on his chin, then flinched at the touch of raw skin. "I don't

know. It was . . . she was saying all these things. About people and distractions and danger and . . . murder. She said I had some part to play. I
don't . . . I don't understand."

Jane let herself stay silent. After a few seconds, Matt shook his head,
staring intently at the mud.

"Something's wrong," he said quietly.

"You're right."

"No," he said, turning to her. There was softness in his voice, but a
shadow in his eyes. "There's something wrong with all of this. With me
being here. I don't . . . I thought it was coincidence. Just bad luck. But it's
not." Matt's hands trembled, but his words stayed steady. "I think someone planned all this. I think there's something going on. I think we're in
danger." There was a distant *pop* followed by the smell of sulfur, and the
sound of raised voices called out over the ruins. Matt's voice dropped. "I
think we're all in danger," he murmured, glancing over at Will and the
approaching Acolytes. "Everyone."

For a moment, Jane stayed silent, simply looking in Matt's eyes. The
wind blew, and the stones creaked, and the scent of ash floated through
the night. Finally, the empath spoke.

"From what?" she whispered, as the Acolytes' footsteps drew closer.
"From who?"

Six thousand miles away in a cold, sterile room, a man the world had
forgotten lay on life support. His body sat unmoving, drips in his arms,
surrounded by monitors and machines—the only sign of life his breathing, that thin, quiet rasping, and his chest's ragged rise and fall. Cameras
gleamed above him, watching every second—though all who saw him
knew it had been years since the man in the bed had freely moved.

The room was large for a cell. Large, cold, and clinical, white floors
and plexiglass, two floors below ground where no sunlight ever touched.
Devoid of human sound, the only noise the whirring cameras, the rhythmic beeps of life support and the air-conditioner's monotonous hum,
pumping chills into the man's frail lungs.

Alone. Dying. Forgotten.

There were staff who came to see him—doctors with their clipboards,
guards to stand against the door. There were checks, changes, and routine cleaning, even jokes outside his cell. Never inside. The prisoner may

not have moved nor spoken but still in his presence they felt wary—still, there came a trickle of fear.

They came. They left. They waited. They watched.

Never knowing there was another.

From a place no one could perceive, a blue-eyed child stood silent, watching the prisoner breathe his artificial air, his slow, imperceptible atrophy; watched some machines give life and others prepare to take it. Watched the living corpse lay motionless, never giving any indication of the thoughts that whirled inside his writhing, boiling mind. Of his swirling pain and fury. Of his dark, unspoken truth.

"Soon," the boy whispered. "Soon."

The man's eyes twitched.

ACKNOWLEDGMENTS

Writing a book is a lot like wrangling an angry baby, and as the saying goes, it takes a village to raise a child. *Superworld* would never have been published without the help and contributions of a large number of people, and I'd like to take a moment to thank them all. First up, to my beta (and sometimes even alpha) readers, Ben M., Julia, Sam, Ayeeda, and of course, my dad, who were the first people to read *Superworld* and who provided me with invaluable feedback, corrections, and notes. It's a huge favor, amongst all the other obligations in one's hectic life, to sit down and read a manuscript, and the fact that you guys made that effort means more to me than you know.

To Kit Carstairs and the Manuscript Appraisal Agency for their excellent and engaged feedback once *Superworld* was out of its infancy—thank you for your insights and support and for reassuring me from a professional vantage point that what I'd written wasn't actually trash.

To the mystery nurse at the Hunter Street blood bank who suggested I start posting my story on Royal Road when I'd never heard of the site before—thank you for changing the course of my life. Though you may never know it, you appeared from the mist to intervene in my story like Rowan Atkinson in *Love Actually* and then disappeared never to be seen again. I'm sorry I can't remember your name, and I promise to keep donating as long as they keep feeding me.

To all my readers on Royal Road, including the many friends and family who jumped onboard—thank you for your positivity, your engagement, your many messages, comments, and reviews. Without all of you none of this would have been possible. It is an amazing feeling to have fans.

A huge thank you, too, to all my supporters on Patreon, be they past or present, whose generosity and passion never ceases to amaze. It is one thing to read a free story, but another thing entirely to pay to support one you could otherwise get for nothing. I cannot overstate how much I appreciate your support, and I hope to continue to entertain you for years to come.

To my fantastic team at Podium, including Kate Runde, Nicole Passage, Hannah Grenfell, and Marina Ferreira, and our fantastic narrator, Luke Daniels—may we one day meet in person so I can apologize for all the Australianisms I unwittingly forced you to edit out.

And last but not least to my loving girlfriend, who continues to put up with me sequestering myself in our spare room and typing endlessly about superheroes when the house is a mess and somebody needs to walk the dog. Thank you for supporting my dream.

I owe you all a beer.

Lots of love,

Ben

ABOUT THE AUTHOR

Benjamin Keyworth is an Australian author born and raised in Newcastle, New South Wales, and currently living in Sydney with his partner and dog. A lawyer by day, Ben has wanted to be a writer since he was five years old (before which he wanted to be a dinosaur). He is pursuing a master's degree in creative writing at the University of Technology Sydney, and in his spare time he enjoys baking and playing video games and *Dungeons & Dragons*.

DISCOVER
STORIES UNBOUND

PodiumAudio.com

Printed in Great Britain
by Amazon

84257116R00176